Paul A. Kazakov graduated from law school in 1978 and was initially employed as a sessional instructor in law for two years. After forty years of practicing civil litigation, he retired in 2020 and finally returned to his initial interest: creative writing.

He quickly realized that composing fiction was not the same as drafting a legal factum or a legal brief, though the fundamentals remained the same. *The Narcissus Touch* is his first effort, and it is the first instalment of a legal trilogy. *The Sharkfish Man* and *Prodigal Passion* are to follow.

The author resides in Calgary, Alberta with his partner and muse, Nancy Brager. He has one son, Mark, who holds a Bachelor of Fine Arts degree and is actively engaged in musical theater.

THE NARCISSUS TOUCH

For Cindy Kreutzenstein

April 4, 2020

PAUL A. KAZAKOV

THE NARCISSUS TOUCH

Vanguard Press

VANGUARD PAPERBACK

© Copyright 2022
Paul A. Kazakov

A CIP catalogue record for this title is
available from the British Library.

ISBN 978 1 80016 339 3

Vanguard Press is an imprint of
Pegasus Elliot MacKenzie Publishers Ltd.
www.pegasuspublishers.com

First Published in 2022

Vanguard Press
Sheraton House Castle Park
Cambridge England

Printed & Bound in Great Britain

Dedication

To my son, Mark, and to my muse, Nancy Brager.

Principal Characters

Michael Bolta	Lawyer and partner in the Calgary law firm of Bolta & Barton
Jacobus (Jake) Barton	Civil litigation lawyer and Michael Bolta's partner
Marlena Bolta	Michael Bolta's estranged wife
Kathy Clemons	Michael Bolta's personal legal assistant
Alexa Bolta	Michael Bolta's prodigal elder sister
Marcel Paradis	Louisiana petroleum businessman operating out of Denver
Ben Cotton	Petroleum engineer who performed services for Paradis' companies and a client of Bolta & Barton
Sterling Layton	Vancouver lawyer and primary adversary of Paradis
Crystal Bachman	Vancouver denturist, originally from New York, and Barton's love interest
Adam Bolta	Michael and Marlena's six-year-old son
Louie Paradis	Marcel Paradis' nephew and business associate
Roger McQuaid	Yukon 'placer' gold mining promoter and Layton's business associate
Bill Gunderson	Michael Bolta's truculent Reno business client
Detectives Peter Krystov and Edward McKeown	Calgary Homicide Unit detectives

Chapter 1

The emaciated old man lay curled up in a fetal position on his right side on the sofa breathing fitfully with excruciating irregular gasps, trying to cling to the last vestiges of his life. His translucent skin was stretched tightly over the skeletal frame of his face. His head was devoid of hair because of the chemotherapy and the radiation treatments he had been forced to endure, which aged him decades. It was only when his eyes fluttered open when the spasmodic pain was especially brutal that the intensity of his azure blue eyes belied the apathy of his physical condition and intimated that he may not yet be prepared to die.

It was past three in the morning and the large empty house was dark and silent. Michael had only been able to inadvertently doze off for a few minutes at a time as he sat on the Persian carpeted floor beside his father. Every time he did doze off, the old man would make an excruciating moan as if a strand of barbed wire were being pulled through his spinal column or even more alarmingly, when he would stop breathing and then gasp involuntarily back to life, jolting his son back to consciousness.

As Michael gazed onto the old man's face, memories of half-forgotten moments percolated through his mind. He recalled how his father would hoist him effortlessly as a child and carry him on his shoulders so that his small size was no longer an impediment to surveying his surroundings. Or when he would throw Michael high up into the air until gravity would arrest his ascent and then delay catching him until the very last moment to maximize his exhilaration. Or observe his precocious attempt to match his father's long stride as they walked hand in hand down the street. Father and son would then knowingly laugh in unison when Michael would look up to his father to see if his father was watching him with approval.

This old man once seemed fearless and invincible. As a teenaged youth, he fought under Tito with Franco Tudjman's partisans in the Balkans during the outbreak of World War II. Subsequently he endured a year in a slave labor camp in Germany, surviving primarily on discarded potato skins for food. Then he survived as a black marketer and an itinerant gambler in post-war Europe before being able to emigrate to Canada, ending up in Calgary. But before he was able to put his ingenuity to work and amass a modest fortune which permitted him to marry, have a family and build this residence on a country estate in the verdant foothills southwest of the city, he had to first repay the Canadian government for his passage by becoming an indentured farm laborer for a year. He had to survive the vicious western winter in a tarpaper shack by keeping the archaic pot-bellied wood burning stove glowing red-hot both day and night. In hindsight, he compared that year of farm servitude to his survival in the slave labor camp; there was not that much of a difference.

Now he was just an old man whose wife had predeceased him a few years earlier, shortly after he paid off his daughter's second ex-husband. Now he was no longer capable of even being able to walk to the bathroom to relieve himself. But perhaps Michael was being a bit too critical of his father, considering the shattered state of his own current personal life.

After she had spent months groundlessly accusing Michael of infidelity, his wife, Marlena, told him that she decided to exact her revenge by initiating an affair with a man who was not only married, but someone whom Michael had considered to be a friend. What she did not tell him, however, was that she could not bring herself to actually do it. She had rejected Michael's denials so venomously that he ceased to bother to make them after a while, even though he had neither the inclination nor the opportunity to be unfaithful. And as if her feigned infidelity was not sufficient revenge, when she made her false confession, she stood proudly before him and taunted him with McNabb's alleged sexual prowess, to exacerbate his pain.

Michael had initially moved into a spare bedroom in their home and they commenced to live separate and apart, and in peace. However, he soon discovered that his wife was attempting to check his cell phone and computer for proof of his infidelity. Then she initiated a practice of having one of her friends stay overnight, allegedly as a supportive companion, but more probably as a convenient corroborating witness to possible acts of alleged misconduct on his part. Finally, he decided to move into his father's home in the country. Shortly thereafter, his father received his fatal diagnosis of stage four lung cancer.

McNabb, Michael's alleged unfaithful friend, vehemently denied the infidelity when Michael confronted him, but Michael did not believe him. McNabb had always told him that he considered Michael to be a lucky man to be married to such a beautiful woman. In hindsight, those comments only served as a final corroboration of Marlena's admission of their affair.

But McNabb had his own marital problems since he was concerned that Michael's wife may be sufficiently vindictive to disclose the supposed infidelity to his wife as well. He had already endured two previous divorces and he did not think he could financially survive another one. He implored Michael to try to intercede with Marlena, but Michael merely shook his head in disbelief and disgust as he turned and walked silently away from his former friend.

After Michael had moved out Marlena had consistently refused to permit Michael to see their six-year-old son. He could have applied for a court order, but he did not want to provoke her or air his personal problems in public, especially since he was a lawyer, himself. That privacy would be short-lived, however, once Marlena commenced divorce proceedings. Then he would have no choice but to apply for a court order if she remained intransigent. Until then, the occasional telephone contact with his son when his mother was not home would have to suffice.

Michael could not understand how or why his marriage disintegrated. They had loved and respected each other at one time, or so it seemed. If he had neglected her because of his work, he had always attempted to compensate through expensive gifts as proof of his love and affection. Those gifts were never refused, but they obviously had not been enough.

And then there was his sister, Alexa, and her ceaseless demands for ongoing financial support from their father. Michael attempted to use his authority as his father's guardian and trustee to shield his father, but those financial demands were going to become even more intense and bitter once his sister learned of their father's testamentary provisions for her.

Then there were his professional responsibilities which always took priority over his personal life. There was the pending judicial ordered mediation scheduled for Denver the following week. Michael's client, a reservoir engineer, had performed engineering work in Colorado and Wyoming on the huge shale deposit named the Jonah Field. Now his company had become entangled in a mega lawsuit between two feuding petroleum companies. Non-payment of the account or legal fees for a long trial: either factor could prove to be fatal to their client.

At the beginning of the next month, he had to fly to Toronto to argue an appeal on a trial he had conducted a year ago. Initially he felt that the trial judge had no option on the law and on the facts, but to find in favor of his defendant client and dismiss the action with costs. However, the judge's negative attitude during the trial and the subsequent undue delay in rendering the judgment did not bode well. The taciturn judge did not try to hide his disdain for this interloping lawyer from Alberta and his client's poor performance as a witness did not make Michael's work any easier.

He remembered the judge's negative reaction to his characterization of the plaintiff's testimony that a curse word had never passed his lips in his dealings with his client. Michael had submitted that it was probably more accurate to state that no *true* word had ever passed the plaintiff's lips. Michael thought that his characterization was not only clever but appropriate as well. The judge's restless body language and contorted facial expression indicated that those sentiments were not shared by the bench.

Michael had strongly recommended that a local lawyer be retained as co-counsel to negate any judicial resentment about an Alberta lawyer usurping legal work in Ontario, but the client was too frugal to agree. His concern about possible judicial bias proved to be correct and the judgment clearly underscored the judge's intention that he was not going to permit any latter-day legal carpetbagger from the west to come to his province and succeed in an action in his courtroom if he could help it.

After reserving his judgment for several months, the judge was able to cherry-pick his way through the evidence and aided by his unfettered authority to make findings of fact and credibility, he cobbled together a substantial judgment, with solicitor-client costs and interest, which totaled almost $1 million, payable by his client. The judgment was appealable, but the outcome was far from certain. At least the client did finally agree to retain an Ontario co-counsel for the appeal.

The following week, Michael had to go to Edmonton, the provincial capital, for an examination on another lawsuit and do his best to help solve another client's legal problem. Then he had to go to Reno for an eccentric client who refused to fly or drive 'in winter'. In addition to those trips, he had to fulfill his regular ongoing responsibilities to the rest of his clients. There was also the scheduled interview for a new associate who wanted to relocate from Toronto to the self-proclaimed oil capital of Canada.

Thankfully, he did not have to worry about the business administration of the firm. His partner, Jake Barton, looked after those matters. Jake was as close to him as the brother he never had. At the end of exams in first year, they had gone to a south-side bar in Edmonton to celebrate with some friends. After a couple of hours of continuous drinking, however, the waiter cut off their table for the third time for being overly boisterous. Instead of trying to use persuasion, which had worked on the first two occasions, Jake impetuously rose and threw an empty beer glass with the intention of striking the mirror behind the bar and shattering the glass as in a Western movie. Unfortunately, the glass struck a bartender in the head and all hell broke loose. Two bouncers jerked Jake outside and then they started to pummel and kick him viciously as he lay prone and helpless on the pavement in retaliation for the bartender's injury.

Michael had followed them out into the parking lot with their other companions, but when another waiter attempted to join in the melee, he tried to intercede and block his path. As a result, Michael sustained a lacerated lower lip when the frustrated waiter struck out at him instead.

After the police arrived and the bartender had been taken to emergency, Jake was too mad and drunk to defend himself and it was up to Michael to try to defuse the situation. The bar manager was threatening to press assault charges against Jake, so Michael countered by threatening to press assault charges against the bar's employee. As this did not seem to have much effect on the manager, Michael added that he also intended to commence a lawsuit for damages against the bar as well, since the waiter was the bar's employee, and the bar was vicariously liable for any misconduct in the course of his employment. He ended his hollow threat by stating that he was looking forward to cross-examining the waiter and the manager at trial. A rather brazen statement for a twenty-two-year-old first-year law student who had never even observed a trial, except on television. At that juncture, the manager's attitude changed from outrage and disgust, to one of exasperation.

Though one year of law school may not have taught Michael much, that threat was enough to convince the manager to relent and not proceed with any charges and Michael agreed to reciprocate. The police were also happy to oblige just to avoid all the paperwork which would have followed if they decided to press ahead with the assault charges on their own initiative.

There had been at least a dozen fellow students present in the bar and then outside, but none of them had stepped forward to give Jake any assistance because of the understandable fear of jeopardizing themselves physically, academically and professionally. Notwithstanding the pummeling Jake had received, aside from some torn clothes, he had come out pretty much unscathed. Michael, on the other hand, had to attend at emergency for three stitches on the inside of his lower lip. Coincidentally, the bartender was being stitched up in an adjoining cubicle at the hospital.

Since that day, Jake remained unfailingly trustworthy and reliable in all matters, with one notable exception. That exception was women. He did, however, adopt the habit of not consuming more than two drinks on any one occasion.

After graduation, completing articles and passing the bar exams, the two friends decided to risk establishing their own firm, Bolta & Barton, rather than joining an established firm. Jake preferred to characterize it as a 'boutique' firm because he believed that characterization gave the firm a more sophisticated cachet which compensated for the firm's small size. They both wanted to specialize in civil litigation. With time, since some of their clients inevitably had legal problems which involved other areas of law, they recruited a small group of lawyers to deal with some of those other areas of law. This permitted the two of them to focus on the one area of law which really interested them.

Michael smiled at remembering Jake's unfailing advice to the associates that *"every billable minute of every hour in every day should be billed out at least once to some client. "*. The associates were not sure if he was serious or just putting them on, but they attempted to diligently heed his advice, just in case.

Chapter 2

Jacobus Barton, better known as Jake, was single, forty years old and above average in height as well in weight. His dark hair was prematurely flecked with grey. His face's most prominent features were his perpetual sardonic smirk and his dark eyebrows which he had learned to arch at will to emphasize either disdain, outrage or interest, as the situation may have required. He would usually dress impeccably in an Italian suit complemented by an exotic silk tie, an embroidered white silk shirt, accented by Italian leather shoes and a matching belt.

The designer suits were purchased at a discount through a former grateful client, but they came with genuine Italian designer labels which he unfailingly showed to anyone who erred in complimenting him on his attire. The silk shirts were also discounted because they were purchased through a Hong Kong sweat shop, but they were silk and discreetly embroidered with the initials 'J B' over the breast pocket and on the French cuffs. The cuffs were complemented by 18-karat gold cufflinks, accented by inset lapis lazuli stones. The cufflinks in turn were complemented by a gold Swiss watch on his left wrist and a two-carat diamond solitaire in a bezel setting on his right hand. He would never fail to ensure that his embroidered cuffs were plainly visible, as well as the cufflinks and the gold watch. He had also developed the knack of being able to flash his ring's reflection at the opposing lawyer's eyes to distract, if not to impress, during boardroom meetings or during examinations. When the other party finally protested, Jake would apologize profusely; however, his sardonic smirk would belie his professed assertion that the action was truly inadvertent.

His ties and shoes were purchased directly from a couple of shops in Rome which Jake had discovered when he had gone there on a vacation a few years earlier. Though purchasing directly from Rome was expensive, he believed that the quality could not be matched and the savings he was able to get by purchasing his suits and shirts at a discount more than made up for that additional cost. But the end result, in his own modest opinion, was spectacular. He believed that he was the best-dressed man when he walked into any courtroom, any boardroom, any office or any restaurant. He could almost taste the envy. He truly believed that most men feared him and that all discerning women desired him. And if his appearance helped to intimidate, so much the better. It reinforced his feeling of superiority, if not his belief in his own invincibility.

But Jake did not rely solely on his appearance to gain an advantage. He also prepared extensively and tirelessly so that he could deal effectively with the known issues, and he attempted to anticipate the unexpected ones as well. Anyone who presumed to think that he was all show and no substance, usually lived to regret it.

***

Jake approached the double glass doors of Bolta & Barton, Barristers & Solicitors, and walked effortlessly into the reception, breezing by the receptionist with a wink and a smile. "You look gorgeous, Ginger… as usual," he gushed with dubious sincerity.

Ginger had heard this salutation before, so she merely smiled and handed him his telephone messages which she had collated from the weekend voice messages his clients had left for him.

"And Ms Christine Breland is in the boardroom."

"Oh? Ms Christine Breland?"

"She is the prospective associate that you and Michael are to interview this morning."

"Right. No problem. Let her know that I will see her in about fifteen minutes. I will interview her myself, but there is another issue I have to deal with first."

Jake walked down the corridor to the two adjoining corner offices divided on the diagonal which he and Michael had reserved for themselves and looked for Michael's assistant.

"Kathy, could you come into my office? There is something I have to discuss with you."

Kathy was the first assistant that Michael had hired as a young nineteen-year-old straight out of secretarial school and now, some fifteen years later, she was the senior paralegal in the firm and the firm's administrative assistant. She was totally devoted to and protective of Michael. Kathy eyed Jake suspiciously for she simply assumed that Jake always had some ulterior motive. She rose and followed him into his office without saying a word while his own paralegal merely glanced up silently out of curiosity and then returned to her own duties.

Jake examined Kathy without being overly obvious. She was an attractive redhead with beautiful light-green eyes and full lips. She wore her hair short, which made it easy to maintain. Though her clothes were professionally appropriate, they could not disguise her nubile hips and her ample bosom. Jake noticed that the hem of her skirt remained discreetly at her knees even when she sat down and crossed her legs. She was confident in her appearance, and she had no need to flaunt any gratuitous leg or cleavage to attract unwanted attention. Notwithstanding her chaste posture, Jake could not help but regret that she was Michael's paralegal and that she was married. That regret did not stop him from fantasizing about her from time to time.

Affecting a serious tone, he advised Kathy about Michael's father's state of health and his obvious imminent death. Even though Kathy had been well aware of the elder Bolta's state of health, she was still caught by surprise at Jake's apparent concern.

"Michael phoned me on my way to work this morning and he will not be coming in today. His father's condition is very delicate, and he does not want to leave him currently. Michael did not sound that well himself. I know that you will assist him as much as you can even though we both know that he will not ask for any help. Furthermore, I do not think that he should go to Denver for that mediation next week, so arrange for me to go instead. I have been working on that file with Michael, so I am ready to take over and it is just a mediation hearing, not a trial."

"Of course, Jacob," Kathy replied.

She could not bring herself to address him as Mr Barton or Jacobus because it was too formal and Jake was too familiar, so she settled on

Jacob, even though Jake's own parents had stopped addressing him by that name. In fact, no one else addressed him as Jacob, just Jake.

"And what does this Christine Breland look like?" he asked mischievously. "She never attached a photograph to her CV if I remember correctly."

"I am sure that you will not be disappointed, Jacob, but do remember that we have strict sexual harassment laws in this province and office policy prohibits fraternization. Perhaps you'd better focus on her professional qualifications rather than her bra size," Kathy answered knowingly.

"Well, you know me. It is not easy, but I shall try my best," he said, shrugging in feigned disappointment.

"But Michael and I have already checked her credentials and references. We have decided that she should get the family law position so you can go ahead and make all the required preliminary arrangements and the interview should just be a formality."

Jake proceeded to the boardroom for his interview with Christine Breland. He had thought about conducting the interview in his own office where it would have been more informal, but decided on the more formal setting of the boardroom to better impress this, Christine Breland.

Chapter 3

On entering the boardroom, he quickly assessed her. Average height and weight, with luxuriant dark brown hair which she wore shoulder length. She had sparkling deep brown eyes. Her cheeks dimpled when she smiled, with full lips which only bore a light gloss. She was dressed conservatively in a well-tailored dark navy business suit, accented by a crisp white blouse which was buttoned discreetly at the top. Her shoes were modestly high, but sensible. He noted, most importantly, that she was not wearing any ring.

He introduced himself casually, extending his hand in greeting as she rose when he entered the room.

"Ms Breland. Jacobus Barton or just Jake to most people and… your future employer, I hope. Would you prefer to skip the formalities and just proceed to discuss your salary and benefits?" he asked flirtatiously.

Christine was momentarily caught off guard by Jake's personal approach, but she noticed his smirk and quickly recovered. Though male chauvinism was declining, Jake Barton, apparently, still retained more vestiges than most of the other males she had met recently.

"Well, if you feel that you have already done your due diligence on me and you are satisfied, then I would be more than happy to become of a member of your firm. And I have done some of my own due diligence on the two senior members and I am impressed. I have reviewed some of Mr Bolta's and your more recent reported cases, but I could not understand that recent decision in Pine Creek Oil & Gas. That was one of your cases, was it not? I could not fully understand why the judgment went against your client."

She smiled demurely, proud of her delicate characterization of a case which Jake recently lost. Now it was Jake who was caught by surprise. He did not anticipate that kind of brazen response and he was not oblivious to the underlying jibe.

"The court awarded substantial damages against your client for failure to pay for certain services it had received or something like that… I am not all that familiar with the oil and gas industry," she added with modest coyness.

Jake's initial surprise turned to amusement. So this young lady wanted to engage in a battle of wits, did she? But he had initiated it so he should not complain. He appreciated her gumption at mentioning the case, but perhaps he could teach her a little lesson in law… and in life.

"Yes, that was one of my cases, but I would not characterize it as a loss. There is more than one way to win," Jake responded ambiguously. "Sometimes you can win, even when you lose."

Christine merely affected a look of feigned confusion as if Jake's comment were too intellectual and beyond a woman's capacity to comprehend.

"The problem was that my client had testified that he was a qualified petroleum engineer during his pre-trial examination. Apparently, he had only picked up the engineer's ring in some pawn shop in Las Vegas as a joke. However, he had been repeating the story that he was a duly qualified P. Eng. for about twenty-five years and it became a reality for him. Unfortunately, the other lawyer decided to verify whether my client had actually obtained an engineering degree and his P. Eng. designation. His skepticism appeared to be warranted since there was no record of my client ever graduating in engineering from any university in Canada.

"I advised my client that since the case was based on an oral agreement between him and the principal of the fracking company, his credibility was critical and that in addition to losing the case, he might end up spending a year in the 'crowbar hotel' for perjury. On the other hand, if he did not have an engineering degree, it would strengthen our defence because he would be more reliant on the professional advice that he was receiving from the fracking company. But after having lied about his qualifications for a quarter of a century, my dear client was unable to disavow his lack of professional qualifications, regardless of those risks. His dubious explanation was that he had attended McGill University under a pseudonym, and he claimed that he had subsequently forgotten the name which he used."

"Forgotten? Fracking?" Christine asked inquisitively.

"Fracking is just an abbreviation for hydraulic fracturing," answered Jake. "Most of the wells in Alberta rely on the process to enhance recovery of the hydrocarbons. It involves a complicated process of fracturing a zone, which is a compressed layer of sand, and injecting substantial amounts of sand through the utilization of very viscous fluids into that fractured zone to increase its porosity so as to facilitate the collection and extraction of hydrocarbons from that zone."

Jake maintained a solemn tone during his explanation, but he watched Christine carefully for her reaction. Her initial insincerity appeared to have transformed into genuine interest.

Christine had not expected Jake to give any explanation, especially one so preposterous. She had merely mentioned the case to corroborate her statement that she had done her own due diligence on the firm and, as an afterthought, perhaps to deflate Jake's obvious ego by referencing a case he did lose.

"I had to learn all about fracking down casing and fracking down tubing and how to read frack reports. I cross-examined the plaintiff's so-called frack engineer for seven hours over two days and I finally got him to admit that commencing the frack with cross-linked fluids would only… excuse me… *constipate* the zone instead of opening it up. Furthermore, utilizing expensive cross-linked fluids in that fashion substantially increased the costs to our client, notwithstanding the fact that the plaintiff was only able to inject less than one tonne of sand over a period of several hours on some frack attempts. I discovered that the alternative was to commence the frack with KCL water, which is very light and relatively inexpensive. As soon as the fracture was initiated with KCL water, you could then switch over to the cross-linked fluid, which is extremely viscous. It looks like a gooey silicon gel, but it can carry and inject about twenty tonnes of sand into the formation within twelve to fifteen minutes. Fracking makes the formation more porous which translates into increased hydrocarbon recovery and increased profit. However, some people claim that the injection of those chemicals also contaminates ground water and contributes to subterranean instability. Fortunately, we do not experience too many earthquakes in Alberta."

Jake assumed that Christine was probably not capable of appreciating the nuances of fracking, but that she should appreciate the legal significance of a key witness lying about his qualifications. Christine did understand the evidentiary significance of the problem of the client's credibility, and she assumed that was the reason the case was lost, but she still did not understand why Jake said that sometimes you can win, even when you lose.

"But if you if have a witness who is obviously lying, how did you end up not losing, as you put it?" she inquired innocently, still unsure if Jake was being totally sincere.

"Well, once we put on our defence my client's direct evidence only took two hours, but we then broke for lunch, and he never bothered to return to be cross-examined. He initially claimed that he had suffered a heart event over the lunch hour, which was probably another lie, but he was able to produce a written medical confirmation from a doctor. The trial judge was skeptical but had no alternative except to adjourn the case for three months to permit my client time to recuperate. Unfortunately, my client never bothered to show up for cross-examination when the trial reconvened."

By this point Christine was seriously intrigued. How could anyone 'not lose' a case when your principal witness commits perjury as to his professional qualifications and, in all probability, lies about his medical condition and then does not even bother to come back for cross-examination?

Jake observed Christine's obvious consternation, but he continued with his chronology in a nonchalant fashion as if everything should be perfectly clear and understandable.

"I assumed that my client had second thoughts about continuing to claim that engineering status and suffering the potential legal consequences. So, like a lot of people who find themselves between the proverbial rock and a hard place, he decided to assume what I call the classic 'ostrich position'. You know, when your client metaphorically sticks his or her head in the proverbial sand and assumes that their problem ceases to exist. Unfortunately, they forget that their posterior is still exposed, and they remain vulnerable to possible sodomy... figuratively speaking."

Jake loved to sexualize his anecdotes. He really believed that if he could reduce an explanation to the lowest form of a sexual analogy or metaphor, no one could possibly fail to understand the point he was trying to make.

"Consequently, the trial judge had no choice but to dismiss his evidence-in-chief which left us with no evidence to contradict the plaintiff's evidence as to the terms of the oral agreement and my brilliant cross-examination was all for naught. Furthermore, the trial judge was so unimpressed that he granted the plaintiff their full judgment with 'enhanced costs' as well."

"And you say that you still did 'not lose'?" Christine asked more seriously.

"Well, my client was the operator of the drilling program, but he only had a 50% equity interest in those dozen wells which were being fracked. The remaining owner was a major player who held substantial leasehold land in western Canada and in the United States, and they were not impressed at all."

"So what did you do?" Christine asked with genuine interest now since it seemed as if the client's position was hopeless.

"I asked the joint owner's legal counsel to authorize me to appeal the trial decision. Even though we had no hope of winning on appeal, filing the appeal would give us time to try to negotiate a settlement."

At this point Christine was even more confused. "But if you lost the trial and the appeal was hopeless, what leverage would you have to try to negotiate a settlement?"

Jake smiled his sardonic smile and arched his right eyebrow in disbelief.

"I said that the joint owner was one of the biggest leasehold owners in western Canada and the United States. I received permission from their corporate counsel to advise the opposing counsel that if they did not settle on more equitable terms, the fracking company would never work for the joint owner anywhere in North America. Once the opposing lawyer spoke with the corporate solicitor who confirmed that position, we were able to settle for one-third of the judgment which was awarded by the trial judge. The settlement struck me as fair because my client did obtain some benefit out of some of those fracks. My client was ecstatic about avoiding jail for perjury. The joint owner was not entirely happy, but the reduction in the judgment more than compensated for their legal fees. I was happy because I was able to mitigate the damages and prevent my client from going to jail. Unfortunately, the law books shall record that the case of Pine Creek Oil & Gas was represented by Jacobus Barton, who went down to ignominious defeat, for posterity. But that is why I do not consider the case to be a loser."

Christine appeared to be lost for words. She did not know how to respond for a moment; however, she was starting to develop a grudging respect for Jake's ingenuity. It really was a case of not losing, even when you have actually lost.

"I apologize, Mr Barton," she stated contritely, "for being so presumptuous."

Christine appeared to be sincerely apologetic and finally Jake asked her a question. "So, what, if anything, did you learn from my explanation?"

Christine was suitably chastened and replied accordingly. "I learned not to presume too much. I also learned that you should be prepared for the unexpected, be flexible enough to adjust to a changing scenario and never give up prematurely."

Jake smiled and then added seriously: "You should also learn, if you have not learned by now, that if you ever quit acting for a client, you should never take them back. It's like going back to an ex-boyfriend or girlfriend or even an ex-spouse. It is a relationship which is doomed to fail because it had failed before. I had quit acting for my client on two prior occasions in the four years preceding the trial after I successfully defended against the plaintiff's applications to have him held in contempt for failing to comply with court orders. Each time he persuaded me to take him back. Sometimes there is not much of a distinction between being a lawyer and being a whore. In the end, he abandoned me and his own lawsuit, but I persevered out of personal stubbornness and pride. Had my client been truthful we would have won the case in any event, but his vanity prevented him from being able to do that. You should also remember to protect yourself at all times—especially against your own client. Some clients have very short memories and retain very little gratitude. You are a hero if you win and a traitor if you lose. And when you lose, do not be surprised if that client decides to turn on you for spite."

Christine was trying to assess Jake carefully and decided that it would be an appropriate time to change the topic.

"If you were serious about that offer of employment, I really would like to work for your firm." She spoke firmly, but with some trepidation in case her queries had offended Jake.

"Well, we have done our due diligence as well. You have practiced family law in Toronto for the last five years. You have no reported cases, but a fairly good reputation with your peers. I suspect that your decision to come west may have been motivated by some personal factors, which should probably remain private."

Christine was surprised at Jake's apparent sympathy as to her possible personal motivations. Though he still seemed to epitomize that proverbial bad boy that her mother cautioned her against, she also sensed that he may have some positive redeeming characteristics as well.

"As I told you at the outset," Jake continued, "you have the position. Go see Kathy Clemens, the senior paralegal and she will set you up. You will be sharing a paralegal with one of the other associates and you can start as soon as possible since we are already a bit shorthanded."

Jake paused and then added somewhat ambiguously: "I am really looking forward to working with you… and getting to know you better." And with that statement, Jake rose to leave the room, casting Christine an enigmatic smile and a conspiratorial wink. He was sure that she would be intrigued.

"And remember this firm's motto: *each minute of every billable hour should be billed out at least once to some client*!"

Chapter 4

Alexa had a luncheon meeting scheduled with Marlena. They had decided upon a new fusion restaurant downtown, but she could not remember exactly what the restaurant was attempting to fuse. Food was not high on her list of priorities this day in any case, but she did order a nine-ounce glass of sauvignon blanc, while she waited for Marlena to arrive.

She was forty-two years old, two years senior to her brother, yet she always had the feeling that she was the junior sibling instead of Michael. She did not consider herself to be unattractive, since men continued to be drawn to her, but the quality of those men had seemed to have declined. She also noticed that her breasts were not quite as perky as they once were, and her buttocks were not quite as firm either. Though she exercised on a regular basis to keep herself physically fit, the passing years were also starting to take a toll on her facial appearance. Those hideous little lines at the corners of her mouth and her eyes seemed to be growing with each passing year. Though she tried to keep them in check with regular Botox injections, the results seemed to be dubious. She also maintained a regimen of highlighting her blonde hair to make the grey hair less noticeable. She had a need to believe that men still found her to be attractive and even more importantly, desirable.

Alexa never thought about how or why she had come to despise her brother so much. It was just accepted as a given fact. Perhaps it was because she believed that her parents seemed to favor him or perhaps it was that everything seemed to come so easily to Michael. He was successful in sports. He was successful academically. He was successful professionally. Their father even selected him to be his guardian and trustee after their mother passed away even though she was the elder offspring. And because of that decision, she was obliged to go to Michael with her hat in hand whenever she was forced to make any financial request even though all she was doing was asking for what she felt was her rightful share of their father's estate. She could not see why she should have to wait until the old man died. After all, he no longer had any use for that money. However, each time she made a request, Michael would presume to lecture her on her choice of husbands or boyfriends or how to utilize those funds more practically and invest the money instead of just spending it as quickly as possible.

Well, that would end fairly soon. Their father was at death's door and after the funeral, Michael would have to release her share of the estate and then she would be free to do whatever she wanted to do. He would not have any control over her, but she was still intent on exacting her revenge by making his life as miserable as she believed that he had made her life.

A cruel smile positioned itself on her lips as she slowly sipped her wine. Her brother may not have been oblivious to many things in life, but he was oblivious to the fact that she was the one who was instrumental in convincing Marlena that he was unfaithful to her. It was a slow and tedious process. A suggestion here and a suggestion there, were made over several months.

When Marlena first raised the issue of Michael's possible infidelity, Alexa initially rejected that suggestion to give herself more credibility. She told Marlena that her concerns had to be unfounded and that she was sure that Michael was a faithful husband. Finally, when she made her own tear-filled admission confirming her brother's infidelity, Marlena was unable to remain unbelieving. After all, it could not be easy for a loving sister to betray her own brother unless it was true. Alexa was especially convincing when she explained that her sole motive was to try to protect her dear sister-in-law from the humiliation of Michael's continuing adultery and all those vile whispers, rumors and snickers which were circulating behind her back.

It had taken a lot of planning on her part and careful execution. She was careful not to disclose or telegraph her true intentions to Marlena. She had to maintain the masquerade of being a caring and loving sister-in-law. She had feigned reluctance to discuss Michael's personal life which had preceded their marriage, but then she proceeded to embellish and even fabricate events to try to corrode Marlena's marital bond of trust.

She had a couple of her friends make anonymous telephone calls and leave voice message requests to have Michael return those calls. When confronted with the voice messages, Michael was unable to identify the caller's purported name and there was no call-back number or the caller's number was blocked. Marlena was bound to become more suspicious as to the identity of the mysterious callers as those calls continued.

Then there was the issue of Michael's unexplained long hours at the office and his frequent trips to various cities in Canada and the United States. After a while they would add to Marlena's anxiety over time, especially with Alexa carefully stoking those fires of suspicion at the same time.

Michael had tried to explain that his professional life involved ongoing arguments to a large extent, with either his clients, the opposing counsel and their clients, and even the court. Since his professional life was so adversarial, he looked forward to some peace and tranquility in his home life which was not possible because of Marlena's continuing unfounded accusations. After a while, he ceased his denials and his absences only increased which only tended to exacerbate his relationship with his wife. But he knew that if he told her that his absences were increasingly motivated by his need to minimize his interactions with her in an effort to avoid that acrimony, it would have only made matters that much worse.

After a while, Alexa was the one who also encouraged Marlena to have an affair herself as an act of cathartic revenge. She even suggested Michael's friend, Bill McNabb. She knew that McNabb would be unable to resist her if Marlena gave him the opportunity. Furthermore, she knew how much Michael loved his wife and how much her accusations hurt him and how her ultimate betrayal would wound him. Though Marlena could not bring herself to have an affair with McNabb, she lied to Alexa and told her that it had happened—once. She was unable to tell Alexa the truth that she could not be unfaithful, because she did not want Alexa to think that she was weak.

Alexa noticed Marlena enter the restaurant and look around for her. She raised an arm in greeting and Marlena proceeded to her table. Alexa was a bit envious of her. Even though Marlena was only four years younger than her, she appeared about a decade younger. Shoulder length curled dark brown hair, flawless skin and an attractive figure clothed in a pale flowered fall dress.

"Alexa, so nice to see you again."

Marlena greeted her with sincere warmth, taking off her dark glasses and revealing her emerald-green eyes.

"And it is nice to see you too, Marlena," Alexa responded sweetly, rising to shake her hand and touching cheeks. She instructed their waiter to bring a second glass of wine for her as well.

"So, how are things going? Is Michael continuing to be difficult or what?"

Marlena's attitude quickly hardened.

"He won't admit it and he won't deny it. He just won't do anything. I thought that he would be a man and give McNabb a thrashing, but he has done nothing. He just doesn't seem to care. And I have even hired a private detective to try to identify that slut he is fucking, but no luck so far."

Alexa decided to goad Marlena some more before she disclosed her next suggestion.

"Well, it is probably that red-headed assistant of his. She may be married, but she has pined for him for a long time. You can tell by the way she looks at him. And if Michael doesn't seem to care that you had an affair with Bill, perhaps he would care more if the guy was someone even closer to him and there is no one closer than Jake?" She raised her eyebrows inquiringly.

"Jake? That male slut."

Marlena spat out the words and curled her upper lip in disgust.

"I don't think I could bring myself to do that. Not even if he was the last dick in the world. I believe that he would be prepared to do Mother Theresa even if she was dead, as long as her body was still warm to the touch."

Alexa feigned a gasp at the outrageous suggestion.

"You are absolutely right about Jake, but at the same time, if you could drive a wedge between those two assholes, that would be quite an accomplishment. Food for thought in any case."

"No, Alexa," replied Marlena. "There is a limit to how far I would be prepared to lower myself and Jake Barton is simply too low for me.

That is something which is simply not going to happen. Once with McNabb was too much for me. I had to take an extra long shower to try to cleanse myself and make sure that I washed off every fingerprint of his."

Marlena hoped that her embellishment of her feigned infidelity would dissuade Alexa from further similar suggestions.

"And you know," she added sadly, "when I told Michael about it, though I could see the hurt in his eyes, it really did not make me feel any better, either."

Alexa took a long sip from her wine glass to give her some more time to collect her thoughts. She realized that she could not push this issue further at this time, but she wanted to continue to create a possible springboard for some renewed suggestion in the future.

"I understand completely, Marlena," she replied. "I would not want to touch Jake Barton with a ten-foot pole even if he was the last living dick on the face of the earth. The thought of him touching me is simply too repugnant to contemplate. But remember, Marlena, it was Michael who betrayed you first."

Chapter 5

Michael had moved out to his father's acreage because he really had no other place else to go and he wanted to be close to his father. His father did have an elderly hired hand who lived in a double-wide mobile home on the property. He was responsible for the general day-to-day maintenance and care of the animals which his father had accumulated for companionship. Michael even started to develop an interest in the animals, himself. There were two dogs. Joe was a cross-bred Doberman who his father had named after his hired hand, an honor the hired hand did not fully appreciate. Sterling, a silver-haired German Shepherd, was appropriately named because of her silver-colored coat. The feral barn cat was named Darryl, but Michael never discovered the reason for his name. There was also a miniature black goat named Buster, which truly looked demonic with its black coat and its two upright satanic horns. He could have been better named Lucifer.

Buster, notwithstanding his small size, had the habit of greeting strangers to the property aggressively by rearing up and butting them in the thigh with his horns. Most people found it hilarious and painful at the same time. To Michael the dogs and the goat seemed inseparable. They played together and they even shared a heated garage bay at night. Finally, there were the two brood mares, one of whom had given birth about a week earlier.

They all had individual personalities and idiosyncrasies which made them unique and interesting. Michael noticed, however, that unlike people, animals did not engage in guile or betrayal. If you treated them with kindness, they reciprocated in kind. Their affection and loyalty seemed unconditional. Even when the dogs misbehaved on occasion and were disciplined by a harsh word or a sharp slap on their hind quarters, they forgave him almost immediately. They also seemed to sense if he was upset or contented. If he seemed upset, the two dogs would go out of their way to show their affection in an effort to distract him from whatever was troubling him or so it seemed.

The two mares were less patient than the two dogs. Michael had arranged with the hired hand that he would feed them in the evening when he came home from work. If he came home late, the mares would be pacing impatiently in obvious disapproval by the feed buckets which were hung on the rail fence which paralleled the long driveway from the highway to the residence. The dogs and Buster were more forgiving. They were just grateful that he had finally arrived, and they would race his car to the garage. Michael had to take care not to hit them as they criss-crossed in front of his vehicle.

Michael was more familiar with Joe than with Sterling and he had taught him a small vocabulary of about a dozen commands. On occasion, instead of saying the words, Michael would just simply spell them out and Joe would listen intently but remain confused while he anxiously waited for some command which was recognizable and which he could then proceed to obey immediately.

"So, Joe," Michael would ask teasingly. "You can't spell? That is most unfortunate!"

When he finally gave him the full audible command, the dog, oblivious to the joke Michael had just played on him, would respond obediently and gratefully.

***

He had gone out to the stable the previous day to check on the brood mare, Wooden Doll, who had just given birth to a female foal the previous week. His father had decided to breed the mare late, so the foal was born in September, instead of March or April. He noticed that the foal appeared to be lame, so he had arranged for Dr Greg Samuelson, a prematurely balding forty-five-year-old veterinarian, to come out that day to check on the foal.

Michael stood on the deck surveying the pastures which were slowly yellowing in the early fall. The cottonwood trees were also slowly shedding their yellowed leaves in anticipation of their coming winter hibernation. The spruce trees remained green, but their deep verdant spring colors seemed to have faded as the days shortened with the passage of summer.

He saw the veterinarian pull up in his van and park in the small, paved parking lot north of the residence as the two dogs jumped up in unison, barking a greeting at the new arrival. Greg saw Michael on the deck, and they exchanged waves, but the veterinarian then proceeded directly to the small six stall stable which was located next to the riding arena to the east of the main residence. Five stalls with removable partitions were reserved for horses. The sixth stall was converted into a tack room, even though the saddles and bridles had not been used by anyone for a long time.

By the time Michael reached the stable he saw the veterinarian already in the stall checking out the foal's pastern while the agitated mare was snorting her displeasure and pacing back and forth against the far wall, eyeing the veterinarian suspiciously. The stall had been enlarged by the removal of a plank dividing wall between two stalls to expand the accommodation for the mare and her newborn frisky foal.

"It doesn't look good, Michael," Greg said soberly. "Here, come take a closer look, but give the mare some rolled oats to eat to keep her occupied."

As Michael entered the stall, Greg was able to hold the foal and pin her against the near wall with his right knee braced behind her front legs. He was using his body weight to keep the foal stationary while Michael picked up her right leg, gently stroking the foal's neck with his left hand to calm her.

"Good God, Greg!" Michael explained with concern. "What the hell happened?"

The foal's pastern was raw, and the skin appeared to have been chewed back to the bone.

"It appears that the foal has been gnawing on her ankle," Greg replied.

Michael was confused and could only ask why.

"I believe the mare may have accidently stepped on the foal's ankle or the foal injured it prancing around the stall. It is obvious that whatever happened, it severed the arteries which feed oxygenated blood to the hoof The hoof was becoming necrotic because of the lack of oxygen and the foal is basically trying to amputate her hoof to try to save her own life," Greg explained matter-of-factly.

"Aright!" Michael replied and though he did not fully understand the situation, he was assuming that the condition could still be treated. "What can we do for her?"

"That is the problem, Michael. Even if you had me come out right after it happened, micro-surgery to correct the arteries would have been extremely tricky and probably unsuccessful. There is really only one option at this time and that is euthanasia, to spare her the agony of enduring more pain and hobbling around on three legs until she dies."

Michael remained silent for a couple of moments. He looked at the foal's doleful eyes which seemed filled with innocent confusion and fear.

"Sometimes, life just sucks," Michael responded. "She is barely a week old, and you are telling me that we have to put her down?"

Greg could only nod his head in confirmation.

"All right Greg. You know what is best." Michael spoke with a heavy resignation which was underscored by the rasp in his voice. "She is not going to suffer though, is she?"

"No need to worry about that, Michael, but I have to go out to my truck to get the appropriate medication."

Greg was quiet and solemn when he came back with the syringe and a vial of clear fluid

"We have to lay her on her side, and you will have to sit on her and hold her head down firmly so that she will not squirm or move too much while I inject her jugular vein."

Michael checked on the mare. She was still eating but watching them carefully. She did appear less distressed than she was when they first entered the stall. The foal was lying on her left side, looking at him searchingly, incapable of understanding what was happening to her.

"Have you ever gotten used to doing this, Greg?"

Michael's question was innocent, but naive.

"If I ever get used to doing this, Michael, that will be time for me to quit," Greg replied quietly.

The regret was palpable in Greg's voice as he injected the syringe into the foal's neck and after approximately fifteen seconds, the foal first closed her eyes and then lay still. She was dead.

"That was fast, Greg. I was thinking about the lethal injections they give convicted killers in the States, and I thought it would take much longer."

"When they introduced the guillotine, they thought it was more humane than manual decapitation or hanging. Hanging usually involved a prolonged strangulation until Albert Pierrepoint, the English executioner, introduced the 'long drop'. He was one of the executioners at the Nuremberg Trials. He utilized the condemned 's own body weight and gravity to break the neck. Then they introduced the electric chair and the gas chamber. They thought it was more humane because a machine did the execution. The first electric chair execution took several minutes, and they pretty much ended up frying that convicted killer. With the gas chamber, the condemned would writhe violently against their restraints as they were slowly asphyxiated with poison gas. With lethal injections they believed the more humane protocol was to first put the condemned to sleep and then kill them. That is why it takes relatively longer. Though it is not really humane to execute anyone, it seems that they try carry out the execution in the most 'humane' fashion possible."

Greg did not appear to have any regret at having to resort to euthanasia since he knew that it was an act of mercy. As Greg stood up, Michael stooped down to pick up the foal and remove it from the stall, but Greg immediately cautioned him.

"Michael, you know how a mare reacts when you first separate her from her foal when you wean it. If you remove the foal right now, you can multiply that reaction tenfold. She will literally kick down your stable or kill herself trying to get back to her foal. You better just leave the foal here until morning and give her an opportunity to realize what has happened."

***

Michael rose early the next day just as the sun was just rising over the horizon. When he got to mare's stall, she was quietly eating her morning ration of rolled oats and supplement which Joe, the hired hand had already provided. He looked around the stall and initially did not see the foal, but then he did notice a lump of straw which was apparently piled up where they left the foal the previous day. He entered the stall and to his amazement the mare had literally buried her foal with straw. Somehow, she was able to accept that her foal was no longer alive, and she was able to accept that loss and carry out that final act of farewell. If she grieved for her foal, that had been completed sometime during the night. Now she was just focused on eating… and continuing to live.

In a few days Michael knew that he would be burying his father just as the mare had buried her dead foal with straw. He could not help but compare the death of the foal with the pending death of his father

Michael carried the foal out of the stall and gently placed her in the front loader of the tractor so that he could take her to the place he had selected for her burial at the back of the property. It was tranquil spot on the south side of the creek that traversed the south end of his father's acreage, beneath some cottonwood trees. The two dogs and the demonic goat followed the tractor out of curiosity. After Michael had dug a small trench to accommodate the foal's body, he carefully covered the body with soil and tried to compact it to dissuade any animals from digging it up.

And just as Wooden Doll had apparently moved on with her life once she had covered the foal with straw, Michael's thoughts strayed to the other pending issues in his life. His father's own imminent death, his disintegrating marriage, his sister, his work, and knowing that he would not be able to get on with his life with the same ease as the mare.

Chapter 6

'UH! UH!"

The old man winced in pain as he attempted to shift his position on the sofa, but he lacked the strength to complete the manoeuvre. Forgetting about his inability to walk, he had also tried to swing his feet down to the floor.

"Would you like another painkiller, Father?" Michael asked respectfully. He had always addressed him formally, because his father had always seemed to be a remote, formal parent.

"UH! They no help, Michael. No help!" His father replied weakly in his broken syntax.

"Do you need to go the bathroom?"

"UH… Shame, Michael… I shamed!"

Michael was aware that the old man was extremely self-conscious about being carried to the bathroom by him, though he was not that self-conscious with his two regular male nurses who had been retained to provide ongoing care in alternating twelve-hour shifts. Michael had decided to give the scheduled nurse the night off and he was asleep in one of the spare upstairs bedrooms in the home. Michael stayed with his father since he was unable to sleep himself. He remained seated on the carpeted floor in the living room beside his father who had chosen to lay and sleep on a sofa on the main floor instead of in his own bed on the second floor.

"No need to be ashamed, Father. After all, you changed my diapers when I was young. Now it is my turn," he added sympathetically.

Michael reached over and placed his right arm under his father's legs. Using his left arm as a support for his back, he lifted his father up. He was surprised at the lack of weight. When he got to the bathroom, he placed him on the toilet and gently pulled his pyjamas down and then turned away to afford his father a modicum of privacy. When his father had finished, Michael carried him back to the sofa and laid him down gently, pulling the comforter over him for warmth.

"Father, perhaps if you took a double dose... or even three painkillers... it may help reduce your pain?"

"UH! No help, Michael...they no help!" His father replied scornfully.

Though the painkillers helped initially, now even a triple dose of the morphine medication was no longer adequate to ease the pain. Michael could see the tears of pain well up in the corners of his father's clenched eyes and he could feel his own tears welling up inside. He felt so helpless and useless. Then the old man's eyes fluttered open again and those piercing intense blue eyes stared back at him.

"UH! Michael... I want. I need die soon."

"Not yet, Father. Not yet!" Michael protested in a quiet soothing voice.

"UH! No Michael... I die soon... not soon enough... No grieve for me, my son... I grieve for you... but enough, Michael!... Time to live! Time to die... now!"

The old man fell silent for a moment, but he continued to stare at his son. His wheezing irregular breathing was still punctuated by spasms of pain. The old man continued to stare at his son with his piercing blue eyes as if he were trying to impose his unspoken will upon his son.

Michael knew what his father wanted him to do, and it was not going to be an easy decision. Whether it was more appropriate to keep him alive for another day or two for his own selfish desire to continue to share his father's life for that additional time or whether it would be more merciful to help end his agony, as with Wooden Doll's foal. He wondered if it were possible that the inherent immorality of an inappropriate act could be made appropriate and moral by certain circumstances if the end result was merciful? He was not sure, but he was able to come to a decision.

Michael rose slowly and went to the kitchen. He looked around absentmindedly, yet he knew what he was looking for: the saran wrap container was on the counter and Michael tore off a long strip and doubled it over and he returned to his father. His father continued to look at him, but he did not speak a word. Father and son shared the understanding of what was about to happen. Michael knew what his father was asking him to do, and his father knew that his son was going fulfil that request as his loving son.

The old man looked up at his son and somehow found the will to form a nascent smile at the corners of his lips.

"Promise, Michael. Promise you try to help your sister. Promise."

"I love you, Father. I wish I had been… a better son… Please forgive me, Father. I…promise."

Michael's voice trailed off after completing that last statement. He found that it was a difficult promise to make. The old man nodded a silent approval before slowly closing his eyes for the last time. Michael placed the saran wrap gently over his father's face and it effected an immediate seal over his nose and his mouth. Then he placed a spare pillow over the saran wrap and gently pressed down.

The passage of time was relatively short, though it seemed interminable, yet the old man did not put up any struggle. Finally, Michael could feel the old man's body shudder slightly and then slacken. Michael released the pressure and it seemed as if his father's soul was finally released as that last breath was expelled from his lungs. Though Michael had stopped being enthusiastically religious a long time ago, for a moment he did believe that his father's soul had been released.

He lifted up the pillow and noticed that there was some mucous and saliva on the saran wrap, so he reached over to pick up a couple of paper tissues and wiped his father's face clean. Then he flushed the saran wrap and the tissue down the toilet. The pillow remained a pristine and mute witness to the part it had just played in the tragic event.

"Forgive me, Father," Michael repeated quietly to himself as he leaned over and kissed his father on his forehead, but he was already starting to regret the promise he made to his father. The old man's face finally looked peaceful and serene. His eyes were shut, and his body was still warm to the touch, but Michael knew that would soon change.

Michael realized that now his tears were streaming freely down his cheeks and over his lips. He could feel their moist warmth and taste their bitter brine. An execution, no matter how merciful or benign, was still an execution, Michael thought. But he could now understand how Dr Greg Samuelson must have felt when he injected the foal and he also thought that he could understand why Greg added that if he ever got used to euthanasia, he would retire. Perhaps an inappropriate act could be perceived as being appropriate if the end result was merciful, but he was not able to expunge his guilt that it was still inappropriate and immoral in the first instance.

He would advise the nurse in the morning and the nurse would arrange for an ambulance to take his father to the funeral home. What he needed now was a double shot of brandy or perhaps a couple of double shots. Hopefully he would be able to anaesthetize himself and perhaps sleep a restless sleep for a little while.

Chapter 7

Michael had been away from the office for a couple of days, but he knew that he had to make an appearance sooner, rather than later. It was only a thirty-minute drive from his father's acreage to his office which was located in the southwestern part of the city, instead of downtown. Though it was still early fall, the fields were continuing to yellow and turn brown. It would not be long before the first winter snows would make their appearance. Sometimes it snowed in September and sometimes people had to pray for snow for a 'white Christmas'. But the first snowfall would confirm that summer had passed, and spring was a long time off. At least the days of summer were long, lasting from the early morning hours and there was still sufficient light until late into the evening. However, the days of winter were correspondingly short. It was dark when he went to work in the morning, and it was already getting dark in the evening when he was heading home.

***

The receptionist greeted Michael warmly as he entered the office.

"Mr Bolta, Kathy and Jake are both anxious to see you. Jake hired that new associate and your sister called to make an appointment. You had an opening at ten a.m. today, so I put her down tentatively for that time, but I can call her back and cancel if you do not want to see her today."

"Thanks, Ginger. I should probably get it over with as soon as possible, but call her back and reschedule it for after my father's funeral. He passed away this morning."

Michael had a pretty good idea as to what Alexa wanted to talk to him about, but he was not inclined to discuss the issue of their father's last will and testament until after his funeral. He really did not want to argue with her about the propriety of the testamentary provisions their father had made for her, which Michael knew she would not appreciate, until after they had first buried their father. Then he would be able to deal with her when she started to argue about her bequest.

Kathy stood up when she saw Michael come down the hall to his office, but Jake saw him coming as well and immediately got up to intercept him before Kathy could say anything. Jake proceeded to follow Michael into his office and then he closed the door, preventing Kathy from following.

"Mike," Jake said, "I just want to express my condolences. The office has been advised of your father's passing. He was quite a man. I always looked up to him, even though I think he tended to look down on me."

"Thanks, Jake. Difficult to describe my feelings. I had always tried very hard to please him, but I always thought that I was disappointing him more often than not. I remember when I first told him that I wanted to go into law. He was incredulous and could only suggest that I get a gun and become an honest bank robber instead, since that was probably a more honorable profession. He always wanted me to go into engineering because he believed that it was a practical profession which contributed to society. I think he forgave me in the end, and I do remember his sage advice once he was able to accept my decision: '*Do not presume to think that you are better than anyone else, but do not let anyone presume to think that they are better than you*'."

But Michael did not want to talk about his father. He wanted to discuss business and his pending schedule which had to be adjusted because of the father's funeral.

"I think your father knew that you were a good lawyer and probably different from most of the lawyers he had to deal with. And I think he knew that if you acted for a morally challenged client on occasion, the other side was usually considerably more corrupt," said Jake.

Michael appreciated the support, but he really wanted to change the topic.

"In light of my father's funeral, there is a conflict with my ability to go to Denver for that judicially directed mediation. I cannot delay the funeral, but I also cannot delay the mediation. Are you are prepared and ready to go in my place?"

"I am," replied Jake. "We have an important obligation to our client and since there are about five other counsels involved, from Vancouver, Denver and Casper, Wyoming, trying to reschedule the mediation would be extremely difficult and time is of the essence for our client."

"As you know Jake, our client's company is a small engineering firm which had performed some reservoir engineering in Colorado and Wyoming for National Hydrocarbons, which currently owes our client about $300,000 for the services rendered. We sued them in Alberta, but their registered office is in Vancouver. It appears that National Hydrocarbons was more into promotion than actual development. It is sometimes referred to as 'pump and dump'. They obtain some good engineering reports and then they drill a few wells. They then promote the company by publishing those engineering reports and their drilling program. Market greed causes the stock to soar, and they proceed to dump their shares and the stock price plummets back down when none of the wells go into production and the company does not receive any revenue. After buying their shares back at the greatly reduced prices, they then proceed to recycle the promotion once again."

"It smacks of blatant dishonesty to me, but greed does make the world go around," opined Jake.

"It comes close, Jake," explained Michael. "But the engineering reports confirming the existence of vast reserves of shale natural gas are legitimate and National Hydrocarbons actually does drill some wells. They simply do not proceed to complete and put them into production. They utilize the reports to create some sizzle in the market, but they probably do not believe their own engineering reports and that is why they do not bother to complete those wells and put them into actual production. In that way they avoid failure, and they avoid incurring those additional completion costs as well."

"So how did our client get involved in a $50 million lawsuit in the US over a $300 grand engineering account?" asked Jake.

"Marcel Paradis is the former CEO of National Hydrocarbons. Paradis was ousted about a year ago in a shareholder revolt which was initiated by some institutional investors who decided that the company's reserves were not being legitimately developed. The problem was that Paradis, who comes from Louisiana, had another company, Bayou

46

Energy, which also had a large participating interest in the reserves held by National Hydrocarbons. Paradis had Bayou Energy commence an action against National Hydrocarbons in Colorado, hypocritically alleging fraud and breach of contract in respect of its failure to legitimately develop its holdings, a practice which was actually initiated by himself. National Hydrocarbons decided to use the Bayou Energy action in Colorado to counterclaim against Bayou Energy and they decided to join our client, claiming that our client's reservoir engineering reports were inaccurate and fraudulent. That gave them a defence to the Bayou Energy action, and it also gave them the excuse not to pay our client's account," replied Michael.

Michael and Jake both knew that the key subliminal issue was that neither National Hydrocarbons' nor Bayou Energy's business practices could stand close scrutiny. And neither could Paradis. Consequently, they got a Colorado state court to direct a mediation to try to resolve the dispute which neither major party could afford to have to go to trial. Their client, on the other hand, did not have much choice since if he did not participate in the Colorado action, his claim might be wiped out.

"Well, our client's claim seems fairly simple and straightforward," said Jake. "The services were requested; they were duly rendered and invoiced, which just leaves the issue of payment. The validity of the reports is confirmed by the fact that National Hydrocarbon utilized those reservoir reports in their public stock promotions."

"The situation is what it is," Michael replied. "Our initial problem is that our client is a bit naive. He appreciates that Paradis is primarily motivated by revenge for being unceremoniously removed from National Hydrocarbons, a company which he had founded, but the lawsuit just does not make any business sense to him."

"I understand," added Jake. "It is also common knowledge that Paradis' own conduct in the whole matter is extremely delicate. He may have commenced the lawsuit, but he does not want to be examined under oath and be obligated to disclose his own stock market dealings. If that happened, Paradis would not be able to be truthful and committing perjury would land him in jail. That would also disqualify him from holding any directorship in a publicly traded company. Failure to testify would also result in Paradis possibly being held in contempt and being made subject to a variety of other judicial sanctions."

Both lawyers also knew that their client, on the other hand, did not have the luxury of time or the financial resources to fight a prolonged litigation in Canada and in the States at the same time. Payment of the $300,000 was also critical to his company's continued survival, but the biggest concern they had was to ensure that in this struggle between National Hydrocarbons and Bayou Energy, that their client would not be made the sacrificial lamb by the two big players.

"All right, Michael, what can you tell me about the other legal counsel?" asked Jake.

Michael proceeded to oblige, commencing with the three other counsel on the opposing side.

"First there is this lady from Wyoming representing some other participant or partner of National Hydrocarbons. I really do not know anything about her. Then there is their local Denver counsel who commenced this counterclaim, but I do not know too much about him either since I have not had any dealings with him either. Finally, there is National Hydrocarbons' Vancouver Counsel, a real slimeball named Sterling Layton, whom I have dealt with in respect of our own action. On our side, there is Mark Jamieson, Bayou Energy's Wyoming Counsel and finally there is Carlos Rodriguez, Bayou Energy's Denver counsel. I do not know anything about the mediator, other than that he is a born-again Christian. So, try to exercise a bit more decorum than usual."

"So, we all alone?" Jake concluded rhetorically.

"Jake, this is a classic case of 'the enemy of my enemy, is my friend… at least for a little while'," Michael replied. "Bayou Energy is actually paying our client for his time and even our client's legal bill. Paradis wants to use our client as a sort of a buffer with the opposing side. Remember, it was Paradis who actually hired our client in the first place. They need us to try to defend against National Hydrocarbons and humble them if we can. But that is not to say that Paradis or Bayou Energy is our client's friend. I believe that they would sell our client out without a second thought if they deemed it to be in their best interests."

"So, since we sued National Hydrocarbons and Bayou Energy has sued National Hydrocarbons, and National Hydrocarbons has countersued both of us back, it should be the two of us against National Hydrocarbons—at least for now?" asked Jake.

"You may assume that, Jake, but do not rely upon that assumption too much," replied Michael, somewhat enigmatically. "I do not believe that Paradis is a man I would be prepared to trust. At least not too much."

"I have never supported mediation, Michael," replied Jake. "It always struck me that the facts and the law became irrelevant. It did not make any difference as to which side is right or which side is wrong, which may be all right if it is your side that is wrong. The only important issue is to obtain a settlement because the mediator always reminds the parties that litigation is uncertain and very expensive. The mediator never tells the parties that though mediation is expedient, be prepared leave dissatisfied. The presumption is that in a successful mediation there is no winner and there is no loser, theoretically. I have always been inclined to only mediate if my client's case was extremely weak or hopeless. The fact that our client is right in this mediation, gives me cause for a lot of concern."

"I agree, Jake,' replied Michael, "just see to it that our client comes back with his account paid in full or are you concerned that it may turn out to be five of them against one of you?"

Jake smiled. "No Michael; I think that would make us about even."

Chapter 8

After Jake left, Kathy came in and quickly closed the door behind her so that she could have more privacy with Michael.

"There is not much I can say, Michael, but I am sorry about your father."

"Thanks Kathy, but Father was in a lot of pain. I would appreciate it if you would arrange for an Orthodox funeral for him as soon as possible. He was not religious, but he was a traditionalist. I would prefer to keep it small and personal. Father would have preferred it that way. And make arrangements for Jake to go to Denver in my place for that mediation."

"I have already made arrangements for Jake to go down to Denver," replied Kathy, "but there is something personal I need to discuss with you if you don't mind. I know that you have a lot on your mind right now, but it is important, and I really need some advice."

Michael did not want to deal with another issue, especially a personal one, but he knew that it had to be important otherwise Kathy would not have brought it up at this point. After fifteen years as his first and only assistant, he thought that he knew her fairly well.

"No, go ahead. I will always make time for you," Michael replied sympathetically.

Kathy sat down with her hands clasped on her lap. She spoke softly but avoided any initial eye contact with Michael by looking down at her clasped hands.

"It's Donny. I have always tried to be supportive wife, emotionally and financially, but his business ventures keep failing and draining our savings. With each failure, his drinking and, I suspect, his drug use, is worsening. He complains about my cooking and even that our sex life is not satisfying for him any more. He criticizes my ability at oral sex and sarcastically declares that if I were French, I would be a disgrace to my race."

"Kathy! Please!" Michael pleaded in desperation because the trend of the conversation was becoming increasingly uncomfortable for him.

Kathy finally raised her gaze so that she looked directly at him.

"No, please, Michael. This is as difficult for me to say as it is for you to hear," she replied, her voice quavering slightly. "Perhaps he is right. Being intimate with him is more of a chore than enjoyment for me as well. I thought I could endure all of his criticism, but my concern now is that I think that he may be becoming suicidal."

Michael, though surprised, remained silent, anticipating that Kathy would want to continue and clarify her last comment.

"Last night I woke up in the middle of the night and he was not in bed, so I went downstairs to see what he was doing. He was drinking, as I had expected, but he also had his shotgun beside him. After he took a drink directly from the bottle, he put the end of the barrel into his mouth and tried to reach down to the trigger. I gasped out loud, but he did not seem to hear me and then he put the gun down and just took another drink. I wanted to talk to him, but I was also concerned that I may provoke him into doing something stupid, so I just went back upstairs. I thought about locking the bedroom door but decided against it in case he decided to come back to bed, and a locked door might provoke him too. I could not sleep for the rest of the night. I was also concerned that if he did come back to bed, he might bring the shotgun with him. When I came downstairs this morning, he had passed out in the same chair. The bottle was empty, but the shotgun was still beside him. I took the shotgun into the garage and unloaded it and took the rest of the box of shells with me when I went to work. I threw the shells in a trash can before I came to the office."

She had a look of anxious desperation and then she placed her hands over her eyes to hide the tears that had started to well up and her body trembled with emotion.

Michael got up from his chair and approached Kathy, who rose slowly to meet him. He put his arms around her to comfort her and she reciprocated. This was the first embrace they had shared in all the time they had worked together. They remained motionless for a few moments as Kathy buried her face on his shoulder and started to sob spasmodically. To Michael's surprise, he could feel her breasts press firmly against his chest and he found the embrace to be embarrassingly arousing. Gradually, she was able to compose herself and Michael was relieved as they separated.

"I just do not know what to do!" she explained. "I just do not know what to do!"

Michael was not sure what he should do or say either, but he knew that he had to say something.

"Has he done this before?" he asked.

"No," Kathy answered. "At least, not to my knowledge."

"Well, you got rid of the shells. Perhaps, if the opportunity presents itself, you should also get rid of the shotgun as well. At the very least, you will eliminate the convenience of permitting him such easy access, but what do you want to try to accomplish at this point?" Michael asked.

"I have been putting up with his emotional disintegration, his drug use and drinking for years. There is nothing else I can do for him if he is not inclined to help himself. He refuses to take responsibility and blames everyone else for his failures—especially me. I just thank God that we do not have any children. I believe that I stopped loving him a long time ago. I just did not realize it. And I know that he certainly does not love me any more, otherwise why would he put me through all this misery and pain?"

Kathy embraced Michael firmly again as she started to cry and he gently caressed her left cheek to comfort her, but once again he felt mixed emotions, arousal and guilt, and he slowly released her and stepped back.

"If that is how you feel and you are certain that it is over, then you should end it as quickly and as cleanly as possible, but he may not be that willing to let you go," Michael responded. "Sometimes, people do not want to let go of a relationship. They reason that, regardless of how objectionable they may be at the present time, they still see themselves to be a marked improvement over how objectionable they were at the outset. That logic prevents them from being able to accept being rejected now."

"Michael, I just want it to be over so that I can start to live again. I dream that I am drowning with him and though I can see the surface of the water above me, I seem to be helpless to break through to the surface and take a breath because he keeps pulling me down, deeper and deeper."

Kathy moved into Michael's arms once again and pressed herself against him. Michael wanted to comfort and support her, but that feeling of arousal shamed him at the same time. He was able to continue to hold her until she was able to compose herself and draw away.

"Kathy, why don't you go to the washroom and freshen up. Take the rest of the day off, if you like, but I do not know if it would be prudent to go home if he is still there. If you want a divorce, I will see if that new associate, Christine, can help you get started,"

"That's all right, Michael," Kathy answered. "I just needed to talk to someone and get this off my chest. I will go and freshen up, though, and if you don't mind, I will take the rest of the day off, but I will settle the funeral arrangements first."

"That will be fine, Kathy. Take all the time you need. Jake is going to Denver, so his assistant can cover for you for a couple of days, if I need help."

Michael hoped that he could say more or do more, but he also felt helpless. After Kathy left the office, he went into Jake's adjoining office and brought him up to speed on what had just transpired between him and Kathy. Mostly, but not completely.

Chapter 9

Alexa walked through reception room of Bolta and Barton and then proceeded straight past the receptionist and down the hall to the inner offices. She was not going to wait to have herself announced. The receptionist, who was sufficiently familiar with Alexa, immediately called Michael's office to warm him that she was coming. By the time Michael was replacing the telephone, Alexa strode into Michael's office and sat down in one of the two chairs facing his desk.

"Just who do you think you are to cancel my appointment?" Alexa asked, not bothering to try to mask her anger and disgust.

Michael observed his older sister calmly, trying to decide how he was going to handle the situation without causing a bigger scene than the one he was anticipating.

"Is that a rhetorical statement, Alexa, or would you like me to respond?" Michael replied politely. "If it is a rhetorical statement, then there is no need to respond. If it is a question, I would like to remind you that Father's funeral is scheduled for Friday afternoon, and I thought it would be more appropriate to bury Father before we dealt with the issue of his will and your bequest."

"Don't you dare try to patronize me!" Alexa spat the words out. "I am his daughter, and I am one of his beneficiaries and I want to see a copy of his will and I want to see it now!"

Michael opened the top right-hand drawer in his desk and pulled out a notarized copy of their father's will and handed it to his sister without saying a word. Alexa grabbed the document out of his hand and proceeded to skim over the preliminary sections and go directly to the beneficiary provisions. Michael watched his sister's face redden as she read them.

Michael had another lawyer attend on his father in the company of his father's family doctor, who confirmed his father's testamentary capacity to prepare the will. He thought it was going to be prudent to avoid any accusation of undue influence or conflict of interest, but he was well aware of the specific provisions relating to his sister's bequest and he had correctly anticipated her response. But those testamentary provisions were their father's last wishes.

There were two critical provisions for Alexa. Firstly, all the advances which their father had given her in the last five years, which were specifically identified and totaled about $500,000, were to be set off against her bequest of one-half of the estate. Secondly, her bequest was to be distributed in equal monthly instalments, subject to Michael's discretion. The residue of her bequest was approximately $700,000.

"What? Just what are you trying to pull?" Alexa sputtered, inadvertently spitting saliva drops on the document. "I am going to take this to court. You are not going to get away with this."

Michael tried to remain calm and responded dispassionately to avoid angering his sister even more. He also remembered the promise he made to his father and the premonition he had that it may not be an easy promise to fulfil.

"Alexa, please calm down and try to lower your voice. I do not want you to air our family issues with my staff or anyone else. I suggest that you go to the section which follows your bequest. It specifically provides that in the event you elect to challenge Father's provisions, that bequest shall be deemed to lapse, and you get nothing. Father's capacity is confirmed in writing by his family doctor and the will was prepared and executed by an experienced estate lawyer from another firm, not this firm. And take a look at the execution date of the will. It is dated some eighteen months earlier so any allegation that his medical condition affected his testamentary capacity would be totally without foundation. Finally, if you bother to read the entire will, you will realize that Father went into a lot of detail as to why he decided to include those provisions for you. Basically, we share equally, but you have received advance distributions of about $500,000 prior to his death."

Alexa was livid with disgust, not only with her younger brother, but also with their father.

"So, my dear, younger, loving brother is going to put me on a monthly allowance, is he?" she asked, without bothering to disguise her sarcasm.

Michael paused before responding. He had given this issue a lot of thought and he believed that his decision, though almost certainly not in the best interests of his sister's financial security, which was their father's primary concern, those testamentary provisions were certainly not in his best interests either. The thought of having to deal with his sister on a monthly basis until her bequest was exhausted was simply unbearable.

"The saving provision in the will is that I am given the right to disperse your bequest in my absolute and unfettered discretion," Michael explained. "I have decided that I will have the estate transfer your entire share in a lump sum as soon as probate is granted. You will receive your bequest in cash and my bequest shall be made up of Father's acreage. I have had Father's acreage appraised and I am going to accept it as my share; my share will be less than equal to your deemed share of about $1.2 million, but I do not want to quibble, and I certainly do not intend to waste my time rendering monthly payments to you. However, before your bequest is transferred to you, you will have to obtain independent legal advice from an experienced estate lawyer. You will have to accept my terms that you shall relinquish all further rights against Father's estate and me, personally. I suggest that you take this notarized copy of the will and this supplementary two-page agreement to your independent legal counsel and once it is duly executed and probate is granted, I will give you your remaining share of $700,000, but I just want to caution you one last time. Once this money is gone, you will have to learn to become self-sufficient because you will not be able to come back and ask for more. So spend it wisely and try to be more selective in your choice of boyfriends or husbands. At very least, try to ensure that they have more money than you have."

Though Michael knew that his comments would be interpreted as pedantic and patronizing, he meant them sincerely, although he knew that his sister would not be able to accept his gratuitous advice.

Alexa was still angry, though that anger did abate a little in the realization that her bequest was not going to be trickled out in monthly installments.

"And how long is probate going to take?" she asked.

"I will tell you what, Alexa. Probate can take about three to four months, but if you can wait until Father's funeral, I will have your bequest paid to you the next day," Michael answered.

Alexa remained seated and quiet for a few moments. Then as she rose, she put the will and the agreement into her purse, but it was obvious that she intended to have the last word.

"Thank you, Michael, for your sage words of advice in respect of my finances and my personal life choices but allow me to reciprocate. I am fully aware of your own martial problems with Marlena and if you want to know why she was unfaithful to you…" Alexa paused for dramatic effect and then added, "…it is because you… you drove her to infidelity!"

Alexa spat out the last words loud enough so that everyone in the office should have been able to hear them as well and then she strutted out of his office, leaving his office door ajar.

Chapter 10

Jake met their client, Ben Cotton, at the airport. Ben seemed anxious and Jake wondered if he had a fear of flying or whether his concern was that Jake had taken over for Michael. After they were airborne, Jake decided to let Ben educate him a bit more in respect of reservoir engineering and shale deposits, even though he was not totally uninformed after the Pine Creek Oil & Gas action.

"Well, the US and Canada have extensive shale deposits, but the cost of extracting the hydrocarbons from those shale deposits, natural gas in particular, was not economical for a long time. After OPEC initiated that first oil embargo in the early '1970s when the price went up from $5.00 a barrel to $25.00 a barrel, the US government got the Army Corps of Engineers to conduct studies as to how to extract gas and oil from shale deposits. In conventional extraction, you first conduct seismic work to try to identify the general location of the deposits. Then you drill a hole and cement the casing to stabilize the hole. Then the seismic charts indicate the location and the depth of the formations which contain the hydrocarbon deposits. The next step is to perforate those formations. Basically, you send down a tool, a perforating gun, to the appropriate depths and it literally perforates those formations by blasting through the casing to crack the surrounding ground. The final step is the frack. You send down another tool to seal off the bottom and the top of the selected formation and you inject a light fluid under tremendous pressure to initiate the fracture of those cracks. Once those cracks in the formation start to fracture, the pumper unit switches to very viscous fluids. They call them cross-linked fluids and they are very expensive, but they have the capacity to carry a huge volume of sand. It is possible to inject about twenty to twenty-two tonnes of sand into that formation in about fifteen minutes. The fluids drain away into the formation and the injected sand makes the formation more permeable which permits the hydrocarbons in that formation to collect and be drained up through the casing up to the surface."

"If that is the conventional approach?" Jake asked. "How is it different for extracting shale deposits?"

"With shale deposits, the formations are narrower. With a conventional deposit, you can seal off the bottom and top of a zone, and then inject about twenty tonnes of sand in one operation. With a shale deposit because the formations are so narrow, you cannot frack the entire zone in one step. You have to conduct a number of mini-fracks to perforate the various formations. This takes more time, more fluid and that drives up the costs considerably. So, it was only recently, when the price of oil and gas went up substantially, that extracting hydrocarbons from shale deposits, became economically viable in America. So viable that oil production in the US increased to such a degree that the US became a net-exporter as opposed to being a net-importer of oil and natural gas. However, that prompted the OPEC producers to increase the volume of their own conventional and less expensive production to drive down the world-wide price of hydrocarbons in an attempt to make this high-cost shale extraction uneconomical. It did work, but then the OPEC producers discovered that they needed the previous high prices to maintain their own economic development, but restoring those prices was not as simple as driving the price down in the first place."

Jake found the explanation informative and interesting.

"So, how does all this relate to the $50 million dispute between National Hydrocarbons and Bayou Energy?"

"Well," continued Ben, "there was not much interest in shale deposits and Paradis used National Hydrocarbons and Bayou Energy to acquire substantial interests in the cheap shale deposits in Wyoming and Colorado. As the price of oil and natural gas went up, so did the interest in shale deposits because the shale extraction studies conducted by the US Corps of Engineers in the 1970s are on file at the Congressional Library—they are not a secret. Paradis used the increasing value of the shale deposits to promote the two companies. First, he sold off a great number of peripheral holdings to raise a lot of cash. Then he hired my engineering company to conduct reservoir studies on their remaining holdings to confirm the estimated size of those reserves, which are substantial. Then he hired a couple of drilling companies to drill a number of holes. However, Paradis was basically a promoter, not a developer. He was getting a lot of action in the stock market, and he made the decision that they would not proceed further. They would keep drilling holes and touting my engineering reports' conclusions, but he would not proceed to complete any of those wells just in case they turned out to be duds. Whenever the companies ran low on cash, he would just sell off some more peripheral reserves. However, his salesmanship was superb, and he got a number of institutional investors to be believers and eventually those institutional investors voted him out of National Hydrocarbons. He was probably grooming Bayou Energy to take over from National Hydrocarbons once the market got disillusioned with National Hydrocarbons. And so here we are."

"Ben, have you ever been involved in a civil trial or a mediation before?" asked Jake.

"No, I have not," admitted Ben.

"Well, they are both adversarial, but they are different," said Jake. "With a trial you have strict procedural protocols and rules of evidence and extensive pre-trial disclosure. With a mediation, it is pretty informal and sometimes things happen which you do not or cannot expect. The mediator meets with both parties, and he also meets with them separately to try to get them to compromise and settle. The important thing to remember is that whatever happens or whatever I happen to say or do, you follow my lead without hesitation and without question. If you do not, you will find out that you will be looking for a new lawyer. Do you understand?"

Ben did not fully understand, but he did understand one thing and that was that whatever happened tomorrow morning when the mediation commenced, he was to follow Jake wherever the hell Jake decided to lead him.

"And do not forget," repeated Jake, "it is an adversarial process. Try to visualize the other side trying to get a tight grip around your throat with one hand and around your scrotum with the other hand. Then they shove you into a corner and start to squeeze until your eyes bulge out of your head and your testicles are totally crushed while they try to persuade you to agree to their position. Do you understand?"

"I… I understand!" replied Ben in a quavering voice, which undercut his assertion a bit.

"And I understand that Paradis is having Bayou Energy pay you for your time and Bayou Energy is also paying our legal account. How did that come about?" asked Jake.

"Paradis knows that I could not afford to finance the action in Alberta and help defend this action down here. He offered to pay for my time and pay my legal bill." Ben paused for a moment. "In exchange for future consideration. He did not tell me what that future consideration might be, and I did not dare ask."

Chapter 11

Denver reminded Jake of Calgary, except on a much larger scale. The airport was iconic, if nothing else, comprising a stylized ersatz canvas mountain skyline which shielded the building infrastructure and its subway system. Driving to the city center, you had the gentle silhouette of the foothills and then the jagged mountains to the west. To the east, there were the flat, dry plains which stretched interminably to the far horizon. Both cities were modern and vibrant, and about a mile above sea level, which predisposed both cities to quickly changing weather patterns, but Denver was substantially larger in size.

Their suite reservations were at a downtown hotel which was proximate to the location of National Hydrocarbons' lawyers' offices who were hosting the mediation. That made it convenient because their offices were within walking distance of their hotel.

It was mutually agreed through text messages that they would hold a preliminary meeting that evening with Paradis and the other lawyers in Ben's suite at about seven p.m.

When Jake entered Ben's suite, the first person to greet him was a large man sucking on a large cigar, oblivious to the 'No Smoking' sign on the inside of the suite door. He reminded Jake of Orson Wells in his later life. Big and obese, with a flushed complexion and an inflated face which did not convey the semblance of good health. He was a tall man with a protruding belly which hung well over his belt to the point that his belt buckle was not visible. His sport jacket, though stylish, remained unbuttoned for obvious reasons. His hair was thin, grey, and receding, which he combed over with great care.

"Hey boy!" Paradis shouted at Jake with a distinct southern accent which struck Jake as more Texan than Louisianan.

"I just want you to know that I am not going to let anyone try to bum fuck me, boy!"

He kept his cigar clenched tightly on the left side of his mouth as he scowled at Jake. Jake examined Paradis for a moment. It was hard to discern if he was serious or just joking, but Jake decided that his rude salutation deserved a suitably rude reply.

"Well, boy!" replied Jake. "And I want you American rednecks to know that as a good Canadian *'boy,* I am not into sodomy... at least not with any males... at least not yet, in any case."

Jake deliberately had arched his right eyebrow and gave Paradis his conspiratorial wink, as if to suggest that he might be persuaded to make an exception in his case.

He had correctly assumed that the person who had addressed him was Paradis. Though Ben Cotton appeared somewhat taken aback by the exchange, he was mindful of Jake's advice during the flight to let Jake be Jake.

The other two men in the room appeared to be amused by the exchange. The short Latin-looking individual with curly moussed hair and a thin dapper moustache was Carlos Rodriguez, Paradis' Denver counsel. The remaining individual with a wry smile on his face and double bourbon in his hand standing behind Rodriguez was Mark Jamieson, the Wyoming counsel.

"Well, gentlemen," said Jake, "allow me to introduce myself. Jacobus Barton, or just Jake to my friends. Or..." Jake added, looking directly at Paradis and affecting a somewhat lecherous grin and giving him a second knowing wink, "You can just call me bum fucker, if you prefer."

Paradis paused for a moment, appraising this upstart from the Great White North, then he slowly smiled. He decided that he could do business with this arrogant son of a bitch.

"Hey, son!" replied Paradis, softening his greeting. "I knew that I was going to like you the moment you all stepped into this room."

Paradis swaggered over to Jake, extending his hand in greeting.

"This may be love at first sight, son," Paradis added with dubious sincerity.

He returned Jake's wink and proceeded to hold him in a hearty embrace.

"Nice to meet you, Mr Paradis," Jake responded. "Ben has told me a lot about you. Some of it was even complimentary. Or should I just call you Dad?"

"Call me Marcel!" Paradis replied, with his drooping cigar clinging to his crooked smile.

As Paradis shook Jake's hand, he attempted to squeeze it with all his might. Jake merely smiled and gripped back as firmly as he could, but Paradis' grip was definitely stronger.

The parties exchanged introductions and Ben acted as the communal bartender, ensuring that everyone had a drink in his hand before any discussions commenced.

Mark Jamieson decided to initiate the discussion and asked the rest of the group about possible strategies to be employed at the mediation the next day.

"Who is going to volunteer to be the 'reasonable and rational' counsel, and who is going to be the 'madman' with the proverbial 'flashing eyes' and 'floating hair'? Jamieson asked half seriously.

"I volunteer to be the madman!" Jake replied quickly. "I always feel more motivated and inspired when I do not have to act like a sanctimonious, supercilious, 'reasonable and rational' son of a bitch."

Jamieson smiled and continued. "In that case, I guess I will be the sanctimonious, supercilious, 'reasonable and rational' son of a bitch."

Rodriguez decided to interject at that point as well. He wanted to give the semblance of contributing even though it seemed obvious that Jake and Jamieson were going to be in control.

"Well, I am a team player, too. What would you gentlemen like me to do?"

Jamieson examined Rodriguez for a moment and then responded.

"Well, Carlos. I am sure that if something comes up, it's good to know that you will be ready, willing and able to do your duty."

Jamieson also decided to add a precautionary note.

"I also think you should all know that the mediator, or so I have been told, is a born-again, Bible-thumping Baptist. So perhaps we should all remember to temper our language tomorrow. Things may get heated from time to time."

"Well, fuck him," said Paradis. "If he wants to go down to the river and stick his head in the water a couple of times and pull it out once, that will be fine with me. This is about money, *my* money, not my salvation."

"And it is just for that reason, Mr Paradis," said Jamieson, "that it would be preferable to leave the talking to the lawyers. Otherwise, this mediation may be over before it has a chance to start. Then the only alternative is that they will be deposing you under oath within two weeks and I do not think you really want to go through that process."

"I have been deposed before and that don't scare me none!" Paradis snapped. "But why don't you gentlemen finish your drinks, and I will take you down to the best gentlemen's club in Denver. All that first-class pussy should really inspire you boys to kick ass tomorrow. My treat."

"Well, Mr Paradis," Carlos interceded, "perhaps we should first conclude this mediation successfully and then celebrate our victory."

Mark Jamieson and Ben Cotton quickly voiced their agreement. Jake delayed responding immediately, but then, affecting a look of mild disappointment, he clarified his own position.

"I would love to see some classy Denver pussy, Marcel," Jake said, "but perhaps my learned friends have a point. No reason to celebrate prematurely. It would be like premature ejaculation. Not really all that enjoyable."

"All right, but I bet that I could drink you two Canucks under the table any day of the goddamn week," added Paradis, proudly patting his overflowing belly.

Jake looked at Paradis' three-hundred-pound physique and he was inclined to agree, but he was also prepared to bet that Paradis would never outlive him. Ever since the bar incident at the end of his freshman year in law school, Jake restricted himself to no more than a couple of drinks per occasion. But perhaps there was a way to stick to that limit and still outdrink Paradis. After all, his drinks did not have to be alcoholic, and it might prove interesting to see exactly how much alcohol Paradis could consume.

"In that case, Marcel, you have a bet," replied Jake. Then he addressed the remaining men in the room. "Gentlemen, all I can say is good night and sweet dreams."

He smiled at Jamieson and Rodriguez and gave them a parting wink.

The other two lawyers exchanged a quick glance and started to feel some trepidation as to what may happen the next day. They had no idea as to what would happen, but they both had a premonition that since Jake decided to nominate himself as the 'madman', he probably intended to live up to that moniker. Hopefully, it would not destroy the possible chance of a successful mediation.

As for Paradis, though he commenced this lawsuit out of spite, he had no intention about permitting it to continue to its conclusion or permit the mediator to decide how it was going to end. If anyone was going to decide how it would end, it was going to be him. Winning was important to him. If he could win honestly, then he would be honest. On the other hand, he was intent on coming out a winner in any case and by any means.

Chapter 12

As Michael drove his car into the church parking lot, he saw that there were a few cars already there. He recognized Marlena's car and he became hopeful at the thought that he might get to see his son, Adam. The autumn sun's rays were glistening off the gold leaf on the church's onion-domed roof as he strode up the steps and entered the Orthodox Church of the Redeemer.

His father's open casket was visible at the end of the center aisle and there was a small scattering of people who had come to attend the last rites. He saw that Marlena and Alexa were seated together near the front, but that his son was nowhere in sight. He recognized a few of his father's friends and business associates. His assistant, Kathy Clemens, was seated by herself on the right side of the aisle across from Marlena and Alexa. Several acquaintances nodded a solemn greeting to Michael as he walked down the center aisle to his father's casket.

He looked down at this father or at least the remains of the person whom he once knew as his father, but aside from the physical resemblance, those remains no longer seemed real. He reached down to touch his father's cheek in homage and the flesh was cold and alien to his touch. The corpse was a mere deceitful pretender. His father's life had ended when his soul left his body in that last breath, though Michael did not know where that soul went. Perhaps there was a heaven and a hell, but he seriously doubted it. But if there was another place, he may be able to see his father again one day. Touch him and even speak with him again. Perhaps?

Michael turned and noticed that his wife and his sister were scowling at him with undisguised resentment, but then he noticed that Kathy was also looking at him and smiling compassionately. Michael remained expressionless as he looked away from Marlena and Alexa, and he turned to join Kathy. These events were not lost on the remaining members of the congregation who were watching Michael and the women carefully.

They had come to pay their last respects to a man they had once known and respected, but if some family gossip materialized, so much the better. Marlena and Alexa merely took his action to be an additional insult.

Nothing was said between Michael and Kathy as he sat down beside her. They merely exchanged a polite muted smile and waited patiently for the funeral service to begin.

The last time he was in the church was a while ago for his mother's funeral. As Michael looked around the church, it had remained basically unchanged. The walls were decorated with faded icons of obscure saints who cast vacant stares at the assembled congregation with their unseeing eyes. His overwhelming awareness was the fragrant order of the vaporized tallow from the burning candles was blending slowly with the smoldering incense. That mixed fragrance seemed to envelope the church. In the loft, the church choir was solemnly reciting some melancholy dirge whose words and meaning remained largely meaningless to Michael, since he never attempted to become familiar with his parents' original Slavic tongue.

The choir continued repeating its solemn chant which seemed to calm and soothe him.

"God be merciful. Jesus be merciful... Give us peace."

As the priest entered the church, the assembled congregation rose respectfully. Michael's remaining recollection of the service remained largely incomplete as if a vital part of him was not present. He recalled only portions of the priest's funeral invocations to the congregation. The chorus continued its solemn monotonous chants in the background with the congregation rising and sitting in unison on cue but Michael felt detached from the service. It was not until he felt his tears slowly welling up in his eyes and gently spilling down his cheeks as he recalled faded memories of his father that he felt that he was fully present. He also noticed that Kathy was watching him attentively and that she was crying quietly as well, but somehow, he knew her tears were not for his father but for him.

***

At the cemetery after the service was concluded and his father's casket was being lowered into the grave, Michael thought that he remembered that it was customary for those assembled, especially members of the family, to pick up a small handful of the excavated soil which was going to cover the lowered casket and drop it into the grave.

"Michael! Do not do that. That handful of soil will weigh heavily on your father's soul."

Those superstitious words were spoken by a familiar face, though Michael could not recall the speaker's name.

"No," Michael responded quietly, "my father's soul is gone. It is gone away."

Michael was numb. He could not feel if the day was still warm. He could not feel if the breeze was blowing. People approached him and he could see their lips moving, but he couldn't hear their words. He merely nodded politely in a feigned acknowledgment and unspoken reply.

***

"When do I get my money?"

The harsh words pulled Michael out of his reverie and back to reality. It was Alexa.

"Oh, Alexa!" Michael said. "Don't you think your timing is slightly inappropriate? After all, they have not even buried Father."

"I was not asking for my money right now; I just want to know when I can get my money. I have plans."

Michael sighed and replied, "You can come to my office with your lawyer tomorrow afternoon at two and pick up your bank draft. You will have to produce the executed settlement agreement and waiver first. I trust that will be soon enough to suit you."

Then Michael turned and walked away from his father's grave without looking at his sister or his wife, who was standing close by. As he approached his car, Kathy was already standing beside it, so he offered to drive her home.

***

Precisely at two p.m. the next day, Alexa attended at Michael's office in the company of her lawyer. He was a short, bespectacled man with disheveled hair, anxiously carrying his briefcase in both hands in front of him. Michael had instructed the receptionist to have the door to the inner offices kept electronically locked so that in the event she arrived early, Alexa would not be able to barge in until the appointed time. He realized that it was a petty act on his part, but he felt a need to do it. Since Alexa arrived precisely at two, Ginger pressed the automatic release button under her desk so that Alexa and her lawyer could proceed down to Michael's office.

Michael did not bother to shake hands with her lawyer whom he knew on sight and with whom he had shared a couple of files. He merely asked them to sit down and asked them to produce the duly endorsed settlement and waiver agreement. Once he had reviewed it and noted that it was duly endorsed, witnessed and notarized, he produced a bank draft made payable to Alexa Alexandra Bolta in the sum of $700,000.00 and handed it to Alexa's lawyer.

"I trust that this concludes matters?" he stated rhetorically, speaking to her lawyer.

Then he turned to his sister who was looking at the bank draft in her lawyer's hand instead of looking at him. He remembered his promise to his father's last request; however, the operative word was that he had to 'try' to help his sister. He believed that he had actually tried and that his promise was fulfilled. If not in the spirit, at least in the literal wording of his promise.

"And now Alexa," Michael said, "listen carefully. I never want to speak to you again. I never want to see you again. And do not even think about asking me for another cent. And if there is a hell, I trust that they will be saving a special place for you. Now get the fuck out of my office before I call the police and have you arrested for trespassing."

Alexa spun around quickly to look at Michael, but before she could formulate any kind of response, her lawyer quickly rose and suggested that they leave. Since he was still holding the bank draft, Alexa rose and followed him out. She turned back partially to try to say something to her brother as she was going through the doorway, but her lawyer quickly ushered her out into the hallway and closed the door behind them.

Shortly after Alexa and her lawyer left, Kathy came into his office. Michael was standing up and looking out of the window which faced west towards the distant mountains. Michael noticed that some of the higher mountain peaks were already clothed in snow. Winter was coming sooner this year.

"Is there anything that I can do for you, Michael?" Kathy asked in a quiet voice as she approached him.

Michael did not respond for a moment, but as he slowly turned around, Kathy embraced him and pulled him into herself, holding him tightly. Michael could feel her warmth and he was sorely tempted to just melt away in her arms. The embrace aroused him, but this time he felt no shame.

"No, Kathy. Everything is fine. Hopefully, at least one of my problems is solved, but you never know," Michael answered as he absentmindedly caressed her cheek.

Kathy was reluctant to release him from her embrace, but she sensed his emotions rising and she became concerned that matters may get out of hand, so she politely released her embrace.

"And what about you and your husband?" asked Michael, as they separated slowly.

"Donny was not home when I came home from the office the other day. In fact, it appears that he packed a couple of suitcases and moved out. Would it be all right if I spoke with Christine Breland to see what she could do to help me?"

"Of course, Kathy," Michael replied solicitously. "And if there is anything that I can do, just let me know."

They were both looking deeply into each other's eyes. Michael tried to discern whether Kathy's sympathy was simply out of pity or something else. Perhaps something more. Kathy was seeking some assurance that her feelings for Michael were being reciprocated, even in a small part. Yet, though they both wanted to share their thoughts at that moment, neither one could muster the will to do so, and their thoughts remained silent and unspoken.

Chapter 13

Jake, Ben Cotton, Carlos Rodriguez and Mark Jamieson arrived together at the 33rd floor offices of Colton, Claridge and Company at precisely nine a.m. The receptionist ushered them into the firm's main spacious boardroom which had seating for about two dozen people. Paradis was speaking with a middle-aged man dressed in a dark suit. His hair was grey at the temples, but still full and not receding. His half-frame glasses were perched precariously near the end of his nose, and he was peering over the lenses as he was listening to Paradis.

"Well, Mr Broadhurst," Paradis said, "allow me to introduce you to the rest of the good guys on my team.

Paradis introduced his team and just as he finished the introductions, the other half of the mediation parties entered the boardroom in single file. Jake attempted to form a preliminary assessment of the opponents by their appearance, dress and facial expressions, as they entered the boardroom.

The woman from Wyoming was tall and thin, with her hair pulled back formally into a tight bun. Her lips were a thin line on an unsmiling stern face which was devoid of any make-up. She was conservatively dressed in a business jacket and skirt. Jake doubted if she ever bothered to display a little extra leg to anyone, even though it was probably her best physical asset. He also doubted that she had been laid for a long time, if ever. He concluded that she had no sense of humor and probably hated most men most of the time.

The Denver counsel was a dapper dresser who, like Jake, apparently also favored monogrammed shirts and gold cufflinks. He entered the boardroom carrying several files, but without his suit jacket. Jake concluded that he was deliberately un-jacketed because his snug shirt was intended to convey his physical fitness. He probably worked out in the gym several days a week, which Jake considered to be a total waste of valuable time.

The Denver counsel generously invited everyone to partake of the arrayed hot and cold beverages, croissants and Danish pastries as he placed his documents on the table. Then, without waiting for an invitation, he walked over to the opposing side and proceeded to introduce himself and shook everyone's hand. Cotton was not initially sure if he should accede or not, after all this guy represented the 'enemy', but he complied politely. Jake concluded that though he may be a bit vain, like himself, the Denver counsel was confident and probably competent.

Sterling Layton, the Vancouver counsel, was an average-looking, thin, middle-aged man who was wearing an expensive Hugo Boss suit that was carefully tailored to ameliorate his poor posture. He shaved his head because he probably assumed that a shaved head conveyed more strength of personality as opposed to displaying a prominent bald spot on a thinning scalp. He wore a smug, thin smile on his face which he wrongfully assumed conveyed self-confidence, but his anemic complexion belied that presumed strength of personality and confidence. To Jake, it only tended to verify a misspent life of overindulgence of alcohol, non-prescription drugs and expensive women who only shared their company and comfort for a prepaid, substantial gratuity. He decided that he did not have much to worry about Sterling Layton, Esquire. What Jake did not notice was that Layton was also making his own assessment of Jake and he was equally unimpressed with this would-be macho peacock.

As the various parties seated themselves on opposite sides of the boardroom table, Jamieson took the seat closest to the mediator, who seated himself at the head of the boardroom table. Rodriguez sat next to him and then Jake took the third seat. Ben Cotton sat beside him, and Paradis sat a couple of seats removed, so as to be in a better position to observe everyone. The Denver counsel sat opposite to Jamieson and the woman from Wyoming sat between him and Layton. No principals appeared on behalf of National Hydrocarbons.

The mediation commenced with the mediator going through the standard litany respecting the advantages of mediation as opposed to the disadvantages of litigation and then he invited the two sides to make their respective opening statements.

73

The Denver counsel and the Wyoming woman advised that they were deferring to their Vancouver colleague to make the opening statement on their behalf. The Wyoming woman barely parted her thin lips as she spoke. Layton remained seated but leaned back nonchalantly in his chair. His legs were crossed, but his right hand remained resting at ease on the table. Overall, a very confident, but cavalier, posture thought Jake.

"Well, this lawsuit was obviously conceived in sin," Layton said. "It is totally without any factual foundation or legal justification. Mr Paradis commenced this action out of spite because he was removed as CEO of National Hydrocarbons. As for Mr Cotton, it is obvious that he was colluding with Mr Paradis and that his reservoir reports fraudulently exaggerated the volume of recoverable gas and oil in the shale formations. In that way both Mr Paradis and Mr Cotton could mislead the public and fraudulently enhance the value of their shares in National Hydrocarbons and, by extension, Mr Paradis' other company, Bayou Energy. To that extent, I suggest that our friends on the other side forthwith discontinue their actions both here in Colorado and in Alberta, pay our legal costs to date and that both Messrs. Paradis and Cotton tender their respective abject written apologies to National Hydrocarbons for initiating this piece of legal excrement in the first place. That last condition is non-negotiable and a condition precedent to any settlement, in my opinion."

Though he had remained reclining in his chair during his soliloquy, he leaned forward and slapped his right hand on the boardroom table to emphasize his concluding statement.

Jake was amused at their proposal. He was surprised that they did not request that Paradis also hump their corporate thigh or perhaps perform corporate fellatio.

Cotton squirmed in his chair every time the suggestion of fraud was mentioned. Jake could sense that Cotton wanted to jump over the boardroom table and grab the smug Vancouver lawyer by the throat. His client was starting to learn what the word 'adversarial' really meant.

Paradis merely leaned back in his chair and continued to calmly chew his unlit cigar. He had gone through enough litigation in his life that he was able to recognize the difference between legal argument and legal flatulence. The words that just emanated from the Vancouver counsel's mouth were largely legal flatulence.

Jamieson paused to collect his thoughts before he responded. When the delay became a bit prolonged, the mediator politely asked him to proceed with his opening response.

"I do believe that if this mediation is going to be successful, it would be prudent for both sides to avoid insults or language which besmirches the integrity or reputation of the opposing parties. We should be able to have a civil discourse without having to engage in character assassination. That will not encourage either side to compromise. Without reciprocal courtesy and respect, compromise will not be possible, and the only alternative will be the heavy cost and uncertainty of a prolonged litigation in which both sides will end up losing. I have instructions from my client to put on the record that our intention to resolve this dispute is sincere and we will do everything we possibly can do to ensure that this mediation is going to be successful. My client would be prepared to discontinue its action if National Hydrocarbons would be prepared to discontinue its counterclaim, on a without costs basis, of course."

Jake concluded that Jamieson dutifully performed as a 'rational and reasonable' counsel, as had been agreed. It was also obvious that Layton took Jamieson's opening statement as a sign of weakness and his smug thin smile only widened as he continued to lean back in his chair with his legs crossed.

"And what about Mr Cotton's position?" Layton snorted in obvious disagreement.

"That would be up to Mr Cotton's counsel," replied Jamieson politely.

Everyone looked at Jake, who deliberately refrained from responding quickly to ensure that he had everyone's attention. Jake then directed his initial comments to the mediator.

"My client's claim is modest. It is for services duly rendered. I have seen no evidence of any engineering report in our Alberta action which contradicts or questions Mr Cotton's findings and conclusions. But after listening to my learned friend from Vancouver gratuitously and repeatedly insult my client, I can advise you that I only have three things to say to the other side."

Once again, Jake paused for dramatic effect. Then, turning to the individuals seated on the opposite side of the boardroom table, starting with Layton, and then proceeding left to right to the other two lawyers, he calmly proceeded to tell everyone what those three things were.

"Fuck you! Fuck you! And fuck you!" said Jake in a firm tone. He struck the table with his fist each time he repeated that obscenity, but with considerably more force than the Vancouver counsel had employed. Then turning back to Layton, he added:

"And if you morally challenged sons of bitches want to fuck around with us, then you are going to find out that we fuck back, hard!"

Rising from his seat, Jake began gathering up his papers. He noticed that Cotton had followed his advice and had risen with him. He also noticed that Layton was caught totally off guard and he finally sat up in his chair, gripping the boardroom table with both hands, looking a bit confused. The Wyoming woman's thin lips had finally parted in surprise, revealing small pristine white teeth. The Denver counsel merely sat back with an admiring nascent smile at the corners of his lips. He seemed to be the only one, aside from Paradis and Jamieson, who was aware of what was happening.

"This mediation is over. I see no point in wasting any more time. Let's go, Ben," Jake said, as he started to put his documents into his briefcase.

The initial reaction from the mediator was shock. Though he expected something to happen, he did not expect what just happened. He did not expect the mediation might be over so quickly. He knew that the National Hydrocarbon group wanted to commence with a hard position and then work down from it. He also knew that they could not seriously expect the Paradis side to accept their opening gambit as a final position, even though that is how it was presented.

The mediator recovered quickly and in order to salvage his mediation, he decided to direct a caucus so that he could separate the two sides and calm matters down. After the opposing side left the room, the mediator attempted to try to pacify Jake as his first priority, to ensure that the mediation would continue.

"And here I thought that this was just about money. Now I see that this dispute is about principles. Please," he implored Jake, "give me an opportunity to speak with the other side and I shall come right back and then we can discuss how we can continue when I return."

After the mediator left, all eyes were on Jake. Rodriguez and Cotton, and even Jamieson, to a lesser point, appeared a bit anxious. They could not decide if Jake's sentiments were serious or just play-acting. Paradis was simply in a state of gleeful awe. His money was being well spent.

"I am not sure if my hair was 'floating' or my eyes were 'flashing', but that certainly felt good to me," Jake announced, quite satisfied with himself, as he sat back down.

"Well, son," added Paradis, "I knew that I was going to like you, you son of a gun! I am starting to like you Canadians. You have balls. Big balls. Did you see the look on that shyster's face? I think he crapped his pants when you told him to fuck himself."

"I thought that you might pull something unusual, Jake, but I certainly did not expect that," added Jamieson. "Good work! And I know who to call if I ever need a 'madman' again."

"I decided," replied Jake quietly, "that I had to do something drastic and dramatic to wipe that smug smile off that motherfucker's face. Hopefully, I have shaken things up enough that they will decide to become reasonable. Otherwise, fuck them! I meant what I said."

Paradis decided that this was the appropriate time for him to advise everyone what he expected to happen from this point on.

"Now this is how this shit is going to go down, since I am paying everyone at this table. First, I want this ended by the end of this day. I see no need to continue this bullshit for another two days," commanded Paradis.

"Second thing is that Ben's account shall be paid in full. Squeeze that Vancouver prick for all you can, Jake, but any shortfall will be made up by me. Also, add another $25,000.00 to your account as a bonus for a job well done. Lord Jesus, but you have balls. You should have seen their collective faces. You scared the shit out of them, but maybe they were even too scared to shit. Once we settle Ben's account, Bayou Energy and National Hydrocarbons are going to bury the hatchet, but not in their respective backs. At least not at this time. I started the lawsuit because they pissed me off. I have made my point, but they can't stand close scrutiny either, so I know they will back off."

Jamieson nodded in agreement, then Rodriguez decided to intervene and try to make a modest contribution, himself, if he could.

"And what can I do to contribute, gentlemen?" he asked politely.

Jake looked at Jamieson and winked. Jamieson did not know what Jake was about to suggest, but he knew that it would probably be interesting.

"Carlos," Jake said, "you told us that you were a team player and you wanted to contribute. Well, I now know what you can do to contribute."

"What?" Carlos asked sincerely.

"You are going to have to do that Wyoming bitch and put a smile on her face. I know that she looks as if her urine would corrode the enamel in a toilet bowl, but someone will have to 'do' her and that someone is you, my friend."

Notwithstanding the fact that Jake answered with a straight face, Carlos got the joke and decided to play along.

"You guys are right. And I understand that 'doing' her would not be an easy task for all you gringos, but for Carlos Rodriguez, a Latin lover, it can be done, and it shall be done. I am a team player and I want to contribute; however, I may have to 'do' her with my eyes shut."

***

As directed by Paradis, though the mediation continued to noon and then resumed and continued until five p.m., at the conclusion of that first day Jake got Layton to agree to have National Hydrocarbons pay Ben Cotton half of his account. There was no further mention of any apology. Jake was sorely tempted to wipe the smug grin off his face by insisting on full payment, but Paradis caught his eye, and he nodded his approval, so Jake relented. His client would receive full payment, albeit the other half was going to be paid by Bayou Energy, but Cotton would also be paid for all his time as well. The main action between National Hydrocarbons and Bayou Energy was settled by way of a mutual discontinuance without costs to either side. The matter was settled quickly and quietly before Paradis' five p.m. deadline.

The Denver and the Wyoming counsel were instrumental in negotiating the terms for their side. Layton remained surprisingly silent, however, as Paradis watched him closely, he would see that he was focused on Jake with unbridled contempt. Paradis decided to remind himself to caution Jake about a possible future retaliation from Layton. He had seen that look on other men's faces.

True to his word, Paradis took Cotton and Jake to that gentlemen's club and the ladies lived up to his praise. Paradis also insisted on carrying out his drinking challenge, so Cotton and Jake decided that Cotton would try to match Paradis drink for drink initially and Jake would drink tonic water. Then they would switch. However, Jake decided that he would continue to drink just tonic.

During the ladies' performances, Paradis introduced Jake to a beautiful strawberry blonde named Amie, who claimed that she only worked at the club on a part-time basis and that she was a full-time stewardess with Frontier Airlines but got laid off recently.

"Well Jake," asked Amie, eyeing Jake with obvious interest. "Marcel tells me that you are a Canadian. Could you share a Canadian pick-up line with me?"

"All right Amie… How would you like to throw those luscious thighs over my shoulders some time, honey?" Jake asked with a mischievous grin on his face.

"How shocking, sir!" replied Amie, however, it was quite obvious that her outrage was feigned. "I only have two words to say to gentlemen who address me in such a crude fashion," she added self-righteously, but still smiling.

"And pray tell, what would those two words be, Amie?" Jake asked skeptically. "Thank you, or Good Boy?"

"Well," replied Amie, smiling, "not quite."

"And though I is inclined to tell youse all to just shut the fucks up," said Paradis, in his alcohol-fractured diction. "Since I is and am a Louisiana gentleman, born and bred, I will just says… hush the fucks up."

***

After that Paradis' remaining sobriety dissipated quickly. He had ordered a last tray of Jägermeister shots which Jake detested and declined to drink. After downing four shots, Paradis wanted to go for a walk to clear his head. Amie had gone to the washroom and Jake had not got her contact information nor arranged to have her meet him at his hotel, so he was somewhat reluctant to join Paradis and Cotton on their nocturnal perambulations. Cotton, however, insisted that he accompany them because he did not think that he would be able to handle Paradis by himself and Jake reluctantly agreed. He knew that he would not have the opportunity to get to know Amie better.

Paradis then collapsed on the sidewalk before they could complete one block. Their walk became more complicated when no cab would stop to pick them up. After all, there were two guys in suits at about three in the morning on a downtown Denver Street trying to flag down a taxi with a third guy lying on the sidewalk. The cab drivers were not sure if the guy was dead or alive. Finally, Jake had to jump in front of a slow-moving cab to make it stop.

After Jake gave the driver a quick explanation and an offer to triple his fare, the cab driver drove them to their hotel. After getting the concierge to loan them a wheelchair, it took the combined efforts of the cab driver, Cotton and Jake to be able to haul Paradis out of the cab and put him into the wheelchair.

There was some formal function going on at the hotel because there were a group of men in tuxedos and their female companions were dressed in long evening gowns standing in front of the elevators when Paradis, though unconscious, commenced to vomit on everyone.

Jake and Ben extended their most sincere apologies, but everyone was aghast. The one good point was that they were able to take the first available elevator since no one else wanted to share the elevator with them. As the elevator proceeded up to their floor, Jake looked at Ben and just shook his head in abject disappointment. Amie had shown some considerable promise.

"Ben, since you are making more money than I am on this file, Paradis can share your room tonight. I will bring you guys a pot of coffee in the morning, but make sure that you keep his head and chest elevated so that if he throws up again, he will not choke on his own vomit. We should try to keep him alive, at least until his cheques clear."

Chapter 14

Jake had received payment of the firm's account and a personal cheque from Paradis for the $25,000 bonus. Consequently, he decided to take an earlier flight back to Calgary the next day instead of laying over for another couple of days. Cotton had business dealings with Paradis, so he was going to stay. Unfortunately, the only flight which was available was at ten that evening, but then that direct flight got delayed indefinitely and the only other flight was via Vancouver, departing at midnight.

While he was seated in the staging area waiting to board the Vancouver flight, he had finished reading his news magazine at least twice. He was totally bored. Jake looked around at the people who were also seated in the lobby when he began to daydream fancifully. What if the world was going to end in a few hours? Was there any woman present with whom he could spend those last remaining hours beneficially or would his fanciful life just end with a whimper?

Looking around the airport lobby, he came upon a young woman he judged to be in her mid-thirties dressed in a black sweater, and black slacks, seated a couple of rows away opposite him. She had black hair, which was stylishly cut, short and simple. He could not make out her eyes, but she had an ample bosom which was accentuated, at least in Jake's mind, by good posture since she sat straight and had her shoulders pulled back. She definitely had promise, so he commenced to stare at her shamelessly to try to get her attention.

He continued to stare at her in the dire hope that she would look up from her magazine and see him looking at her at which point he would give her a friendly smile. If she reciprocated, he would join her and try to get to know her. This continued for about twenty minutes, but she never looked up once. He finally concluded that it was not meant to be. The world was going to end; he had lost out on a chance to get lucky in Denver with Amie and it did not look as if his chances were going to improve on the flight to Vancouver. He remembered that line from T.S.

Elliot's poem, 'The Hollow Men': *'This is how the world ends? Not with a bang, but a whimper!'* How fucking true, he thought. But his preference would have been to go out with a bang.

Finally, Jake tossed his magazine into the trash receptacle and walked over to Starbucks to order an additional coffee.

"A large latte," said Jake. "With whole milk."

"Oh," the barista answered pedantically, "you mean a grande latte?"

"If a 'grande' is a large latte, then that is what I want," Jake replied in an indulgent fashion.

"And I would like a grande latte too," a female voice chimed in behind Jake.

Jake turned around to see that it was the voluptuous lady in black. He immediately smiled at her and commenced to savor his presumed change of fortune. He adored her dark-violet eyes He graciously instructed the barista to put the second grande latte on his bill.

"Jake Barton, your most humble and obedient servant, madam," he said slavishly, bowing slightly and inviting her to introduce herself in return.

"Crystal," she said, extending her hand in greeting, but reserving her surname for the present time. "But I am not a madam, I assure you."

"Oh, not that kind of 'madam'," echoed Jake. It is just a quaint Anglo-Saxon salutation which I save for exceptionally attractive ladies like you."

"Well, thank you, kind sir," Crystal replied, affecting an abbreviated curtsey.

"Well Crystal, shall we share our grande lattes and discuss life in general, and you in particular?" Jake asked flirtatiously. "Does the name Crystal come with a surname?"

After all, if the world was going to end in couple of hours, he did not have that much time to waste on senseless preliminaries. The best approach in these circumstances was his Neanderthal caveman approach. Be direct. Overwhelm her with flattery and throw her over his shoulder as she swoons and then carry her off to his metaphorical cave.

"The name is Bachman and hopefully, we can discuss you as well," Crystal answered coyly.

After they got their lattes, they found adjoining seats and commenced to complete their introductions. Jake told her that he was a litigation lawyer from Calgary, not attached, never married and with no children. He was returning to Calgary via Vancouver after concluding a mediation in Denver.

Crystal told him that she was a denturist in Vancouver, originally from New York City, but that she had been residing in Vancouver for about eight years and that she had even become a Canadian citizen a couple of years earlier. She had been married twice, but both those marriages failed, she candidly admitted, because she had affairs with her husband's best friends. When she confessed that she found fidelity to be confining, she watched him carefully to see if he was going to be judgmental. She also had no children and was currently in between relationships and returning to Vancouver after visiting friends in Denver.

Jake concluded that she was great prospect, at least for a little while, so he decided to confess his fantasy about the world ending and his futile search to try to find someone suitable in the airport lobby to share those last few fleeting moments.

"So you were hoping that, like a condemned man, you would be granted one last wish. But you were not necessarily interested in just a last cigarette before dying, were you?" Crystal asked.

"Well, I don't smoke," answered Jake, quite honestly.

"So what were you hoping for, Jacob, a mercy hump, perhaps?" Crystal chuckled as she answered her own question. "I trust you don't mind if I refer to you as Jacob?"

"I would prefer to characterize my last wish in more romantic terms since I consider myself to be an incorrigible romantic, Crystal. But I must confess that a mercy hump would suffice," Jake answered sheepishly.

"So you must be a believer in true love?" Crystal asked.

"Actually, I am," answered Jake. "I was weaned on all those stories which commenced with 'Once upon a time' and ended with 'and they lived happily ever after'. But I am also a realist, so if you cannot find true love, some hot, sweaty, frivolous fornication will do just fine for me."

Crystal did not respond. She merely examined him from top to toe as if she were evaluating his suitability for a possible last act of mercy, but she continued to smile. She was obviously enjoying the conversation and the battle of wits.

"Oh, what onerous demands we women are called upon to perform from time to time," she lamented, dramatically clasping her hands together and resting them over her heart. "I am not sure if it is out of some duty we owe mankind, or what."

"You may not have noticed," Jake confessed, "but I was staring at you for at least a half hour in the dire hope that you would look up and see me."

"Actually, you were staring at me for only twenty minutes," Crystal corrected him cheekily. "I was actually wondering how long you would continue to stare until you built up the courage to come over and speak to me."

Jake quickly realized that there might be more to Crystal than what he had initially assumed.

"Sometimes a guy, a gentleman, needs a sign of encouragement," he replied. "Especially a gentleman like myself who would never presume to intrude upon a lady's privacy... without some small gesture or sign of interest."

"I assumed that had to be the case, Jake," Crystal replied disingenuously. "That you were just too much of a 'gentleman' to presume to intrude upon a lady's privacy. That is why I decided to give you a second chance and join you at Starbucks. By the way, thanks for the latte."

Jake smiled. He sensed that he could love this woman... at least for a little while.

"Well, I have a confession to make, Crystal," said Jake, trying to adopt a serious tone.

"And do you confess on a regular basis?" asked Crystal, taking another sip from her cup.

"I think I really, really like you, Crystal... at least a little bit," Jake replied

"And here I thought you were just hoping for a little... lust at first sight, Jacob," Crystal replied. "But why do you first profess affection and then modify it with that qualifier, 'a little bit'? Are you concerned about rejection?"

"That is an interesting question," replied Jake. "Would you mind if I took it under advisement and got back to you on that in due course?"

They continued their flirtatious conversation until they were scheduled to board their flight. Jake implored the stewardess to arrange to have them seated together, 'in the name of love… true, true love' and the stewardess finally relented, persuading another lone passenger to switch seats with him. During the flight they talked some more, exchanged business cards, and promised to keep in touch. It seemed like the start of a promising relationship for both of them.

On the short flight back from Vancouver to Calgary, Jake could not get Crystal out of his mind. He fantasized about her. Kissing her and caressing her. Tasting her and making love to her. He concluded that this trip was a success on both a professional basis and a personal basis. Perhaps the change of his return flight through Vancouver was ordained by whatever gods there may be and who was he to question something if it was divinely predestined? Crystal Bachman was definitely full of promise for the future. He felt great. The mediation was concluded successfully. He met an amazingly attractive woman with a great sense of humor who seemed to be interested in him. Life could not get much better than this.

He reminded himself to have his assistant send Crystal a dozen roses when he got to the office that morning. He was sure that the romantic gesture would impress her and probably motivate her to reciprocate, albeit not in kind. But he also felt a pang of possible regret. What if Crystal would turn out to be just another heartbreaker? He reminded himself to keep the relationship on a casual level. It was obvious that she knew how to play the game as well, if not better than him. But he was not going to permit himself to become infatuated with her. In that way, he would not make himself vulnerable. He did find her comment about 'finding fidelity too confining' very reassuring, but he also had to come up with an answer to her question about his qualifying comment that 'he liked her, at least a little bit'.

Chapter 15

Michael was seated at his desk with his back to the window which looked out to the mountains to the west when he heard a polite knock at his door and then Kathy entered quickly.

"I do not want to bother you, Michael, but I need some quick advice," she said as she remained standing in front of his desk.

'Please sit down, Kathy," replied Michael.

"I just discovered that Donny cleaned out our joint bank account and that he had also issued a couple of cheques to some woman in Edmonton, who I assume is a girlfriend because I certainly do not recognize the name. The cheques were made out for only $500 each, but it is still upsetting."

"You should open up your own bank account immediately, Kathy, and do not deposit any further funds to that joint account. Cancel all joint credit cards and you should even get a locksmith to change the locks on your home. And I would like to have Christine Breland advise you of what legal steps you should commence to take if you truly believe that your marriage has broken down irreparably."

"As I told you before, Michael," Kathy answered quite somberly, "I believe that we had both stopped loving each other a long time ago, but I never dreamed that he would do this to me."

Michael called Christine and gave her a summary of the status of Kathy's situation and asked her to see Kathy and do whatever she could for her.

***

Christine smiled and rose to greet Kathy as she entered her office. Kathy quickly summarized her five-year turbulent marriage and the current status for Christine, who took copious notes on a yellow legal pad. When Kathy finished, Christine followed up with some additional questions to fill in some of the blank spaces in Kathy's narrative and then she simply asked her what she would like done at this point. There were no children to complicate the divorce proceedings and the remaining financial assets were not that extensive and basically held in joint title. Christine did recommend that Kathy initiate proceedings for a divorce and a division of the matrimonial property, to maintain some control. She also recommended that Kathy obtain an order for exclusive possession of the matrimonial home which would permit her to change the locks and prevent her husband from returning whenever he wanted. The funds which her husband had wrongfully appropriated would be adjusted for when their family home was sold or bought out by her, so she would not be out of pocket at the end of the day. Fees were not discussed because Christine assumed that she would be acting on a pro bono basis since Kathy was the senior partner's paralegal.

***

Jake only got back to Calgary at five that morning. He went to his apartment for a short nap, shower and change of clothes, and then he arrived at the offices of Bolta & Barton about one in the afternoon.

"You look gorgeous, Ginger, as usual," Jake said as he entered the reception. However, this time he appeared to be unusually euphoric, and he stopped by Ginger's desk instead of just going down the hall to his office.

Leaning over her desk, Jake asked. "Have I ever told you how the reception lights bring out the highlights in your eyes?"

Ginger merely smiled back. Jake's innocuous lines always amused her.

"No, you haven't. At least not this month, Mr Barton," Ginger replied formally in the hope that it might dampen Jake's obvious elation. "Was the mediation successful?"

"Of course it was successful. How could you possibly think anything else? And I am back early so that I can make even more money for the firm so that we can pay you at the end of the month. And Ginger... I think I may be in love. I met this gorgeous creature on the flight from Denver."

With that statement, Jake effected a pirouette and proceeded to skip boyishly down the hallway to his office. He instructed his assistant to send a Ms Crystal Bachman c/o Vancouver a dozen red roses, but he could not choose between what transmittal message to attach. He usually relied on his recollection of favorite poetic quotations from his freshman English course. He could send Marlowe's couplet: *"Those who love, love at first sight; Those who hesitate, their love is slight."* His second choice was from Shelley: *"I throw myself upon the thorns of life… I bleed".* Even though he thought it was a bit melodramatic.

His assistant, when asked for her preference, selected the quotation from Marlowe which immediately convinced Jake to use the Shelley quotation, since Crystal Bachman struck him as an unconventional woman. Unfortunately, Jake failed to explain his rationale to his miffed assistant.

After dropping off his briefcase in his office, Jake knocked on Michael's door and entered the office before Michael had any chance to respond. Michael could see that Jake was full of adrenalin, but Ben Cotton had phoned him that morning to apprize him of what had happened.

"We kicked ass, Michael. We really kicked some ass down in Denver," Jake announced emotionally.

"Please sit down and relax, Jake. I also heard that you almost gave our client a heart attack down there with some of your antics. Are you familiar with the concept of 'conduct unbecoming'? Our Code of Professional Conduct applies to behavior both in the province and out of the province. Telling opposing counsel to go fuck themselves and calling them morally challenged sons of bitches should qualify to be deemed 'conduct unbecoming' in my opinion," said Michael, half seriously.

"Calling them sons of bitches was not really that pejorative in this situation. In fact, if I insulted anyone, it was the proverbial bitch that gave birth to those sons of bitches. Talk about lowlifes, Michael, but calling them sons of bitches was anatomically accurate, I assure you."

"Well, sometimes you have to do what you have to do. But both Cotton and I are happy that matters worked out well for us," replied Michael.

Jake took out the two cheques which Paradis had given him after the mediation had concluded. One cheque was payable to the firm. The other cheque for $25,000 was made payable to Jake, personally. In jest, Paradis had even drawn a little caricature of himself on the cheque with remorseful tears streaming down his cheeks as if endorsing that cheque was really painful for him. Jake assumed that the cheque was still negotiable.

"I am going to give the firm cheque to accounting, but I shall give you a personal cheque for $12,500 for your share of Paradis' charitable gift. Now that is one smart guy with a sense of humor, unfortunately the 'Big Boy' simply cannot hold his liquor," said Jake, laughing.

Michael was not surprised at Jake's generosity, and he tried to decline, stating that Paradis intended the gift for Jake, alone. He had no idea of what Jake was talking about in referencing his drinking capacity, since that matter had not been mentioned by Cotton.

"No, Michael!" replied Jake. "You did all the preliminary work. We are partners. We share the agonies of defeat, and we also share the spoils of victory. And… I met the most gorgeous woman on the face of the earth on the flight back from Denver."

Michael had heard this refrain on many occasions in the past and mentioned that fact to Jake.

"But this time, Michael…" Jake replied, "This time I really think it is different. And she is even smart, too."

"Well, I am glad that you are not being totally superficial and only focused on this lady's physical attributes. And I am even a bit relieved that you are perceptive enough to admire her intellectual traits as well," answered Michael, facetiously.

After Jake left Michael's office, Kathy came in. Though she had been able to maintain her composure during her meeting with Christine Breland, as soon as their eyes met, Kathy burst into tears. Michael got up and the two embraced tightly. Kathy's body convulsed gently and rhythmically as she clung to Michael. Michael held his right arm tightly around her back, but his left hand compassionately caressed her right side. Without even realizing it, Michael's left thumb also gently caressed the side of Kathy's right breast. When he realized what he had done, he immediately froze, but Kathy did not draw away. She merely placed her right hand over his hand and drew his hand over her whole breast, pressing down firmly. They looked at each other and then they kissed intensely. It was a long, hard, bitter kiss. They both realized that they had crossed a line and neither one of them was sure what was going to happen from here.

"Kathy…" Michael spoke first. "I am sorry. I did not realize what I was doing."

"No need for an apology, Michael," answered Kathy. "I knew what I was doing, and I know what we were doing was right, for both of us."

"Kathy," Michael continued, "we are still married. We work together. This is not going to be a simple matter."

"Michael," Kathy answered, still holding his right hand firmly over her breast, "let's see what happens. I just want to see what happens and regardless of what happens or how things may turn out, I know that for myself, I shall have no regrets. Besides, we cannot undo what has been done."

Chapter 16

Marlena was sitting in the living room watching Adam play with his toys. He seemed so happy and contented. So oblivious about what was transpiring between his parents. Perhaps ignorance may be bliss in some circumstances, she thought.

Her mind turned to Michael. She found his refusal to sit beside her and Alexa at his father's funeral to be reprehensible and insulting. Regardless of the state of their relationship, it was important, she felt, that family issues not be aired in public and that the family display appropriate appearances and decorum on those occasions.

She was convinced that Michael had breached his marital vows and that he had been unfaithful to her. She had some misgivings about lying to him about having a tryst with McNabb, but she was wounded deeply when Alexa finally confirmed her suspicions about Michael's infidelity, and she wanted to wound him back.

Now their relationship was in a stalemate. Neither party had commenced any legal proceedings, though Michael continued to be persistent in requesting more contact with their son and even suggesting overnight access. She knew that Michael was a loving father, but just as she could not bring herself to actually have that affair with McNabb, she found herself equally unable to accede to his requests for additional access to Adam.

She was aware of the telephone contact between Michael and Adam from the monthly telephone statements, but she was reluctant to terminate those calls because she knew that Adam might misunderstand and just blame her, even though Michael was the real culpable party.

Alexa had told her of the testamentary provisions her deceased father-in-law had made in his will and that the agreement reached between Michael and Alexa meant that Michael would be inheriting his father's acreage. It was good that Michael would have a home of his own, but Marlena did not feel that it was totally fair. After all, their city home was registered in their joint names. Michael was paying all of the monthly expenses and providing her with a comfortable allowance, but since their marriage had ended she felt she needed to be financially independent rather than in a position of continuing dependence on Michael's generosity. She felt that she should receive what she was entitled to receive, as a right. After all, she had been a faithful, loving wife; a good homemaker and she had provided Michael with a son.

***

Kathy called Michael's private line to advise him that Marlena wanted to speak with him and asked if he wanted the call put through or politely deflected. Michael confirmed that he would take Marlena's call.

"Michael, it was unfortunate that we did not have a chance to speak after your father's funeral, but can we have that discussion now?" asked Marlena.

"Alexa did not make it convenient to have any discussion with anyone after the funeral, but what would you like to discuss, Marlena?" Michael asked politely.

"Well, I think we should proceed with the divorce in a civil manner. I do not want to fight," Marlena replied.

"How do you suggest we proceed, then?" asked Michael. "I do not want to fight either and if we are going through with a divorce, I would prefer that we remain civil, at least for Adam's sake. He is only six years old, but separations and acrimonious divorces can have a devastating and lasting impact on children, especially as they get older. They usually hold themselves responsible for the breakdown of their parents' relationship. Sometimes they develop depression or get rebellious and end up destroying their own lives by punishing themselves for their parents' marital breakdown."

Marlena did not respond directly, but she thought that if Michael had been as considerate about her and her feelings, they would not be having this discussion right now.

"I have gone to see a divorce lawyer and he recommends that I commence the proceeding and apply for a no-fault divorce on the grounds of a one-year separation. I can commence the divorce now, though the divorce decree would not issue until that year has expired. However, we would be able to settle the financial matters in the interim," said Marlena.

Michael noticed that she was quite informed, but that she had made no mention of settling the issue of his access to their son, so he decided to inject that issue into the conversation.

"And we can also settle the issue of my access to Adam as well, can't we?" he asked.

"Oh! Of course, Michael," Marlena answered absentmindedly. "We should be able to settle all of those...*collateral* issues."

"All right, Marlena. Please have your lawyer contact Ms Christine Breland at my office. She is a new lawyer we have hired to look after our family law practice. Since we both agree that we are going to be civil and not contentious, having Christine... Ms Breland act should not be an issue."

***

Jake was in his office checking his e-mails before commencing to work on some of his ongoing files when he noticed that he had received an e-mail from Crystal.

"Just a gracious thank you to my Prince Charming for sending me those beautiful flowers. The girls at the clinic were quite envious and kept pestering me for details about my new beau. May I call you tonight at ten Calgary time, if that is convenient for you?"

Jake immediately typed his ostentatious reply.

"I await to hear the dulcet tones of your mellifluous voice with unbridled anticipation, My Lady. And I remain... your most humble and obedient servant."

He reconsidered his message before sending it, thinking that it may make him sound inanely foolish, but then he decided that was the precise sentiment he wanted to convey, so he sent it, nevertheless. He could always tone it down later on, after they got to know each other a bit better.

***

Precisely at ten p.m., Jake's telephone rang and as he had hoped, it was Crystal.

"Good evening, Jacob."

"You may call me, Jake," he responded.

"If you don't mind, I would prefer to call you Jacob. It is such a beautiful name with such a great religious and historical tradition," Crystal replied. "He was quite a virile specimen, biblically speaking."

"In that case, you may call me anything you like… as long as you call me," replied Jake, acceding to her request in a teasing fashion.

***

Their conversation continued for another hour during which Crystal revealed that she was scheduled to go back to New York City to see her family and friends for the first time in about nine years at the end of the month. She was going away for about two weeks, but she would love it if he would be able to fly out to Vancouver and spend a weekend with her before she left. She suggested, with surprising modesty that since the relationship was new that perhaps Jake should arrange for accommodation at one of the hotels, downtown, to start with. She would meet him at the hotel and take him out to dinner and they would take matters from there. It was agreed that he would fly out the following weekend. Jake was truly exhilarated by their conversation.

Just as he finished the telephone conversation with Crystal, however, Jake received another call but this time it was from Paradis, and he sounded extremely angry.

"Jake! I would like to retain you and your partner to look after a little problem that has come up on one of my business ventures in your country. Those sons of bitches are trying to give me an auxiliary anal orifice which I neither want, nor need. My choice right now is to either hire a couple of good, tough, no-holds-barred lawyers to resolve it legally… or just hire someone to get this job done right the old-fashioned way. No son of a bitch is going to steal from me and get away with it."

"Slow down, Marcel," Jake responded. "What is this all about?"

"Don't have time to explain all of the details right now, Jake. My cab is downstairs waiting to take me to the airport. I shall get back to you when I get to Calgary. Just advise your partner to keep tomorrow afternoon open for me."

With that closing statement, Paradis abruptly terminated the call.

Chapter 17

The next morning Jake went into Michael's office to advise him of the telephone conversation with Paradis the previous evening. They decided that if the matter was urgent and lucrative, Michael would even cancel his scheduled trip to Toronto the next week and permit his Ontario co-counsel to argue the appeal, even though the client would probably have mixed feelings. If the appeal was successful, he would blame Michael for having to pay him needlessly since the Ontario co-counsel could have argued the appeal. If the appeal was not successful, then he would probably blame him for not going. In any case, that final decision could wait until Paradis got to Calgary that afternoon.

***

At two in the afternoon, Paradis showed up at the offices of Bolta & Barton. Ginger escorted him and his younger associate down to Michael's office. Jake and Michael were seated at a small round conference table and rose to meet their guests. Jake introduced Paradis to Michael, but since he was not familiar with his companion, he left that courtesy to Paradis.

"Nice to meet you all," Paradis said. "Lord God have mercy, but it is sure colder here than in Denver."

Shivering for emphasis, he continued. "First, I want to thank both of you for the excellent work on that National Hydrocarbons mediation. That was fun, Michael, but your partner here almost killed me later. Jake must be a founding member of Alcoholics Anonymous, but the son of a gun outdrank me fair and square. I must be getting old."

"This here," he added, turning to his companion, "is my nephew, Louie Paradis. My deceased brother's only son, whom I seem to have inherited. He is a good boy, just not all that bright, sometimes."

Louie Paradis did look like a younger version of Marcel Paradis. He was as tall as his uncle and though only in his late twenties, his hair was already thinning and receding. He had not acquired Marcel's prominent belly just yet, but he also spoke with a southern accent. He also seemed completely submissive to his uncle. Like his uncle, he came decked out with his Stetson hat, ostrich cowboy boots and a huge silver belt buckle. Jake estimated that their boots, buckle and the hats alone must have set them back by a couple of thousand dollars each.

"Nice to meet both of you," replied Michael. "Jake has told me a lot of good things about you, Mr Paradis, and I would like to thank you for that bonus, as well."

"I try to hire good people to work for me and if they perform well, I like to show my gratitude. That stunt that Jake pulled in Denver almost gave those sons of bitches a heart attack and I almost lost control of my bladder trying to keep a straight face. But let's get down to business."

"So, Mr Paradis, what is this new problem?" asked Jake as the four men sat down at the conference table.

"Are either of you familiar with placer gold mining?" Paradis asked.

"Not really," answered Jake. "I think I have watched a couple of those television programs from either Alaska or the Yukon where they dig a lot of dirt and wash it clean and try to collect the gold dust. But gold is selling for over $1,500 Canadian per ounce and even though the season is short, between the spring thaw and the fall freeze-up, it can be lucrative. The days are long, and they run those rigs almost twenty-four hours a day, seven days a week. Don't understand why they call it 'mining' though."

"That is a good start, Jake. You need to obtain a claim and have a good source of water. But basically, you dig up a lot of dirt and try to recover the gold dust and nuggets in the soil that Mother Nature left in the ground after the last Ice Age receded. You need a scraper to remove the topsoil, first; a front-end loader and a heavy tandem truck to move the pay dirt, and a centrifuge or a shaker to recover the gold dust and small nuggets from the dirt. So your front-end costs can be substantial, but you do have a chance to possibly double your investment in about four months. And that brings me to my dear fool nephew," said Paradis.

"Uncle Marcel. I may have made a couple of mistakes, but I sure do wish you would stop insulting me in front of these two gentlemen," Louie pleaded.

"Marcel," added Michael quickly in the hope that it would distract Paradis from launching into a longer diatribe about his nephew, "Jake tells me that you got cheated by someone or that someone has stolen from you. Can you fill in those details?"

"Late last month my dear nephew came to me with a great investment opportunity."

Paradis went on to relate how his nephew decided to get into a placer mining joint venture with a couple of guys in the Yukon. A Roger McQuaid and his silent partner had acquired the right to a mineral lease, but they needed a partner with some capital to close the deal. They needed $600,000 from their partner to match their own $600,000 to acquire the necessary heavy equipment so that they could commence the mining operation the following spring. They expected to not only recover their respective initial investment in the first year, but to share another $600,000 promised return between Paradis' nephew and McQuaid in four short months. Since their capital cost would be recovered the first year, the following year should provide them with at least $1 million to split.

Louie approached his uncle for a loan for that $600,000, promising to split his 50% share with his uncle once the initial capital investment was repaid first. The proposal was not in Paradis' usual line of business, but he felt obliged to try to assist his nephew and if it was possible to make a quick profit at the same time, so much the better. Consequently, Paradis decided, somewhat reluctantly, to advance the $600,000 to his nephew and see what would happen.

He specifically instructed his nephew that he wanted a first charge on the mineral lease and on the equipment, to minimize his risk in the event the venture proved to be unsuccessful. He also reminded his nephew to ensure that McQuaid deposited their $600,000 contribution at the same time. Paradis further instructed his nephew to deposit the funds in a bank account which would require McQuaid's and Louie's joint signatures to withdraw or transfer any funds.

He sincerely wanted to help his nephew get ahead in the world, but it was still a business deal to him, and certain standard precautions had to be taken. However, though he neglected to conduct his own due diligence on the proposed venture, he did wire the $600,000 to Louie at Calgary in any case.

***

Louie and McQuaid had agreed to meet at the bank one afternoon and deposit the funds at the same time; however, McQuaid's silent partner got delayed in traffic and phoned them to advise that he would not be able to make it in time that afternoon. McQuaid suggested that they meet at the bank the following morning at eleven. When McQuaid asked Louie what he wanted to do with his $600,000 draft in the interim, Louie did not want his proposed partners to think that he did not trust them, so he agreed to deposit it to that joint account, against his uncle's instructions.

The following morning, Louie and McQuaid met outside the bank. After waiting fifteen minutes a dapper, bald-headed individual approached them waving a bank draft made payable to McQuaid in the sum of $600,000 for deposit to their joint account. Louie was so relieved that the money had actually materialized that he did not bother to arrange for any security or even insure the joint signing authority on that account, again against Paradis' specific instructions.

Paradis subsequently discovered that the money he had wired to his nephew was just deposited to a joint account which did not require the joint signatures of McQuaid and his nephew. Secondly, his nephew forgot to register any security interest against the mineral lease or the equipment which was supposedly being purchased. Finally, the money simply disappeared from that account and now McQuaid was nowhere to be found.

"Sounds like a clear case of fraud to me, Mr Paradis," said Michael. "Why don't you simply go to the police and file fraud charges against McQuaid?"

"Please call me Marcel, Michael," Paradis answered. "And the reason I am not interested in pressing criminal charges is because I do not care about getting McQuaid and his silent partner jailed. I just want to get my money back. The one thing I learned about dealing with crooks like McQuaid is that the worst thing you can do to them is recover the money. Going to jail for them is just a necessary price they have to pay in the conduct of their criminal affairs. Besides that, I have looked into your legal system and this country is a civil fraud paradise. You can get a three-year sentence for robbing a grocery store, but you get the same sentence if you are convicted—and that is a big '*if*'—for defrauding someone out of $600,000.

Furthermore, if you don't have a prior criminal record, I think you only have to serve about one-sixth of that sentence. Besides that, if I wanted revenge, I know people who know people who could look after that for me—very well and very quickly."

"Michael," interjected Jake, "I swear I just went deaf there for a brief minute." Then turning to Paradis, he added quite seriously, "Marcel, you have to remember that we are officers of the court and that precludes us from becoming accessories before, during or after the fact to the commission of a crime. I fight hard for my clients, but I fight by the rules, and I do not intend to get disbarred or go to jail for a client."

"And, Marcel," added Michael, "getting a judgment is one thing. Collecting the money may be another matter. I see no problem in obtaining a judgment in this case. We can prove the $600,000 came from you and was deposited to that account. The bank's records would be able to permit us to discover where the money went from there. Tracing those funds and discovering their present location is one thing, recovering those funds may not be that easy."

"So here in my proposition, gentlemen," said Paradis. "The amount of money is not that significant. It is the principle which is the issue here. These sons of bitches took advantage of my flesh and blood, and then they did the unthinkable. They knew the money came from me, not him. That means they stole from me. And no son of a bitch is going to get away with that, not as long as I am alive. I don't mind being out-negotiated fairly in a business deal. But I *do* mind if I am lied to and then stolen from. Louie is my flesh and blood. When they lied to him, they lied to me and when they stole from him, they stole from me. This is a matter of family honour."

"Marcel," answered Michael, "I may have to go to Toronto to argue an appeal this coming week, but Jake can commence the preliminaries such as obtaining the necessary bank documents for that joint account and preparing a statement of claim. Then we will have to locate McQuaid to serve him and examine him and see what admissions we can get out of him. Then we can apply for a summary judgment and try to locate and recover your funds. But I want you to know that even though we will try to do our best, we cannot guarantee that we will be able to recover your funds."

Paradis paused for a moment, scrutinizing both lawyers carefully, then he replied, "That is understood and accepted. However, I want my name stipulated to be the plaintiff in the action. Louie here was only acting as my agent throughout his dealings with McQuaid. If they decide to examine someone before the summary judgment application, they will have to be satisfied with examining me, not Louie."

"Thanks, Uncle Marcel," Louie chimed in with a sigh of relief as if a very heavy burden just got lifted from his shoulders.

"Secondly," continued Paradis, "there is no written agreement detailing the specific terms. The only documents which I can provide you are just several e-mails which Louie, here, sent to McQuaid. McQuaid would only communicate with Louie by telephone. I can also provide you with Louie's telephone records which cross-reference McQuaid's telephone calls to Louie's e-mails. Fortunately, Louie's e-mails are fairly detailed. And you can commence to look for McQuaid in Edmonton. He uses Edmonton as the base of his operations to give his placer mining scam in the Yukon more credibility. Finally, I want to be copied with every correspondence that goes out or comes in on this file. Do we understand each other?"

"Marcel," answered Michael, "our standard protocol is that we provide our clients with a timely and detailed periodic summary. Usually monthly, at the latest."

"No, Michael," Paradis responded, "that will not do for me. I wanna be informed on a timelier basis. I wanna feel the heartbeat of this action. I cannot think of how you can do that for me other than doing what I have asked you to do. Furthermore, I wanna be able to interpret the correspondence myself, as well as receiving the benefit of your comments and opinions. I am not asking to shove my forearm up your alimentary canal. I just want to be kept informed."

Michael and Jake exchanged a glance and Jake shrugged his shoulders to indicate that it did not make any difference to him.

"Well, Marcel," Michael said, "That would keep you fully informed on a timely basis, and it would save us the additional task of having to periodically summarize matters for you at the same time." He paused then added, "All right your terms are acceptable. Jake can prepare a retainer agreement and—"

Paradis interrupted Michael before he could finish his sentence. He was extremely relieved. Some of the lawyers he had dealt with were not prepared to have him maintain such a close scrutiny on the day-to-day conduct of his file.

"No need for a retainer agreement, Michael. I am a man of my word, and I can see that you and Jake are the same," Paradis responded, and pulling out his billfold from his jacket pocket he extracted a bank draft made payable to their firm in the sum of $100,000.00. "And here is your retainer."

Michael examined the draft, but he also considered Paradis' unwillingness to enter into a formal retainer agreement.

"No, Marcel," Michael answered slowly, "we accept your terms, but on one condition. That one condition is that we *do* have a retainer agreement. You say that you trust us and that is reassuring, and I want you to know that we are prepared to trust you as well. If we were not prepared to trust you, we would not agree to act for you. But I do not want any future misunderstanding to arise between us."

Paradis paused for a moment and then he smiled. "Gentlemen, I do believe that we have a deal. Now let's go and kick some McQuaid ass."

Chapter 18

It was mid-afternoon when Kathy entered Michael's office to advise him that Christine Breland was outside and wished to see him and discuss the divorce issue with Marlena.

"Please send her in, Kathy."

"Mr Bolta, we have heard from your wife's lawyer, and I would like to discuss their proposed terms with you before you go to Toronto, so that we can keep the momentum going," Christine said as she entered Michael's office and joined him at his conference table.

Michael considered suggesting to Christine that she address him informally, but then reconsidered. He would let her decide when she felt comfortable enough to address him informally.

"All right, Ms Breland," Michael reciprocated. "What are they asking for and what are they offering?"

"Mrs Bolta wants sole title to your home in the city and its contents. She wants non-taxable spousal support for five years so that she would be able to complete her university degree and become self-supporting. Her vehicle is already registered in her name, so that is not an issue. And she wants child support for your son, pursuant to the Federal Child Support Guidelines, so that is not a contentious issue."

Christine had responded nervously, looking up at Michael occasionally to gauge his initial reaction to the various points she was announcing. Michael's countenance remained impassive.

"Is that all?" Michael asked calmly.

"Well, she also wants to be named as your irrevocable beneficiary on a $500,000.00 life insurance policy, with your son named as a designated alternative beneficiary in the event she predeceases you."

"Is that it?" Michael asked calmly again, since he could see that Christine was nervous.

"She is also asking for half of the value of your shares in your professional corporation by way of a cash payout in lieu of receiving any shares."

"Anything else?" Michael asked again.

"She also wants you to pay her legal fees on the divorce," answered Christine and before Michael could ask the same question again, she added. "And that is it. Overall, she is not being that unreasonable… compared to some of the initial settlement proposals I have dealt with."

"Was there any mention of custody and my access to Adam?" Michael asked.

"The usual generic proposal of 'joint custody', with residential care vested in her and 'reasonable access' for you," Christine responded.

"Thank you, Ms Breland. You may respond on a without prejudice basis as follows: she may have the city residence and contents in full satisfaction of her property claims, including a waiver against any claim in respect of my law practice; she may have five years of spousal support so that she can finish her university degree and get established, but it will be taxable to her and deductible to me. I believe she was in her third year of a Bachelor of Arts program. She is entitled to receive the appropriate child support and any supplementary payments on a non-taxable basis; the life insurance is not an issue, but she shall be responsible for her own legal fees; I certainly do not want to commit myself to paying her legal fees in the event this really gets contentious."

"And what kind of child access would you like to have with your son?" Christine asked politely.

Michael had his fingertips on both hands touching together in a steeple position as he gazed to the distant mountains to the west. He noticed that the snow caps on the mountains were getting more pronounced with each passing week. Finally, after considering the various alternatives, he was able to formulate his position.

"I would like to have my access defined. I do not want to keep going back to court trying to determine what 'reasonable' means. Besides that, defined access will give both of us an opportunity to organize our respective lives more effectively. So I would like every second weekend from Friday evening to Monday morning. I shall be responsible for picking Adam up from his school on Friday afternoon and I will be responsible for dropping him off Monday morning. I want alternating ten-day terms at Christmas and Spring Break and a month during the summer. I would like to have the right to take Adam on holiday somewhere for a fourteen-day period each summer, but we can deal with that on a case-by-case basis so we need not mention that right now. Please intimate to my wife's counsel that this is basically a package proposal, and I am not going to entertain any cherry-picking where they select some points and reject others and then try to negotiate from that position. If this matter does have to go to court, I cannot see how a court will give her more and me less. Do you have any further comments or suggestions?"

"I had some preliminary discussions with Mrs Bolta's counsel and the reason she is asking for both the residence and a share of your practice is because you have just inherited your father's acreage," Christine said.

"And what was your reply to that statement, Ms Breland?" Michael asked.

"I reminded my learned friend that because the acreage was inherited by you, it was not matrimonial property, and it did not come into play. I further advised him that your share of the residence and its contents, on a tax-free basis, was more than fair compensation for half your current share of the practice," Christine responded with increasing confidence.

"Do you think that I am being unfair at this point, Ms Breland?" Michael asked.

"As your counsel, I can sincerely say that I think that you are not only being fair, but generous in the circumstances," Christine responded firmly.

"In that case, please pass on our counterproposal with my full endorsement."

***

Michael had trouble getting back to work after his discussion with Christine. He simply was not able to concentrate on any of his files that required his attention. He just kept looking out his office window, staring off to the far distant mountains. He regretted how certain events, over which he had no control, seemed to have taken over his personal life. His father's death. The apparent irreconcilable differences with his sister and the irretrievable breakdown of his marriage.

Michael remained seated at the small conference table, lost in his thoughts as he ruminated over some of those events in his personal and professional life when Kathy re-entered his office and quietly locked the door behind her.

"Michael. Everyone has left and it is almost six p.m. Look at how dark the evening has turned. Is there anything else that I can do for you?" she asked politely, as she approached him. Michael looked up at her and realized that she was truly an attractive and a desirable woman. He was also reminded of the fact that he had not been intimate with anyone for months.

Kathy approached him from behind, placed her hands on his shoulders and started to massage his tense muscles. After a few moments, Michael rose from his seat and turned to face Kathy. They both reached for each other and kissed, slowly and tenderly, with parted lips and darting tongues. Slowly pressing their lips together more firmly and hungrily

"Uh, we should be careful, Kathy," Michael cautioned.

"I have locked the front door and the door to the hall, as well as your office door. The cleaning staff have strict instructions not to enter or clean any private office with a locked door. We will not be interrupted," Kathy replied quietly, her eyes downcast, concerned about his reaction.

Michael walked her over to the office sofa he had acquired a few years earlier so that he would be able to catch a short nap when he was working late or pulling an all-nighter. He was just wearing his slacks and dress shirt, but he proceeded to take off his tie. Kathy reciprocated by taking off her heels and reclining on the sofa. Michael took off his shoes and lay down beside her. They commenced to kiss gently and explore each other with their hands.

Michael started to fondle her breasts. He casually unbuttoned her blouse and exposed her green lace bra which was cradling her full breasts. Kathy reached down to undo Michael's belt and zipper and reach inside his boxer shorts. She wanted to hold him and fondle him and feel his arousal. Then they proceeded to remove their remaining clothes without any further discussion.

Michael was enthralled with Kathy's breasts. They were firm and conical, tipped with small pointed pink nipples and he proceeded to put his mouth over each one of them in turn. Teasingly licking them slowly as Kathy moaned and arched her body in response. She still continued to hold Michael's organ which had grown firm with arousal by this time. She could feel the pulsation of the blood engorging it with each heartbeat and she held it even tighter.

Slowly, Michael ran his tongue down between her breasts, down to her navel and then below her manicured red pubic hair. She parted her legs to afford him access to the lip-shaped folds of her labia, which he parted with his wet tongue and tasted her for the first time. Kathy moaned again with muted excitement, trying desperately to control her passion.

"Please, Michael," Kathy pleaded, "please come inside me. I want to feel you inside me."

Michael placed his hands under her buttocks so that he could raise her pelvis to facilitate his entry. Kathy felt moist and warm as he entered her. Then they both commenced to enjoy each other in a slow choreographed thrust and parry... until they finally reached a simultaneous climax. Neither one of them was aware as to whether they had come quickly or if it was prolonged. They were both covered with a sweat which glued their bodies together, as their breathing started to subside.

Michael finally decided to speak.

"I really do not know what to say, Kathy. 'Thank you' seems to be a bit inappropriate."

Kathy giggled in response and embraced him even tighter.

"It would be nice to take you out for a nice dinner now, but we both look a bit too disheveled to go out in public," Michael added, giggling a bit in return.

"We can go out to dinner another time, Michael. And if anyone should thank anyone, I should be thanking you. If this was just sex, it was the best sex I have had for a long time. If it was more, then it is what it is. I want you to know that I have nurtured feelings for you for a long time, but even I did not fully appreciate what those feelings were to start with. I thought it was just admiration and respect… and then slowly, as my own marriage… which was a mistake from the start slowly disintegrated… I realized that my feelings for you were deeper, but you were taken… you were married. You were unavailable."

Kathy buried her head in Michael's chest so that he would not be able to see her tears which accompanied her confession.

"Kathy," Michael responded, "I have always liked you, respected you and trusted you. But I have to also confess that I was not blind. You are an extremely attractive and desirable woman, but I had to banish those thoughts from my mind because you and I were both married. It did not feel right for me to entertain those thoughts… those sensual thoughts. But this has exceeded my wildest dreams and it does not feel that we have done anything wrong. I feel no guilt, just satisfaction and exhilaration and relief."

Kathy reached up to kiss him again.

"My office bathroom does not have a shower," Michael said. "So we can't share a shower, but you can use it to freshen up and then I think we should call a night. I would like to take you out to dinner before I go to Toronto next week, though."

"That would be nice, Michael," answered Kathy. "But perhaps we should be more discreet before our respective marital issues are resolved."

"In that case, why don't you come out to the acreage on Sunday after I get back from Toronto and I can make dinner for you?"

Chapter 19

The next week was hectic for Jake. He had to draft the retainer agreement, the statement of claim, prepare an application and a supporting affidavit to obtain an *ex parte* order directing the relevant bank to produce the bank statements and copies of all incoming and outgoing cheques, bank drafts or wire transfers. Jake felt he had grounds for the order on the basis that Louie had deposited those funds and it was a joint account. He wanted to expedite the production of those bank documents before he examined McQuaid. Since it was apparent that the agreement crystalized in Calgary, that made Alberta an appropriate forum for the proposed lawsuit irrespective of the fact that Paradis operated from Denver and McQuaid operated from White Horse in the Yukon or possibly Edmonton. Then he still had to arrange for service of the statement of claim on McQuaid.

Michael was in Toronto for his appeal, so Jake was the effective partner in charge. The staff and the firm associates were familiar with Jake's standard hectic work schedule, but everyone was surprised at Jake's heightened zeal this time. He was like a whirling dervish, relentlessly moving from one case to another case. Everyone was really impressed with his current heightened dedication, but then they were not aware that Jake had an additional collateral motive this time, in the form of his scheduled flight to Vancouver to meet Crystal. They had been phoning each other on almost a daily basis and it amazed him how their interests and opinions and discussion meshed so well.

***

The flight from Calgary to Vancouver took just over an hour and because of the one-hour time difference between the two cities, Jake was able to work until mid-afternoon on Friday, get to the airport and fly to Vancouver and register at the Georgia Hotel by six p.m. Vancouver time.

The Georgia was an elegant and stately older hotel located conveniently in the heart of the downtown core. Crystal was going to meet him at the hotel and take him to the restaurant. After she had phoned his room from the lobby to announce her arrival, Jake proceeded down to the lobby to meet her.

"Hello, Crystal," Jake announced nonchalantly as he approached her slowly. He was concerned that his excitement at seeing her again would be betrayed by his voice or by his eyes or even by his walk. He wanted to convey the impression that he was calm, cool and confident.

"And do you do this often?" he added innocuously. "This assignation kind of thing?"

Crystal wore a stylish black beret which was tilted to her right and she was wearing a black Brooks Brothers thigh-length double-breasted fall jacket. Black seemed to be her favorite colour, since she was also wearing black faded jeans which were tucked inside her knee-high black boots.

Crystal was unsure how to greet Jake. She considered sharing a hug, perhaps a gentle peck on his cheek during that brief embrace but she decided that a handshake would be the most appropriate greeting at this time.

"Hello Jacob," she replied. "And I just do this assignation thing once in a special while."

She smiled, extending her right hand before Jake had an opportunity to initiate a more personal greeting.

"It is really nice to see you again in person, too. However, I have to ask a small favor. Could you refrain from sending me a dozen roses almost every second day? I do appreciate the sentiment, but it is just that my office and my apartment are overflowing with roses. I may be obliged to start giving some away soon to my clients or my staff, if you keep it up."

Jake merely smiled.

"I guess my assistant misunderstood my instructions. I just asked her to send you that initial batch... has she been sending you roses every second day?" he asked innocently. "I shall have to speak to her."

Crystal returned his smile and said, "Well, in that case, perhaps I should send your assistant my thanks and appreciation instead of you.

And I hope you like seafood. I have made a reservation at one of my favorite restaurants and it has a very subdued ambience, so we shall be able to chat in relative tranquility."

"Before we do that, can you come up to my room for a minute? I have a surprise for you," Jake replied.

"Not more roses, I trust?" Crystal responded.

"You will have to come up and see for yourself," said Jake.

***

Jake presented Crystal with a thin rectangular box which was wrapped in gold paper and bound with a rich purple ribbon. *Thank God,* he thought pleasantly, *that I have a generous client who is a jeweler. Paying wholesale certainly beats paying full retail.*

"And what is this? A box of chocolates?" Crystal asked frivolously, as she untied the ribbon and carefully removed the wrapping paper, even though the box was much too thin for even a small box of chocolates. Inside the box was a Tahitian black pearl set of earrings and a matching pendant on a thin gold chain. Jake could tell that she was surprised. And pleased.

"Do you like them?" Jake asked nonchalantly.

"Oh, I do. I adore them. But what is the occasion? It's not my birthday," Crystal replied, still enthralled with the dark luster of the black pearls. Obviously, she concluded, Jacob did not have to be too perceptive to notice that her favorite colour was black. The pearls especially complemented her dark-violet eyes and would be a beautiful accessory to most of her wardrobe.

"Just consider it an early pre-Christmas gift. I wanted to ensure that you would not forget me on your trip to New York next week," Jake replied modestly.

Crystal paused and looked up curiously at Jake.

"But surely you realize that I am a Jew. Look at my profile. My nose. My name…"

Without missing a beat, Jake replied calmly. "Then just consider it an early pre-Hanukkah gift."

***

The restaurant was within walking distance of the hotel and as promised, the food was amazing, and the ambience was suitably tranquil. Though Crystal told Jake that Jews do not drink, at least, not that much, she agreed to share a glass of burgundy which, as Jake explained, had to be aged at least six years before it was fit for consumption. Their non-stop conversation continued throughout the dinner. As soon as one stopped speaking, the other picked up the conversation. Soon they realized that they were the last remaining guests and that the staff were congregated at the bar, occasionally looking discreetly in their direction to see if they were getting ready to leave.

Finally, Crystal beckoned their waiter to come over, but as she reached for her purse, Jake put out his hand in protest. Confessing to being an old-fashioned male chauvinist, he insisted on paying for the bill.

There had been a mild rain that evening while they were eating, and the sidewalks glistened and reflected the adjacent storefronts and passing traffic as they walked hand in hand back to his hotel. Jake had really enjoyed the evening and he had given some thought as to how the night might end. He sincerely enjoyed Crystal's company. When they reached his hotel, they finally shared their first embrace and an innocuous short kiss.

"Well, kind sir," Crystal said coyly, deciding to take the initiative, "aren't you going to invite me up to see your 'etchings'?"

Jake was actually taken aback for a moment, but when he recovered, he politely asked her if she would indeed be interested in 'seeing his etchings', and Crystal confirmed that she would.

When they got to his room and took off their coats, Crystal approached Jake and said: "Believe me or believe me not, but I usually do hold out until at least the second date, though I confess that on a rare occasion I have succumbed earlier. But I want you to know that a first date for me is a very special occasion. So, I trust you were sufficiently optimistic, and you came suitably armed with a few condoms for this weekend?"

Things were unfolding quickly and unexpectedly. Though Jake prided himself on being quick, himself, he was obviously having a problem trying to keep up with Crystal this night.

"I have another confession to make," he said, "I do not have any condoms with me, but I assure you that I do not have, nor have I ever had, any STD. I so swear on the eyes of my saintly, departed mother." Jake placed his right hand over his heart to underscore his avowed sincerity.

"Jacob! I am going to have to start calling you 'Jacob, the Confessor', if you keep confessing all the time. But seriously, you do not know me that well or where I have been or what I have done, and the same applies to you. So I am prepared to love you gentle and long, or hard and fast, whatever you prefer, but we really should use a condom to start with."

"Well, they usually have them for sale in the men's washroom," Jake replied. "Let me go and get a couple."

Unfortunately, there was no condom dispenser in the men's washroom. Crystal checked the women's washroom and there were none there either. Finally, Jake suggested that he check with the hotel desk, but when he asked the young female attendant if he could purchase a couple of condoms, she was truly insulted and she proceeded to reprimand him for his 'amoral' query. She stated that the Georgia was reputable, and it did not lower itself to dispensing condoms.

Finally, Crystal suggested that they take a cab back to her apartment and she assured him that she was fully stocked and prepared. She even hinted at owning some interesting toys, as well.

While they were standing on the corner on the still glistening sidewalk impatiently waiting for their cab to arrive, Jake noticed that there was another more modern hotel just across the street.

"Let's check that hotel," he suggested, not wanting to waste more time.

"My dear sir," Crystal responded. "I trust that you shall not get too anxious and possibly come… prematurely?"

Jake smiled back at Crystal and assured her that she need not be concerned about that happening. He entered the hotel and approached the two young women at the front desk, who looked up at him in a solicitous fashion, ready to cater to his needs. To his surprise, they did not blink or blush when he asked if it was possible to purchase some condoms. They merely inquired as to how many, what size and whether he wanted it billed to his room or not. Crystal stood back a few feet observing and smiled in amusement. Jake suggested four would be sufficient and family size; however, he would pay cash since he was actually staying at the hotel across the street. The young women smiled knowingly, so Jake concluded that he was not the first Georgia Hotel guest to make this kind of purchase at their hotel.

As they walked back to his hotel, Crystal could not help herself and inquired out of curiosity.

"Family size?" she asked quizzically.

"Well, I am a modest man and I do not like to boast, but I do remember that condoms do stretch a little bit," Jake replied and winked, "so family size should be sufficient.

When they got back to his room, each undressed separately and quickly. They embraced and kissed, exploring each other with their hands and mouths. They finally collapsed on the bed and Jake was prepared to mount Crystal, but she pushed him down on his back and proceeded to mount him.

"Condom on, Jacob, and since it is our first time, it should be lady's choice, if you don't mind."

Unfortunately, since Jake was not inclined to use condoms that often, he was unable to become fully erect and pull on the condom. Crystal attempted to provide him with her own personal encouragement and ministrations by taking him into her mouth and caressing his scrotum with her other hand at the same time, but when she attempted to pull the condom over his penis, it continued to deflate. Finally, Crystal threw caution to the wind and threw the condom aside.

"Come on," she said, "obviously, you are one of those guys who suffers from condom phobia but let me mount you. You come from Calgary, which is cowboy country, so let me ride you cowboy style."

Crystal rode Jake hard and fast, and though he found her shouted exhortations to fuck her deeper a bit disconcerting, he tried to oblige as best he could.

"Well, Jacob," Crystal finally said in a satisfied voice, "could you get me some cold water from your hotel fridge? I am really dehydrated. After all, I did most of the work tonight. But you're not too bad for a Gentile. Aside from that... condom phobia."

"So, I am not the first Gentile that you have had?" Jake asked disingenuously and affecting disappointment. "Well, you are not too bad for a Jew, either."

"I lived with a guy in Vancouver for a year and he was a Gentile," Crystal answered. "He really could not get over me being a Jew, so I deliberately celebrated every Jewish holiday which came around. The contorted agony on his face was amusing to observe. He tried to acquiesce and indulge me, but it was obvious that he was not being sincere. He just wanted me around to fuck him."

"Well, I have had a few Jewish girlfriends, myself, Crystal," replied Jake, but then he corrected himself quickly. "Well, two of them were just one-night stands, but I think they still count. However, one of the things that I have never understood about Jews and Christians, Crystal, is that both groups seem to forget that Jesus was a Jew. So why all the reciprocated suspicion?"

"That's right. But he was a Jew, first," replied Crystal to Jake's somewhat cryptic question.

"And since you have had your preference tonight, young lady, I just want to caution you that I am assuming that all orifices are open for business when it comes time for me to exercise my preferences tomorrow?" Jake asked directly.

"You shall have to wait and see, kind sir," Crystal answered ambiguously, but she was still smiling mischievously.

***

On a purely sexual level, it was the best sex Jake had experienced in a long time. Crystal was passionate, experienced, uninhibited and apparently, insatiable. After the first night, Jake was not sure that he would be able to continue to perform at the same level or even survive until Sunday evening when he was scheduled to fly back to Calgary. But as matters unfolded, he found that Crystal's exhortations and oral ministrations inspired him to muster all of his reserves and he was able to persevere and perform.

***

Crystal shared a cab with Jake to the airport Sunday evening. Both were quiet and subdued during that trip. They were both being contemplative about their pending separation. Crystal had agreed that she would phone him from her family's apartment in New York and Jake was sincere when he told her that he was going to wait anxiously for her calls. Crystal could tell that it was not just another flippant statement and that Jake meant it sincerely.

Crystal had only been in contact with her family and friends by social media, text messages and e-mails for the preceding nine years. She was anxious and apprehensive at the same time. New York was filled with a lot of memories for her, some good and some bad. She held a sincere affection for Jake. He was amusing, interesting and satisfying on both a personal and a sexual level... even if he was a Gentile. However, she hoped that his level of feeling for her was the same as hers. It was just friendship and hot, casual sex. It was not love at first sight. That was something she wanted to avoid at all costs, because it had never worked out for her before.

Jake's thoughts were similar, though his concerns were different. He had no personal issues awaiting him when he returned to Calgary. If there was any current trepidation in his life, it was Crystal. Though he deliberately tried to prevent himself from becoming infatuated with this intoxicating woman, he harbored a sincere concern that he may not have been entirely successful. He even briefly fantasized about possibly having a more lasting relationship with this dark-eyed Semitic beauty. At the same time, he also had a feeling of a growing dread gnawing away somewhere deep inside himself.

As the cab neared the airport, Crystal finally spoke.

"Jacob, that was a very expensive gift you gave me last night. Are you sure you want me to have it?"

Jake looked at Crystal and he could see that she seemed somewhat uncertain of herself.

"Yes, I want you to have it," Jake replied and then added teasingly. "You should know that I like you by now... at least a little bit."

Chapter 20

Michael decided to fly to Toronto even though Paradis' case seemed urgent, it was not that critical. Jake would be able to handle the preliminary steps himself.

He always wore Western boots when he had to travel to eastern Canada. It never failed to amuse him as he walked through a hotel lobby or when he was in an elevator that someone would inevitably notice the boots and ask him if he was from Alberta. He would affect a western accent and just laconically reply: "Yup!"

Then he would quickly add before they could ask the inevitable follow-up question. "And yes, I even have a horse which I actually ride."

Their reaction usually depended upon the international price for oil. If the price was high, the reaction was one of envy. If the price was low, the reaction was one of feigned commiseration.

***

The current appeal involved an oral variation of a written contract which, to say the least, was very problematic. The client had recruited an engineer from England to manage a small manufacturing plant in Ontario. The written agreement was for a five-year term at $75,000 a year. Unfortunately, once the engineer was hired, he quickly developed a 'Napoleonic complex' according to Michael's client. The engineer assumed a severe case of self-importance and, coupled with the fact that his client was headquartered in Calgary, that distance resulted in a quick and inevitable breakdown in communication between the client and engineer. A lawsuit was not that far away.

Since the client did not intend to tolerate the engineer's alleged insubordination, the initial remedial step was a unilateral reduction of the annual salary, which the client attempted to justify on the grounds of economic necessity since the manufacturing plant was losing money.

The client also alleged that the engineer had agreed, orally, to that reduction in salary. The client also wrongfully assumed that the new amended agreement did not have to be reduced to writing.

Several months thereafter, the client discovered that the engineer was engaging in a noon-hour tryst a couple of times a week with a married secretary whose husband was also a company employee. When the husband commenced to object to the affair, the engineer decided to terminate the cuckolded husband. That prompted the husband to commence an action against the company for unlawful dismissal and vicariously, for the engineer's alleged alienation of his wife's affection.

When the client became aware of the lawsuit and its allegations, he decided to terminate the engineer's employment without notice on the alleged grounds of moral turpitude. To compound matters, the company had also generously provided the engineer with the use of a company vehicle which mysteriously became registered in the engineer's own name. The client, continuing his managerial ineptitude, decided to deem the vehicle as a 'gift' in lieu of any severance payment to the engineer. Since the vehicle was already registered in the engineer's name, the likelihood that the vehicle would be returned to the company was nonexistent.

The engineer then sued the client's company for unlawful dismissal and breach of contract.

Michael's defence had attempted to mitigate the damages by trying to argue that the engineer's continued employment at the reduced salary corroborated the engineer's agreement to the reduced salary through his conduct. He also attempted to claim as a set-off, the damages the company had to pay to settle the cuckolded husband's action on the grounds of the engineer's managerial misconduct.

The trial came before a taciturn Ontario judge who did not bother to disguise his disdain for Michael, whom he considered to be just a 'legal carpetbagger' from Alberta. After a three-day trial, the judge reserved his decision for a couple of months and then rendered a judgment against the client's company based on the original $75,000 per year from the date of the unilateral reduction in salary for the three and a half years remaining on the contract. He also held that the vehicle was a corporate gift and could not be set off against the judgment. He did not even bother to refer to the 'cuckold set-off defence', as the judge contemptuously characterized it during the trial.

Not surprisingly, the client remained oblivious to his own contributing errors in judgment. He just considered the whole mess to be a gross injustice to himself. The engineer caused his company to be sued by the husband; the engineer had basically misappropriated the company vehicle and now the engineer had a judgment against the company for close to $300,000, when you added in the costs and interest.

Michael tried to explain to the client that when stupid decisions are made…one should not be surprised if stupid results quickly follow. He knew his sage advice was not going to assuage his client's feelings. However, he did know that if his client did not learn any lesson this time, he was just doomed to repeat those mistakes in the future. Simply put: it was not prudent to modify a written agreement, orally.

***

Michael's co-counsel argued the appeal as effectively as any competent lawyer could argue, considering the facts that he had to deal with. The Court of Appeal decided to reserve its decision which gave Michael some hope that the quantum of damages might be reduced. After all, the engineer continued to work for the company for several months subsequent to the reduction in salary without any complaint and that surely corroborated, on a balance of probability, the allegation that there was a mutual agreement to reduce the original salary.

Furthermore, the engineer was quite proud of the fact that he had cuckolded the company employee and then wrongfully dismissed his lover's husband. He had readily admitted those facts at the trial. Michael assumed that the appellate panel should be inclined to reduce the damages at the very least, but they would have to wait to receive the written decision.

***

Michael phoned the client to advise him that the appeal had gone well, in his opinion, but that the panel had reserved their decision.
The next person he called was Kathy.

"Kathy, how are you? How are things at the office?" he inquired politely.

"Everything is fine here. What about the appeal?" Kathy reciprocated.

Neither one was really interested in the status of the office or the status of the appeal. They just had a mutual desire to hear each other's voice.

Michael paused for a couple of seconds and then he confessed. "I really miss you even though it has only been a couple of days."

"And I assure you that my sentiments are the same, Mr Bolta," Kathy responded impersonally.

Michael was surprised at Kathy's formal response and assumed that she was not at liberty to speak freely.

"Am I to assume that you cannot talk right now?" he asked.

"That is correct, Mr Bolta."

"In that case, I just want you to know that I am flying back on the red-eye tonight and that I shall see you tomorrow. And... I want you to know that I really do miss you and I look forward to seeing you soon," said Michael.

"All right. Goodbye, Mr Bolta," Kathy responded neutrally.

Michael decided that the first question he was going to put to Kathy when he saw her tomorrow was... 'who was standing by your desk when I called you?'

Christine Breland was not oblivious and she had not missed the transient deep blush that reddened Kathy's cheeks as she ended her telephone conversation with the senior partner and hung up her phone

"Kathy, I have heard back from your husband's lawyer. Could we speak privately in Mr Bolta's office? And how did the appeal go?"

"Mr Bolta said that it went as well as could be expected, but he was not expecting too much in any case. He will be back in the office tomorrow. And what is Donny asking for to settle our affairs?" Kathy responded.

As they entered Michael's office, Kathy fleetingly glanced over to the sofa and smiled before they seated themselves at the small conference table.

"He has offered to sell you his interest in your family home, but I think that he is asking too much. You have no children, so that is not an issue. Even though he is unemployed, to the best of my knowledge, he is not asking for any spousal support, but he is eager to have the financial matters settled quickly. It seems that he may have gotten his girlfriend in Edmonton pregnant, and he is anxious to, as his lawyer so charitably characterized it, *make an honest woman out of her.*"

"How considerate of him," Kathy answered quietly. "You know, Christine, I wanted to start a family as soon as we got married, but Donny wanted to wait. He wanted us to be free for a while before we got 'burdened' with children. I guess I have him to thank for that small mercy. Please advise his lawyer that we should just list the property for sale since I do not want to keep it. It holds too many sad memories for me. But since he removed that $20,000 out of our joint savings account, I want to recover my $10,000 share out of his sale proceeds, even though I probably contributed the bulk of those savings in the first place."

"Makes good sense to me, Kathy," Christine replied.

"And Christine," added Kathy, "if Donny is so anxious to be free, can't we amend our divorce documents to plead his adultery? In that way, the Decree Absolute would issue more quickly and my 'dear'… soon to be my 'dear ex' husband… would be in a position to make his girlfriend an 'honest woman' that much sooner."

"I agree again, Kathy," Christine said. "Let me look into the details for you."

***

As Christine walked back to her office, she could not get Kathy's momentary blush out of her mind. Perhaps it was just a comment Mr Bolta made at the other end of the line. Though it certainly was none of her business and she did not want to be judgmental if anything was transpiring between Kathy and Mr Bolta. No matter how improbable it may seem, it was still possible. If there was anything, it might very well affect their respective legal positions in their respective divorces. That certainly would not simplify their positions if their respective spouses found out and that would make it her business. It might even create a conflict of interest for her, personally, since she was acting as their respective legal counsel in both divorce proceedings. She decided to keep the issue to herself for the time being, but to watch and see if she could confirm or deny her suspicions.

Chapter 21

Jake's euphoric mood had continued after he returned to Calgary from Vancouver. He truly had a difficult time keeping Crystal and their erotic weekend off his mind. He was really looking forward to receiving her first call from New York; however, his reverie was distracted by a call from someone else.

"This is Jake Barton," he answered.

"Jake, this is Marcel Paradis calling from Denver. I guess that dumb nephew of mine is not as dumb as I thought. It turns out that we *do* have additional evidence against McQuaid. My dear nephew took the precaution of recording some of the later telephone calls he had with McQuaid, since he never bothered to respond in writing to his e-mails."

Jake was surprised at the potential good news, but he needed to have more background.

"Why didn't Louie mention this when you guys came up to Calgary?" Jake asked.

"You should remember that even a dumb person can do a smart thing, from time to time, Jake," Paradis replied. "But Louie was not sure if the recorded telephone calls were legal in Canada or if he would be exposing himself to some criminal charge."

"The general rule, to my knowledge, Marcel," Jake responded, "is that you need a court order to intercept a telephone conversation between other people, but if you are party to a telephone conversation, you are free to record it. Generally, judges tend to frown on the practice, but it depends on the particular facts in each case. In this particular case, I cannot see any judge becoming prejudiced against us if Louie, for good reason, chose to record his telephone calls with McQuaid. Please make a copy of the recordings and then courier the original recordings to our office. We shall have them transcribed by a certified court reporter to ensure accuracy and authenticity."

"Shall do, Jake," Paradis replied. "By the way, have you filed my claim and served that son of a bitch, yet?"

"It's all set to go, Marcel," answered Jake, "but I will hold off until I see what, if anything, the recordings contribute first."

***

Later that evening, as they had agreed in an earlier text exchange, Crystal did call Jake at about eight, which made it ten p.m. New York time.

"Well, Big Boy!" Crystal addressed him with the new nickname she had coined for him. "Do you still miss me, or have you found someone else already?"

"Hello Crystal," answered Jake. "I can assure you that I am not even looking. Too busy at work on a new file. So I don't even have time, even if I were so inclined. Besides that… you would be a hard lady to replace."

"Ah shucks, lover," Crystal replied in an affected drawl. "You just say the sweetest things. You make my poor little heart go pitter-patter, pitter-patter."

***

Their conversation lasted over an hour. Crystal told him about her heartfelt reunion with her family and some of her friends. She told him how New York seemed so different, yet so much the same as the city she had left over nine years ago. She told him that she intended to go sightseeing, shopping, wining and dining, though not necessarily in that order. She sounded very elated and at the end of the conversation she told him that she missed him and that she was looking forward to seeing him again soon. She promised she would call him the next evening at the same time.

The next evening, Crystal called Jake at about nine thirty p.m., which made it eleven thirty p.m. in New York. He could tell by her voice that she had been drinking, but she seemed truly happy about being with her family and friends in New York again.

Jake waited for her call the next night until midnight, which made it two in the morning in New York, but no call came in.

On the fourth night, there was no call by eight p.m. Calgary time, so Jake checked his telephone call record and noticed that her first two calls did not come from her cell phone. He assumed that the calls came from her family's apartment, so he called back on that number. After three rings, a male voice answered the telephone.

"Hello. Bachman residence," the male voice replied, waiting for a further inquiry from the unknown caller.

"Hello," answered Jake, "my name is Jacob Barton." He decided to use his more formal name since it sounded a bit more Semitic, rather than Gentile. "I am calling from Calgary, Alberta. I am a friend of Crystal Bachman, and I am trying to get hold of her. Can you help me?"

"Oh!" answered the unknown male voice. "Well, that explains why the call display did not provide me with any help. I am Aaron, Crystal's younger brother... Would you mind if I asked you about how you know my sister? I only ask because she is here on vacation."

His question struck Jake as a bit strange, but he decided to answer as best he could.

"Well, we met on a plane from Denver to Vancouver a while back and we have become close friends, I think, since that time. Why do you ask, Aaron?"

Aaron paused briefly before responding in order to collect his thoughts and frame his response as appropriately as he could.

"Crystal is my one and only sister and I love her," Aaron replied. But she does have some habits, to be truthful. She met a former friend a couple of days ago... a former boyfriend, in fact. A guy she got to know during her second marriage. I hate to tell you this, but she seems to have decided to move into his apartment a couple of days ago and we really have not seen or heard from her since then. I am only telling you this since you must have feelings for Crystal to call from Calgary. She is my sister, but I am still a man, and we have to stick together from time to time. I hope that you do not think that I am betraying her."

"I see," said Jake, somewhat taken aback. "No problem, we are both... as I said, we are just... friends and we only met a short while ago. Crystal asked me to look into a matter for her," Jake lied. "I am a lawyer and I just wanted to let her know what I was able to find out for her."

"If it is important," Aaron replied, somewhat relieved, "I believe that I might be able to find his telephone number and pass it on to you. I am sure that you would still be able to reach her tonight at his apartment."

"That is all right," replied Jake. "It can wait until she gets back to Vancouver. There is no need to interrupt her vacation with an unimportant business matter. There is no urgency; I was just anxious to let her know, that's all."

After the two men politely exchanged farewells and hung up, Jake felt his body starting to chill and tighten. He had permitted it to happen again. He had permitted himself to become vulnerable with a woman and that woman betrayed his trust, again. Jake went over to his computer and logged on. On occasions when he felt low or disgusted with his life, he took refuge in seeking low and disgusting companionship on an adult internet dating site. He selected a category where husbands or boyfriends wanted to watch their female partners have sex with other males. Within twenty-five minutes he was able to locate a suitable match. Though the woman's photos were cropped and headless, her exposed nude body was certainly desirable. After a quick exchange of e-mails, Jake provided the woman with his auxiliary cell phone number to maintain a degree of confidentiality and they were able to arrange a meeting at a downtown bar the next evening. If the meeting went well, they would adjourn to their apartment and consummate their newfound friendship.

If this is how Crystal wanted to play their relationship, then he could play it her way as well.

Chapter 22

The next day Jake tried to immerse himself in the Paradis file. The overnight courier had delivered Louie's recorded conversations and they certainly showed significant promise. Jake arranged to have a certified court reporter transcribe the tapes in chronological order on an expedited basis. He spent the remainder of the morning trying to formulate a strategy as to the best way to incorporate McQuaid's oral admissions within the case as a whole. He was also waiting for Michael to come to the office, though that probably would not happen until noon, since his flight from Toronto came in fairly late that morning.

As anticipated, at precisely noon Michael strode into the offices of Bolta & Barton only to be simultaneously besieged by Jake, Kathy and Christine Breland. Kathy and Christine immediately demurred and gave priority to Jake. Michael promised to accommodate the two ladies as quickly as possible.

***

"Michael…" Jake spoke solicitously, which communicated to Michael that it was more likely a personal matter, not a business matter. "Do you believe in love or is it just lust and sex out there?"

Michael placed his briefcase on a desk and turned to his long-time friend. He could see that Jake was serious and troubled. He hoped that he might be able to help him in some way.

"Women problems, Jake?" he asked, "or just one woman in particular?"

Jake paused and considered Michael's question before answering.

"I guess you can say that it is just one woman in particular…?" Jake replied. "I told you about that woman I met on the plane back from Denver and that she had invited me to come out to Vancouver and visit

129

her, which I did. And that she was going to see her family in New York…"

Michael remained silent as Jake related the telephone conversation with Crystal's brother.

"Have you had a chance to speak with Crystal about what her brother told you?" asked Michael.

"No!" answered Jake. "Not yet. In fact, what would be the point of talking to her after what she did? After all, even though we had agreed that we were not committing… unfortunately, it appears that I became committed against my own will, but that does not make me feel any better."

"You realize, of course, that you are asking advice about the distinction between love and lust from a guy whose own marriage recently imploded and who is currently going through a divorce?" Michael replied kindly. "What makes you think that I could possibly give you some helpful advice, my friend? Besides, you probably know more about lust in any case."

"I trust you, Michael," replied Jake. "More than any other living soul on this damned planet. If you cannot help me, then nobody can."

"All right, Jake." Michael spoke reluctantly. "I am going to speculate somewhat, so if any of my assumptions are wrong, do not hesitate to interrupt and correct me. I think that you are feeling what you are feeling right now because Crystal's brother told you about her betrayal. And notwithstanding your repeated assertions that you would never permit a woman to get so close to you, you did just that. It may have been unconscious and not deliberate, but there was something about this woman that touched your soul. You became attached to her even though that was probably the last thing you wanted to happen.

"You also expected or assumed that she would reciprocate those feelings to some degree. Jake, whenever you permit someone to get close to you, there is always the chance that you might be disappointed or become disillusioned or even be betrayed. Life, like litigation, does not come with any iron-clad guarantee of happiness in the former or success in the latter. It is the possibility of happiness or success which makes the attempt worthwhile. And if you are fortunate, it will make your life all the more meaningful and fulfilled.

"The key is that those feelings of affection, trust, commitment and respect, have to be reciprocated. Easy to say, not so easy to do because we all seem to be so self-obsessed to a point—as if we were infected by a *Narcissus Touch*, you might say. That preoccupation with ourselves seems to blind us to the other person's feelings and needs. It makes any meaningful relationship difficult to achieve, but that does not mean that it makes it doomed to failure. Sometimes people can learn to perceive life with more clarity through personal adversity. But you also have to be able to forgive, forget and move on."

"If the chances of success seem so slight, Michael, what is the point in even trying?"

"Because you cannot succeed if you do not try, no matter how many times you may have failed," responded Michael. "But if you do succeed, your life will be truly enriched."

"And what about you and Marlena?" Jake asked.

"I believed that I had found that kind of relationship with Marlena," answered Michael. "My mistake was that after having found her, I permitted myself to get preoccupied with work and other matters and I neglected to continue to nurture that relationship... and after a while, those feelings atrophied and died... I am paying the price right now, but the one redeeming vestige I cling to is my son, Adam. His existence makes my pain bearable and my life still truly meaningful."

"Thanks for sharing, my friend," Jake replied and then embraced Michael. "But I do not know if I am capable of forgiveness or deliberately placing myself in a position of such vulnerability on the off-chance I would come out successfully. But you have given me some food for thought, and I thank you for that."

***

After Jake left his office, Kathy ushered in Christine acting on the assumption that business should precede personal matters. Since Kathy was standing behind Christine, Christine could not see that Kathy had flirtatiously blown a kiss to Michael. What she could see, however, was Michael's surprised reaction and sudden smile, which he attempted to stifle with only partial success. Christine decided to pretend that she had not noticed anything and proceeded to just deal with her issue.

"Mr Bolta." Christine spoke formally. "There have been a couple of positive developments on your divorce, but the mundane details can wait a little while. I know that you must be exhausted after the appeal and the flight back to Calgary. I can advise that I formally submitted your proposal, and it appears that your wife's counsel is recommending acceptance. Most importantly, her lawyer has persuaded Marlena to agree to weekend overnight access to your son, starting this weekend."

"Well!" responded Michael, "that certainly is good news. Thank you for your good work."

With that, Christine turned and exited the office, appreciative of Michael's gratitude because she knew how long it had been since he had been able to see his son on any extended basis. However, she also heard the unmistakable click of the door lock being activated as Kathy closed the door behind her. She paused and smiled to herself. Her premonitions may have been correct. Being intimately involved with the details of both divorce proceedings, she felt a sincere elation at the possibility of these two decent people possibly finding happiness together at this difficult time.

***

After Christine left and Kathy locked the door behind her, she turned slowly to face Michael with a happy conspiratorial smile on her face. Michael responded in kind, and they approached each other slowly, until they embraced and exchanged a tender kiss. Kathy had the presence of mind to break off the embrace first.

"Well, Mr Bolta," she said, "it certainly is a pleasure to see you back home again and to hold you and kiss you. By the way, what time should I come over this Sunday for dinner? I hear that you may be cooking. Perhaps we can consummate our friendship again after dinner?"

"Well, Ms Clemens," Michael replied formally as well, "I can assure you that those sentiments are reciprocated. And why don't you come over about mid-afternoon? That would give me an opportunity to introduce you to my father's menagerie… and as Christine has just advised, we shall also have the company of my son, Adam, whom I hope you will get to know a bit better."

Chapter 23

Jake deliberately arrived at the bar earlier than scheduled. He wanted to reconnoiter the surroundings and be able to watch for his anonymous companions; however, they were already seated and watching out for him. The woman was attractive and obviously the one in control. Though her hair seemed dyed, she had ample breasts which were accented by a generously disclosed cleavage, great crossed legs which were accented by a generously disclosed length of thigh… and a very inviting lascivious smile, accented by a row of gleaming white teeth.

Jake wondered to himself why a man would permit his woman to have sex with another man in front of him. Either they both had to be extremely kinky, or the husband was so totally submissive to his wife that he was prepared to indulge her in anything she wanted, regardless of the toll it may take on his personal dignity. After exchanging introductions and some banal pleasantries, he concluded that with this couple the motivation seemed to be simple: mutual lust. The wife got off on having sex with other men and the husband got off seeing his wife have sex with them as well. But Jake did not really care this night.

After they ordered a round of drinks. Jake excused himself before the waiter returned so that he could intercept him and instruct him to just bring him a virginal Coke and ice, no rum, notwithstanding the fact that he ordered rum & Coke. He further instructed the waiter to bring him the bill, promising him a substantial tip and giving him a preliminary $20 bill as a sign of good faith.

The three had ended up ordering four separate rounds and after the fourth round was finished, Jake could see that the alcohol was starting to have a strong effect on both of his companions. As Jake was about to suggest that they proceed to go to their apartment, the woman rose and linked arms with Jake and made that suggestion herself with a slightly slurred voice. She also implored Jake to follow them carefully because she did not want him to get lost.

When they got to their apartment on the eleventh floor, the husband unfolded the living room sofa to reveal a double, somewhat disheveled bed and then he silently left the room. The woman approached Jake and asked flirtatiously if he had done this often, as she ravenously groped to undo his belt and start to pull down his zipper.

"Not often enough, Honey," Jake replied, as her husband re-entered the living room totally naked. He was overweight and he was tugging at his penis in an attempt to arose himself.

"Say man," the husband asked, "you don't mind if I watch and masturbate, do you?"

"Not at all, man," Jake replied. "I do not have a homophobic ligament in my body."

As the woman continued to fumble with his pants, Jake undid the buttons on her blouse and her bra from the front, releasing her pendulous breasts which he proceeded to fondle as she led him to the bed by his semi-erect penis.

"Say look, honey." The woman addressed her husband, who was still busy trying to arouse himself, as she pointed to Jake's genitals. "Talk about being well-hung!"

As she sat down, she took Jake's penis in her mouth and proceeded to suckle him. Jake could only focus on the top of her head which confirmed that she dyed her hair. The part was grey, not dark brown. He placed his hand on her head to gently encourage her to engulf him deeper.

As an afterthought, Jake became concerned that they may be taping his performance surreptitiously; consequently, he tried to make sure that he turned his face away from the husband and buried his head in the wife's breasts as much as he could.

Though he reached climax before her, he dutifully continued until he felt her shudder as well. Her husband had obviously ejaculated before him since he was wiping his hands with a couple of tissues. Though they offered him another drink, Jake declined and after acceding somewhat equivocally to their request for an encore performance sometime soon with his trademark wink, he left the apartment. But he was totally dissatisfied, especially with himself.

***

Jake entered his condo just as his landline started to ring. He looked at the caller ID which confirmed that it was Crystal, and she was calling on her own cell phone. He reluctantly decided to take the call and see what she had to say for herself. He assumed that her brother probably told her that he had called.

"Hello Crystal," Jake said. "Still having fun in New York? I missed your call last night?"

Crystal did not respond immediately, but just as Jake was ready to put down the receiver, she finally relented.

"Jacob. I would like to sincerely apologize," she said, adding quickly. "I was out with friends; we met by chance in a bar in Manhattan and I had too much to drink. I woke up the next day nude in his bed. It was not something I planned or wanted to happen."

Then it was Jake's turn to pause and try to collect his thoughts.

"And then you decided to spend the next couple of days with him in any case?" Jake stated rhetorically. "I take it that you did not remain in a continuing state of inebriation all that time. There were some evanescent periods of lucidity... of sobriety, weren't there?"

"Jacob, please!" Crystal implored. "I have apologized, and I am sincerely sorry."

"Apologize for what?" Jake asked sarcastically. "Just what do you want to apologize for? For betraying my trust? For fucking your ex-boyfriend? Or just forgetting to call me because you were so preoccupied?"

"All of the above," Crystal replied contritely, "and probably more."

"You know something, Crystal," Jake said. "Words are pretty cheap. You do what you do, but just because you apologize after, that does not absolve you of your conduct."

"Jacob, I am truly sorry for what I have done... and for hurting you. Have you never got drunk and done something stupid and wrong, and then regretted it enormously? I had no intention of being intimate with him. Though I was happy to see him, I no longer had any interest in him."

"But you did fuck him, anyway?"

"As I told you, Jacob," Crystal replied, "I woke up nude in his bed the next morning. I may not have fucked him, but he probably fucked me. But I do understand that it was my fault. I put myself in that position without considering the possible consequences and now I have hurt you."

"Do not worry about hurting me, honey," Jake replied. "Better people than you have hurt me a lot more and I am still here, still standing."

"Jacob, you do not know what I have gone through these past couple of days," Crystal tried to explain. "I was drinking when he joined our group and then I got drunker. I do not know how I got into his bed.

"Then when I woke up the next morning, he told me that he had been on some form of lithium medication, but he decided to take himself off. He would not let me out of his apartment for the next two days. He took away my phone and my clothes. He even threatened to hurt me, if necessary.

"It was only this morning when he went into his bathroom that I had a chance to get away. I was just dressed in a short slip, but I got out of the apartment and ran out into the street to get some help. The police arrested him and took him to a psychiatric hospital for observation. I have been trying to call you all night, but you were not answering your cell or your landline."

Jake remained unrepentant and unforgiving.

"Well, Crystal, you are not the only one who can choose to fuck around," Jake said. "Tonight, I had a threesome with another couple. I did the guy's wife in front of him, while he was masturbating away. How does that grab you, honey?"

Crystal paused and then asked quietly. "Did you enjoy yourself, Jacob?"

Jake paused and thought for a moment. He was sorely tempted to try to hurt her some more, but he thought that she would be able to see through a lie, so he decided to answer her truthfully.

"No, Crystal," Jake replied quietly, "I did not enjoy myself. I did what I did to try to pay you back. To hurt you, but it seems that I only hurt myself."

"Well, Jacob," Crystal replied solemnly. "It seems that we both hurt each other. You did hurt me, but I guess you were entitled because I had hurt you first. But for what it is worth, Jacob, and this comes from personal experience, I can assure you that revenge fucks do not work."

Jake was unable to respond. He simply did not know what to say and so, remained silent. He hoped that Crystal would say something which would erase what had happened to them.

"I have decided that I should also return the Tahitian Pearl set you gave me as that 'early pre-Hanukkah gift', Jacob, because I do not deserve it. You should give it to someone else. Someone more deserving."

Jake paused again before responding.

"No, Crystal," Jake said. "I gave it to you because you totally captivated me at the Denver Airport and on the flight back to Vancouver. I gave it to you because I not only liked you, but I was totally and hopelessly infatuated with you. I wanted you to have it so that you would know that I was not interested in just that mercy hump. I still want you to keep it... perhaps just so you would remember me."

"We all make mistakes, Jacob," Crystal responded. "And as we go through life, doors open and doors close, but sometimes it may be possible to pry open a closed door... if both parties are so inclined and prepared to forgive and give themselves a second chance."

Jake remained silent again. He was not sure if he could or should respond.

Crystal finally spoke slowly. "You said you gave it to me, because you liked me. May I ask you something, Jacob? Do you *still* like me... even after everything that has happened... just a little bit?"

Jake considered her question carefully. Was it preferable to be honest with her and admit that he still cared about her and that he wanted to have a relationship with her or to lie and reject her heart-felt entreaty and deny those feelings in an attempt to hurt her more? Even a little bit more. However, at this point, he lacked the courage to be honest with her... and he also lacked the enmity it required to lie to her and to disavow his true feelings. So, he elected to take the coward's third option.

"Crystal, I really do not know what I should do, never mind what I would like to do."

"All right, Jacob," Crystal replied. "Since it was my error in judgment which initiated this mess for both of us, I feel I owe you some time, at the very least for you to consider whether you believe that we should or could salvage something out of what we had. Notwithstanding what has happened in the interim."

Jake was still unable to respond.

"However, Jacob," Crystal continued, "I am not a naive debutante any more who may believe that 'love conquers all'. And I may not be 'chaste' any longer, though I have been 'chased'. However, I do believe I have a good heart and that my intentions are pure. I want you to know that I do have feelings for you. Deep feelings and that I do want to have a relationship with you. I also want to assure you that I will try my best to fulfill the expectations which you may have of me, and I trust that you will be prepared to reciprocate.

"However, this is not an unlimited time offer. After you have had some time to consider what, if anything, you would like the two of us to do, please let me know. If you would like us to try again, I will be ecstatic to do so. If you choose to leave it ended, all I can do is thank you for sharing a small part of your life with me… even for this brief period… and hopefully we can part as friends as we go our own separate ways. Ending in bitterness seems to be so needlessly self-defeating and self-destructive."

Chapter 24

Michael was hurrying to finish preparations for the dinner he was going
to serve that evening before Kathy came over so that they would have
more social time together. His culinary skills were modest, but he did
want to make a good initial impression. He also wanted to introduce her
to his father's menagerie and more importantly, he wanted to introduce
her to Adam, who was busily playing some electronic game on his
computer. Marlena had dropped Adam off Saturday morning and it was
agreed
that Michael would drive Adam to his school Monday morning. After
dropping Adam off at school, he decided that he would drive up to
Edmonton for that scheduled examination, since it was going to
commence at one p.m. and the drive up would only take about three
hours.

For dinner, Michael decided on some simple favorites of his own
which would hopefully increase his chances of culinary success. A fresh
Caesar salad with actual crushed anchovies, instead of just anchovy
paste, followed by a generously garlic-buttered spaghettini and mild
Italian sausage main course, accompanied by pan-seared Brussels
sprouts garnished with toasted pancetta. How could he possibly go wrong
with a generous portion of anchovies, garlic butter, pancetta, black
pepper and sea salt? He decided upon a fresh fruit medley garnished with
cane sugar and some whipped cream for dessert to freshen the palate. He
also selected a twelve-year-old Amarone wine to accompany their meal
and he hoped that Kathy preferred red wine to that ubiquitous sauvignon
blanc that he thought that most women seemed to prefer.

Adam was playing his electronic game, but he was getting a bit
frustrated in controlling his penguin's slide down a slippery slope and he
seemed to be on the verge of having a temper tantrum, so Michael
decided to intercede and try to diffuse the situation.

"Adam," Michael said, "it is just a game. Do not let it frustrate you and make you mad. If you lose your temper, you know what is going to happen. I will have to send you to your room for a time out."

"Oh," responded Adam. "Er… for how long, Dad?" he asked inquisitively, as if the proposed punishment might be bearable or even negotiable. He was weighing the relative merits of losing his temper and being punished against the effort it would take to control his frustration and not lose his temper.

"That depends on how long it takes you to decide that you are going to behave like the well-mannered young man I know you to be," replied Michael.

"Maybe five minutes, Dad?" asked Adam.

"Or maybe an hour, Adam," replied Michael. "It all depends on you."

Adam continued to furrow his brow and weigh those alternatives as Michael heard the dogs start barking. It was their announcement of the probable arrival of Kathy. He had tried to explain to Adam that a friend was coming to join them for dinner and that he wanted Adam to impress his friend by being on his very best behavior. Adam assured Michael that he would really try his best.

Michael decided to hurry outside so that he could try to intercept Buster and prevent him from his usual greeting of rearing up and butting newcomers to the property. By the time Michael had reached the small parking lot, Kathy had already exited, and she was surrounded by Joe, Sterling and Buster, who, somewhat uncharacteristically, was being quite social and permitting Kathy to run her hand down his neck and then scratch his back.

"Allow me to make the introductions, Kathy," Michael said. "This is Sterling, a purebred silver German Shepherd." Then directing himself to Sterling, Michael commanded her to 'sit and stay', and Sterling immediately complied.

"Then we have Joe, who is not a purebred. He is a part Doberman and part something else, we are not quite sure what. He has the black-and-tan Doberman colouring, but his body hair is longer, and Father did not bother to have his tail and ears clipped when he was a pup. Then he commanded Joe to 'sit and stay' and Joe immediately complied.

"And last but not least, we have Buster. He is a miniature black goat, obviously, but that is about all I know about him. And he is not as obedient as Joe and Sterling by a long shot. The three of them share a heated bay in the utility garage and they are let out in the morning and then put away for the night for their own safety. We have some bears, wolves, and the occasional cougar, which follow the creek down this valley from the mountains, looking for easy prey.

Michael noticed that Kathy seemed happy to meet the 'gruesome threesome'. She was dressed casually in form-fitting faded jeans and a loose-knit sport shirt which was discreetly buttoned at her neck. She was also wearing flat casual walking shoes. Kathy and Michael briefly embraced and parted as Adam formally announced his presence behind them.

"I am Adam, Ms Kathy," he announced formally and then added proudly, "my father's one and only son."

Michael's father had instilled the habit of Adam addressing adults by the prefix Mr or Ms, followed by their first name, as a sign of respect for his elders and Michael approved that practice.

Kathy smiled and looked over to Michael inquisitively, but Michael simply shrugged his shoulders in silent capitulation.

Without invitation or prompting, Adam approached Kathy and extended his hand in greeting.

"And how do you do, Ms Kathy?" he asked... adding quickly, "you are a very pretty lady."

"Well, Adam," Kathy replied. "I am quite fine, thank you. And you are a very handsome young man."

Adam was obviously impressed with himself, and he wanted to continue the conversation.

"Thank you, ma'am," he said with feigned modesty and a snide smile. "I do try my best."

"All right, you two," Michael interjected. "I believe that this mutual admiration society has gone far enough. Let's go up to the house and have a drink and then we can eat. I will introduce the two mares which are out in that pasture by the arena and Darrell, some other time.

"Darrell?" inquired Kathy.

"Darrell is an orange feral cat who came from God knows where and moved into the stable a few years back. He seems to keep the mice under control, but he is also fed on a regular basis. I do not believe that anyone other than Father was ever able to actually pet him, but even Father couldn't pick him up. Darrell may let you approach him but that is the extent of his social interaction.

***

The dinner was relaxing and enjoyable. As Adam and Kathy got to know each other better, Adam was able to relax and be more himself as well instead of deliberately trying to affect a maturity which he did not yet possess. After dinner, Adam invited Kathy to play his penguin electronic game and she was able to assist him to get the penguin to slide down the full length of the slide, which, as Adam quickly explained, gave him access to different shields which would protect him from other hazards and obstacles in his continuing journey through the game. Michael put away the dishes and the cutlery and then joined them with a couple of glasses of the remaining Amarone for himself and for Kathy.

"Well, Adam," Michael announced. "It is getting pretty late, and it is way past your bedtime. I will have to wake you up a bit earlier tomorrow morning, so it is off to bed, my one and only son."

Adam smiled at his father's reference to him being his 'one and only son' and he only put up a brief resistance before acceding to his father's instructions. After changing into his pajamas and brushing his teeth, he repeated the Lord's Prayer with his eyes reverentially closed and his palms clasped together. Michael stood beside him by his bed and Kathy watched discreetly from the doorway. However, Adam was not quite ready to capitulate that easily and he politely pleaded that Michael read him one of his bedtime books. Michael attempted to speed up the reading by deliberately missing a couple of pages on occasion; however, Adam had the story memorized. Each time Michael attempted to skip a page, Adam would point out his oversight. Kathy, in observing the two of them, was sure that they both knew what the other was doing and that this was merely a rehearsed performance which they had been repeated from time to time.

Michael escorted Kathy to the deck which partially surrounded the southern portion of the residence in a semi-circular fashion. The day's warmth had dissipated, and they put on a couple of light jackets to fend off the night's chill. They looked out at the cottonwood trees which were continuing to slowly shed their remaining yellowed leaves and they could hear the distant creek as the water babbled softly over its pebbled bed.

They turned together in unison. Their wine glasses were drained, so they placed the empty glasses on the rail and then they embraced. The embrace commenced in a gentle fashion, but it quickly became more intense as if they were trying to fuse their two bodies into one. Finally, Michael looked down into Kathy's eyes and he noticed that tears were starting to well up in her eyes. He was initially surprised and then confused, but Kathy read his confusion and tried to allay his concerns.

"Michael," she said softly, "I do not believe that I have ever been happier in my life than at this precise moment. Do not be concerned. My tears are just tears of joy."

With that statement she raised herself up on her tiptoes and kissed Michael on his lips. Michael swept her up in his arms and carried her to his upstairs bedroom. This time he chose to undress her, himself, slowly. He practically found himself worshiping her nude form as he kissed and caressed her before he undressed himself.

They made love without speaking. Without making any verbal demand of the other as if each instinctively knew what the other wanted and expected. When they drifted off into a deep sleep, their arms and legs remained entwined together. Their peaceful slumber was disrupted only too quickly when the alarm announced that it was six thirty the following morning.

***

Kathy only wanted a strong coffee for breakfast, while Adam required a full breakfast. Kathy volunteered to put together a healthy lunch for him and then she intended to go home to change before heading to the office.

Michael advised her that he was going to drop off Adam at this school and then he was going to head to Edmonton for the scheduled examination that afternoon. He did not believe that he would be able to return to the office before closing time, so he simply told her that he would see her on Tuesday morning.

While Adam was preoccupied with his scrambled eggs, raisin toast and orange juice, Kathy and Michael had an opportunity to drift off into the living room and briefly embrace and share a short, tender, discreet kiss before she left.

When Michael came back into the kitchen, Adam had a mischievous smirk on his face.

"You like Ms Kathy, Dad. Don't you?" he asked smugly.

"Yes, I do, Adam," replied Michael. "And I hope that you get to know her and that you will get to like her too."

"Is Ms Kathy going to be my new mom?" Adam asked, a bit confused.

"No, Adam," Michael replied. "Your mom will be your mom forever, but I hope that you and Kathy can become close friends."

"Oh!" Adam said with relief. "Good! So Mom is my mom and Ms Kathy is my friend."

Chapter 25

Jake was in his office waiting for Paradis and his nephew to arrive. He was reviewing the transcribed telephone conversations and trying to strategize as to how to incorporate those transcripts with Louie Paradis' e-mails to McQuaid when the receptionist phoned to advise him that his clients had arrived. Jake decided to meet them in the reception room and personally escort them back to his office.

"Hey, good buddy!" Paradis bellowed, the ever-present unlit cigar dangling precariously from the right side of his mouth. "How's it hanging?"

Jake was not sure if he preferred some of the previous appellations which Paradis had directed at him, such as 'bumfucker'. He decided to spare Ginger any further embarrassment by not bothering to respond to Paradis' more personal query.

"Mr Paradis, Louie," Jake replied and proceeded to shake both men's hands in turn. "Nice to see both of you gentlemen again. Please follow me to my office."

"Never you mind the 'Mr Paradis', Jake," Paradis said. "After that performance in Denver, I feel like you and me is kin. I would appreciate it if you would just call me Marcel."

***

As soon as they seated themselves at Jake's round conference table, Paradis asked Jake as to the status of his lawsuit in general and what he thought of the transcribed telephone conversations.

"I decided to file a statement of claim in order to obtain an *ex parte* order directing the bank to produce the relevant bank statements and particulars of all cheques, bank drafts and wire transfers. *Ex parte* just means without notice to the defendants because I had not served McQuaid... in case I had to amend that statement of claim. I named

McQuaid as the primary defendant and 'John Doe', as the pseudonym for his silent partner. Once we identify him, we can substitute his real name. After reviewing Louie's e-mails and the telephone transcripts, I believe that the one transcript which precedes Louie's transfer into that joint account is critical. McQuaid repeatedly assures Louie and makes a couple of very significant admissions. First, he confirms that he would deposit his $600,000 to that joint account as soon as your wired funds arrived. Second, he confirms that the operating instructions for that joint bank account required the joint authorization of Louie and himself. However, the bank records show that a couple of days after your deposit arrived, McQuaid wire transferred $300,000 to a Vancouver bank account and that he also wired the remaining $300,000 to another bank account in Edmonton. It was a joint account, but either named signatory had full authority to deal with any funds."

"So, we've got him by his balls!" replied Paradis, slapping his hands together and feinting in an attempt to grab Louie's genitals, who jumped back, startled, and almost falling out of his chair.

"I think we are in a pretty good position, Marcel," said Jake, adding, "but we will still need to conduct a quick examination of McQuaid in order to fill in a couple of blank spaces. For example, who is his dapper silent partner? Who are the beneficial owners of those two bank accounts in Vancouver and Edmonton who received $300,000 each? But it is clear that McQuaid lied about depositing his $600,000 and that the funds would be used for that placer gold mining operation in the Yukon and that it took both signatures to operate that account. It seems probable that he was primarily responsible for the misappropriation of your funds."

"Then it should be a slam dunk!" Paradis exclaimed and joyfully slammed his open hand on the table for emphasis, startling his nephew almost out of his chair again.

"I do not want to assume anything at this point, but I believe that we have the makings of a very good case," replied Jake, modestly.

"You're just too goddamned cautious, Jake!" bellowed Paradis. "I know a sure-thing winner when I see one. This is a *guar-an-teed* winner. I can feel that son of a bitch McQuaid's money in my pocket already."

"Well, Marcel," Jake politely reminded him, "it is your money to start with in any case. We are just trying to get it back."

"I say that this is a goddamned guaranteed winner... I tell you!" replied Paradis, almost spitting out his cigar in his excitement.

"You know Marcel, I heard tell of a criminal lawyer in town who used to promise guaranteed wins for an additional cash bonus payment of $10,000. He was a very good criminal lawyer, and he won a lot of cases... but not all of them. Because he did not win all his cases, some of his disappointed clients, or so they say, took offense at having paid him that cash bonus and then still ending up in jail."

"So, what the hell did he do?" asked Paradis, obviously intrigued.

"They say," continued Jake somewhat ambiguously by keeping his alleged sources confidential, "that he obtained a license to carry a firearm. And they say that he also had an unlicensed sawed-off shotgun which he kept under the driver's seat of his car for personal protection."

"Jake... good buddy," replied Paradis, with a sly smile on his crooked lips, "I would be prepared to pay you a substantial cash bonus... if you would be prepared to guarantee that we will win this damn case."

"But you have not heard what happened to the lawyer," answered Jake.

"All right... what the hell happened to the lawyer, then?"

"They found him outside his car in a back-alley parking lot downtown early one morning. Shot in both knees and to add insult to injury, with a final shotgun blast to the face, from his own shotgun. Needless to say, the police checked the records to see which one of his unsuccessful clients had been released recently, but they all had convenient alibis... and the case remains open."

"But you know me, Jake," Paradis replied, trying unsuccessfully to arch his broad thin lips into a believable smile, "I am not that kind of person."

"I *hope* that you are not that kind of person, Marcel, but as you told me in Denver, you know people who know people," said Jake, smiling back at him.

Paradis remained silent for a moment, slyly watching Jake carefully.

"All right. Let's get serious, Jake. What is your strategy for a quick victory in this case?"

"I am going to proceed to serve McQuaid... who is in Edmonton at this time. After service, he will have twenty days to file a defence, but he will probably wait until the very last minute before he has his lawyer contact me and ask for a further thirty-day extension so that he can 'obtain instructions and familiarize himself with the case', which is a polite euphemism to indicate that he has not received his retainer yet. I shall decline and just give him an additional five days to file a defence, since I am obliged to extend professional courtesies under our Code of Professional Conduct, or we will proceed to note him in default and apply for a summary judgment since this is a liquidated claim…or a specified sum and we do not require a trial to quantify our damages. If his lawyer files a defence, I will serve him with a notice to admit and introduce the telephone transcriptions and the bank records. Keep in mind, they can file a simple denial of everything in their statement of defence, but they are obliged to provide cogent reasons to deny any fact or document in a notice to admit. They have twenty days' grace to file their response and I expect them to come up with a variety of legal flatulence to justify why they were unable to admit anything. I will apply for a summary judgment. But I really want to know who is behind those two bank accounts which received those two wire transfers."

"Are you sure you won't go for that guarantee, Jake? Paradis asked again, licking his cigar with his lips and rolling it over seductively in his mouth.

"Marcel, if I could testify for you at the examinations and at the trial," replied Jake, "I might be interested in taking you up on that offer, but since the Rules of Court and the Code of Professional Conduct preclude me from doing so, that means I have to rely on my witnesses and my client's performance… and they have been known to screw up from time to time. So, NO! I cannot accept your kind offer."

"Jake," Paradis said resignedly. "You are one son of a bitch, but I am glad you are *my* son of a bitch."

Chapter 26

After dropping Adam at his school, Michael decided to drive up to Edmonton rather than taking the shuttle jet, even though he could fly up in less than an hour. It would take him at least two and a half hours to drive up, but he would have to exceed the posted speed limit all the way. The drive would, however, give him that time to relax and collect his thoughts. As he headed north, the mountains to the west gradually faded into the distance and soon they were not even visible.

The scheduled examination involved his inventive client coming up with a very clever and lucrative business operation. The traditional disposition of discarded concrete from demolished buildings and bridges, as well as discarded asphalt from road renovations, involved trucking that material to distant dump sites. This involved substantial costs in trucking fees and dump fees, as well as stringent compliance with the province's environmental regulations which were put in place to ensure that these dump sites would not become future pollution sites, themselves.

Michael's client came to the realization that by crushing and mixing this unwanted material, it could become a more effective surface dressing for industrial yards and even for resurfacing rural roads. For one thing, vehicle traffic would compact the mixture and make it more durable, since it would not spray or scatter like loose gravel, which required regular and expensive replacement. Secondly, it was environmentally friendly.

Michael's client had a further epiphany. He would offer to accept the discarded concrete and asphalt at his industrial yard for a nominal fee which was substantially below the cost of trucking the material to distant dump sites. In effect, his clients would pay him to accept the raw material which he would then process through a small crusher and mix accordingly to a client's specific needs and then resell it. In that fashion, he would receive revenue upon receipt of the unwanted material and receive further revenue upon its resale. Furthermore, he would not have to pay for the raw material, itself.

Clever as his client seemed to be to recognize this business opportunity, he was still naive regarding the machinations of the business world. In the instant case, he had entered into an oral agreement with a businessman who had a large industrial yard to maintain. They had come to an agreement that the entire yard would be covered with this recycled aggregate mixture to a specified depth for the all-inclusive price of $100,000. However, after the aggregate was delivered and spread out, the purchaser refused to pay, claiming that the material was not suitable. Michael's client offered to send in his trucks and his loader to scrape up the aggregate and take it back to his yard at his own expense, but the purchaser refused that proposal as well. He did offer to pay $25,000 in full satisfaction of the alleged debt. The only remaining alternative was to sue; however, there was no written contract.

Michael smiled to himself at that thought. Considering that the last matter he had to appear on in the Ontario Court of Appeal also involved an oral variation of a written contract, he ruefully mused that he may be trying to develop a sub-specialty in his litigation practice in respect of trying to enforce oral agreements.

He had discussed the case with the opposing counsel, a woman who bore the French-Canadian name of Monique Dupuis, who spoke, however, without a trace of her French heritage.

Dupuis had asked Michael if he was taking the position that her client, a man named Mohamed Omir, and who had emigrated from Lebanon twenty years earlier, was a liar? Michael did not want to get into personal attacks, however, on a strictly off the record basis, he pointed out that he had produced two signed and dated statements from two independent witnesses, who, fortuitously, happened to be present when his client and Omir shook hands to confirm their agreement. Michael advised Dupuis that one of their respective clients had to be lying. However, since those two independent witnesses corroborated his client's position, he personally felt that it was her client who was being untruthful.

This was not an unusual discussion between counsel. However, the protocol was that neither counsel would use any portion of the off the record conversation against the other.

***

Michael had arranged to meet his client in the lobby of the thirty-five-story office building at one thirty p.m., so that they would have a brief time to review. Michael admonished his client to pay attention to the questions asked and to answer those questions without volunteering additional information because that additional information would only result in additional questions. The overriding instruction was his reminder to his client that anything he said could be used against him at the trial, but he was precluded from using his own examination evidence at trial, himself. However, some clients unfortunately felt that if they could only persuade the opposing counsel that they were right, the matter would be settled. Consequently, they usually ignored that cogent advice.

"You could have made matters a lot easier for yourself if you had reduced your agreement to writing," said Michael. "But there is a chance of a possible settlement today."

***

Dupuis' offices were on the thirty-fourth floor. As they entered the reception room and introduced themselves to the receptionist, a swarthy middle-aged man stormed out of an office and stomped down the hall to what was obviously the law firm's boardroom.

Though Michael's client remained oblivious to the possible significance of this development, Michael immediately felt a dread developing deep inside himself that there probably would be no settlement today.

The receptionist escorted Michael and his client to the boardroom. The court reporter was already set up with her clasped hands poised on her lap. She smiled in acknowledgment as the two men entered and sat down. Omir was not seated. He was pacing back and forth on the opposite side of the boardroom table, obviously agitated.

A young woman followed Michael and his client into the boardroom. She was carrying a couple of files and had a smug smile on her face. As she bent over to lower the files to the table opposite Michael, she deliberately and proudly displayed her low-cut top.

"Ms Dupuis, I presume?" Michael asked politely. "Could you have your assistant provide me with more legible copies of these three pages from your client's documentary production?"

Michael did not really need more legible copies. What he wanted to do was to stall for a couple of minutes to afford Omir an opportunity to settle down. Once he received those needless replacements, he asked the court reporter to swear in the witness. However, Omir refused to sit down and insisted on affirming his oath to tell the truth, standing up.

"Mr Omir," Michael asked in a firm, but quiet voice. "I take it that you are being presented today as an officer to testify on behalf of your company, the corporate defendant in this action and to that extent, could you repeat your name in full for the record."

"What? You want me to repeat my name?" Omir responded insolently. "Are you deaf? I just identified myself to the court reporter. I told her my full name."

Michael looked over to Dupuis to see if she intended to advise her client to be polite and co-operative, but she merely stared back blankly at him, indicating that she was not going to intervene.

"Mr Omir, will you confirm that your answers to my questions today shall be binding on the corporate defendant in this action?" Michael asked politely.

These were standard introductory and non-contentious questions; however, it was apparent that Omir was not going to be co-operative, and his counsel was not going to try to maintain any kind of decorum over the proceedings either.

"You want to know something?" Omir asked rhetorically. "You're nothing but a two-bit shyster and you call me a liar?"

"Perhaps we should go off the record?" said Dupuis, finally deciding to intercede since she did not want a recorded transcript of what her client might proceed to say. "Both sides should try to calm down."

Michael looked at Dupuis and smiled. "I assure you, Ms Dupuis, that I am quite calm." Then turning to the court reporter, he instructed her accordingly.

"Madam reporter, this is my examination, and no one is going to tell me when to go off the record. To that extent I want you to keep transcribing everything which is said by anyone in this room, until I advise you otherwise."

Dupuis attempted to interject herself again so that she could put some self-serving comments on the record and to give herself an opportunity to lecture Michael. However, to preclude her from doing so, Michael deliberately proceeded to speak over her so that the court reporter would not be able to transcribe anything. The court reporter finally pleaded and implored both counsels not to speak at the same time for that very reason. Dupuis finally gave up and Michael proceeded to address her client who had remained adamant and standing, his arms crossed defiantly against his chest.

"Now, Mr Omir," Michael stated calmly. "I assume that you want to insult me by calling me a 'two-bit shyster'. But surely, if you want to really insult me, perhaps I am only worth fifteen cents? Perhaps I am just worth a nickel? Or perhaps we should just ask everyone here to leave the boardroom so that you and I can discuss this issue in private… like men."

Michael was not sure what he would do if Omir decided to take him up on his suggestion; however, Omir became incredulous and temporarily speechless. Consequently, before Omir or Dupuis could recover, Michael rose from the table and started to pick up his file material and place it back in his briefcase.

"And Ms Dupuis," Michael said, "I am formally waiving my right to conclude my examination of your client; however, the partial transcript which we do have clearly indicates that Mr Omir has no intention of fulfilling his responsibility under the Rules of Court. It will also be my intention to apply for a summary judgment as soon as possible, based on our corroborating statements."

Then he turned to his client and advised him that they were leaving.

"But I thought we would be settling today, Michael?" his client asked, somewhat confused by the recent developments.

"And I have not had the opportunity of examining your client yet, Mr Bolta," Dupuis added, anxious to avoid an aborted examination.

"I served your office with a filed notice to attend, and we paid the appropriate conduct funds so that I would be able to examine your client by right, Ms Dupuis," Michael replied. "However, I was producing the plaintiff today on a purely voluntary basis. You have not served me with a filed notice to attend, nor have you paid us the required conduct funds. Therefore, you have no right to examine my client today, if I choose otherwise… and I do so choose."

"But we are just wasting this opportunity and increasing our clients' respective legal costs," Dupuis protested.

"I do not want to lecture you, Ms Dupuis," replied Michael, disingenuously. "But you should have considered that before you decided to disclose that 'off the record' comment and before you decided to permit your client to fail to fulfil his legal obligations as a party to this litigation. But since you are so concerned about my client's legal fees, I will now formally confirm for the record that I will not be charging my client for any of the preparation, travel time or the wasted time in trying to examine your client this afternoon. I trust you will be inclined to follow my example and state, for the record, that you will not charge Mr Omir, either."

Dupuis did not respond verbally. She merely glared at Michael as she rose from the table and proceeded to deliberately cover her decolletage with her left hand as she leaned over to collect her documents. She had obviously concluded that Michael was not deserving of a further gratuitous glimpse. But Dupuis did not accede to Michael's suggestion that both counsels, in the financial interests of their respective clients, agree to waive their respective legal fees for the day.

"Mr Bolta," the court reporter asked politely. "I have continued to try to transcribe what had occurred this afternoon to the best of my ability. Would you like to order a transcript?"

"Of course I would, Madam Reporter," Michael replied and returned her smile.

He knew that this would compel Dupuis to order a transcript as well and ensure that the court reporter would not only be paid for her time, but for the transcripts as well.

"And Ms Dupuis, would you like to order transcripts as well?" The court reporter inquired politely.

"I... Uh..." Dupuis was obviously flustered, but then she agreed that she wanted a set of transcripts as well, simply because Michael had ordered a set.

***

In the lobby, Michael's client was confused and disappointed.

"You told me that we would be settling this case today."

"Actually, if you think back to what I actually said, I did not say that exactly," Michael replied, knowing that it was going to be a waste of time trying to explain the nuances of what occurred that afternoon.

"As I said upstairs," Michael added, "I will not be charging you for today, but I will be applying for a summary judgment. Furthermore, I was watching Omar watching Dupuis and it was obvious that he was not impressed with her today. I believe that he will be changing lawyers and that we shall be settling this matter quickly once that application is filed. Omar is an experienced businessman and I have checked his litigation record — he is quite the litigious fellow — more often sued successfully, than suing successfully. With those two corroborating independent witness statements, he knows that he cannot win at trial. He merely went through this exercise to try to save himself $50,000. He had offered you $25,000 to start and I believe that he would have agreed to pay you up to $50,000 by way of a settlement, which I probably would have been inclined to recommend that you accept because a trial would have probably cost you $35,000, anyway. But thanks to Ms Dupuis' miscalculation, your legal fees will be minimized, and your recovery shall be maximized."

Michael's client furrowed his brow as he tried to understand what his lawyer just told him and then he finally understood and smiled... and proceeded to shake Michael's hand and thank him profusely.

"However!" Michael added. "If you phone me again to tell me that you have a contractual dispute and that you did not bother to reduce it to writing... or if you had a written contract, but you did not bother to fax or e-mail it to me to permit me to review it before you signed it... I swear

156

that I will not take your case… at least not at any reduced rate like today. In fact, I may be inclined to double my hourly rate."

"Michael… and I mean this sincerely," his client replied. "It will be money well spent, but I insist that you bill me out for everything. Today included."

Chapter 27

Jake continued to work on the new Paradis file, but his heart was not really into it. He found that his mind would wander, and he would have to go back and reread material from time to time. Invariably, he would find himself thinking about Crystal… her wit… her lust, her infidelity… and even her time-limited offer of a possible reconciliation.

The following week he had received an anonymous delivery of roses. Ginger and his own paralegal were amused that some woman was attempting to court him. Jake's own initial surprise and obvious confusion did not help clarify matters for the women. But he realized who had sent those roses, even though they did not come with a card. It hindered his concentration even more because he knew that the roses were intended to remind him that his allotted time was fleeting.

His own attempt to draft a preliminary legal brief in contemplation of a summary judgment on the Paradis file was being unduly delayed. Finally, he decided to give up and delegate that task to someone else.

Christine Breland, even though she was specializing in family law, was a good researcher and a good writer so Jake decided that she should prepare that preliminary draft. He could have phoned her on her office line and asked her to come and see him, but he decided that he would go to her office instead.

Jake knocked at her office door, then proceeded to enter without waiting for an invitation and placed the Paradis file on her cluttered desk. After all, he was one of the two firm partners, and he did not think he had to wait to be invited to enter.

'Christine," Jake said, "I was wondering if you could help me to prepare a preliminary legal brief on a litigation file I am working on right now."

Christine looked up from her desk, a bit surprised. She really did not have much to do with Jake ever since that initial employment interview she had with him in the boardroom.

"Of course, Jake. Oh, I'm sorry, Mr Barton," said Christine, correcting herself quickly as she rose to greet him.

"No need for any of those formalities, Christine," Jake responded and sat down, again without any prior invitation, gesturing that she should sit down as well. He then proceeded to outline the material facts and the legal issues, as he perceived them, on the Paradis fraud file. After he had finished, he asked if she had any preliminary questions.

"So, since McQuaid was successful in persuading Louie to deposit the Paradis $600,000 into that bank account and he had the unilateral right to withdraw those funds, why would they go through that exercise the next morning when McQuaid's silent partner showed up with their $600,000?" asked Christine.

Christine also noted that there was something different about Jake's attitude this morning. He was not his usual cavalier self. He was polite, but unsmiling. He was serious, but he also appeared to be distracted at the same time. He certainly was not examining her physically in any prurient fashion as he had done during that initial interview, even though he had wrongfully assumed that he was being subtle and coming across as totally innocuous and professional.

"Oh, I forgot to mention that a review of the bank account records confirms that there was only one $600,000 deposit into that account. It was deposited the preceding afternoon by Louie and withdrawn shortly thereafter by McQuaid through a draft made payable to himself. That same draft was the draft which the dapper silent partner presented the following morning to McQuaid, and which was then endorsed by McQuaid and deposited back into that same joint account," Jake explained.

"If they intended to defraud Paradis out of his $600,000 and since they did not deposit their own matching $600,000, why have those funds been deposited, withdrawn and then redeposited again?"

"Christine," Jake explained, "it did not make much sense to me either at first, but I believe that their reasoning was as follows: First, they had to get Louie to decide, ostensibly on his own initiative, to deposit his funds in that account… presumably as an act of good faith on his part in his new business partner and their joint venture without insisting on their own reciprocal deposit. Second, by utilizing the Paradis funds, they were able to present a $600,000 bank draft as their own matching contribution the following morning. In that way they would be able to assuage any concern that Louie may have developed overnight about the security of his own deposit. Third, after their bogus deposit was made, Louie would have had no concern about the presumed safety of that $1.2 million, since he was operating under the assumption that the account required their joint signatures to utilize those funds."

"I'm sorry," said Christine. "I still cannot follow that logic."

"Time, Christine," Jake replied. "They needed time to cover their tracks and that little switch gave them that time. The placer mining operation would not commence until the following spring. In the interim, McQuaid could access those funds as he deemed fit, and wire transfer them around the world if he felt that was appropriate. Neither Louie nor Paradis would really be asking any questions until much later. By then, McQuaid and the $600,000 could have simply disappeared. Unfortunately for McQuaid and his silent partner, Louie has demonstrated more intuition than McQuaid had anticipated. Louie had the presence of mind to start to record some of his telephone conversations with McQuaid since he never responded in writing or via any e-mail. A few days after the alleged McQuaid deposit was supposed to have been made, Louie, for reasons even he does not fully understand, decided to check that bank balance. He told me that he just wanted to see that $1.2 million bank balance figure since he felt that it represented quite a substantial business achievement. He was proud of what he thought he had accomplished, and he wanted to go online and look at that balance to reaffirm his feeling of accomplishment. When he discovered that the bank balance was nil... he panicked and immediately notified Paradis and so here we are."

"Seems like a lot of effort to expend for just $600,000, which presumably would be divided between McQuaid and his partner," Christine observed. "But even though the initial trail should not be that hard to follow, locating the final destination of the money is not guaranteed. But perhaps the solution to that problem is to locate McQuaid and identify his partner and possibly recover the money through them, personally."

"I agree," replied Jake, in a slightly patronizing fashion, but he was impressed that she had the insight not only to recognize the practical problem of actual recovery of those funds, but a practical alternative solution to that problem as well.

"It does seem like a lot of effort," Jake continued, "but keep in mind, McQuaid and his partner do get the benefit of $600,000 on a tax-free basis. However, I have the feeling that there is a collateral motivation here. hopefully we will be able to discover it in due course, but in the interim, I want a preliminary legal brief to support the summary judgment application I am contemplating. Keep in mind that the judicial threshold is no longer just to show that there is no triable issue, but to show that the claim is bound to be successful on a balance of probability, notwithstanding any triable issues."

"The new test for summary judgment does try to expedite the litigation process, Jake," replied Christine. "It is a potential remedy which eliminates the need for years of litigation and avoids substantial legal costs. Just because the parties may be disputing certain facts and allegations, that no longer necessarily requires a trial to resolve those issues, if you can show that the trial judge can decide that it is probable that Paradis would still win, despite those triable issues. On the other hand, if the issue of credibility of the parties is involved, a trial judge would have to hear that evidence and observe the respective witnesses and make a determination as to which party the court is inclined to believe."

"And how do you think that McQuaid and his partner will likely respond to any such summary judgment application?" asked Jake.

"If I were them," answered Christine, "I would try my best to show… that there is a credibility issue and that there should be a trial to resolve that issue."

"And what do you think would be the best way to negate any such alleged credibility issue?" asked Jake, still curious as to the extent of Christine's initial insight into their potential problems.

"Documents!" Christine replied quickly and unequivocally. "Documents are the best form of corroboration which should show which party is being truthful and which party is embellishing or lying. The next best form of corroboration is their conduct. The witness may say whatever he or she may want to say, but if you can cross-reference it to their conduct and their conduct contradicts their oral evidence, a court can draw the appropriate inference and come to the appropriate conclusion."

"Well, Christine," Jake stated quite positively, "in this instant case I believe that we have both the documentary proof in the form of tape-recorded telephone conversations between Louie and McQuaid, as well as Louie's e-mails to McQuaid and then we have the bank records. As for 'conduct', that little charade which McQuaid and his partner engaged in by withdrawing and then redepositing the Paradis funds speaks for itself."

***

After Jake had left her office, Christine surveyed the pile of documents which he had left behind for her. The legal brief would take her away from her family law files, but if she worked evenings and weekends, she should be able to prepare a preliminary legal brief within a relatively short period. Hopefully it would impress Jake. She did not have much of a social life in Calgary yet, so that was not a problem. It would also give her an opportunity to collaborate more closely with him and to possibly pick up some pointers on civil litigation. She might even get to know Jake a bit better on a personal basis. He seemed to be a more complicated man on closer inspection, as opposed to the initial facade he presented as the smug litigator or the expensively attired womanizer, which he preferred to exhibit to the world. He also struck her as a somewhat confused and conflicted man, though he did not appear to be fully aware of that fact, himself. She understood that he had a high opinion of himself, both personally and professionally, but there also was an additional troubling factor which she was unable to identify at this point.

Chapter 28

Michael was scheduled to participate in a teleconference examination of his elderly client who was currently residing in Reno. His client, Bill Gunderson, was a founding member of a manufacturing business in Calgary. He had decided to retire and agreed to sell his interest to his two younger partners. The sale price was $3 million with $1 million payable on execution of the agreement and the remaining $2 million to be paid on the second anniversary of the sale.

It was intended to be especially fair to the buyers since Gunderson really did not need the full $3 million on closing, Furthermore, the interest on his remaining unpaid funds would give him a good monthly income but leave sufficient funds in the company so that it would continue to grow without having to borrow. In that way, it was Gunderson's final act of assistance to his two junior partners. He was, in effect, giving them the use of that $2 million to continue to build up the business during the transition in the corporate ownership.

The proverbial fly in the ointment was that the sale agreement was prepared and supervised by one law firm which presumed to act for both sides, but with the respective parties' express written consent. The law firm had acted for the company since its inception some twenty-five years earlier. The Chief Financial Officer, Arnold Butler, had been employed initially as a bookkeeper for the company while he was completing his Bachelor of Commerce degree. After he was certified as a Chartered Professional Accountant, he was appointed the company's CFO. The third partner was a long-time associate of Butler, who had introduced and recommended him to Gunderson. He became responsible for the company's management and its manufacturing operations.

Gunderson had brought both individuals into the company as a long-term exit strategy which he had formulated in his mind. He was planning ahead. He wanted someone young who could assist him during the company's formative years and then eventually take over the company when he decided to retire.

At the appropriate time, Gunderson would sell out his share in the company to his two junior partners. He would leave financially secure, and his two partners would have the benefit of taking over a prosperous company with sufficient internal capital for continued expansion and prosperity. Unfortunately, Gunderson failed to appreciate the value of independent legal advice to ensure that the sale agreement was fair to both sides. He did not even stop to consider that if the law firm chose to prefer one party over the other party, the law firm's loyalty would probably be to its continued representation of the company, not to a retiring shareholder.

However, after the two years had elapsed and Gunderson requested the final $2 million payment, he was advised by Butler that since the company did not have the available cash, pursuant to the terms of the sale agreement—at least to the CFO's interpretation of that agreement, no funds were payable at that time.

The law firm's bias was underscored by the fact that it was even brazen enough to presume to act on behalf of the company and file a statement of defence in reply to Michael's statement of claim, even though it had been acting on behalf of both the seller and the buyers when it drafted that sale agreement. The law firm quickly ceased to act after Michael brought their egregious conflict of interest to their attention and conduct of the file was transferred to another law firm. The new firm had to first agree to an undertaking not to accept the company as a client for any other matter for the next decade. The previous firm intended to retain the company for itself for as long as possible.

After Michael commenced the lawsuit against both the company and the individual shareholder/directors and he obtained the defendants' copious documentary disclosure, what was apparent was that the company had expended substantial funds in the preceding two years to acquire related businesses in Vancouver, Edmonton and Winnipeg. It had also implemented a management decision to substantially increase its inventory, thereby increasing its costs and dramatically reducing its cash reserves to the point where the financial statements and latest balance sheet confirmed that there was no available cash with which to pay out

Gunderson. Consequently, though the company did appear to have made an excellent profit and the value of the company had increased substantially, there were insufficient cash reserves to render the final payout.

The only motivation that Michael could formulate for that conduct was that Gunderson's partners were hoping that he would predecease the obligatory date for payment of his balance. He felt that he could prove bad faith on the part of the two business partners and that it could be proven through the various documents the company had produced itself. To that extent, he decided to waive examinations of the defendants and try to expedite having the action set down for trial.

The defendants, however, insisted on being able to examine Gunderson, personally. But Gunderson refused to fly at any time, and he was not prepared to drive from Reno to Calgary in the late fall since he believed that driving through the mountains at that time of year was dangerous. Consequently, one alternative would be to have Michael fly down to Reno, via San Francisco for a proceeding which would be completed within a couple of hours or have the opposing side examine Gunderson through a videoconference. The disadvantage was that Michael would not be sitting beside his client but seated across the boardroom table in Calgary opposite the opposing counsel who would be questioning Gunderson via a closed-circuit hook-up.

Gunderson struck Michael as a strong-willed and a strong-spoken person who was experienced in the civil litigation process. Michael's primary concern was that the personal aspect of this litigation, as opposed to a general commercial dispute, might affect Gunderson's ability to testify effectively. After all, the two young men who he had introduced to the business and whom he had nurtured and made prosperous, had disclosed their greed in the end. and they had also betrayed his trust. It was that betrayal which concerned Michael because he was concerned that instead of testifying dispassionately and effectively, Gunderson may lose his temper and take the opportunity to just lash out. That kind of loss of control might encourage the opposing side to proceed to trial.

After spending a couple of weekends rehearsing Gunderson in sham examinations, Michael believed that Gunderson's personal feelings would be controlled sufficiently that he would perform well. Michael believed that Gunderson would adhere to the advice and instructions which he had tried to instill in him during those sundry rehearsed examinations which were tape recorded and then played back so that Michael could get Gunderson to recognize his mistakes in expression or choice of words. The goal was not only to testify honestly, but effectively as well.

***

Gunderson had pleaded with Michael to fly on down to Reno and Michael had acceded to that request the previous year. Gunderson had picked him up at the airport in a stretch limo with a fully stocked bar. There was a bottle of twenty-five-year-old Balvenie which Gunderson had chilled in an ice bucket. By the time the limo reached the hotel, Michael and Gunderson had nearly drained the entire bottle.

Gunderson had told Michael that he chose to stay in Reno as opposed to Las Vegas, because he would only be a minnow in Las Vegas, while in Reno he was a big fish in a little pond.

After dropping off his suitcase and briefcase in his room, Gunderson proceeded to take him down to the sushi restaurant and Michael had lost track of the number of bottles of hot sake they had consumed. The first thing he did remember was waking up in his room totally dehydrated and only able to crawl to the bathroom in order to get a drink of water. If it were not for the copious number of grapes that were part of the gratuitous fruit basket Gunderson had arranged for him, Michael was not sure that he would have been able to make it to the bathroom.

The following morning Gunderson woke him up and advised him that he had arranged for a foursome to play a round of golf and he was not taking no for an answer. He had also instructed Michael to bring down two bottles of Glayva liqueur to Reno since they were not available in Nevada. Gunderson proceeded to drink and share the Glayva with all the golfers, one of whom was the sushi chef who had prepared their dinner the previous evening. Michael was amazed at Gunderson's constitution. While he could not bring himself to eat breakfast, Gunderson, who probably outmatched him drink for drink the previous night and who was at least thirty-five years his senior, was in an excellent condition and eager to play high-stakes golf.

Michael declined to accept any wager from Gunderson in respect of their golf game because he knew he had no chance of winning. In fact, it seemed that every third ball he hit went off the fairway or out of bounds.

"Michael, you can say *Adios* motherfucker to that one!" Gunderson would exclaim each time Michael's shot went out of bounds.

By the time they got to the second nine holes, the obese sushi chef started to experience severe chest pains and pleaded with Gunderson that he be permitted to withdraw and go to the clubhouse, but Gunderson would have nothing to do with that suggestion. He had a large wager going and he was giving the sushi chef the alternative of either forfeiting the $400 Gunderson claimed he was owed or completing their golf game.

"Bill!" Michael implored, "that guy could be having a heart attack or something and you want him to play out the round? Jesus Christ Almighty!"

Gunderson finally decided to take Michael into his confidence. In a hushed voice which would not be overheard, he said. "Michael, it is not a heart attack. It is heartburn. That Glayva is so sweet, and he has been drinking it like camel in the Sahara Desert. He has just given himself heartburn. That fat son of a gun is not going to die, but his indigestion may make him consider suicide. But a bet is a bet, and he is behind and if he wants to quit, then he has to forfeit the bet."

***

Michael smiled at that memory as the opposing counsel had Gunderson sworn in to testify.

"Sir, can you identify yourself for the record?"

"My name is William Gunderson, and I am seventy-eight years old. I am not on any medication, nor have I had any alcohol in the preceding eight hours," answered Gunderson, anticipating the questions which were going to inevitably follow.

"Thank you, sir," the defendants' counsel replied in a condescending fashion, literally tilting his head back and almost snorting in Gunderson's direction. "But I had not asked for your age or your current medical

167

status, so I would appreciate it if your responses would be restricted to answering the specific questions I actually ask."

Gunderson did not bother to reply, but Michael noticed a gleam in his eyes and a slight smile form at the corners of his lips.

"And you go by the nickname 'Gunner', is that correct?"

Gunderson still maintained that nascent smile, but Michael could see that his eyes had hardened. However, Gunderson elected to respond in a calm and quiet voice.

"Yes, 'Gunner' is my nickname. But I only permit my close friends to address me by that nickname… and you and your goddamned clients are no goddamned friends of mine, so you have no right to address me as such. My legal name is William Gunderson and since I am probably twice as old as you, you may address me as Mr Gunderson and in no other way if you want me to answer any more of your insipid questions today. My nickname is not relevant to these proceedings."

Turning towards the camera, he addressed Michael.

"Mr Bolta, do you agree with my position?"

"Absolutely!" Michael replied quickly and turning to the opposing counsel, he added. "I object formally for the record to that last question on the grounds of relevance."

"Well!" responded the opposing counsel, electing not to let the matter go. "I take exception to your client's language and his tone… and to your objection…" And he could not help getting pedantic and so he added, "Just for the record, of course."

"Well!" replied Michael, deliberately imitating him. "Try to imagine how much I care! Now, are you going to get on with your examination or should we just terminate it because you take exception to my client's language and/or his tone and to my objection, albeit just for the record?"

***

Those opening salvos pretty well set the tone for the balance of the examination. The opposing counsel did try to desist, as best he could, from presuming to lecture Gunderson on his responses, language or tone and Gunderson did try to desist, as best he could, from presuming to lecture the opposing counsel in reply.

The opposing counsel then attempted a new tactic by requesting a voluminous number of undertakings from Gunderson to try to swamp the plaintiffs with a legal obligation to provide better answers or further documents. Gunderson would not respond as each request was made, as per Michael's instructions and each time Michael would either decline the request on grounds of relevance or, in the alternative, he would advise that he was taking the request 'under consideration', knowing full well that the request would be subsequently denied by him.

After all, the contract spoke for itself and the matter of its interpretation was a matter that the presiding judge would have to determine. As for the balance of the requests, Gunderson did not do or say anything. All he did was live up to the letter and the spirit of the agreement which he signed. He waited patiently for two years and then requested the balance of his payment which was refused… improperly in his opinion, but that was another matter for the presiding judge to decide.

Before concluding, the opposing counsel decided to introduce Butler's letter denying Gunderson's request for the payment of the balance of the purchase price.

"Mr Gunderson, there is some handwriting on Mr Butler's correspondence denying your request for any further payment, including interest payments, which came from your production. Is that your handwriting?"

"Yes, it is," Gunderson replied.

"And can you state for the record what is it that you wrote on Mr Butler's correspondence and why you wrote it?"

"I wrote 'AMF on that letter."

"And what do the letters 'AMF represent?"

"They represent a favorite golf expression of mine. They are an acronym for 'Adios Mother Fucker'. I wrote those letters on that correspondence because that was my interpretation of what Butler was telling me to do. Instead of having the company, which I founded and sold in good conscience, fulfill its contractual obligation to me… Butler was basically telling me to fuck off."

"Really, Mr Gunderson. I must object to your language."

"Really, Mr Counselor, or whatever your name is," Gunderson replied, "I object to your clients failing to fulfil, in good faith, their

169

contractual obligation to me. When they fulfil that obligation, I would be more than willing to apologize to you for my language if it offended your delicate nature... but your clients' conduct in this case offended me a lot more."

***

After three hours, the opposing counsel ended his examination, but not before he threatened to apply to the court for an order to compel Gunderson to respond to those denied or postponed undertaking requests.

"Well," answered Michael. "As I said at the outset... *try to imagine how much I care.*"

He knew that the threat was hollow and that the lawyer just wanted to try to impress his two clients, who seemed to have become a bit more anxious and concerned as the examination proceeded. Perhaps, Michael mused, they are considering the possibility that in trying to cheat Gunderson, they may have outsmarted themselves.

Chapter 29

Kathy had offered to come out to the Bolta acreage and make dinner for Michael and Adam the next time Michael had his weekend access. They had agreed on the Sunday, so that Adam would not get confused by Kathy spending the entire weekend with them. That would come in due course as Adam became more familiar with her and as he became more acclimated to their relationship.

As she turned onto the long driveway up to the house, Joe, Sterling and Buster charged down the driveway to greet her. When she parked her car and exited, Michael came out of the residence to meet her in turn. He remained surprised at his pets' exuberant, yet friendly greeting.

"Hello, Kathy," Michael said, giving her a quick peck on her cheek. "Can I give you a hand with those packages? Not sure what you decided to make for dinner, but it looks as if I may be having leftovers for a few days as well."

"I was not sure what groceries you have here, so I decided to bring all the fixings. I decided to make a traditional fried chicken dinner with rice and vegetables. I also baked an apple pie yesterday for our dessert. I even brought along some vanilla ice cream," Kathy replied proudly. "I want you to know that most people say that my crusts are the best. But you can decide for yourself after you have tried the pie."

Michael could not mistake her obvious joy in seeing him and he believed that he was as happy and contented as she was in being able to spend another casual day together.

"Apple pie?" inquired Adam. "That's my favorite. Can I have a piece right now? Please?"

"*May* I, not can I," corrected Michael.

"Adam," Kathy replied, "it is so nice to see you again. But if you are patient for a little while, I promise that you shall get an extra-large serving with two scoops of ice cream."

That promise mollified Adam somewhat and as the dogs escorted them to the residence breezeway, the goat trotted obediently behind everyone.

"Dad, can I show Ms Kathy the horses? One is called Wooden Doll and the other one…" Adam paused dramatically. "She is called *Kathy's Dream*!" He looked at Kathy to see if his surprise pleased her. Turning quickly to Michael, he asked, "Dad, you named her after Ms Kathy, didn't you?"

"Actually, your grandfather named her Kathy's Dream, but I do believe that he may have named her after Kathy," Michael replied. "Your grandfather knew Kathy from the office, and he liked to name the animals he really liked after people he really liked."

Michael was satisfied that the possibility that his father may have named the mare after Kathy was sufficiently truthful so it would not disappoint his son, since it may be true. But he wanted to be careful that Adam did not think that the mare was named by him, in case his son decided to repeat and share the story with his mother. Their divorce was proceeding smoothly, and Michael did not want anything to upset matters before it became finalized.

After putting away Kathy's ingredients, Adam and Michael decided to introduce Kathy to the two mares. As they went through the gate, Adam cautioned Kathy to always make sure that the gate was closed behind them.

"Dad always reminds me to make sure the gate is closed because those horses are pretty smart. They watch carefully and as soon as you go away a little bit, if that gate is left open, they will run up to it and get away. And then we will have to chase them down the driveway," Adam cautioned her seriously.

"Thanks for reminding me, Adam," Kathy replied, acknowledging Adam's advice. I promise to remember to make sure that the gate is always closed after I go through it."

As the three of them entered the mares' paddock, even though the mares were at the far north end, they quickly broke into a gallop to join them… sliding on their haunches to stop quickly within a few feet of the visitors.

"Adam," Kathy asked, "would you like to make the introductions?"

"Of course," Adam replied. "The brown mare is Wooden Doll. She had a foal a little while ago and I did not even have a chance to see her, but it died. And this is Kathy's Dream. Isn't she pretty?"

Kathy's Dream was a beautiful chestnut with four white stockings and a white symmetrical blaze on her face. They both had kind eyes and were nuzzling Michael because they knew that he usually had a treat for them. Their favorite was a thin, sweet carrot. Michael could see that Kathy was a bit apprehensive because both horses weighed at least a thousand pounds each.

"Kathy do not be too worried by their size," Michael advised. "If you are concerned, just make sure that you maintain eye contact with them. That will reassure the mares that they do not have anything to worry about from you."

They proceeded through a second gate so that they could show Kathy the riding arena and the stable. As they entered the shed row to the stable, there was an orange flash that streaked from one stall to another stall which contained bales of hay and straw. After a moment, Darrell peeked over the edge of the uppermost bale so that he could examine the intruders in relative safety. Joe and his companions had been locked out of the stable and he started to bark loudly at the commotion inside.

"Joe! Shut up, for Pete's sake!" shouted Michael.

"I really wish you would rename that dog, Mr Bolta."

It was his father's hired hand whom Michael decided to keep on after his father's death.

"You could call him Charley or Max or something… anything, but Joe. So when you start yelling or cursing at 'Joe', I won't get confused and think that you were yelling at me."

The smile on Joe's face belied his stated concern. Everyone knew that he was kidding.

"Father was the one who named him, and I don't believe trying to rename him at this point would work," Michael answered. "But perhaps we can get *you* to change your name, Joe?"

"That's right, Mr Joe," Adam chimed in. "Then I could call you Mr Charley or Mr Max."

"Maybe I will just keep my 'Joe' name, if you all don't mind."

***

They had finished dinner and had started on Kathy's apple pie and as promised, Adam got a slightly bigger piece, though he did not think it was big enough. He also received two scoops of vanilla ice cream.

The doorbell rang unexpectedly, and Michael excused himself as he went to see who it was. He certainly did not expect any visitors. As he opened the door, he saw it was Marlena, and she did not look pleased at all. For a moment, Michael remained dumbfounded at her unexpected appearance.

"Well, are you going to invite me in or are you just going to let me stand outside?"

Though the tone of her voice seemed civil enough, the rage seething through her body was evident in her facial expression. Michael remained frozen, enable to speak or even move.

"Mom! Mom!" exclaimed Adam. "I thought I heard your voice. We just finished dinner, but there is still some dessert left. Ms Kathy's apple pie is delicious."

"Hello, Adam," Marlena replied. "Thank you, I am sure it is delicious, but I did not come here to eat."

At that moment, Kathy made a shy appearance in the doorway.

"Good evening, Mrs Bolta," Kathy said, attempting to be civil.

Marlena did not bother to respond. She knew full well if she said anything, the words would definitely not be suitable for Adam's ears.

"Michael," Kathy quickly added, "since dinner is finished, I believe I should go."

"Yes, Kathy!" Marlena responded. "I do believe that you should go."

***

Kathy packed up her belongings and politely squeezed past Marlena, who remained unmoving and almost blocking the doorway. She had no intention of moving in the slightest. After Kathy had left, Michael invited Marlena into his home and suggested that Adam go into the family room to watch television or play one of his computer games, while he finished his apple pie and vanilla ice cream.

***

"So Michael!" Marlena asked sarcastically, "is Kathy as good in bed as she is in the kitchen?"

Michael was not sure how to deal with Marlena initially, but he decided that showing any guilt or shame was not the appropriate reaction. They had executed their settlement agreement and their divorce would become final in a few more weeks after their stated one-year separation had expired. And since she was the one who was unfaithful by having that affair with McNabb, he could not understand why he *was* feeling some shame and embarrassment at that moment.

"Actually, Marlena," Michael calmly replied, having recovered his composure to a small degree. "Her fried chicken was excellent and the crust on her apple pie was simply amazing. If you would like, I can get you her recipe."

"What!" Marlena sputtered in rage. "You know what you can do with her recipe. But is this how you intend to introduce your son to your... mistress?"

"Well, I am glad that you did not lower yourself to Alexa's level and call her a slut or a whore," replied Michael. "But since our marriage is over, we are both free to pursue our respective lives as we may deem fit and appropriate. I thought that this is what you wanted? To end our marriage."

"You ended our marriage when you started to have those affairs," Marlena responded. "Alexa told me all about them. We both suspected that the bitch secretary of yours was one of them. By the way, she is married, isn't she?"

"Kathy is going through her own divorce, which should be finalized even before ours. It appears that her husband got his girlfriend in Edmonton pregnant. Furthermore, I do not understand what Alexa may have told you, but it was not true. I have been faithful to you until you commenced our divorce proceedings. I swear that on the eyes on my mother and father. You, in fact, were accusing me of being unfaithful when you were the one who had that affair with McNabb."

175

"But... I was never intimate with McNabb!" Marlena confessed contritely.

"But why did you repeatedly tell me that you were!" asked Michael, somewhat confused.

"Alexa told me about your screwing around and she was the one who suggested that I have an affair with McNabb, since he was your friend and our neighbor. But I could not bring myself to do it. I did not want Alexa to think that I was a coward, so I lied to her and then I decided to lie to you as well."

"Why?" Michael pleaded. "Why would you do such a cruel, stupid thing? It might have been kinder had you actually *had* that affair, rather than simply lying to me about it. What is the matter with you?"

"You think that I am stupid? You think that something is the matter with me?"

Those questions may have been rhetorical, but Marlena's voice was angry and rising in volume. Michael was concerned that Adam would hear them arguing and get upset himself.

"Please keep your voice down, Marlena. You don't want to upset Adam, do you?" Michael implored.

"You started this by screwing around. Why did you decide to be unfaithful? I wasn't good enough for you any more? What did I do wrong?" pleaded Marlena as she burst into tears.

"I had never been unfaithful to you... before you commenced the divorce proceedings. At that point, I decided that there was nothing that I could do," Michael answered her somberly.

"Are you accusing your sister of betraying you and lying? Why would she do that? Go on, tell me. Why would she do that? You are the only remaining blood relative she has in Canada."

"Marlena, I am telling you that I was never unfaithful to you. And why Alexa decided to do what she has done to destroy our marriage... I simply do not know. I know that she hates me for some reason... but those reasons are unfathomable to me. I could never understand what motivated her to do some of the things she did... to herself... and it seems, to us. She is one unhappy woman, and she cannot stand to see anyone else be happy, so she schemes and tries to make other people's lives miserable as well."

176

Michael and Marlena were both emotionally spent and for a few moments neither one uttered a word. They would simply exchange a fleeting glance and then quickly look away.

***

"Michael, I don't know, but I may have made the biggest mistake of my life... if you are telling me the truth," Marlena finally answered after she had collected her thoughts. "Do you think there is any chance that we can set everything aside and try again?"

Michael did not respond immediately. He looked into her eyes, and he could see her fear and her confusion, but he could also see some residual resentment.

"But Marlena," he answered quietly, "you still do not believe me... because you qualified your statement by saying, 'if you are telling me the truth'. That is a pretty big 'if'. So obviously, you still do not believe me. We have exchanged a number of fairly unforgivable accusations and insults. I just do not believe that we will be able to go back and make it work. What we should focus on is to do what we can to ensure that Adam is going to remain happy. with both of us. Who said that life and relationships are easy?"

Marlena remained silent for a moment trying to collect her thoughts and decide what she should do; however, no firm answer was forthcoming. All the alternatives which came to her mind had respective pros and cons. There did not seem to be a clear answer or solution.

"If you do not mind, Michael, I would like to take Adam home with me right now. I do not want to be alone tonight."

Now it was Michael's turn to consider the alternatives and decide which one was the most appropriate. "All right, I understand. Let me get Adam."

It seemed predestined that it was he and Kathy who would remain alone that night.

***

Adam had appeared to be engrossed in some new computer game and he was just finishing his pie and ice cream. He was not eager to go, but he did sense that if he did not go, that it would make his mother sad. She did not look very happy. Perhaps he could bring a smile to her sad face.

Adam deliberately reached out to hold his mother's hand as they walked out to her car. Driving back to the city in the lightly falling snow, they both remained quiet, but Adam kept looking up at his mother who seemed to be preoccupied with her own thoughts. Finally, she glanced down and noticed that Adam was watching her intently.

"Is everything all right, Adam?" Marlena asked kindly.

"I love you, Mom. Please do not be sad," Adam replied

Those reassuring words had their desired effect on Marlena, who immediately broke into a broad smile and started to cry at the same time.

"How can I be sad when I have such a wonderful young man as my son," Marlena replied. "And I want you to know that I will always love you… for ever and ever and ever."

***

After Marlena had left, Michael poured himself a double shot of Camus, his favorite brandy, and then he sat in his recliner chair before the fireplace and tried to think as he sipped his drink slowly.

Though he felt he could forgive Marlena for her groundless accusations and even her cruel deception about having an affair with McNabb, he did not think that he could bring himself to forget it. Though he believed Marlena completely in respect of what she told him about Alexa's involvement in that deception, he could not bring himself to believe that he and Marlena could simply sweep what had happened between themselves under that proverbial rug and simply resume their lives as if nothing had happened. Sooner or later one of them was bound to raise those issues again. He was also positive that Marlena would ask him, sooner, rather than later, about the depth of his relationship with Kathy. Furthermore, if he agreed with Marlena, it would be impossible to have Kathy continue as his personal paralegal, not that she would have wanted to stay on in that position in any case. That would have been an intolerable situation for her as well.

By the time Michael had finished his copious portion of brandy, he felt that he had made up his mind about what he should do. He realized that he did not want to resume his previous life with Marlena because he knew, in his mind and in his heart, that it could not — *would* not — ever work again. At the same time, he realized that he did want to be able to have a new life with Kathy if she would still have him. And perhaps he and Marlena could create a new separate relationship… one which hopefully would be devoid of rancor and spite, so that they could continue to raise Adam as loving parents.

Chapter 30

As Michael drove from the acreage to his office the following Monday, he was not sure what would be waiting for him when he arrived. He also had to drive a bit slower, since the first snows of the coming winter season had materialized overnight and though the snow was not deep, the roads were slippery. Winter driving skills had to be revived quickly. Michael did not want to slide off the road this morning. He could see in his rear-view mirror that the mountains were completely snow covered, instead of their peaks merely being snow-capped. They would remain that way until spring.

In thinking about the snow, he had decided that he should introduce Adam to downhill skiing, and he had made plans to take him for some introductory lessons and practice before they would venture out to one of the ski hills which were located in the nearby mountains. Perhaps Kathy would join them as well.

At that thought, memories of what had transpired the day before came flooding back into his mind. There was no way he could have stopped Kathy from leaving when she did, because he and Marlena had to try to bring their personal matters to some form of resolution. However, Marlena's suggestion that they try to set aside their issues and resume their relationship had caught him by surprise. It was the last thing he expected her to say or to ask.

Suddenly Michael's car hit some glare ice under the light snow covering. The snow had initially melted before the temperature continued to drop and that melted snow had pooled on this lower stretch of the highway. As the snow continued to fall, the melted snow turned to ice and then was discreetly disguised by the subsequent falling snow. Even though Michael's car had four-wheel drive, either his vehicle was not absolutely perpendicular as it struck the glare ice or perhaps, he had accelerated a little bit at the wrong time or sightly turned the steering wheel, but suddenly his car went into a complete spin.

That immediately brought Michael out of his reverie as the adrenalin hit his bloodstream. Fortunately, Michael did not apply his brakes and his car completed an entire pirouette and to his utter amazement, ended up in its original easterly direction on the highway. Michael slowed his vehicle a bit more and whispered a silent prayer at his good fortune. Perhaps that miraculous pirouette was a divine sign of better things to come this day and in the days to follow.

***

Michael greeted Ginger as he stepped into the reception of Bolta & Barton, but he was not inclined to sharing those routine salutations and pleasantries which the two of them usually exchanged after a weekend break. As he strode down the hall, he could see Kathy seated at her desk in front of his office and he assumed that she did not look up deliberately. *Well,* he thought, *at least she showed up for work. That was a positive sign.*

As he approached her desk, Kathy finally looked up. Though her posture and facial expression remained neutral, he could see that she was tense and concerned.

"Good morning, Kathy." Michael spoke as kindly as he could as he approached her desk.

"Good morning," Kathy replied politely as she looked up inquisitively, searching for some hopeful indication as to what was about to transpire.

Michael noted that she did not address him by name, either formally or informally.

"Could you come into my office, Kathy, and please bring your coffee. I believe that we have a few things to discuss."

Kathy rose obediently and followed him into his office, clutching her coffee mug in front of her with both her hands as if she was afraid that one hand was not going to be sufficient and that it might drop. Michael held the door open for her and then locked it after she had entered.

"I would like to apologize for Marlena, yesterday," Michael stated matter-of-factly, but as kindly as he could. "It was a rather rude intrusion which disrupted what promised to be a very enjoyable evening. By the way, I loved your fried chicken and that apple pie crust was even better than you said it would be."

He noted that Kathy continued to grasp her coffee mug firmly with both hands in front of her. He assumed that it might be just a convenient excuse to prevent him from embracing her.

"I think I owe you an apology," Kathy replied. "In hindsight, I believe we should have waited until our respective divorces had been completed. But as I told you at the outset... whatever happens... or however events turn out... I am not going to regret anything." Then in an almost hushed voice and downcast eyes she asked the critical question. "What did Marlena have to say after I left?"

Michael continued to watch Kathy closely and carefully. He knew that she was close to tears, but she was trying desperately to maintain a brave facade.

"She said a number of things, Kathy," Michael replied. "But she does not want your recipe for the fried chicken or your apple pie."

Michael noticed that Kathy winced at his poor attempt at levity, so he quickly approached her and took her coffee mug away so that she could no longer use it as a shield. After he placed the mug on his conference table, he turned towards her and gently placed his hands on her shoulders. He sensed that sharing an embrace at that moment was not appropriate. Kathy continued to avoid direct eye contact by continuing to look down in a non-committal fashion at his chest.

"I'm sorry about that last comment, Kathy. We have some serious matters to discuss, and this is not a time to joke around."

Michael continued to speak in a soft, gentle, reassuring voice.

"She told me, that it was Alexa who convinced her that I was unfaithful. She also told me that she did not have an affair with McNabb. She lied about it to Alexa because Alexa was the one who suggested it and kept encouraging her to do it for revenge. Marlena did not want Alexa to think that she was a coward, but she lied about it to me because she *did* want to exact some revenge."

"Oh!" said Kathy, with mixed feelings. She had expected worse news.

"She also asked me to try to set matters aside, so that we could try to resume our marriage," Michael added sadly.

"OH!" Kathy, sputtered in emotional surprise. Her worst fears had materialized.

Her initial relief had been premature. Her anxiety that Marlena would be able to persuade Michael to reconcile and resume their marriage had apparently come true. Marlena had the upper hand and Kathy had recognized that from the outset. After all, Marlena had provided Michael with a son and that gave her an almost insurmountable advantage. She turned away slowly and moved towards the door, her disappointment quite evident in her body language.

"Hold on, young lady," Michael said quickly, but calmly, as he put his hands on her shoulders with a gentle firmness to prevent her from leaving. "Just what kind of guy do you think I am? Do you think that I have just been toying with your emotions these past few weeks? You have not heard what I said to her."

Kathy stopped, but she did not turn around. She could not bear to face Michael if he was about to say those dreaded words…*well we are still married… and we do have Adam to think about… and his best interests should come first.* In fact, she closed her eyes, though that was not evident to Michael.

"I thought long and hard about it, last night, Kathy," he finally said. "I do not want to hurt Marlena… not only because she is Adam's mother but because we do have a history… and she is a good person at heart. She was just vulnerable to Alexa's manipulation."

Kathy remained unmoving, but Michael could feel her body stiffen as she tried to restrain any shudder which would betray the true gravity of her personal feelings at that moment.

"But I decided," Michael exhaled deeply as he completed his confession, "that I really wanted to try to build a new life with you… and with Adam."

Kathy remained still, but he could feel her tension slowly ebb away. As that strain left her body, she slowly turned around to face him directly. Her tears had welled up in her eyes and were gently spilling down her cheeks, but her eyes radiated happiness, as did her smile.

"You better kiss me, mister, right now!" she commanded... then softening her voice, she repeated her statement, but it was more of a polite plea.

"Kiss me, Michael, please."

Chapter 31

Jake knocked twice on Michael's office door and then proceeded to try to barge in, as was his habit. He was surprised to find the door locked, so he knocked again, but more firmly.

"Michael," he said, "your door is locked, but we need to talk."

Then he heard the lock being unlatched as Kathy proceeded to exit the office.

"I am sorry, Jake," she answered innocently as she moved quickly past him. "I must have locked the door by mistake." Jake was not aware of the smug smile on her face as she walked away with her back to him.

Fortunately for her, Jake was so anxious that he did not take note of the fact that her face seemed slightly flushed. Jake also did not immediately notice the fact that for the first time in the fifteen years they had worked together that she had addressed him informally as 'Jake'. Then he paused for a moment and looked back at her as she proceeded to walk away and be seated at her desk, her face still turned discreetly away from him.

Jake was still so self-absorbed that he did not even notice that Michael's face seemed to be a bit crimson as well.

"We need to talk, Michael. First, about the status of the Paradis file. The statement of claim has been filed and we did obtain copies of the bank documents for that joint account which McQuaid had set up for that placer gold mining partnership."

Jake went on to detail the charade which had been apparently perpetrated on Louie Paradis. First to subtly encourage him to deposit the Paradis investment of $600,000, as a sign of trust and good faith on his part, contrary to his uncle's specific instructions. Then the withdrawal and subsequent redeposit of those same funds the following morning, but which were represented to be McQuaid's investment. Followed by the immediate withdrawal of those funds in two equal wire transfers to Vancouver and to Edmonton. He also summarized the preliminary legal brief which Christine Breland had prepared at his request for the proposed summary judgment application.

"We have an address for McQuaid in Edmonton, and he should be served in the next couple of days by our process server. I have also asked Christine to prepare a draft notice to admit facts, so that we can serve him with that document as soon as his lawyer files his statement of defence."

"Excellent, Jake," Michael said approvingly. It was obvious that Jake was motivated and when Jake was motivated, the opposing side should start to worry.

"So the new mystery is: *Who were the recipients of those two wire transfers?*" Michael asked, adding, "But try not to monopolize Christine too much. After all, she has her own work, and she is also working on my divorce and on Kathy's divorce as well."

"No need to worry about Christine," Jake replied, "she is a really efficient and competent young counsel. I am glad we hired her, but I will be preparing the final legal brief and the final version of the notice to admit facts, myself."

"You seem to have everything under control, Jake. Is there anything else?" Michael asked, quite oblivious to the fact that Jake displayed no intention of leaving his office at that point.

"Yes... you know that matter we had discussed briefly before, Michael," Jake said, as he seated himself on Michael's office sofa, his arms outstretched on top of the sofa cushions. "About that woman... lady I met on the flight back from Denver. She seems to have complicated my life."

Jake quickly summarized those details again, just in case Michael had forgotten some of the more salient points, then he went on to detail their last telephone conversation after Crystal had returned from New York.

"The primary question, Jake," Michael replied, "is what do you want to do at this point?"

"To be honest, Michael, I have to admit that I seem to have feelings for her... which is somewhat unusual for me. You know my usual modus operandi: catch them then release them and then definitely, forget them. But she is proving to be a difficult lady to release and forget."

"And what about her, Jake? What is her position, or has she told you?" Michael asked.

Though Jake proceeded to repeat the details of the telephone call he had shared with Crystal after she returned from New York, he did not bother to mention his revenge threesome, because he felt embarrassed and childish for resorting to that behavior. He went into considerable detail about what Crystal had told him and that she also professed to have feelings for him as well. The issue that bothered Jake, however, was his apparent inability or unwillingness to forgive her for her error in judgment.

"It is a worn-out cliché, Jake, but life is not always that simple," Michael replied. "From what you have told me about Crystal, she seems to be a very interesting woman—possibly a very suitable match for you. She is intelligent and apparently quite witty, who can give as well as she can take, which seems to be an important personality trait you seem to appreciate in women. But what happened is that she made a mistake: she drank too much in her excitement of being reunited with her family and friends. after not seeing them in quite an extended period."

"About nine years," interjected Jake.

"And she was used… but not with her knowing and willing consent… and she was made a hostage for almost two days and even threatened," Michael continued. "We judge a civil case on a balance of probability, a sufficiency which is measured at a minimum fifty-one percent… that leaves forty-nine percent which is either ignored or deemed irrelevant. I believe that if you apply that standard to Crystal, she would even pass beyond the criminal standard of reasonable doubt and possibly approach the higher medical standard of certainty."

"So you think that I should take her back?" Jake asked anxiously.

"I would not phrase it in that fashion, Jake," Michael replied. "After all, women are not chattels… to be given away or taken back." And then he added half-seriously. "They have even had the right to vote for about one hundred years. And I am not going to tell you what to do. That must remain your decision. All I am going to do is just share my perspective. I believe that you should both be prepared to consider giving yourselves a second chance. I think you would probably have a more interesting life together rather than apart. Crystal seems certainly willing to try."

Jake remained silent and apparently unconvinced, consequently Michael decided to continue to formulate an argument to try to persuade him to make the right decision for himself.

"By the way, Jake," Michael asked, "just out of curiosity, how many women have you been intimate with in the course of your life to date?"

"Well, it is not as if I have a little black book… and keep a count of them all," Jake replied modestly, "but I think it is about four hundred, give or take a few. And I do not sleep with every woman I meet. In fact, I have even declined the opportunity on occasion, albeit a rare occasion." Jake smiled to himself at his humble modesty.

"And are you happy? Are you satisfied with your life right now?" asked Michael.

"Usually," replied Jake. "Usually, it is enough for me. But Crystal seems to have taken a piece of my flesh… and even a drop of my blood."

"Perhaps, she may have even touched your soul, Jake?" Michael asked almost rhetorically. "I am not suggesting that you get down on your knee and propose marriage. All I am suggesting is that you give both of you a chance. I have a good feeling about what you told me about Crystal and what you have also told me about how you feel about her."

"Like what, Michael?" Jake asked, somewhat confused, since he did not think that he had disclosed that much.

"Like the fact that she offered to return that gift you gave you and the fact that you declined to take it back. I remember a couple of times in the past when some woman offered to return your gifts, you readily accepted their return. Then you proceeded to re-gift those returned gifts to someone else. You just characterized that 're-gifting' as 'money well spent'. Those gifts did not mean anything to you in the first place and neither did their return or the subsequent re-gifting to someone else. However, you tell me that you told Crystal that you wanted her to keep that pearl set… so that she might remember you by it."

"Well, I did not want her to think that… that I was cheap or something… that's all, Michael," Jake replied somewhat unconvincingly.

"Really, Jake? And so why could you not have simply responded to her question about whether or not you still held any feeling for her. You said that you could not bring yourself to lie to her and tell her that you

188

did not care any more, because you said that you did not want to hurt her. You usually do not spare that kind of restraint to women you wish to shed or forget, Jake. Yet you were unable to admit that you still cared about her, even after she told you that she had feelings for you."

"Are you on my side or hers, Michael?" Jake asked, somewhat confused by Michael's analytic summary.

"I will always be on your side, Jake," Michael replied. "It just seems to me that Crystal showed a lot of courage in being truthful about what happened, when she could have just as easily lied about it to protect her personal dignity. She also apologized to you for her error in judgment, Jake. And most importantly, after she told you the truth and apologized, she said that she still wanted a second chance. That means that she cares a lot."

"She even sent me a dozen red roses a week later, Michael," Jake mused weakly. "She is the only woman who has bothered to do that for me, but it was probably just her sense of humor, because I showered her with flowers after our flight to Vancouver."

"Or it could have been a sincere reciprocal token of her affection, Jake," Michael replied.

***

Michael decided it was time for him to remain silent. He could see that Jake may be starting to see some of the positive reasons why he and Crystal should take the opportunity to try again, instead of just focusing on the negative reasons for not even trying. But Jake had to convince himself so that it was his decision in the end. After a long pause in their discussion, Michael decided to add some final pragmatic logic to assist Jake in his final decision.

"Jake, if you decide to at least try to see if you and Crystal might be able to make it work, whether it works out or not, at least you will have the certainty of knowing. If you do not bother to even try, you may remain cursed in not ever knowing that it may have worked out for the two of you. And even if you two decide to try again and that effort fails in the end, perhaps you may remain friends. I do not believe that a person can have too many friends. true friends as you go through life."

"Thank you again, for your sage advice, Michael," Jake finally replied. "I may have to start paying you for all of this personal counseling. You are truly my one best friend."

The two men embraced each other affectionately and then separated slowly. Michael watched as Jake exited his office and slowly closed the door.

"And the best of luck to you, my friend," Michael mused to himself. "Whatever decision you decide to make."

***

As Jake passed Kathy's desk, he was oblivious to the fact that she had been able to regain her composure, but then he stopped and looked at her and then he remembered and smiled.

"Ms Clemmons... I do believe that you addressed me as 'Jake' when you came out of Michael's office. And I take that salutation as a sign that after working together for about fifteen years... you are finally starting to develop a little affection for me?" Jake asked, with his mischievous smirk displayed prominently on his face.

To his surprise, Kathy's response was kind, friendly and quite personal.

"You may assume that, Jake," Kathy replied, smiling in return. "As long as you remember that any affection which I may hold for you is and shall always be... strictly platonic."

***

Jake smiled as he walked away from her desk and approached his own assistant.

"Could you arrange for another dozen roses to be sent to... that woman in Vancouver for me?"

Jake did not mention Crystal's name deliberately, so that his assistant would not assume any undue infatuation on his part, however, his assistant knew Jake better than he knew his assistant.

"And does that... *woman* have a name and an address?" his assistant inquired politely.

Kathy was overhearing their conversation and she was amused at the fact that for once Jake's assistant was playing word games with Jake, instead of the other way around.

"Jake, should I also send her the same card… you know… something about 'thorns' and 'bleeding hearts', I think?"

By this time, it dawned on Jake that his assistant was toying with him, and he could also see that Kathy was having minor difficulty in restraining herself at his expense as well.

"All right, ladies," Jake said, directing his comment at Kathy and at his assistant. "I trust that you have both amused yourselves sufficiently at my expense."

"I believe that you can locate the… lady's address by yourself and her name is Crystal Bachman. Ms Crystal Bachman. And the card should read as follows:

"*'And a man lies here all tied and bound.*

Making no sound on the cold wet ground.

Remembering moments in far distant places.

Fragments of kisses from forgotten faces."

Kathy and Jake's assistant exchanged a puzzled look as he went into his office and closed the door behind himself.

Chapter 32

Ten days had passed, and Jake continued to work on the Paradis file. He was getting a bit obsessed with resolving some of the mysteries on the file. Why had Louie Paradis been approached by McQuaid in the first place? Jake did not believe that it was simply a coincidental event. Who were the recipients of those two wire transfers? Why did the malefactors in this case decide to perpetrate this kind of fraud in the first place, at this point and on these particular clients?

He was getting impatient with the normal litigation process - first you have to draft the statement of claim, then you have to serve it; then you have to wait at least twenty days before the other side is obligated to serve you with their statement of defence. Almost inevitably, the opposing counsel is only retained at the last minute and then there is the request for a professional courtesy of an extension to file that defence, which usually is either a request for an indefinite extension or a request for a further twenty days. Jake had anticipated that probability and he had decided that he would agree to no more than a token couple of additional days. After all, all they had to do was deny everything. He was anxious to proceed... and his client, Marcel Paradis, was growing even more impatient.

Paradis had expressed his impatience by repeatedly stating that he wanted the defendants' testicles removed with a rusty scalpel... and sooner, rather than later. Jake was not sure if Paradis only meant that in a figurative fashion.

Jake was also impatient about not receiving any reply from Crystal. Perhaps he waited too long to respond? Perhaps... perhaps she may have changed her mind?

***

Kathy came into Michael's office with a disappointed look on her face. In her hand, she held a copy of the appellate decision in Michael's Ontario appeal.

"I hate to be the bearer of bad news, Michael," Kathy said, "but the Ontario Court of Appeal dismissed our client's appeal. They did indicate that they may have quantified the damages differently—translation: at a lower amount, I believe, but they decided to defer to the trial judge's assessment of damages. On a more positive note, however, in the Omir case, that recycled aggregate matter in Edmonton… his new lawyer is proposing a settlement. Payment of our client's $100,000 on an all-inclusive and forthwith basis."

"All right, thanks, Kathy," Michael replied. "I will phone our client and give him the bad news from Ontario. Hopefully he has learned not to try to modify a written agreement, orally. And I would like you to fax and e-mail the offer on the Omir case to our client and advise him that I recommend acceptance, because the legal costs were not that extensive and an expedited recovery of that $100,000 makes good sense."

Kathy was busily taking down his instructions and she did not notice that Michael was smiling at her as he watched her take them down with meticulous care.

"And on a more personal level, Kathy… would you mind locking that office door and then joining me on the sofa for a discussion on… perhaps some aspects on the true meaning of life?"

Michael had raised his eyebrows inquisitively as Kathy looked up from her notes and returned his smile.

"As inviting as your suggestion may be, Michael, I do not think that would be a good idea… in the middle of the day… and in the middle of a busy week. But perhaps we can share a quick hug and a kiss."

With that, Kathy went to the office door and locked it. When she turned around, Michael had laid down on the sofa and had his hands clasped in a fake supplication, silently beseeching her to join him. Kathy deliberately took her time and she attempted to stroll as provocatively as she could from the office door to the sofa without bursting out in laughter, herself.

"Have mercy on me, honey," Michael said, as he playfully placed his right hand over his heart. "We are going to have to start meeting on a more regular basis. Some days when I come into the office, and I see you seated at your desk working away at your computer… I almost feel like pole-vaulting over the desk and doing you right there on the spot."

"Well, Jake and his assistant would probably find that very interesting, to say the least," Kathy replied flirtatiously as she lay down beside Michael and kissed him fiercely on the lips and pressed her body up against him. She could feel that he was becoming aroused quickly, but before they could get more serious, Ginger called from the front office to advise Michael that Alexa was in the reception room and that she wanted to see him about something very urgent. Like a flat tire, Kathy could feel Michael's passion deflate as well.

"Damn!" Michael whispered so that Ginger would not hear him, while Kathy tried to mollify his obvious disappointment. "All right, Ginger, send her down in five minutes, no sooner. I am in the middle of something."

Turning to Kathy, Michael asked urgently, "Would you like to come out to the acreage tonight, Kathy?"

Then he rose from the sofa and ran his fingers through his hair and tried to ensure that his shirt was tucked in and that his tie was straight.

"I can pick up some take-out. What would you prefer: Chinese, Greek, Italian, French… or perhaps some sushi?"

"That sounds like an inviting idea," answered Kathy, "but if you do not want me to put on another five kilos, perhaps we can make it sushi this time…with some green tea or sake, if you have it?"

"A little extra weight would just be more of you to appreciate, Kathy," Michael replied teasingly. "But I will pick up the sushi and stop by the liquor vendor for the sake."

***

Ginger was on the intercom again to advise Michael that Alexa was on her way. Just as Kathy got to the door first and unlocked it, Alexa actually knocked on the door, which was very unusual for her. Kathy greeted Alexa politely, which greeting Alexa ignored. Holding her notepad and pen prominently in her hand, she permitted Alexa to enter Michael's office as she let herself out.

Alexa entered the office with a distraught look on her face. Michael was able to get seated at his desk and he looked up at his older sister without saying a word. Considering what he told her the last time they spoke, he was surprised that she would be brazen enough to come back, but he had an inkling about what might be distressing her.

"And I would ask at the outset… no, I would *beg* that you… do not presume to lecture me before I tell you what has happened," Alexa said.

Alexa then went on to tell Michael that her new friend was an entrepreneur and an investor. He had come across a high return investment (which Michael silently translated as a high-risk investment) in which he was investing, himself. It had something to do with a comity protocol between banks whereby banks or private entities would lend money to banks so that they could meet short-term overnight shortfalls, to comply with certain banking regulations respecting their liquidity requirements or something. The minimum investment was $50,000 and the minimum term was for one month. These investment funds were pooled and advanced to various banks as they were needed and then the collected interest and principal was returned to the investors at the end of the thirty days. The minimum promised return for one month was twenty percent.

Michael quickly assessed the 'high-return' investment to be a scam. For one thing, having banks cover respective shortfalls would make sense, but banks had a lot more money to affect this kind of accommodation than a group of private individuals. Furthermore, since this comity or accommodation was of mutual benefit to the banks, it did not make any sense that banks would want to pay twenty percent interest for a relatively short term to private individuals. Michael further assumed that Alexa would only have documentary proof of a wire transfer to some corporate entity somewhere offshore. He was sure that she did not have any formal written agreement, but he remained silent to afford Alexa her opportunity to continue her sad story.

Alexa told Michael that she did practice some due diligence, because even though her new friend had recommended that she match his proposed investment of $500,000, she decided to only risk $50,000.

When she received $60,000 at the end of the thirty-day period, she felt that the investment was legitimate and consequently, she decided to invest the sum of $500,000, which she had wired to the same company in the Bahamas. However, at the end of the next thirty days she did not receive her anticipated $600,000 return. Furthermore, her new friend had also disappeared.

Michael was familiar with this kind of fraud. It was usually referred to as 'priming the pump'. The fraud artist would get a gullible investor to make a modest investment, which would be paid off as represented. Then the fraud artist relied upon gullibility and greed to take over, as it had apparently occurred with Alexa. She received a $10,000 return on a $50,000 investment for a thirty-day period. If she invested $500,000, she would receive a $100,000 return within thirty days. Her greed even dissuaded her from bothering to consider that a 240% annual return was totally unreasonable and probably not legitimate. That greed also dissuaded her from even considering why banks would not be averse to paying such usurious rates.

"So you invested $500,000 of your inheritance in this high-return investment and that money is gone. What do you think I can do about it, Alexa?" Michael asked.

"Well you can sue these people and get my money back?" Alexa replied desperately.

"And who, pray tell, do I sue on your behalf? Your 'new friend', whose current whereabouts are unknown and the name he gave you is probably fictitious. Or perhaps we can sue that company in the Bahamas, which is probably just an empty corporate shell with a post office box as a business address, controlled by unknown people with fictitious names?" Michael replied quietly, watching his sister's reaction very carefully. "And by the way," Michael added, "what documentation do you have in respect of this high-return investment? Just your wire transfer?"

"You...! You promised Dad that you would protect me and help me!" replied Alexa, her desperation increasing with every passing minute. "It was his dying wish... and you promised."

"Well, firstly Alexa," Michael answered her quietly, aware that if he raised his voice, Alexa would reciprocate tenfold, "why didn't you bother to seek my advice when you were first approached with this investment idea?"

"You told me that you would have me arrested for trespassing!" Alexa sputtered, attempting to shift the blame to Michael.

"Well, that is true, I did say that, but your irreverence for our father's death made me extremely upset. But if that is the reason you did not approach me before... why are you approaching me now?" Michael replied logically.

Alexa remained silent, though she pursed her lips and squirmed uncomfortably in her chair.

"Because there is no one else who can help me," she answered.

"Let us clarify some preliminary matters first, Alexa," Michael replied. "How did you know about what I may have promised Father before he died?"

"I would phone dad from time to time when you were working at the office, and we talked. We discussed things. One day Dad told me that he was going to ask you to promise to protect me."

"Why is it, Alexa," Michael asked, "that I think it is more probable that you made the suggestion to Father, rather than the other way around?

"Secondly, the only promise I made Father is that I would *try* to protect you. 'Try' is the operative word, Alexa.

"Thirdly, though I may have protected you had you sought my help and my advice before you wired your funds, how am I supposed to protect you from yourself now that your money is lost?"

"Well, damn it!" Alexa swore, her voice becoming louder with agitation. "I am asking for your help now!"

Alexa decided to use her only trump card again, as a last resort.

"You are my brother and... and you promised Dad that you would protect me."

"From a strictly legal perspective, Alexa, and I mean this sincerely, there is nothing I can do for you. We do not know who to sue and we do not know where your money is. What do you think that I can possibly do for you now?" Michael asked.

Michael remained quiet for a moment. He knew that there was nothing he could do for her, legally. But knowing what he knew after he had his discussion with Marlena at the acreage when his wife explained

Alexa's involvement in Michael alleged infidelity, Alexa's duplicity appalled Michael beyond belief.

"Yes, I am your brother… and I did promise Father that I would try to protect you… but you are my sister… my older and wiser and loving sister, right?" Michael asked, though his questions was strictly rhetorical. "But you, as my older, loving and only sister… you fed lies to Marlena and somehow convinced her that I was unfaithful. You even persuaded her to have an affair with McNabb and you even suggested that she try to seduce Jake, as well. You… my older, loving and only sister… you did all that, didn't you?"

Alexa's initial response was one of surprise. She never anticipated that Marlena would disclose what she had done. The question, though, was what she should do or say now. Notwithstanding her desperation, she had an intuitive feeling that Michael would not help her, that he would not protect her… even though he made that promise to their father… and it was their father's dying last wish. It was not an issue that he *could* not, it was the fact that he *would* not.

"I can see the writing on the wall, Michael. I can see that you will not help me… that you will not protect me. Our father is probably turning over in his grave at the realization that his favorite son is breaking the promise he made to him as he was dying. So all I am going to say is fuck you, Michael! At least I have the satisfaction of knowing that your marriage is destroyed and that your wife fucked your friend, McNabb."

As Alexa rose from her chair and turned to leave Michael's office, Michael decided to have the last word with his sister… at least this one last time.

"Marlena knows now that you deceived her, so I would not count her as a friend of yours. She will probably despise you—no, allow me to correct that last statement… she will probably pity you as much as I pity you right now. You have ruined your own life and though you may have ruined our marriage, I am going to try my best to nurture a sincere friendship with Marlena, for our son's sake and for our own sake. Neither one of us ever did anything to you to deserve what you have done to us. But one last thing, Alexa… Marlena has more class and character than you give her credit for. Marlena did *not* have an affair with McNabb. She lied to you about that because she thought that you would ridicule her for being weak. But, unlike you, even though you convinced her that I was unfaithful, she could not lower herself to have an affair with McNabb."

Alexa remained standing quietly, with her back turned to Michael. She tried desperately to think of something suitably caustic to say to Michael in response, but she could not think of anything. Her concern was about how she was going to be able to support herself for the remainder of her life. She slowly walked to the door and left, but she did not bother to close the office door.

When Alexa exited the reception, Kathy rose and entered Michael's office, closing the door behind her. Michael rose silently to meet her and then they embraced.

"I have not said these words to anyone in a long, long time, Michael," Kathy said as she held herself tightly to him. "I love you... and I promise that I shall try my best never to hurt you."

Michael realized that her statement had brought tears to her eyes, and he kissed her.

"I suppose I should confess and tell you that I... care very deeply for you as well," Michael replied teasingly.

Kathy immediately kicked Michael's shin playfully. Although she did not intend to use much force, the toe of her shoe was firm and pointed and she struck Michael directly on his shin bone.

"Ouch, that hurts, Kathy," Michael said honestly, then quickly added. "I love you, too. But I thought you just said that you would try your best never to hurt me?"

He bent down and feigned massaging his shin. Kathy looked into Michael's eyes as he straightened up; her own eyes were still radiating joy.

"Perhaps I should have been more specific," Kathy replied. "I promise to try my best not to hurt you *emotionally*... physically? Well, that shall depend on your continued good behavior."

"And I shall give you an opportunity to atone for this physical abuse tonight, after we have dinner," answered Michael.

Chapter 33

Kathy drove carefully since the highway was snow covered from the city to Michael's acreage. Though the snowplows had cleared the pathways in both directions, the remaining snow was compacted and slippery. As she approached the entrance to the acreage, she tried to follow the tire tracks which Michael's vehicle had conveniently left for her. As she was passing the three-bay utility garage, Michael exited from the most westerly bay, and she could see the two dogs and Buster trying to follow him out. Obviously, Michael was shutting them up for the night. They waved to each other and Kathy stopped so that she could give him a ride up to the residence.

"That was good timing, Kathy," Michael said, and he slid in beside her. "I have just fed the gruesome threesome and locked them up for the night."

"They won't get cold, will they?" Kathy asked.

"No. Not at all," Michael replied. "The thermostat is set at 18 degrees Celsius. The dogs sleep on a carpeted bed which is elevated off the cement floor. Father also put some insulation underneath their bed as well. Buster likes to sleep on the seat of the tractor. So they will be fine."

To her surprise, Michael had a remote garage door opener with him and as she approached the double garage, which was attached to the residence itself, he activated the remote to open the garage door so that she could park inside the garage beside his vehicle. Between the garage and the residence was a glassed-in, carpeted breezeway which had two convenient sliding-door entrances on either side. It was a convenient place where you could shed your outer garments and footwear, if necessary, before entering the residence itself.

The interior was warm. Michael had the fireplace burning robustly and Kathy could feel the warmth radiating out as the birch firewood crackled as it was licked and consumed seductively by the yellow flames. The extensive array of sushi and sashimi was displayed on the coffee table between two armchairs and the fireplace itself. Kathy noticed that there were both chopsticks and forks. There was also some classical music which was quietly wafting through the room as well.

"Are you trying to seduce me… or feed me, Michael?" Kathy asked mischievously.

"Hopefully, both," answered Michael as he came out of the kitchen carrying a ceramic vessel, which was obviously warm to the touch from the way he was gingerly shifting it from one hand to the other, before he placed it on a glass plate on the table.

"And I decided that since it was a cold evening, that you deserved some warm sake to warm you up a little."

"Thank you. Michael," Kathy replied. "That was very thoughtful of you."

***

They both ate slowly, trying to savor each mouthful, which they washed down with a mouthful of warm sake. Kathy explained that she had an accepted offer on her home and that her ex-husband had immediately married his pregnant girlfriend as soon as their decree absolute had been issued.

Michael explained what had happened with Alexa, though he thought that Kathy had probably heard most of what had transpired between the two of them.

"I still find it hard to believe that she could be so cruel to you and Marlena," Kathy said. "You are her nearest blood relative, and you have only tried to be helpful and supportive, from what I have been able to observe."

"It is hard to understand what motivates some people to do what they do," replied Michael. "I suppose that in her own mind, she thinks that her actions are totally justified. What really offends me is her hypocrisy. She tried to destroy my reputation… and my marriage… and then she comes to me to bail her out after she continues to jump from one puddle of excrement to another. And then she had the temerity to throw my promise to my dying father in my face."

They had finished eating and were savoring the last remaining drops of the sake as Kathy rose from her cushioned chair and went over to sit on Michael's lap before fireplace.

"Michael, why don't you move the coffee table away from the fireplace and bring out a spare comforter or a blanket, while I put away the remnants of our dinner," Kathy said, adding, "I feel like experimenting tonight. What about us making love on the comforter in front of the fireplace?"

"You do not have to ask me twice, Kathy," Michael replied, as he quickly put her aside and proceeded to move their improvised dining table away. "I shall be right back with that comforter."

Kathy smiled and proceeded to empty the remains of their dinner into the plastic bags and then she discarded the plastic bags into the appropriate garbage containers. She had started undressing as Michael came back into the room.

"Allow me to assist you, madam," he said, as he proceeded to unlatch her bra and lift it off her shoulders, letting it drop down to the floor. Then he undid her belt and unzipped her slacks, letting gravity slowly pull them down over her hips and drop at her feet.

"And allow me to reciprocate, kind sir," Kathy replied seductively as she undid his belt and unzipped his jeans, letting them fall down of their own accord. She could see that he was aroused already and anxious to commence their lovemaking as he pulled his sweater over his head and threw it carelessly to the floor. His shorts were quick to follow.

Kathy proceeded to lay him down on the comforter and then she proceeded to examine the physical injury she had inflicted on his shin earlier that afternoon. She touched his bruise gingerly as Michael feigned a flinch and then she bent down to kiss it back to health. Michael was reclined, supported only by his elbows as he watched her minister to his injury and then gradually proceed upwards as she kissed his knee, then his thigh and then finally his erection… taking him deeply into her mouth as she massaged it with her tongue holding him tightly with both her hands.

Michael could only moan softly as he enjoyed her enjoying him. But he wanted to be inside her… engulfed by her warm, moist opening. Since she was still partly clothed, he eased her silk panties down over her thighs. Then he positioned her so that she would be facing the fireplace on her side as he entered her from behind, cupping her breasts in the palms of his hands and caressing her erect nipples with his fingers and thumbs. Now it was her turn to moan softly and beseech him to make love to her as she arched her back to maximize his penetration. Finally, Michael moaned again as he came inside her and though he was not sure that she had reached climax herself, he was physically and emotionally spent.

***

Neither one knew how much time had elapsed, but the first thing either one noticed was that the flames in the fireplace had consumed the firewood and that only glowing embers remained. Since the fireplace was no longer radiating as much heat, they remained embraced and rolled up inside the comforter for warmth. They were both tempted to remain there until the morning. They both felt so safe and secure. So happy and so contented.

***

"Kathy, since your home is sold… have you considered possibly moving in with me?" Michael asked softly.

"I would love to move in with you, Michael," Kathy replied. "But I am not sure if the timing is right. Perhaps we are just rushing things a little bit. What would the people at the office say? What would Marlena say…? What would Adam think?"

"I have given it some thought, Kathy," Michael replied slowly. I think that most of the people in the office… if not all of them, would be understanding and supportive. As for Marlena, I am going to try my best to have a positive relationship with her, for our respective sakes… and for Adam as well. As for Adam, he seems to have really taken to you. He did express a concern about how to relate to you and to Marlena… but I explained that Marlena would always be his mother… but you could be his best friend… and he seemed to be pleasantly relieved by that statement."

"You have a lovely son, Michael," Kathy said. "He is truly adorable."

"But listen, Kathy," Michael said. "Why are we so concerned about everyone else? What about the two of us? For one thing, would you like to have a child of your own? A pretty little girl with red hair and emerald-green eyes? I know that I would love to have another child, preferably a girl who I would spoil shamelessly. And Adam would love to be a big brother and he would not be alone... which is how I felt when I was growing up, even though there was Alexa."

Kathy looked into Michael's eyes, and they radiated sincerity.

"I would love to have a child... a little girl would be nice... but that is in God's hands so I would not be disappointed if my child was a boy. Adam would have a little brother... and you would have another son. But aren't we just engaging in some delusional, wishful thinking, or do you think that there is a chance?"

While Kathy was engaging in her soliloquy, she did not notice that Michael had reached under the comforter and was rummaging through his slacks. He brought his hand back clutching something with a boyish grin on his face.

"All right, madam," he said. "Please close your eyes and open you hand."

Kathy, though somewhat surprised and confused, followed his instructions.

She felt something metallic... but she dared not open her eyes until Michael prodded her to see what he had placed in her hand. She was immediately overwhelmed with conflicting emotions. Hoping for the best... yet dreading possible disappointment.

It was an emerald ring. A rather large rectangular emerald ring, surrounded by a ring of glittering tiny diamonds.

"Well, what do you think?" asked Michael. "Is it nice enough for you...? It certainly brings out the highlights in your eyes. And if it is not large enough, I am sure that Jake's jeweler would be happy to provide us with a bigger one."

"I... I do not know what to say. What is this all about?" Kathy asked, somewhat surprised and confused at this development.

"I do believe that I am proposing marriage to you, young lady. Michael answered. "So what do you say? Yea or nay?"

"But your divorce is not final yet, Michael," Kathy answered.

"I am not proposing that we engage in bigamy… though that might be an interesting suggestion," said Michael. "Surely you do not think that I would suggest that we live together in sin, as they say? Though that may be another interesting suggestion. No, darling… I am asking you to marry me after my divorce is final… but that should not preclude living in sin in the interim."

Kathy remained dumbfounded… she really did not know what to say, though she could not remember experiencing such inner joy in her life.

"And if you do not think the ring, alone, is sufficiently impressive to persuade you to accept my humble proposal… take a look at this."

Michael extracted another ring but it looked somewhat different. Though it had one joined base, which appeared to have been leveled, two arms emerged from that common base, which were also encrusted in small diamonds.

Since Kathy was even more confused, Michael took the emerald ring from her hand and inserted it between the two arms of the second ring and then he placed it on the coffee table and the combined ring remained upright.

"It is called a 'jacket'," Michael said. "And it was Jake's idea to enhance the engagement ring, itself, rather than just getting a pedestrian wedding band. This jacket is a substitute for the wedding ring, and it is joined, actually married in a way, to the engagement ring itself. Once they are put together, they become one. And the level base permits the wearer to straighten the ring from underneath with a thumb, if the ring becomes turned to one side or the other, so that the total ring is always presented perfectly."

"I do not know what to say… I just do not know what to say," said Kathy.

"Just say *Yes, my Lord and Master…*" said Michael. "I humbly accept your proposal."

"On, don't be silly, Michael… but… yes, yes, yes… and yes!" Kathy answered emotionally. "I want to be your wife… I want to be the mother of your child… and I want to share the rest of my life with you. Yes!"

"But are you sure, Kathy?" Michael asked ingenuously. "Are you really, really sure?"

Kathy embraced Michael without speaking and kissed him fiercely.

"Yes, Michael," she finally answered as she broke their embrace. "I am really sure."

Chapter 34

It had been about a couple of weeks since Jake had those roses sent to Crystal's office, but there had been no response. No telephone call, no text and no e-mail. His disappointment was palpable and it was affecting his ability to concentrate on shepherding the Paradis file forward. Fortunately, Christine Breland's assistance was an adequate substitution for his lack of focus in the interim.

And as expected, just as the twenty-day grace period after service of the statement of claim was expiring, he did receive an e-mailed request for the courtesy of an extension to file a statement of defence on the Paradis file the preceding day. What was totally unexpected was that the request came from Sterling Layton, Esquire, of Vancouver. The Sterling Layton who was the counsel of record for National Hydrocarbons, whom he had sued on behalf of Ben Cotton, and on whose behalf he had attended that mediation hearing in Denver, several months ago.

Since the request came in on a Thursday afternoon, Jake decided to e-mail an immediate confirmation that he was extending the courtesy for five additional days, including that same Thursday. This meant that Layton would have to serve a filed statement of defence by noon on the following Wednesday. He believed that this extension was sufficient compliance with the Code of Professional Conduct, since the statement of defence, in all likelihood, would just be a simple denial of all of the allegations in any case.

Jake did conclude that this 'coincidence' could not be a real 'coincidence' and he had quickly relayed this development to Paradis. Paradis concurred that it was just too much to be a coincidence as well because he also recalled the look of utter hatred on Layton's face when Jake told him and his other two colleagues to fuck off.

"I believe that we are starting to see the possible reason Louie was approached and defrauded," Jake said. "I had a feeling that McQuaid's approach to Louie, coming so soon after the Denver mediation, had to be connected. The fact that Layton was National Hydrocarbons' counsel of record in Ben's civil action and now he is the defence counsel in your action against McQuaid… it is just too much to be strictly coincidental."

Jake could visualize Paradis rolling his cigar in his mouth with his tongue, as he collected his thoughts.

"I think you may be right, Jake," Paradis finally replied. "In which case, this is not just a case of simple fraud. It is fucking personal. Someone is trying to fuck with my family's honour… and there is no way that I am going to permit anyone to get away with that."

"I just had an idea, Marcel," Jake added. "Remember that little charade that McQuaid had orchestrated to trick Louie into thinking that McQuaid had contributed his $600,000 to that joint account? McQuaid's silent partner… someone who Louie described as a dapper dresser — well, Layton is certainly a dapper dresser — showed up the following day with a bank draft which was supposed to represent McQuaid's contribution. Do you think it might have been Layton?"

"Anything is possible, Jake," Paradis replied. "Louie never described that son of a bitch as being bald, but Louie is the only one to have seen him. I will ask Louie to confirm or deny whether that son of a bitch was bald, but I will also ask him to check on the internet for Layton, himself. He probably has his profile on prominent display. The sooner we can confirm that McQuaid's partner was Layton, the better."

"And another coincidence is that half of your $600,000 was wired to Vancouver and Layton is in Vancouver and now he is purporting to act on behalf of McQuaid," Jake added.

"The wire transfer could have been sent to some anonymous account, though," replied Paradis. "But let me get a hold of Louie and I will get back to you ASAP."

***

Jake looked west towards the snow-covered foothills and the distant mountains to the west. It was Friday and it was getting late in the afternoon. He did not feel like working this weekend, but he certainly did not feel like staying home and watching Netflix again. Just as he started to contemplate an encore performance with that kinky couple, he received a call on his cell phone. It was Crystal.

"Jake Barton," he answered tersely, pretending that he had not noticed the call display.

"Hello Jacob," Crystal said. "I have been wanting to call you for some time, but I had to think about the possible implications before I did call."

"Well, you finally did call. Does that mean that you were able to resolve those possible implications?" Jake asked politely.

Though on the one hand, he was upset that she had not called him sooner, on the other hand, he was relieved that she finally did call.

"And what does a nice girl like me have to do to get a dinner invitation in this cow-hick town of yours?" Crystal asked smugly. "Stand on a cold street corner in the snow and accost passing men with the greeting: *Hey sailor...are you new in town? Will you take me out to dinner?*"

"Well, Crystal... if you ever come out to this cow-hick town, I am sure that you would be able to find lots of would-be suitors who would love to invite you out to dinner. You may even get lucky and meet someone in the lobby at the airport at Vancouver... or possibly be seated beside some wealthy, well-hung Adonis on the flight over."

"How about my chances at getting lucky at the offices of Bolta & Barton, Jacob?" Crystal asked.

Jake's relief that Crystal had finally called had dulled his wit and senses to a degree, and Jake, to Crystal's delight, was not picking up on her subliminal clues.

"I would say that your chances of getting a dinner invitation and... lucky... at the offices of Bolta & Barton are excellent. In fact, I would personally guarantee it," replied Jake.

"Then why are you leaving me seated in your reception room... practically all alone, except for Ginger? Is that an appropriate way to treat a friend who took the afternoon off so that she could fly out to meet you and hopefully get a dinner invitation?"

"What?" Jake exclaimed. "You are here? Right now? Don't move! I will be right out to get you."

Jake rushed out of his office so quickly that both his assistant and Kathy looked up from their respective computers.

"I have not seen Jake move so fast since that time that irate husband showed up to confront him about having an affair with his wife," Jake's assistant observed. "Jake had ushered him into his office innocently assuming that he was a possible new client. Then the man confronted him with that accusation, but he also asked Jake for his professional opinion as to his wife's relative merits compared to the other women Jake had known intimately. Jake, quite stupidly, instead of praising her charms and telling the guy that he was a very lucky man, chose to characterize the guy's wife as merely mediocre. At which point, the guy started to threaten Jake, who, concerned that the man might be armed, rushed out of the office as fast as he could."

"I remember that incident," replied Kathy. "But that was over five or six years ago. Jake is rushing to meet someone this time, instead of running away from a cuckolded husband."

***

Jake slowed down as he approached the door that connected the bank of offices to the reception room. He wanted to catch his breath before he entered. He opened the door in a normal fashion and Crystal was seated on one of the two reception room sofas, smiling up at him. She was dressed in black, as usual. A black beret, an open black hip-length leather jacket, black faded jeans and knee-high black boots. He could also see that she was wearing a black turtle-neck sweater and the Tahitian pearl set, whose luster glistened in the reception room's lights.

He also noticed that Ginger had a slight smirk on her face as well, but by this time Jake had sufficient time to recover and he was starting to become more fully attuned to the developments.

"Mr Barton," Ginger said, trying to affect a serious tone, "Ms Crystal Bachman was in the neighborhood and came in to see you. I was just about to advise you on the intercom."

Jake gave Ginger a withering, though not a cruel look, so that she understood that he understood… but that he was not angry with her in respect of the little pantomime which she and Crystal had decided to concoct.

"Thank you, Ginger," Jake replied. "Please remember to remind me how loyal and professional you are... at your next annual review."

His veiled threat was quite transparent to both women, who just smiled and waited for his next reaction.

"Please do not hold this against, Ginger," Crystal said. "I begged her to play along with my little game. I assured her that it was totally innocent and that we were... *are* such close friends that you would never harbor a grudge... because you have such a wonderful and forgiving sense of humour."

Jake looked at Crystal and just slowly shook his head, conceding defeat, since she had effectively disarmed him with that last flattering comment.

"So Jacob, who do I have to sleep with around here before I get that invitation to dinner?" Crystal asked irreverently as Ginger attempted to suppress a giggle, albeit not with complete success.

"You wouldn't happen to have a wealthy, well-hung Adonis hanging around here, would you?" she went on.

At that point Ginger lost her remaining composure and with her right hand over her mouth to stifle her laughter, left the reception room quickly, mumbling something about needing to go to the washroom.

"No, Crystal," Jake answered, "we don't have such an *Adonis*, but this may still be your lucky day because, if you behave... you may have me."

At that he walked over to her, and Crystal rose to embrace and kiss him.

"You know, Jacob," Crystal whispered, her head buried in his chest. "I have missed you... at least a little bit."

Jake smiled at her clever reference.

"Well, to be honest, Crystal, I missed you a hell of a lot. You have almost driven me out of my mind. Let's go down to my office and get my jacket and coat, and then I will take you out to dinner someplace."

***

When they got to his office, Jake sheepishly introduced Crystal to his assistant and to Kathy as his 'good friend'.

"And I would like to thank you for all those flowers you sent me in the past two weeks. It is a good thing that Jacob is so generous with his good friends," Crystal said, addressing his assistant.

"All those flowers?" Jake asked, somewhat confused and looking at his assistant for clarification.

"Just with his 'very special good friends'," Jake's assistant answered, sharing a wink with Crystal to which Jake remained oblivious.

"And I can vouch for that as well," added Kathy.

"Well, I am quite relieved that I am a 'very special good friend'," replied Crystal, looking back at Jake, who was slightly embarrassed at the thought that Crystal and Ginger, and now his assistant and Kathy, had somehow conspired to get the better of him. But his defeat felt good, nevertheless.

"All right ladies," Jake said. "I surrender, though it took the combined efforts of the four of you to take advantage of poor, little, old me."

Then looking affectionately at Crystal, he added. "I do believe that I am suddenly famished. Shall we go to dinner?" He took Crystal by the hand and said a parting farewell to the two paralegals.

"Goodnight, ladies… and thanks."

***

The dinner was sumptuous but subdued. After dinner, Jake drove Crystal to his condo. She only had one small suitcase with her. He also noted that she went out of her way to display the Tahitian pearl set. Either fondling an earring or readjusting the pendant from time to time.

"So you still like the pearls?" Jake asked.

"They are one of my favorite pieces of jewelry," Crystal replied. "You would be surprised at the number of compliments I receive. The sheen of the gold setting seems to complement the luster of the pearls themselves. And then I am inevitably asked about who gave them to me."

She deliberately stopped at that point to see if Jake would ask her how she would reply, but he simply smiled and waited her to complete her story.

"I usually just say that it was a gift from a friend. A very good friend... whom I hold dear to my heart." She continued to fondle the pendant as she watched Jake carefully. Jake watched her carefully in return. Her dark eyes seemed sincere and caring.

***

Though their dinner conversation was sparse, their never-ending exchange of glances and smiles seemed to be sufficient. There would be time enough to discuss other matters after they got home.

***

After they entered his condo, as was his habit, Jake noticed that his telephone answering machine was flickering its red light, beckoning him to check for his voice messages. As Jake pressed the message button, a loud, rude response filled his living room. It was a male voice which was uttering a death threat, as well as a crude genital mutilation and the desecration of his corpse. The message ended abruptly, and Crystal initially assumed that it was just a practical joke

"Well, Jacob," Crystal said, "I would have expected some disgruntled girlfriend or husband threatening to emasculate you, but this seems to be a bit different."

Then she noticed that Jake's face was drained of all colour and that he had a look of mixed fear and hatred in his eyes. A look which she had never seen before.

Chapter 35

Crystal quickly came to the realization that the telephone message may not be a prank. She was curious, to say the least, but she was not unsure how she should proceed.

"Jacob, what was that all about?" she asked. "At first, I thought it was a joke, but the voice seemed too angry to be just a prank. Do you know who left that message?"

Jake tried to calm down before he answered. The call caught him by surprise as well. He had received a couple of anonymous death threats in the preceding fifteen years of practicing civil law, but this one sounded different. He recalled about five years ago when he was successful in tracing a $1 million loan to a small mining company, which was subsequently converted into a secured corporate debenture. That debenture was then converted into ten million common shares of that public mining company. Those shares were then transferred by the father, who was the majority owner of that penny stock mining company, to his daughter, in consideration of a non-interest-bearing $1 million promissory note.

Since the penny stock value had increased from ten cents per share to seventy cents per share, the face value of those shares had increased to $7 million. Though the ability to convert that many shares of a penny stock at that value was not very likely, the recovery of the original $1 million investment was absolutely assured.

After examining the father and then his daughter, Jake was able to establish that the father had affected a fraudulent preference by having the company transfer those shares to his daughter. His daughter also admitted that she had not paid any consideration for those shares, and, in fact, she had never even bothered to execute any promissory note in an alleged payment for those shares.

Jake applied for an order declaring that the transfer from the father to the daughter was a fraudulent preference and furthermore, that the daughter was simply holding those shares in trust for the original corporate debtor, her father's company. The order also provided that the trust company holding those share certificates was to transfer those share certificates to the Clerk of the Court of Queen's Bench of Alberta, Judicial Centre of Calgary. Once those share certificates were delivered to the clerk's office, Jake could apply to have them released to his client, in repayment of his original loan plus accrued interest.

On the day he had received, filed and served that court order, he had come home to his condo and received another recorded voice message. It was a woman's voice, but it was shrill, vulgar and angry. The threat was simple and direct. The woman intended to kill him, but her reasons were not specified.

Since Jake had no disgruntled ex-wife or ex-girlfriend at that material time, it was logical to assume that the woman who left that death threat on his phone was the woman who lost ownership of ten million penny shares of a mining company whose stock was trading at seventy cents a share. Her realization that she had lost $7 million obviously drove her to make the death threat.

Jake duly reported it to the Calgary Police Service, who took the original recording and attempted to trace the call, albeit unsuccessfully. Fortunately, nothing further was forthcoming and after a few months, Jake just put the entire incident out of his mind.

"No, I agree," replied Jake. "It does not seem to be a practical joke… but these things happen in civil litigation from time to time. After all, it is an adversarial process. But there is nothing to worry about. This is not the first threat I have received. I shall report it to the police and let them look after it. They will try to trace the call, but that is not guaranteed. They will also have the phone company monitor incoming calls for while as well."

Though Jake's intent was to reassure Crystal, he was not entirely successful.

"Honestly, Jake," she replied. "I just do not understand how you can take it so calmly. That man is not only threatening to kill you but to mutilate you as well."

"Crystal, I assure you that I am taking the threat seriously, but in my experience, people who choose to voice or communicate their threats, rarely attempt to carry them out. They are merely venting. It is the disgruntled people who do not say anything, who you should really worry about."

"I cannot understand how you can remain so calm, Jacob," Crystal replied anxiously. "I do not want anything to happen to you. or to lose you again."

She embraced him tightly and buried her head in his chest.

"I almost lost you once already… I really do not want to lose you again. Promise me that you that you shall take all appropriate care, otherwise I am just going to worry about you day and night."

"I promise, Crystal," Jake replied. "I assure you that I prefer, and I intend to live for a long while. Hopefully with you."

"I know we joke around a lot, Jacob," Crystal replied. "But let us have a very serious conversation right now, so we can understand each other a bit better. When I told you when we first met that I found fidelity 'confining'. I did not mean it. It was just a defence mechanism I picked up along the path of my life. By saying that, I was just trying to protect myself in the event those men were not prepared to commit to me or be faithful to me. I know that it was childish in a way, but it helped preserve my self-esteem. But from time to time, I also was not faithful to some of the other men in my life, even though in hindsight, they deserved a lot better from me. Do you understand?"

"I think we all develop defence mechanisms as we go through life. Crystal. My primary defence mechanism is to avoid any deep attachment or commitment. I believed that if you failed to do that, then you would only nurture expectations which would be remain unrequited. Why would someone want to deliberately put himself through that kind of disappointment and frustration?"

"I am really sorry about what happened in New York, Jacob," Crystal interceded emotionally. "I was initially attracted to you physically… and as we talked, I also became attracted to your sense of humour. After you came out to see me in Vancouver, that was one of the most interesting and enjoyable weekends I had experienced in a very long period. I realized that I was developing a deep affection for you, but I still wanted just an arms-length relationship at that time. After what happened in New York, I thought I blew my chance with you, but something compelled me to continue to try to be honest, even after you told me what you did in revenge."

"And I would like to apologize to you for that but I was disillusioned and hurt… and I wanted to hurt you back, even though I believe I only hurt myself," Jake confessed.

"For what it is worth, Jacob," Crystal replied, "though I tried to maintain a cavalier attitude about the whole incident, it did hurt me. I realized that I did not want to share you with anyone, even if it was just casual sex."

"And I want you to know that I did not want to share you with anyone, either," Jake said. "I want you exclusively. It may sound selfish, but that is how I feel."

"And that is what I wanted to hear, Jacob," Crystal replied. "So why don't we set aside our defences and give ourselves a chance. Why don't you open up a nice bottle of red wine and then we can go to bed and have some great make-up sex. But I do not want you to just fuck me, Jacob. I want you to make love to me, as tenderly as you can, as an act of mutual atonement. Proof that we have forgiven each other for our respective errors in judgment."

Jake lifted Crystal up and carried her to his bedroom and lay her down gently on the bed.

"Give me a minute and I shall be back with that wine," he promised.

When he came back, Crystal was still lying on her side, waiting patiently for him to return. "You're still dressed," he said. "Can I give you a hand with those clothes?"

Jake undressed her slowly, throwing her clothes down carelessly on his bedroom floor. He examined her body as he undressed her. Her full breasts were firm, and her nipples were erect and yearning to be suckled. He kissed her lips gently, prying them apart with his tongue. Then he kissed her breasts, savoring each nipple, one at a time, while he caressed her breasts in turn, working his way down slowly. He tasted her gently, exploring her with his tongue as she moaned quietly in satisfaction.

Then he quickly undressed himself and as he stood beside the bed, Crystal held and caressed him in turn.

"Please do not come in my mouth, Jacob," she pleaded. "I want you to come inside me." Then she took him into her mouth. Jacob tried to

217

restrain himself as much as he could, but then finally he had to get her to release him so that he could lie down on top of her and enter her slowly. He tried to be as gentle and restrained as he could, and as they lay coupled together, they kissed each other with open mouths and darting tongues. Their bodies heaved in unison like parallelograms, until they both climaxed together.

"Thank you for that, Jacob. I promise that I will be more energetic another time. I just wanted you to make love to me this time."

Jake looked down at her and though her eyes were closed, he could see that tears had pooled at the corners of her eyes and that she was trying hopelessly to hide that fact. He kept hold of her and remained inside of her until his ardor finally abated. By the time he gently withdrew himself, he could see that Crystal had fallen into a deep sleep.

His thoughts returned to that telephone death threat. Timing was important and the only two people who could be responsible for that death threat were McQuaid, since he was the only new party which Jake had sued recently, or perhaps his lawyer, Layton. It could not be anyone else. But why would either of those two bastards want to threaten him at this point? Making a threat like that was simply stupid, in his opinion. People usually do things for a reason. What could they possibly hope to achieve? It was something he had to discuss with both Michael and Paradis.

Jake was initially frightened by the gross monstrosity of the unexpected threat. Having your genitals removed could never be a pleasant experience to contemplate, never mind actually experience. But then his initial fear turned to anger and to thoughts of retribution and revenge. The brazen nerve of those sons of bitches. Well, if they wanted to throw a scare into him, they better be prepared to receive one in return.

But then he looked at Crystal lying beside him, their arms and legs still intertwined. She was no longer clinging to him tightly. Her grip had gradually lessened as she drifted off into her peaceful dreams. Jake was unable to drift off into his own sleep. He remained awake for a considerable period, thinking about what an appropriate retribution would be and how to put it into effect. He did not consider himself to be a vindictive man, but he did believe in insuring that all undeserved slights and injuries were duly reciprocated. Finally, he was able to drift off to sleep, himself.

Chapter 36

Jake made a light brunch for the two of them, since they remained in bed until almost noon. Then he drove Crystal to the mountains, and they stayed overnight at the Banff Springs Hotel. Though the hotel was over a hundred years old, and its furnishings could be deemed to be a bit seedy, it was also palatial at the same time. A literal granite mansion nestled in the Rocky Mountains, high above the town site in the valley below.

They enjoyed walking around the town site and then driving back to the city on Sunday afternoon so that Jake could drive Crystal to the airport for her return flight to Vancouver. He tried his best to put the threat aside and not talk about it at all for the balance of the weekend. He hoped that Crystal would be more inclined to believe that it was just someone venting, even though he had felt that it may be more serious than just an empty threat.

***

"Promise me that you will be careful, Jacob," Crystal implored him after he drove her to the airport. "And make sure that you report the threat to the police."

"I promise," replied Jake.

Taking a small packet from her purse, Crystal handed it to Jake, along with a sealed card.

"I want you to have this as a... token of my affection, Jacob," Crystal said. "Of course, I do not make the money a lawyer makes, so it is just a modest gift, but please do not read the card or open the little packet until after I have boarded my plane."

The packet contained a key with a note confirming that it was a key to her Vancouver condo and an open invitation to visit whenever he deemed it fit and appropriate. When Jake opened the card, it contained a smiling photograph of Crystal and on the back of the photo, she had written the following note:

"From my heart to yours.
Love, Crystal"

***

The following Monday, Jake decided to file a police report and when he got to the office, he wanted to bring the new development to Michael's attention. After listening to the recorded threat, a couple of times, Michael suggested that they contact Paradis in Denver and apprize him of this new development as well.

To their mutual surprise, Paradis merely listened quietly as they played the recorded threat, and he did not respond immediately after the voice message had concluded.

"Do either of you recognize the voice?" Paradis finally asked.

"Neither of us recognize it, but the speaker may be trying to disguise it somewhat, or he just may be so angry that his anger is distorting his voice. He also sounds as if he may be a bit drunk as well, but who knows," Jake answered.

"And you have reported it to the police?" Paradis asked.

"Yes," replied Jake, "I have reported it to the police."

"Any reason the threat was directed at you, Jake, instead of Michael?" Paradis asked.

"Well, even though both of us are working on the file, I am the solicitor of record on the statement of claim. It is my name on that document," Jake replied.

"And your best guess is that it is either Layton or McQuaid?" Paradis asked.

"That is our best guess," replied Michael. "We have reviewed the most adversarial dealings that Jake has had in the past few months and Layton and McQuaid are the only new individuals who we believe would stoop to doing something like this."

"Well, I was really pissed when McQuaid insulted my family honour by taking advantage of my nephew," Paradis said, "but I want you two to know that I consider you to be family too. And I will be damned if I permit any son of a bitch to threaten a member of my family. It is like they are threatening me, and no one threatens Marcel Paradis, or his family and I can have a friend take a trip…"

Though Paradis broke off without finishing his sentence, Jake and Michael exchanged a quick glance since they both concluded that Paradis may have intended to end the sentence by adding words to the effect of… *and they will regret it.*

"Marcel, please do not think about taking matters into you own hands," Michael said firmly. "The authorities have been notified and Jake also told them that it might be Layton or McQuaid, but it may be someone else. The police are conducting their investigation and the telephone company is monitoring Jake's incoming calls."

"That's right," added Jake, "and I can look after myself. This may be just a prank or some disgruntled boyfriend who found out that I had a fling with his girlfriend, and he is just venting. There is no need to permit this to get out of hand."

"Marcel," added Michael, "we need your assurance that you will let us and the police handle matters legally."

"All right!" Paradis replied. "All right! You all relax now, boys. Since I consider you both to be… not just my lawyers… but my friends and even family, I was prepared to offer to help out whichever way I could. But if you do not want that help, that's all right with me. You can just look after this problem all by yourselves. Just get me back my money."

***

After their teleconference, Jake remained in Michael's office. It was obvious that they had to review whether they made the right decision in informing Paradis about the threat.

"Well, Michael, what do you think? Do you believe that he will stay out of it?"

"I really do not know," answered Michael. "I sure hope so. But if he does decide to get involved personally, God only knows how everything will get complicated in a big hurry. We must be on our guard and not take anything for granted. But we need to try to recover his money as quickly as possible. If we can affect a quick recovery, that may satisfy him and get him to focus on something else."

"Remember when he first came up to Calgary with his nephew," Jake added. "Remember that comment he made about *'knowing people who know people'*? It sure sounded like a veiled threat to me."

"I took it the same way, but I was hoping that he was just blowing hot air to impress us," Michael said. "What is the status of the action at this time?"

"They have to serve us with a statement of defence by Wednesday and as soon as they do that, I will be serving them with our affidavit of records, our notice to admit facts and a notice to attend to force McQuaid to attend at our offices to be examined by me."

"In light of the fact that you were the one who received that death threat, Jake," Michael said, "do you think that it would be a good idea that you are the one to examine McQuaid? I would be more than prepared to examine him, myself."

"Thanks Michael," Jake replied, "but I assure you that I do not just want to conduct the examination just because I received the threat. I will keep my personal feelings in check. That should aggravate McQuaid and Layton even more, regardless of who may have made the threat. If I show that I am not concerned about it, it may prompt one of them to reveal something which may identify who actually made the threat in the first place. If they want to play games, I am more than prepared to reciprocate."

***

After they finished their discussion, Michael asked Kathy to come into his office. As usual, she brought her pen and her notebook with her, hoping that it would seem that their meeting was professional, not personal.

"I noticed that you are not wearing your ring, Kathy," Michael said somewhat anxiously. "Is there any problem?"

Without speaking, Kathy withdrew a gold chain from the top of her blouse to show that the emerald ring suspended safely at its end.

"I thought it might be more prudent, at least until your divorce is final. I do not want to wear the ring openly on my finger," Kathy replied. "I hope that you are not offended. After all, I am wearing the ring and fairly close to my heart."

"No, I am not offended," Michael replied. "On the contrary, you never cease to amaze me with your sensitivity. No wonder I adore you so much. It seems that every day you do something or say something that totally surprises me. Pleasant surprises, I may add."

He embraced and kissed her.

"I was thinking about taking Adam out to the Olympic Park for some introductory ski lessons this weekend. Would you like to come with us?" asked Michael.

"I would love to join you two. I have not downhill skied for about ten years. I could use some practice… as well the exercise," Kathy replied. "By the way, did you have a chance to meet Jake's new lady friend on Friday?"

"No, unfortunately, I did not," Michael replied, "but Ginger and Jake's assistant told me about how you girls played him. That had to be amusing to watch Jake squirm a little."

Michael then briefly told Kathy about the earlier discussion he had with Jake and the advice he had offered him.

"Jake has a good heart, even though he is not inclined to show it or share it with too many people," Michael said. "I think he deserves to meet someone who he can truly appreciate and most importantly, trust. I know that he cares more about Crystal than he is prepared to admit to anyone, including me."

"Crystal had called our office a few times in the past week, but she only wanted to speak to Ginger, his assistant or me," Kathy confided. "At first all three of us found it to be a bit unusual, but within a couple of minutes we all concluded that she was sincere in trying to get to know more about Jake. Then when she showed up at the office Friday afternoon, unannounced, we all concluded that she had to be serious about him. She certainly demonstrated that she has a great sense of humour. By the way, I was the one who suggested to his assistant that she continue to send roses to Crystal. I will be sure that the expense gets billed to Jake, since it appears that he is going to be the beneficiary of his unintended generosity."

"As I said, Kathy," Michael replied, "there is barely a day that goes by when you do not surprise me. Was I blind before, or have you changed so much?

"You were not totally *blind*, Michael," Kathy said smugly. "You were just a little nearsighted.

Chapter 37

Paradis had remained seated in his office chair after his telephone conversation with Jake and Michael. He kept rolling his unlit cigar in his mouth with his tongue, moving it from one side to the other as he peered out his office window onto downtown Denver. The winter snows were late this year, notwithstanding the mile-high elevation of the city, but as sure as he was that the winter snows would be coming soon, he was even more sure in his mind that Layton and McQuaid were both involved in the fraud and that the death threat was also connected.

It used to be, when he was younger and much lighter, that he would handle his personal issues himself. But the passing years had weathered him considerably. His body was bloated as much as his face and carrying over three hundred pounds did not help much either. He remembered that in his youth he was lithe and fast and totally capable of meting out the appropriate retribution to those who presumed to cheat him or soil his or his family's honour, but that was then. Lately, he had become more reliant on other people.

Growing old really sucked, he concluded. Just as you become more experienced in the ways of the world, you become less potent in being able to deal with those issues yourself. Paradis considered himself to be a simple man who lived by simple rules. In business, if you could make money honestly, then you were honest. If you could not make money honestly, then you did what you had to do to still come out on top in the end.

Family honour, however, was one of the things which he held especially dear. If someone tried to cheat him, he was not just insulting him, he was also insulting his family honour. And if someone threatened a member of his family, that was akin to them trying to threaten him as well. That was something which Paradis was not prepared to tolerate… from any quarter.

He regretted now that he had never married, but he either seemed to lack the opportunity or the inclination at the relevant times. That left his nephew as his nearest blood kin and sole beneficiary of his estate. McQuaid and Layton probably decided to take advantage of his trusting nephew and made a fool of him because his nephew chose to trust McQuaid. In so doing, they had also made a fool out of Marcel Paradis, himself. Now those chicken-shit sons of bitches were making death threats to his lawyer when his lawyer was only trying to recover his money. In trying to intimidate his lawyer, they were, in fact, trying to threaten and intimidate him, personally. He did not believe that the threat would frighten Jake, after seeing him perform in Denver on that National Hydrocarbons mediation, but it might very well distract him, and that distraction would assist them.

No sir! Marcel Paradis was not going to permit that to happen, not if he could help it, regardless of whether or not his lawyers approved. What they did not know would not hurt them and it definitely would not hurt him.

He believed that both Michael and Jake were competent, but he also considered them to be a bit naive in the ways of the world. Just because you happened to be right, ethically and legally, that did not guarantee success and most importantly, satisfaction! Sometimes, just winning did not seem to be sufficient. The fact that the other side was prepared to engage in fraud and death threats, meant that they were not going to play by the rules of the game. Paradis concluded that he may have to take matters into in his hands to ensure the correct ultimate result.

He proceeded to dial a number on his cell phone which he had memorized a long time ago. He had met Tommy Consella about twenty years earlier when he needed some special help in New York. Consella was a veteran of the Vietnam war. He had just gotten married to his high school sweetheart, but after a couple of weeks of marriage, she was tragically killed in car accident in Brooklyn. She was crossing a street on a green light in the crosswalk when she was struck by a car which was operated by someone who was high on drugs. Though the driver was duly charged with vehicular homicide, he never showed up for trial. In fact, he was never seen again. Paradis did not have to ask Consella if he had anything to do with that non-appearance.

227

Though many young men his age tried to avoid, if not evade, the draft, Consella volunteered and completed his tour of duty. A few members of his family thought that it was his way of just trying to commit suicide, because of his grief.

Tommy was in Vietnam on April 30, 1975, and only nineteen years old when Saigon fell. He was a guard on the second-last helicopter which left the American embassy grounds that day. He could still remember those desperate Vietnamese clinging to the runners of the helicopter as it left the embassy grounds, until they could not hold on any longer. One by one, their numb fingers released their grip and they seemed to flutter swiftly and silently down to the distant ground.

After he was honorably discharged, Consella was not able to fit into what was left of the society he had left. He was unable to develop another relationship with a woman, though his relatives attempted to introduce him to a 'nice marriageable Italian girl'. Hookers and call girls had to suffice. The only marketable skill he had learned was how to terminate another person's existence. Fortunately for him, there was an ongoing demand for such services. Even now, when he was a senior citizen, the passage of time had not dulled those skills—it only seemed to sharpen them.

He was of average height and a bit overweight, but in pretty good overall physical condition for his age. His dark hair was thinning and greying at the temples, but his eyebrows remained full and dark, as did his unkempt handlebar mustache. He had a slight limp in his left leg as a result of a shrapnel injury from the war, and he was starting to feel the onset of rheumatism in both legs. Though he was still reasonably agile, he knew that he had slowed down substantially and that is what motivated him to plan meticulously and take extra precautions in the execution of any assignment.

He also adhered to a couple of cardinal principles. Firstly, he had to personally believe that the assignment's target was deserving of punishment on some level. Secondly, the client only had two responsibilities: to identify the target and to render timely payment. If his client presumed to instruct him on how the assignment was to be carried out, the assignment was rejected. Consella was not a sadist. If his client wanted the target be made the subject of special treatment, his response was that the client was at liberty to do it himself or herself. They were only hiring him to affect a specific end result. Consella would decide when, where and how that result would be brought about.

***

Consella picked up his phone and uttered his usual monosyllabic response. "Yes?"

"Hello, Tommy. This is Marcel Paradis calling from Denver. How are things in New York?"

Consella responded in a thick Brooklyn accent.

"Eh, Marcel. You know that some things don't change too much. Haven't heard from you in a while, good buddy. What's up?"

"I may need a favor, up in Canada, a place called Calgary, Alberta. It is a couple of hundred miles north of Montana. By the way, do you ski?" Marcel asked half-seriously.

"Not too many ski hills in Brooklyn, Marcel," Consella replied. "Besides that, I think the rheumatism in my legs is getting a bit worse. May have to retire soon."

"Well, we are both getting older, Tommy, but this should not be too difficult, and it may turn out to be nothing at all. But I want to be prepared, just in case. I would like you to fly up there and reconnoiter and become familiar with the place in case I do need you," Paradis said.

***

Paradis went on to briefly outline the characters and the issues involved. It struck Tommy as a routine assignment, but he agreed that it would be a good idea if he flew up earlier so that he could become familiar with the city. It was important that he either leave town quickly as soon as the assignment was completed or if he had to go to ground, he had someplace to lay low for a while until matters had settled down. He had to avoid unnecessary attention as much as possible in either case. Then he could leave town, calmly and quietly. Consella preferred the former alternative. Hanging around just increased the risks and complicated matters.

***

"All right Tommy," Paradis added. "Usual protocol. We both get burner phones and we do not use either my regular personal number or your regular personal number to communicate with after today until this assignment is finished, one way or the other. Neither phone sees the light of day in any case. I will wire your usual retainer to cover your expenses and preliminary payment. Balance will be payable in any event, whether the assignment proceeds or not."

"What do you think, Marcel? Is this likely to be a 'one-fer' or a 'two-fer'?" Consella asked.

"Not sure right now, Tommy," Paradis replied, "it may turn out to be nothing at all."

***

Paradis looked out again at the downtown high-rise towers with their office lights gradually being shut off in a sporadic fashion. The people were scurrying around on the sidewalks down below, anxious to get home. The streets were full of cars and their headlights gleamed eerily in the early dusk, meandering slowly up and down the streets. They were trying to avoid each other and the jaywalking pedestrians who dared to dash across. Paradis tried to focus and collect his thoughts.

He would send Consella up to Calgary and give him time to get familiar with the city. Before Jake commenced his examination, he would know the whereabouts of McQuaid and Layton, and he would know how to proceed by that time. Depending on how matters unfolded, it may just end up as a holiday trip for Consella. On the other hand, he would be in a position to restore his family honour, if that was still necessary. The recovery of the funds was Jake's responsibility. Paradis proceeded to call his nephew who had an office down the hall from his office.

"Louie, something has happened up in Calgary. Some son of a bitch sent Jake, my lawyer, a death threat. Threatened to cut off his dick and his balls and shove them up his ass. You said that McQuaid's partner, the dapper dresser, showed up the next day with McQuaid's bank draft for $600,000. Can you tell me what he looked like?"

"Well, Uncle Marcel," Louie replied, "he was sort of prissy. You know, the type who makes you feel that you are not good enough to kiss his ass. Average height and weight, and he was bald as a billiard ball. I swear I think he polished his head with oil to make it shine. Why do you ask?"

"There is just something I need to confirm, Louie," Paradis said. "You are reasonably good on the computer so I want you to dig up whatever you can on a lawyer in Vancouver named Sterling Layton. He was National Hydrocarbons' lawyer on that mediation I was involved in a few months ago. I also want you to download a couple of recent photos of the guy."

"Why would you want any photos of Layton? You have seen him, so you know what he looks like," Louie asked.

"You're right, dear nephew, but I want to know if you had seen that son of a bitch before. too."

"All right! You got it, Uncle Marcel." Louie replied, though he was still a bit confused. "How fast do you need this stuff?"

"Yesterday, Louie!"

***

Within one hour Louie had completed his task and he was striding quickly down the hall to Paradis' office, clutching a few loose pages in his hand.

"Uncle Marcel!" he announced, "you ain't gonna believe it. That prick who brought McQuaid's bank draft that day in Calgary. That guy is this Sterling Layton."

Louie handed Paradis a couple of photocopied pictures of a smug, bald-headed, middle-aged man. Though he was trying to affect a look of congeniality with a broad smile and capped teeth, his shrouded eyes did not seem to convey such a friendly disposition.

"Here, take a look," Louie said, as he handed Paradis the photos he had downloaded.

"All right, Louie! Well done," Paradis replied. "Scan and e-mail this material to Barton in Calgary and advise him that the 'dapper guy' who provided that $600,000 bank draft to you in Calgary, is his learned friend, Sterling Layton. Who also just happens to be, McQuaid's lawyer."

Chapter 38

Alexa was seated on a stuffed wing-back chair in the living room of her apartment. She purchased it because she loved its vibrant floral pattern; however, it did not give her much pleasure this day. She held a half-full glass of white wine in one hand and a smoldering cigarette in the other. She simply did not know what to do. She finally decided to call Marlena to verify if she had told Michael about her involvement in the infidelity accusation.

"Hello, Marlena," she announced a bit tentatively. "It's Alexa. I would like to speak with you if you are willing."

Marlena was surprised to receive her call. She simply could not fathom what, if anything, the two of them could possibly want to discuss after Michael had finally convinced her that Alexa had lied to her.

"I don't want to be rude, Alexa, but I don't think there is anything for us to discuss."

"Please Marlena, we have been friends for over seven years." Alexa beseeched her. "I would like to have an opportunity to explain matters from my position."

"What happened, Alexa, was that you lied to me, and you destroyed my marriage. I do not understand what would possess you to do what you have done. What have I, not to mention Michael, what have we done to you to drive you to do the vile things you have done? That is the only thing I am prepared to listen to. If you are not prepared to explain your actions, I really do not want to speak with you about anything," Marlena replied in a firm, but calm voice.

"If I told you that I really believed what I told you, would you believe me?" Alexa asked anxiously.

"No!" Marlena said tersely. "You have chosen to lie to me repeatedly for over a year about Michael's infidelity and he is your only brother. While you were pretending to be my friend and confidant, you continually misled me. I will not permit you to mislead me again. You wanted to destroy your brother and our marriage, well you succeeded in destroying our marriage, but you have failed to destroy your brother and you have failed to destroy me, though you did come close."

"Well, I certainly did not want to hurt you, Marlena, just Michael, for reasons I do not fully understand, myself," Alexa answered anxiously, her voice trailed off guiltily.

"How could you possibly think that you could destroy Michael and our marriage, and not hurt me at the same time? How self-centered can you be that you would be blind to the inevitable consequences of your contemptible lies?"

***

Marlena's thoughts drifted back to her discussion with Michael. He told her that though he could not lie and tell her he still loved her, he did tell her that he still cherished her, and he would always cherish the time they had together. He did confess that he did truly love her… for that while. He also sincerely thanked her for sharing her life with him and he truly wanted them to try to remain cherished friends, if possible. But he did not believe that it would be possible to undo the things that were done to them and which both of them had done to each other. She now understood that her unfounded accusations had destroyed her marriage and driven her husband into the arms of another woman, simply because she chose to accept Alexa's lies over Michael's denials. If Alexa thought that she could forgive her for such a deception, she was being truly delusional.

***

"May I at least apologize to you, Marlena?" asked Alexa. Her apprehension at Marlena's likely response was palpable in her strained voice.

"Unfortunately, your apology will not restore my marriage. Your apology will not restore Michael's love. So what would be the purpose of your apology, assuming that it was actually sincere and not just another vile lie?"

"Well, I would like to maintain a relationship with you and Adam. After all, he is my only nephew."

"Well, Alexa," replied Marlena. "I was your only sister-in-law and Michael was your only brother, but that did not dissuade you from engaging in your dishonesty. So my answer is a definite NO! Furthermore, considering what you have done to me and to Michael, I do not want Adam to have anything more to do with you. You have succeeded in causing both of us to suffer a lot of anguish over this past year and there is no way that I am going to give you the opportunity to hurt me again or Adam."

With that, Marlene abruptly ended their conversation.

Chapter 39

When Jake received Louie's e-mailed material and confirmation that the 'dapper man' he had met in Calgary was Sterling Layton, his mind was truly boggled. Why would anyone, especially an experienced lawyer like Layton, put himself into that kind of a position? Basically, he made himself a party to the fraud. Furthermore, he was in a truly egregious conflict of interest by presuming that his involvement would not be discovered and that he would be able to defend McQuaid. Jake knew that he could have him removed from the file, but that resolution struck him as insufficient. He decided to consult with Michael as to the most effective way to exploit this opportunity.

"This case keeps getting more bizarre with each passing week, Jake," said Michael, after Jake explained the new development. "Why would Layton do something like this?"

"That is what I asked myself, Michael," replied Jake. "It is either brazen contempt or extreme stupidity or possibly both."

"Well, let's review what we do know," Michael said. "First, we have McQuaid approach Louie about a plausible, though high-risk investment opportunity. Louie arranges to have Paradis provide him with the required financing. Then we have McQuaid —with Layton's personal participation — engage in that little charade about providing McQuaid's share of the financing. I am sure that Layton could have financed McQuaid's share anonymously. The signing authority on that account would have still permitted McQuaid to remove those funds immediately after they were deposited. There was no need to risk disclosing his identity. He and his involvement could have remained confidential. In the event of a lawsuit, he could have then proceeded to defend McQuaid with relative impunity. But he had to know that if a lawsuit resulted, Louie would be a relevant witness who could identify him. The final unresolved issue is why would either one of them decide to threaten you?"

"I agree that Layton's actions do not make much sense," replied Jake. "But the issue now is what do we do about it? We can remove him from the file and join him formally as the second defendant to the action or, since we are not obligated to disclose our knowledge of his unethical involvement at this point, we can wait until we conduct the examinations and see what happens."

"There is one additional matter that bothers me, Jake," Michael added, "but perhaps I am getting a bit paranoid in my middle age. If anything happens to Louie before the trial, how do we prove that it was Layton who provided that bank draft to him that day?"

"We still have the transcripts of the telephone conversations between McQuaid and Louie, and we have Louie's telephone logs which confirm the date and the duration of those calls, coupled with his texts and e-mailed messages to McQuaid," answered Jake.

"But that evidence does not identify Layton as the 'dapper man'," replied Michael. "Furthermore, Layton's possible exculpatory explanation is that he was just acting as McQuaid's counsel and on his instructions in transferring that bank draft to Louie. After all, only McQuaid could have withdrawn those funds from that joint account, not Layton."

"That's right, Michael," Jake said in agreement. "But why would he get himself so personally involved when it was totally unnecessary?"

"I once met a guy several years ago who had a few odd primal characteristics," Michael answered. "He believed that he was superior to everyone else, so for his own amusement he would deliberately get himself entangled in sticky situations just to prove that he was smart enough to extricate himself. His second characteristic was that he seemed to value obtaining dishonest money over earning money honestly. If he could trick or cheat someone out of a hundred dollars, that meant more to him than earning a thousand. At the same time, though he would lie and cheat as he deemed appropriate, he still expected the other side to be truthful and honest with him. I suggested to my client that it could be his Achilles heel. Perhaps Layton is similar kind of guy. A guy who deliberately increases the risks he is prepared to take because it gives him a bigger hard-on. The only reason I can think of is that it was not enough for him to defraud Paradis through surrogates, he wanted to participate personally. Like a fool who deliberately introduces his wife to his mistress at a dinner party and assumes that she will remain oblivious. Perhaps we may be able to use Layton's own arrogance against himself."

"Should we caution Paradis about the new potential risk to his nephew?" asked Jake. "Though that risk may be farfetched at this point, I think we should at least bring it to his attention, just in case."

"I am starting to think that since Layton decided to take the risk of personally and openly participating in McQuaid's fraud, there may be no limit to what additional risks he may be prepared to take to protect himself. I certainly do not see him trying to eliminate Louie, personally, but perhaps, like Paradis, he may know people who know people too," Michael replied. "As I said, this case is becoming more bizarre with each passing day. Perhaps Paradis' retainer was not quite as generous as we had both presumed. We may have to work for every cent and even assume potential risks that we never even contemplated."

***

Jake proceeded to phone Paradis and advise him of their new concern, though he did characterize the risk as probably being extremely low. Paradis did not seem to express any concern or surprise about their caution. He did say that he would take appropriate steps to ensure that his nephew would remain safe.

After the phone call, Paradis decided to light his cigar, irrespective of the non-smoking prohibition in the building. He really needed to try to relax and assess the new development. Leaning back in his chair, he threw his legs up on his desk and took a long deep draw, holding it his lungs as long as he could bear it, before expelling the fragrant blue smoke at the ceiling. By the time he finished his cigar, he had decided on a modified plan of action. He proceeded to phone Consella in New York. Neither party had obtained their burner phones yet, so the discussion had to be in disguised much as possible, but he felt that it was a minor risk at this point.

"Hello Tommy," Paradis announced, "Marcel Paradis, here. A couple of wrinkles may have surfaced, and I thought it was best to discuss them with you."

Paradis proceeded to acquaint Consella in partially coded language. Louie was referred to as the 'kid'. The potential threat to Louie was referred to as the 'infection'. The reference to 'medication' was obvious and ominous. Paradis explained that the 'kid' had a delicate disposition and may be susceptible to becoming exposed to an 'infection' if he braved Calgary's cold climate at this time of the year. He had the required 'medication' if the 'kid' became infected, but it may be difficult getting that 'medication' past customs. To that extent, he did not think that it was prudent for the 'kid' to come up to Calgary, since Denver afforded a more amiable climate. However, notwithstanding that risk, travel to Calgary may become inevitable. In that case, he would appreciate it if Consella would be able to look after the 'kid', since Paradis was going to be involved in the litigation. Paradis invited Consella to share whatever thoughts or suggestions he may have on the matter.

"If the risk of 'infection' is that real, Marcel," replied Consella, 'the 'kid' can probably get infected just as easily in Denver, as in Calgary. Perhaps even easier, because there would be no need to travel across an international border or take any required 'medication' past customs."

"So what would you recommend if you were in my shoes, Tommy?" Paradis asked.

"It may make sense that I fly out to Denver tomorrow and make suitable arrangements to minimize the risk of 'infection' in Denver, and then fly up to Calgary as we had agreed before. If the 'kid' does end up going up north, I will be there to provide whatever assistance he may need."

"All right then, Tommy," replied Paradis. "Let's do this thing."

Chapter 40

Christine Breland came to Kathy's desk, and she was smiling.

"May I see Mr Bolta, Kathy? I have some good news for him."

After Kathy notified Michael, Christine let herself into his office. Michael was seated at his desk reviewing some documents, but he looked up with a smile to greet his young associate.

"Mr Bolta, your divorce was just finalized yesterday, and the court runner dropped off your decree absolute this morning. Since you and your wife, your ex-wife, have agreed to all of the proposed revisions respecting your settlement agreement and that revised agreement has been executed by both sides, I am happy to announce that your divorce is final and so, if you are so inclined, you are free to go forth and marry again."

Michael noticed that Christine had an impish twinkle in her eye as she presented her good news.

"Are you implying something, Ms Breland or just making a personal recommendation?" Michael asked curiously.

"Not at all, Mr Bolta," Christine replied and then she repeated her noncommittal response as she left his office with that impish smile and a twinkle still sparkling in her eyes. "Not at all."

***

Michael buzzed Kathy on his intercom, and she quickly entered with her ever-present exonerating notebook and pen in hand. As she approached his desk, he rose to meet and embrace her. Then he reached down to her neck and took hold of her gold chain and lifted out her emerald ring. Holding her left hand gently, he placed the emerald ring on her finger.

"Christine has just announced that my divorce is final and that I am free to marry again," Michael announced. "And I suspect that she may know more about the two of us than she is prepared to admit."

"Does that mean that I do not have to bother locking your office door any more?" Kathy asked mischievously.

"Well, hopefully it means that you will be moving out to the acreage, where we can have all of the privacy we may want and whenever we may want it."

Kathy reached up to give Michael a quick kiss on his cheek and then as she left the office, she lifted her left hand to proudly admire the sparkle of her engagement ring.

***

Jake was fully prepared to examine McQuaid the following week, so he decided to phone Crystal to see if she would be free for a day or two this weekend. They usually spoke for an hour on the phone every second night, but he did want to see her again in person.

"Crystal Bachman, please," he asked politely, and she was on the line almost immediately.

"Hello Jacob. Pray tell, but are you interested in coming out here for some dental work or something?"

"You must be a mind reader, Crystal. I can fly out and be in Vancouver in about a couple of hours. Can you meet me at the airport? I have really missed being with you."

"Feeling is mutual, lover," Crystal replied. "The clinic is not busy this afternoon, so I can go home to freshen up and then come out to meet you. But instead of going out for dinner, perhaps we can order some take-out and just stay in tonight. The weather forecast is cool and wet for the entire weekend."

"Sounds like a plan, honey. My flight is coming in at quarter to seven this evening, your time."

***

As Jake deplaned and walked down the exit aisle at Vancouver International, Crystal stood out prominently at the rail separating the disembarking passengers from the people who had come out to greet their family and friends. As usual, she was dressed in black from head to toe, anxiously waving to him to get his attention and smiling. He thought that she looked exquisite. He only had his carry-on luggage and after Crystal greeted him with an embrace and a quick kiss, they proceeded to the airport short-term parking lot.

Jake had a hard time keeping his hands off Crystal while she tried to navigate the heavy traffic from the airport to her third-floor condominium in the southern part of the downtown core. Crystal tried to distract him from his amorous overtures by keeping up a steady stream of innocuous dialogue. Jake would simply smile and nod in agreement on occasion. He was extremely happy to be close to her again, but he was finally compelled to ask a question out of curiosity.

"Crystal" Jake began earnestly, "and please do not take this as a pejorative observation, but do you ever wear something other than black?"

"Well, I am wearing a red silk bra and thong right now, but you were going to find out about that soon enough in any case."

"Please forgive me and forget my stupid question," Jake replied contritely. "You look glorious and black does become you, with your black hair and those dark..."

"Foreboding eyes?" interjected Crystal.

"No. I would characterize them as 'mysterious', 'inscrutable', even 'mystical'," replied Jake.

"Well flattery will get you everywhere, kind sir," replied Crystal, smiling delightfully as Jake's compliments.

"And I have a question for you, Jacob," she asked. "What was the meaning of that quatrain you sent me on the card with the dozen roses. Something about *'memories of moments'* and *'fragments of kisses from forgotten faces'*? I took an English survey course in my freshman year, but I never came across that poem. I even tried to google it, but I could not find it or who wrote it."

"Well, what do you think it means?" asked Jake.

"I got the overall impression that the writer was a melancholy old man. Though he may have been to many places and met a lot of women, he was still sad and unfulfilled at the twilight of his life and looking back on that life, he seems to be filled with a lot of regret."

"Perhaps it was just written by a young man, who had not been to many places or met a lot of women. Perhaps it was just prophetic and that even after he will have traveled to many places and met a lot of women, he was still destined to remain sad and unfulfilled," Jake replied, somewhat cryptically.

"So, how old were you when you wrote that quatrain, Jacob?" Crystal asked.

"I was seventeen and I just had my heart broken by the first girl I was infatuated with. In hindsight, it was just infatuation, but at the time I thought it was true love and I just wanted to die. However, I chose to live, to travel and then I learned to love and leave. The only remaining vestiges of my life seemed destined to be *'memories of moments in far distant places'… 'fragments of kisses from forgotten faces'*. But then I found you," Jake replied seriously.

"I would love it if you would share the entire poem with me, Jacob," Crystal said shyly. "I knew in my heart that there was a lot more to you than you were prepared to show me that first night."

"I remember the poem by heart, even though I composed it over twenty years ago. I will be glad to recite the whole piece for you, but later tonight," Jake replied.

***

After dinner, while the persistent rain continued to fall outside and the raindrops continued to ceaselessly tap away against the windowpanes, Jake and Crystal adjourned to her bedroom with a couple of glasses of a rich red wine. They undressed themselves and then sat on her bed in a kneeling position, facing each other. They commenced to kiss and caress each other and then Crystal mounted Jake in that kneeling position, wrapping her arms tightly around his neck. She lifted herself and then lowered herself, gradually increasing the tempo. Jake reciprocated by gently nibbling at her earlobe while they slowly heaved in unison. He caressed her breasts and occasionally assisted in lifting her up so that they could maximize the penetration.

"I love making love to you, Jacob," Crystal said in a muffled voice. "And I love the way you make love to me."

"You talk too much, honey," Jake replied, somewhat breathlessly.

This position was getting him to exert extra energy and he was not interested in talking at that moment. He was extremely satisfied and relieved when he finally came and the two of them collapsed on their sides, still clinging together.

"Would you recite your poem for me now, Jacob?"

"All right. I believe I titled the poem *'Feathered Wings'*," Jake replied. "Because nothing better came to my mind at that time."

Feathered wings soar through skies so high
Skies so high, so blue and dry
While a man lies here all tied and bound
Making no sound on the cold wet ground

Emerald fins glide through seas so deep
Seas so deep, so green and steep
While a man lies here all tied and bound
Making no sound on the cold wet ground

Lilting sighs drift through azure skies
Silent tears fall from amber eyes
While a man lies here all tied and bound
Making no sound on the cold wet ground

Remembering moments in far distant places
Fragments of kisses from forgotten faces

"That is beautiful, Jacob," Crystal said as he concluded his recitation. "I think I will appropriate the poem for myself if you don't mind. I will tell my friends that you composed it for me, even though you were not aware that I existed at that time."

"It is just a juvenile, melancholy, verbal contrivance," Jake replied modestly. "I was just trying to fool around with images, words and rhymes."

"But the end result now has a life of its own and I can interpret it anyway I want," Crystal replied firmly. "Besides that, I do not believe that your self-deprecating humility is all that sincere. By the way, have you ever told a woman you love them when you actually meant it?"

"Humm!" Jake replied playfully. "There have been so many, oh so many. Why do you insist on asking such difficult and profound questions?"

Crystal responded with a stinging slap against his right buttock.

"Confess, Jacob. After all, you are known as 'Jacob the Confessor'," Crystal said teasingly.

"Actually, though I may have used that expression once or twice, I have never said those words when I actually meant them, until now. Crystal Bachman, I do love you!"

Crystal rolled on top on him and started to kiss him fiercely while her tears spilled onto Jake's face as he attempted to kiss her back, until they both separated.

"And I may have used those words once or twice myself, but they were just hollow words, Jacob. Until now. I do love you, Jacob Barton!" Crystal exclaimed. "I do love you!"

Crystal, emotionally spent, collapsed on top of Jake, but she continued to cling to him.

"You know something, Jacob?" Crystal asked rhetorically. "Those words are so much sweeter when they are truly sincere. And the sex is so much better too."

"A silly thought just crossed my mind, Crystal," Jake replied. "Even though we are not teenagers any more, right now I do feel like a juvenile experiencing that bittersweet taste of an initial infatuation."

"I think we have already experienced the bitter portion, so I want to focus on tasting the sweetness which is oozing from my heart to yours," Crystal answered softly. "I want to be with you with when we are both old and grey, rolling our wheelchairs down the hallways in some extended care facility. Me in front and you behind, desperately chasing me with all your remaining energy, with your tongue hanging out of the side of your mouth and spittle dripping down your chin."

"Since you are fantasizing at the present time, perhaps you should fantasize that I actually overtake you and have my way with you, right in that hallway, while the other inmates of the institution experience heart attacks. I pick up your flat breasts and praise their beauty and…"

"No flat breasts for me, Jacob," Crystal replied. "I intend to get implants as soon as I need them. They are going to remain firm and perky until the day I die!"

"And no flaccid dick for me, Crystal," Jake said. "As long as my family doctor keeps renewing my Viagra prescription, but unlike you, I have no desire to die with an erection."

"So we should live happily ever after, right Jacob?" Crystal asked playfully.

"I am going to do my best to try, Crystal," Jake replied.

Chapter 41

Consella was checking his favorite weapon. A Beretta 92 FS. The 92 model was initially built in 1975 and then modified continually. It was smaller than a Glock 17, with its seventeen-round magazine, and the SIG Sauer 320, but its muzzle velocity exceeded both the Glock and the SIG Sauer. For its size, it was a bit heavier because of its all-metal construction, but its accuracy at its optimum distance of fifty meters also exceeded both of its principal competitors. It was the pistol of choice of the United States military such as the Navy SEALs, as well as many police departments across the country.

He had originally adopted the use of a Walther PPK because that was the pistol that Ian Fleming had his fictional hero, James Bond, use. The Walther PPK was originally manufactured in Germany in 1929. It was small and easy to conceal, but very functional. In fact, Hitler used one to commit suicide in the Führerbunker in 1945.

But Consella decided to switch to the Beretta because it was Italian. *Fabbrica d'Armi Pietro Beretta*, the armory which manufactured it, was established in 1526 and it is the oldest pistol manufacturer in the world. Though Consella held that fact in high regard, what was most important to him was that the manufacturer was, like him, of Italian heritage.

Though the Beretta grip was slightly thicker, Consella had it modified by reducing its magazine capacity from fifteen rounds down to ten. This permitted the circumference of the grip to be reduced to accommodate his hand more comfortably. He felt that if you couldn't get the job done with ten hollow-point rounds, you were not fit for the profession in any case. Though the Glock 17 could carry seventeen 9-millimeter rounds, he had no intention of getting into any shoot-out since the Glock magazine capacity did provide an advantage. His Beretta was semi-automatic, so his standard procedure was to inflict two quick shots to the body to incapacitate the target, with a final shot to the head. He found that the target was usually fatally wounded by the damage caused by the initial double shots, but a final shot to the head was mandatory. After all, Rasputin was poisoned and shot twice, before the fatal third shot between his eyes.

His Beretta was more accurate, more reliable and more easily concealed. He also had it adapted for a laser sight under the barrel, as well as a suppressor. It was also possible to substitute the laser for a mini flashlight, if necessary. He found those accessories to be indispensable. Since he was right-handed, the spent shell was ejected to his right. Finally, its parts were also easily replaceable. Consequently, it was not a difficult to change the firing pin and the barrel after an assignment. That made it difficult, if not impossible to connect his weapon with any particular homicide.

He had also developed an efficient technique whereby the pistol could be broken down into its component parts and skillfully integrated with other innocuous metallic items in his luggage, which facilitated his passage through airport security.

His auxiliary back-up weapon was three-inch switchblade which he usually secreted in the sole of his left boot. The primary advantage of a switchblade was that it could by activated with one hand. He had an Italian switchblade since his high school days in Brooklyn, but its bayonet blade was only effective for thrusting, not slicing. Furthermore, the guard, which prevented the hand from sliding down onto the blade and being cut by the sharpened blade, protruded awkwardly to its sides.

Consequently, he had a special switchblade knife custom-made for himself. The length of the handle, with the blade closed, was only three inches and extremely easy to conceal in one hand. Furthermore, both sides of the blade were sharpened to a razor's edge, so it could be used for thrusting and for slicing. The handle was ergonomically designed to accommodate his forefinger within a curved recess below the blade to eliminate the risk of the hand slipping down to the blade and being cut, thereby eliminating the need for that awkward protruding guard.

His shrapnel injury from Vietnam was his convenient explanation for not having to take the boot off in the first place and for activating the security alarm in the second place. Airport security was usually quite solicitous to an older gentleman who had served his country and now walked with a limp with shrapnel in his left leg.

His first priority was to fly out to Denver and ensure that Paradis' nephew was adequately protected. Once he had accomplished that task, he would continue his journey to Calgary, Alberta, and become familiar with that terrain. He would center on the law offices of Bolta & Barton and review the radiating avenues of ingress and egress. Once Paradis advised him of the whereabouts of Layton and McQuaid, he would check out that area and cross-reference it to the law offices as well, since they would obviously have to travel back and forth between those two locations. Paradis had estimated that the examinations would take possibly two days to complete, so there was no final decision as to whether or not the assignment would be executed.

The complicating factor was that if the nephew had to come to Calgary as well, his duties would be doubled. He would have to ensure that Louie remained safe and secure, while he had to finalize plans on how to execute the assignment if Paradis decided to proceed. Finally, he had to arrange for an alternate location to stay a few days in the event he was not able to leave the city once his assignment was completed. He called it his 'safe house' and its location would not be disclosed to anyone.

***

Paradis was on the phone to Jake, and they were reviewing the final preparations for the exams which were scheduled to begin in a couple of days.

"I know the fundamentals, Jake," Paradis stated matter-of-factly. "Listen to the goddam question. Do not start answering the goddamn question until the goddam lawyer has finished asking his goddam question. Answer that goddam question. Do not volunteer any additional goddam information. Shut the fuck up once you have answered that goddam question. Did I forget anything?"

"No, Marcel," Jake answered, "Those are the fundamentals. But also remember the adage that you can't win the trial during an examination, but you can definitely lose one. Keep your emotions in check. Do not vent. Calling him a 'bumfucker' may make you feel good, but it is not going to expedite the process or facilitate obtaining a judgment. Also, try to avoid using the good Lord's name in vain so much."

"I would swear on the eyes of my children, Jake, that I will behave like a choir boy, but then I don't have any children," Paradis replied in jest. "But do not worry, I know what to do. You just do your job, and I will do mine."

***

The day before the examinations were scheduled to begin, Jake had a final meeting with Michael on possible examination strategy in Michael's office.

"What approach do you think you will take, Jake?" asked Michael.

"Well, what I try to do is to size up McQuaid when he comes into the boardroom. His appearance, his dress, the way he walks, the way he sits at the boardroom table. Then I will try to get a read on him during the preliminary background questions. Is he arrogant or timid? Does he seek eye contact, or does he avoid it? Does he appear to be experienced or inexperienced in respect of the examination procedure? Is he responsive to the questions I ask or is he evasive? Once the preliminaries are over with, I intend to have him admit his telephone number and his e-mail address. That will lay the foundation of the subsequent questions in respect of Louie's telephone records and their numerous exchanged calls. It will also lay the foundation for questioning him on Louie's transcripts of some of those recorded telephone conversations and the admissions those transcripts contain. It will also lay the foundation of examining him in respect of Louie's unanswered e-mails. Finally, I am interested to hear what he has to say in respect of that little charade about his alleged $600,000 contribution to the joint bank account."

"How do you intend to deal with Layton if he presumes to be disruptive and interrupt your examination with fatuous objections?" Michael asked.

"Probably in the usual fashion," answered Jake. "But I shall try to avoid telling him to shut the fuck up, since it will be on the record. I promise that I will do my best to be erudite in trying to keep him under control."

"As we both know, since there is no signed agreement, credibility is important. If you can get him to contradict himself as you proceed, you should be able to apply for a quick summary judgment," Michael concluded.

"And on an entirely different matter, Michael," Jake said seriously. "I noticed that Kathy is wearing that emerald ring. Allow me to be the first to offer both of you my most sincere congratulations."

"Thank you, Jake. For everything," Michael said. "Especially the help with the ring. It is just fabulous. And I might as well tell you that Kathy will be moving in with me on the acreage. She has sold her home and I see no point in her buying a condo or a townhouse and then making mortgage payments. Perhaps in a year you can be my best man."

"It will be my honour, my friend," replied Jake. "And I mean that sincerely, but I think it is time to offer my congratulations to Kathy, if I may be so bold."

Jake rose from his seat and exited Michael's office. Then he approached Kathy's desk.

"Say, young lady, that is quite a rock you are carrying on your ring finger. If you ever need any assistance in holding your left arm up when you are walking down the hall or some aisle, just let me know." Jake spoke facetiously, but before Kathy could respond, he quickly added. "Seriously, Kathy, I just want to wish you and Michael all the best. I know that you will both be truly happy, and I want you to know that from this day forth, I consider you to be my sister-in-law."

Kathy was not sure how to respond. Jake was jesting and being serious at the same time, but she rose and embraced him gently and kissed him lightly on his right cheek.

"I want to thank you for your best wishes, Jake," she replied happily. "And I hope that we can get to know each other much better. Since we have been working together for the past fifteen years, I think it is about time, don't you?"

"That's the second time you addressed me as 'Jake'," he answered. "That means that you must really, really like me... at least a little bit."

"All right, Jake," Kathy smiled and replied, "I do like you a little bit, but strictly platonically."

Neither Jake nor Kathy noticed that Michael had exited his office and was standing in the hallway with his arms crossed, smiling at both of them.

"May I join this mutual admiration society?" he asked and then he embraced them both.

Chapter 42

The following morning, Christine Breland approached Kathy's desk in a happy mood. She was going to sit in on Jake's examination of McQuaid that morning, but she wanted to extend her congratulations to Kathy on her announced engagement.

"Morning Kathy," she said. "I want to congratulate you on your engagement. I hope you two will be very happy."

"Thank you, Christine," Kathy replied as she rose to greet her. "But Michael thinks that this may not have come as a complete surprise to you."

"Perhaps not a complete surprise," she replied, "but it was still an extremely pleasant confirmation." Then she proceeded down to the boardroom to join Jake.

***

Though the examination was going to start at ten a.m., Jake wanted to arrange all his materials in advance. He would be seated next to the court reporter and McQuaid would be seated immediately opposite him, with Layton seated to his left. At precisely 9.59 a.m., McQuaid entered the boardroom, followed by Layton, who was only carrying a slim briefcase. The parties did not bother to shake hands, they merely acknowledged each other with a curt nod.

McQuaid was above average in height, in his early fifties, modestly overweight and dressed in an off-the-rack business suit which fitted him snugly. His hair was thinning and greying, but it was combed neatly. As he sat down at the table, Jake could see that his enormous hands had not done any manual labour for a considerable period. The nails were professionally manicured, and the large hands showed no evidence of any callouses.

McQuaid reciprocated by focusing intently on Jake, examining him and trying to seek out potential weaknesses. He was not intimidated to any degree, but he was annoyed at having to be there and being obliged to answer questions which he preferred were not asked. There also seemed to be a certain arrogance in the way he remained seated, with one hand on the table and one hand on his lap, and the way his right upper lip arched up at the corner into an arrogant sneer every time he looked at Jake.

Layton, on the other hand, could not disguise his contempt for Jake. He had not even bothered to open his briefcase as if the proceeding was just going to be a total waste of time and he wanted Jake to know that was what he was thinking.

Jake could see Paradis seated a couple of seats away from him and to his surprise, Paradis did not disclose any emotion at all. All he continued to do was roll the unlit cigar in his mouth and occasionally move it from one side to the other side.

Christine was seated next to him, and she was trying to control her emotions as best she could. She decided that she should sit with her legs crossed, her notepad on her lap and her pen in her hand ready to take down any relevant notes. She wanted to remain as impassive as possible. She hoped that no one noticed that her hands were trembling slightly with anticipation at what was about to unfold before her eyes. Her hands were not trembling out of fear.

After McQuaid was sworn in, Jake took him through the preliminary matters. He confirmed that he was fifty-two years of age; divorced a couple of times; no formal education past high school and he described himself as a 'jack-of-all-trades'. He had worked in the oil industry, in construction and finally, in mining—both hard rock and placer mining. Lately, he was basically just an investor who sought out business prospects, raised the required funds and had other people do the 'grunt work', as he characterized it, while he reaped the profits.

As for his meeting with Louie Paradis, it was just a chance meeting at a downtown bar a few months earlier. He had located a placer gold mining property in the Yukon, and he was pitching the proposal to a couple of potential investors. Louie had been listening in on their discussion and after those investors left, he told McQuaid that he might be interested in his proposal. Consequently, their discussion continued. The bourbon and the beer chasers continued to flow until they reached an agreement.

"So, Mr McQuaid," Jake asked, "what, if anything, did you and Mr Louie Paradis agree to by the end of this meeting?"

"Firstly, Mr Barton." McQuaid replied in a patronizing fashion, "I do not know why the named plaintiff in this action is Marcel Paradis. I never had any dealings with him. I never even met the guy. My agreement was strictly with Louie Paradis."

"In that case, Mr McQuaid," Jake replied, "my question still stands. What, if any, agreement did you reach with Mr Louie Paradis that evening?"

Instead of responding to the question, McQuaid attempted to deflect the question again and go back to Marcel Paradis.

"I just want the record to show that I never entered into any agreement with this Marcel Paradis. I never even met the son of a bitch," McQuaid replied vigorously.

Jake could see that Paradis did not react in any fashion. His facial demeanor and his body language remained unflappable.

"In that case, Mr McQuaid, allow me to introduce you to my client, Mr Marcel Paradis of Denver, Colorado," Jake replied, pointing in Paradis' direction.

McQuaid simply made some guttural sound as if he was clearing his throat and arched his sneering lip even higher as he looked in Paradis' direction.

Paradis, on the other hand, slowly removed his cigar and pointed it at McQuaid, but he moved his thumb down on the cigar like a hammer on a gun and smiled in acknowledgment. Though some people may have interpreted the gesture to be just an innocuous acknowledgment, to Jake the motion had a more sinister meaning and by the change in McQuaid's facial expression, he was also aware of that possible alternate subliminal message.

"I object! I object! I object!" shouted Layton.

"Object to what?" Jake inquired, genuinely surprised since there was no question to which Layton could possibly object to.

"Your client has just threatened my client. He has just threatened to shoot my client. I will not stand for this kind of intimidation!" sputtered Layton, though his outrage seemed to lack sincerity. Unfortunately, the court reporter could only record the spoken words, not the speaker's facial impression.

"Since your client stated that he had never met Mr Paradis, all I did was introduce him," Jake replied calmly. "Mr Paradis never said a word. He merely acknowledged your client and he happened to remove the cigar from his mouth, which I take to be just a civil gesture. Are you suggesting that Mr Paradis threatened to shoot your client with his cigar? And since you are presuming to accuse my client and lecture me, perhaps you should lecture your own client and advise him that it is neither polite, nor proper, to refer to an opposing party as a son of a bitch. Especially on the record."

"I say that it was a threat. A symbolic threat," Layton persisted emotionally. "He pointed his cigar at my client as if it were a gun, and then dropped his thumb as if it were a hammer, and the obvious intent he wanted to convey was that he wanted to shoot my client."

***

Usually in civil litigation when one lawyer prefaces a comment to another lawyer with the words 'with all due respect', the intended meaning is usually the exact opposite.

"*With all due respect*, Mr Layton," Jake replied calmly, "you are only entitled to object to an improper question, and I am sure that when you check the record it will confirm that no question, proper or improper, was asked. In fact, I do not believe I have asked an improper question in the past three years. Secondly, you have succeeded in getting that improper accusation, which unjustly besmirches my client's reputation, on my examination record. Finally, I do not believe that you have clairvoyant powers which enable you to read my client's frame of mind as to his intention. However, the record will clearly show that you have repeatedly interrupted my examination with fatuous objections and if that conduct continues, I will adjourn the examination and apply for a court order to have a Master supervise the continued examination and who will be able to grant rulings on the spot. And all those additional costs shall be payable by you, personally. So we can continue and hopefully be finished with Mr McQuaid today or we can take all week. I really do not care."

"With all due respect," Paradis interjected, "I just want to assure Mr Layton and Mr McQuaid that all I did was remove my cigar and gesture an acknowledgment to Mr McQuaid, a gentleman whom I have not previously met, because in Louisiana that is just how we demonstrate that courtesy. It is akin to taking off one's hat when one enters another's home or lifts the toilet seat when using their bathroom. I emphatically deny that I intended to shoot Mr McQuaid, either symbolically or actually. And I have been called a son of a bitch by better men than Mr McQuaid. Much better men and I have never taken any personal offence. So I just want to assure Mr McQuaid that I take no such offence this time either."

Though Jake maintained his composure, he was extremely proud of Paradis who not only had exonerated himself on the record and neutralized Layton's accusation, but he also simultaneously succeeded in insulting both McQuaid and Layton. If they wanted to have a battle of wits with him, Paradis would win hands down.

"Perhaps, we should just take a brief adjournment," suggested Layton, "and give everyone a chance to calm down."

"Neither Mr Paradis nor I need calming down, Mr Layton," Jake replied. "After all, it was your client who decided to gratuitously insult my client by disparaging his ancestry and it was you who decided to beat his chest in righteous indignation and improperly accuse him of threatening your client. However, perhaps we should take a ten-minute adjournment to give you two gentlemen an opportunity to calm down. Mr Paradis and I will leave the boardroom and adjourn to my office to give you two the privacy you may need."

Turning to the court reporter, Jake advised her that she was free to take a break as well, but the reporter merely smiled and thanked him for his consideration.

***

As Jake and Paradis walked back down the hall to the boardroom to resume the examination, they noted that the court reporter had also been excused from the boardroom. Obviously, Layton and McQuaid did not want any witness to what had transpired between them during that short break. Her expulsion did give Jake an opportunity to resume his examination with a surprise of his own.

***

"Mr McQuaid, you confirm that you are still under oath and that you intend to tell the truth, the whole truth and nothing but the truth?

"I do," McQuaid replied tersely.

"During the brief adjournment, did your lawyer give you any new instructions on how to answer that last unanswered question I had asked before the break?" asked Jake.

"What? I object!" Layton was sputtered again, but this time it appeared to be sincere, not feigned. "That is an improper question. It intrudes on solicitor/client privilege. I object!"

Jake decided that it was an appropriate time for him to shake up Layton. His strident denial seemed like an affirmation of his accusation.

"I heard you the first time, Mr Layton," Jake replied. "But as we both know, I am in the middle of an examination and it is totally improper for opposing counsel to coach their client on how to respond to any question which is asked, for the duration of that examination."

"Well, I never have been so insulted in my life. Especially by a junior counsel who obviously does not know what he is doing!" Layton responded vigorously.

"In any case, prior to the break, I had asked Mr McQuaid as to what, if anything, had been agreed to between him and Mr Louie Paradis," Jake said. "And my question stands. Mr McQuaid, did you receive any instructions from Mr Layton on how to answer that question during the break which has just been concluded?"

Before Layton could interject and object again, McQuaid decided to respond in exasperation.

"No! Mr Layton did not advise or instruct me on how to answer that question. I hope that you are satisfied."

"Then what, if anything, did the two of you discuss which motivated you to expel the court reporter from the boardroom?" Jake continued to ask calmly.

"Nothing much." McQuaid replied. "It was just a meaningless conversation. I think we talked about the weather in Vancouver, as compared to Calgary."

Jake remained silent for a moment while he looked at McQuaid intently. He wanted McQuaid to know that he knew when he was lying.

The remainder of the examination that morning and afternoon passed quickly and relatively uneventfully. McQuaid's version of the agreement with Louie was that Louie was receiving a 50% equity interest in the placer mining claim in the Yukon for that $600,000. Further development funds had to be raised to actually conduct the placer mining operation which would commence in the coming spring, if those additional funds were raised. He denied that there was any agreement that he would be matching the Paradis investment. His investment was 'front-loaded' through his acquisition of the mining claim in the first place.

When asked about his failure to respond to Louie's sundry e-mails which confirmed an agreement that both McQuaid and Paradis would be contributing $600,000, McQuaid simply showed his large hands to Jake and his excuse for not responding via e-mail was because his fingers were too large for a computer's keyboard.

In respect of Louie's certified transcripts of some of their telephone conversations wherein McQuaid could be heard confirming that he would be personally investing $600,000 as well, he denied that he was the speaker and claimed that those transcripts were fake.

When those transcripts were cross-referenced to Louie's telephone logs, McQuaid admitted that it appeared that either Louie would be phoning him, or he would be phoning Louie. However, even though the date and the length of those calls corresponded to the transcripts, McQuaid continued to adamantly deny that it was his voice on those recorded calls which had been transcribed by a certified court reporter.

"Do you recall meeting Louie Paradis in Calgary, the morning after Paradis had deposited that $600,000 into that joint bank account?" Jake asked.

Once again, before Layton could come up with a timely objection to delay and give McQuaid a subtle hint to be cautious in answering, McQuaid ventured to respond quickly.

"Yes, I do. I remember it well."

"What was the purpose of the meeting, Mr McQuaid?"

"Louie was getting cold feet and he wanted to withdraw the money. So, I made arrangements to withdraw those funds and give them back to Louie if he did not want to proceed."

"But the bank records show that the bank draft was made payable to you, not to Louie Paradis, Mr McQuaid. Can you explain why the bank draft was made payable to you, when you say your intention was to refund those funds to Louie?" asked Jake.

"That was just a bank error," McQuaid replied smoothly. "I told them to make the bank draft payable to the depositor and by mistake, they made it payable to me. I was prepared to countersign it over to Louie."

"Did you also advise Louie the first time you two met, that you had a silent partner in this specific proposal?"

McQuaid was growing increasingly confident and proceeding to respond to Jake's questions quickly, denying Layton the opportunity to object and delay.

"I did!" McQuaid replied emphatically.

"And what is that silent partner's name?" Jake asked.

This time McQuaid hesitated, and it gave Layton an opportunity to object.

"I object, Mr Barton! I object most strenuously!" Layton sputtered.

"And pray tell, Mr Layton, what are the grounds of your objection this time?"

"Relevance, Mr Barton," Layton replied, "your question is not relevant!"

Layton thrust out his chin in confirmation of the righteousness of his objection, reminding Jake of a photo of Mussolini projecting his chin and bald head defiantly at the world.

"*With all due respect,* Mr Layton," Jake replied. "First, the witness has admitted that the $600,000 represented the agreed Paradis investment in this business venture. Second, your client has admitted that he had advised Louie Paradis that he had a silent partner in this venture. Thirdly, according to the Rules of Court and the case law in Alberta, you may not withhold the name of a potentially relevant witness. So, I would submit that your objection is improper, and I want you to reconsider your objection and I want the witness to answer."

"I have made my objection and stated the grounds, and if you do not accept it, then you may apply to the court for an order compelling the witness to answer."

***

Jake paused for a moment and merely looked at Layton. Layton was becoming increasingly flustered as to how the examination was progressing because he had failed to duly prepare McQuaid, and he wanted Layton to know that he was aware of that failure. Turning back to McQuaid, he returned to his line of questioning.

"Mr McQuaid, I am advised that another gentleman met you and Louie at the bank that morning and that bank draft was in that gentleman's possession. It was he, not you, who handed that bank draft in the sum of $600,000 to Louie Paradis, even though it had been made payable to you. Do you confirm those facts?"

Again, McQuaid proceeded to answer the question quickly in the affirmative before Layton could register an objection.

"And who was that gentleman, Mr McQuaid?" Jake asked as a logical follow-up question.

At that point, McQuaid realized that he may have committed an error and he paused in responding, which gave Layton an opportunity to object.

"I object, Mr Barton." Layton stated tersely. "Same objection as before and on the same grounds. Relevance, Mr Barton. Relevance."

***

Jake paused for a moment and merely looked at McQuaid this time, who was starting to lose his self-assurance. He was starting to perspire profusely, and his throat was bone dry since he was quaffing one glass of water after another to relieve his dehydration. Usually, a sure sign of a witness who is not telling the truth, the whole truth and nothing but the truth. McQuaid was not necessarily someone who was concerned that his eternal soul would be condemned to hell after he died. He was a person who was concerned with more temporal consequences such as going to jail for perjury in this life.

***

"Mr McQuaid, can you tell me what happened to the Paradis $600,0000 investment?" Jake asked innocently.

"Mr Barton, I believe that you are operating under a fundamental misunderstanding," McQuaid replied confidently. "That money was paid to me for a 50% interest in this placer mining concession in the Yukon. Pursuant to the terms of our agreement, that money became mine and I was at liberty to do whatever I wanted to do with it."

"To be clear, is it your position that since the payment was for a 50% interest in that mining concession, you are not prepared to answer my question?"

"That is absolutely correct, Mr Barton!" McQuaid replied emphatically.

"Then I am asking for an undertaking that you to produce a copy of that executed document which confirms that you had acquired this placer gold mining concession in which you sold Mr Louie Paradis a 50% interest, since it strikes me as a very relevant document which was not disclosed in your documentary production. Do I have that undertaking Mr Layton?" Jake asked, turning to Layton for formal confirmation.

"Uh, well, Louie never asked for a copy, so I guess I never provided it," McQuaid replied.

"Well, we are asking for it now," replied Jake, turning back to McQuaid.

"I believe you may be entitled to it," interjected Layton. "But for now, I am just going to take it under advisement. I shall try to respond to that undertaking request as expeditiously as possible."

I bet you won't, mused Jake to himself.

"I would like to rephrase my previous question, Mr McQuaid. The $600,000 was deposited to a joint account on which Mr Louie Paradis was a joint signor. The bank records confirm that the next day that the $600,000 was withdrawn and then redeposited back to that joint account. Then you arranged for a wire transfer to a bank account in Edmonton for $300,000 and the remaining $300,000 was transferred to a bank account in Vancouver. What I want to know is who were the recipients of those two $300,000 wire transfers?"

Layton immediately objected to ensure that McQuaid did not even start to answer that question.

"I object, Mr Barton. I most vehemently object to that question. Same grounds as before. Relevance, Mr Barton. Your questions must be relevant to the issues in this action. My client is not here to simply satiate your curiosity."

"I have a follow-up question, Mr McQuaid," Jake replied. "If that $600,000 was intended to be in payment for a 50% interest in that mining concession and, therefore, your own personal funds to do with as you deem fit, why were those funds deposited to a joint business account which was set up for this joint venture?"

"I object, Mr Barton!" Layton sputtered again. "I object. That question has been asked and answered and rephrasing it does not make it more relevant the second time around."

***

Jake paused again and first looked at McQuaid, whose respiration rate had not abated, so he decided to share a conspiratorial wink with him, which, as Jake had anticipated, merely confused him even more. Then he looked at Layton who appeared to be also perspiring unduly himself. He smiled innocently at him as if to convey the notion that though he had tried his best, he failed to penetrate Layton's fatuous objection defence.

***

"Well subject to the undertakings which were given or taken under advisement, and subject to the questions which were objected to, which I do intend to refer to the court, I am adjourning my examination."

"I object again, Mr Barton." Layton interjected again.

"On what grounds this time, Mr Layton? Jake asked.

"You stated that you want to 'adjourn'. I insist that you *conclude* your examination, albeit subject to those outstanding matters you have mentioned."

"This is my examination and in light of your improper and unfounded objections, I am unable to complete my examination because a number of the questions to which you have objected to form the foundation of a number of follow-up questions. To that extent, I am adjourning this examination because your objections prevent me from concluding it today," Jake stated with finality.

Jake turned to the court reporter and instructed her to conclude her transcription of the proceedings and rose to leave the boardroom, leaving Layton staring at him with his mouth agape.

Chapter 43

Paradis, Jake, Michael and Christine met in Jake's office to review the proceedings which had just been concluded. Christine sat beside Michael at the conference table, while Jake and Paradis slouched down together on the office sofa, throwing their legs up on the coffee table.

"Well, I think it went fairly well," said Jake, initiating the discussion. "McQuaid's version of the events are as porous as Swiss cheese. Furthermore, he simply does not exude any credibility. We will get a court order to compel answers to those objected questions and we will get a court order to compel them to produce those documents, especially that lease agreement that McQuaid volunteered he had. If they do not comply with those court orders, the court will dismiss their defence and enter a default judgment in our favor."

"I agree, Jake," replied Paradis. "I think what really threw McQuaid was your question about why the money was deposited to a joint business account when he was claiming that it was just in payment to him, personally, for a 50% interest in that mining claim. He simply could not come up with an answer and then Layton objected again. Perhaps you should have objected to his fucking objections."

"That is what I will be doing when I make those applications to the court to compel compliance," Jake answered.

"And Christine, what do you have to add to this discussion?" Michael asked politely.

"I tried to focus on how Layton and McQuaid were reacting to each other during the questioning," Christine replied. "Layton was definitely not impressed that McQuaid was volunteering answers to sensitive questions without giving him an opportunity to object."

'That is a good point to remember when you are examined tomorrow, Marcel," Jake said. "Wait a couple of seconds... and if I do not object, then proceed to answer. It does not come across well if you are answering and I am objecting at the same time."

"I also got the impression that Layton was in charge, not McQuaid, even though the latter was the client," Christine continued. "Layton seemed to be more upset at McQuaid's conduct and answers than his various procedural disputes with Mr Barton. But it was also clear that Layton holds you, personally, in total contempt."

"Oh, I got that feeling myself, Christine," Jake replied. "I thought he was ready to spit at me across the boardroom table at times."

"Well, let's go get some dinner," Paradis suggested. "I trust there is a good steakhouse you can recommend that's close by Jake?"

"And I will respectfully decline, gentlemen," Christine said. "I do not believe you need me for anything else this evening and I would not want my presence to inhibit you gentlemen in any way."

***

Jake took Michael and Paradis to his favorite steakhouse, which was operated by one of his former clients, a Greek named Nick Theodorakis, who greeted the trio warmly. He assured them that he was going to seat them in the private dining alcove with a semi-circular padded seat, which would afford them sufficient privacy, but which was located proximate to the glassed-in grill to permit them to observe the chef prepare their steaks. Michael and Jake ordered ten-ounce rib-eyes, medium-rare. Paradis ordered a sixteen-ounce porterhouse, well done. They also selected a twelve-year-old Barolo, an exuberant, deep-flavoured red wine to complement their manly entrées.

They were almost finished with their meal when an older gentleman with dark eyebrows and a dark handlebar mustache approached their table. Michael noticed that the man walked proudly and confidently, but with a slight limp.

"Excuse me, Mr Paradis," Consella asked politely. "I need to speak to you about a couple of matters. It shall not take long."

"Oh, Tommy!" Paradis replied, quickly standing up. "Allow me to introduce you to my lawyers: Michael Bolta and Jake Barton," Paradis then paused before introducing Consella. "And this is my associate... Tommy... er... Smith."

Jake rose to greet Consella since he was seated on the end of the seat and extended his hand in greeting. To his surprise, Consella, quickly stepped back and declined to shake hands.

"I must apologize for Tommy, gentlemen," Paradis said. "Tommy served a hard tour of duty in Vietnam and since that time, he avoids certain practices, such as shaking hands."

"I mean no offence, Mr Barton," Consella added. "I just do not shake hands with anyone, at any time."

Jake and Michael also noticed that 'Tommy' spoke with a thick New York city accent.

"No offence taken, Tommy," replied Jake. Then turning to Paradis, he offered to arrange for a private room in the back of the restaurant, which both Paradis and Tommy declined. They elected to go near the main entrance and carry on a brief conversation near the coat check.

Michael and Jake continued to gaze in Paradis' direction. Paradis and Tommy appeared to engage in a calm discussion which ended relatively quickly, as had been promised. As Paradis started to return to their table, they exchanged a questioning glance between themselves.

"Obviously, his last name is not Smith," Jake stated quite seriously. "Could he possibly be 'someone whom someone knows?"

"My thoughts exactly," answered Michael. "Let's wait and see what Paradis may have to say by way of explanation."

***

When Paradis joined his dining companions, he could sense their unspoken curiosity.

"You gentlemen are probably a bit inquisitive about my associate, Tommy, which is his real name, though I should not have disclosed it. And as you both have probably guessed, Smith is not his real last name. Tommy is in the security business. Since you advised me of the potential risk to Louie, I arranged to retain him to ensure that Louie would not come to any harm. Though Louie is in Denver, safe as a babe in his mother's loving arms, in the event he had to come to Calgary for this examination, I asked Tommy to come up and make appropriate arrangements here as well. Any questions?"

Michael and Jake exchanged another knowing glance which communicated that their mutual decision at that point in time was not to venture into areas which they did not fully understand What they did not know should not hurt them, too much.

"No, Marcel," Jake replied. "If there is nothing further you want to tell us, we do not have any questions."

"Damn!" Paradis exclaimed. "That was one of the best steaks I have had in a long time. I probably could have cut it with my fork, but now it is cold. I am almost tempted to have it warmed up, but that is the problem with ordering it well done in the first place. It would probably come back like charcoal, but my momma always cooked my steaks well done."

The three of them then parted, agreeing to meet at the office the next morning at which time Layton would conduct his examination of Paradis.

***

Layton attempted to commence his examination by proceeding through the usual litany of standard questions. However, after Paradis identified himself by name and confirmed that he was the named plaintiff in the action, Paradis refused to answer any other personal questions, such as his age, his education and business experience. His standard response was that those questions were not relevant to the issues in the lawsuit and if he wanted to know his age, etcetera, he could ask those irrelevant questions at trial.

***

"Mr Paradis, what is your relationship to Louie Paradis in this matter?" Layton asked scornfully, upset that he was being upstaged by a semiliterate hick from Louisiana.

"Louie Paradis is my only nephew," Paradis replied laconically.

"I was not asking about your *biological* relationship, Mr Paradis. I was asking you to clarify your *business* relationship." Layton replied, somewhat exasperated by Paradis's reply.

"*With all due respect*, Mr Layton," Paradis replied sarcastically. "You are going to have to phrase your questions more accurately. All you asked me for was my 'relationship' to Louie and I believe I responded to the specific question which you had asked.

"All right then, Mr Paradis, what *business* relationship, if any, did you have with Louie Paradis in respect of the subject matter of this lawsuit?"

"Good specific question, Mr Layton," Paradis replied. "Louie Paradis, at all material times in respect of the subject matter of this lawsuit, was my agent."

"Can you explain to me why you nephew never disclosed that 'agency' to Mr McQuaid?"

"I do not believe that is a proper question, because you are presuming to ask me to speculate what may have been in the mind of my nephew," Paradis replied. "But since you have asked me to speculate, perhaps it was the same reason Mr McQuaid did not disclose the identity of his silent partner, which you claimed was 'irrelevant' yesterday in Mr Barton's examination of your client."

Layton paused for a moment to collect his thoughts and to try to get his increasing contempt for Paradis under control. He rummaged through a few loose pages, pretending he was looking for something important. Jake almost expected him to exclaim 'eureka' before he asked his next question.

"Mr Paradis, would you agree that you, personally, did not have any dealings with Mr McQuaid in respect of the subject matter of this litigation?"

"That is correct," Paradis replied.

"So would it be fair to say that all of your information would have come to you from what your nephew, Louie Paradis, told you?" asked Layton, in a self-satisfied fashion as if he had led Paradis into a trap.

"No, it would not be correct to say that," Paradis replied somewhat cryptically.

"What do you mean it would not be correct?" Layton asked, obviously frustrated. "You just admitted that you did not have any personal dealings with McQuaid."

"Well, your specific question was if 'all of my information' came to me from Louie and I responded that it did not. Unlike your client, I actually went to the trouble of trying to inform myself. Consequently, I have reviewed my nephew's telephone records; I have reviewed his e-mails and text messages to McQuaid; I have listened to the recorded telephone discussions, and I have reviewed the transcripts which were prepared by a certified court reporter, which McQuaid has chosen to stupidly disavow. Furthermore, I have also reviewed the bank statements and related documents from that joint account. That is why I answered your stupid question that it would not be correct to say that my knowledge is based solely on what Louie may have told me."

"I object, Mr Barton. It is incumbent upon you to control your client," Layton sputtered in obvious frustration. "I object to Mr Paradis' repeated characterization of my questions being 'stupid'."

"First you objected to practically every second question I asked, now you are attempting to object to my client's answers, even though they are responsive. Unfortunately for you, Mr Layton," Jake replied nonchalantly, "it is up to me to object, not you. And I believe that my client is responding directly to the questions as you have deemed to phrase them. As for my client's pejorative characterization of your client's disavowal of the transcribed telephone conversations or the propriety of some of your questions, it was your client who initially and gratuitously characterized my client as a 'son of a bitch'. I do not recall you controlling and lecturing your client upon appropriate language at that point in time. Therefore, I take the self-righteous posture you are attempting to assume at this point to be a bit hypocritical and most unbecoming the stature of such an experienced litigation counsel, like yourself."

***

Layton visibly seethed with anger, but he attempted to regain personal control before he continued with his examination.

"Mr Paradis, am I correct in assuming that you believe that your nephew is totally truthful in respect of what he may have told you in respect of his alleged dealings with McQuaid?"

"Thank you for finally asking me a very good question, Mr Sterling Layton, Esquire," Paradis replied sarcastically again. "Indubitably! My nephew is totally truthful, which makes your client a lying, cock sucking, son of a bitch!"

While Layton was totally dumbfounded by Paradis' outburst, Jake quickly intervened and suggested that the parties take an immediate break to cool down. McQuaid was equally dumbfounded, though he seemed to want to debate the accuracy of Paradis' vulgar characterization of himself. Layton did muster the presence of mind to usher McQuaid out of the boardroom, who reluctantly complied.

***

When McQuaid and Layton left the boardroom, Christine continued to try to stifle her laughter. Paradis merely sat back in his chair with his arms crossed proudly across his chest, almost biting through his unlit cigar. Jake decided to address what Paradis had just done with some resignation. After all, what was done was done. What was said was said.

"You may be anatomically accurate in your characterization of McQuaid, but I have to advise you that it was not really appropriate to say what you said, especially knowing that it was being recorded. Those words will not portray you in the most favorable light when those comments are read in front of a judge on any application. They will not be fatal, but you have not made my work any easier."

"Fuck him and fuck McQuaid!" Paradis relied calmly, which was in dramatic contrast to the vehemence of his most recently spoken insult. "McQuaid called me a son of a bitch and he had no call to say that. I know that he was just trying to insult me, but goddamn it, Jake, he also insulted my mother. And then Layton had the gall to accuse me of threatening to shoot that cocksucker. I ain't going to put up with that kind of shit—not from them bumfuckers."

"Well, thank God that all of this is not on the record as well, Marcel," Jake replied. "But this is what is going to happen. When they come back, I know that you will not apologize, so I am going to apologize on your behalf for the record. I will explain that your emotions got the best of you, and you retract your comments without reservation. Then we shall proceed to conclude this examination. Also, I really would appreciate it if you would just answer whatever other questions he may have, so that this examination can end, and your action can proceed."

"You are my counsel, and you may do whatever you deem appropriate, Jake," Paradis replied, but he still retained a smirk on his face. He was quite proud of what he thought he had accomplished.

"And I would appreciate it if you would adopt a more contrite facial expression, Marcel. Pretend that the parish priest just caught you with you hand in the donation jar. You should look a bit ashamed, even if you really do not feel ashamed. That impression would make my apology appear to be more sincere."

***

When Layton and McQuaid returned, both their faces were still flushed with anger. McQuaid, because of the vulgar insults which were put on the record by Paradis. Layton, because Paradis had also insulted him by disparaging his questions.

***

"For the record, Mr Layton... Mr McQuaid..." Jake spoke solemnly, addressing both men. "I would like to apologize on behalf of Mr Paradis for the language he used in responding to that last question. Mr Paradis was unable to control his emotions in that moment and I apologize on his behalf without reservation. I trust you gentlemen shall accept his apology and let us continue and conclude this examination."

"Further to discussion with my client," Layton responded, barely keeping his own anger in check, "I do not believe that further questioning is warranted and to that extent I am concluding my examination."

***

After Layton and McQuaid left, Paradis declined an invitation to another dinner to celebrate the relative success over the preceding two days. His excuse was an urgent business commitment in Denver and that he had a flight to catch in two hours. Paradis did confirm that he would get in touch with Jake within a day or two.

Chapter 44

Jake came into the office the following morning at about nine. He was still feeling pretty good in respect of his assessment regarding how the examinations had proceeded. He did not expect too much from McQuaid, but what he had actually received still exceeded those expectations. On the other hand, Paradis had performed in an excellent fashion, except for his emotional outburst at the end of his examination. Jake believed that his apology ameliorated some of the damage Paradis had created.

Crystal had phoned him late both evenings to ensure that no one had attempted to carry out that death threat. Her concern was sincere and endearing.

Jake was annoyed that some pusillanimous prick had the nerve to actually utter that death threat in first place, but he never had any serious concern that someone would try to actually carry it out.

***

"Good morning, Ginger!" Jake exclaimed with more enthusiasm than usual. "And may I add that as most women just age with the passage of time, you simply continue to blossom like a flower in the spring."

"Thank you, Mr Barton," Ginger replied with a smile. "I only wish that my husband would flatter me with such sincere compliments, especially since I am only twenty-three years of age and there is a howling snowstorm outside right now, not spring."

"It is just a figure of speech, Ginger, just a figure of speech. But most deserving in your case."

***

Michael and Christine met Jake as he was walking down the hall to his office. Jake's elation decreased when he observed the serious countenance on Michael's face. He was carrying a copy of the *Calgary Herald* newspaper in his left hand.

"Let's go to the boardroom, Jake," Michael said. 'There has been a serious development overnight on the Paradis file."

Once they sat down, Michael opened the paper and pushed it toward Jake. The first page heralded a murder in bold type on the front page and the story was summarized in the City Section.

"Businessman Murdered in Hotel Room"

Jake looked up at Michael and Christine and he could only mutter. "Who was murdered? Not Paradis?"

"No," replied Christine. "It was McQuaid."

"Calgary Police Services contacted me first thing this morning to advise me that McQuaid was shot last night in his room at the Delta Plaza Hotel," Michael continued. "They received an anonymous tip that he had been involved in an examination for the past two days in a case with our firm and that is why they called me, but that was all they would disclose.

"They asked me about the litigation, and I told them that the claim accused McQuaid of a $600,000 fraud, but that was on the public record. They asked me to arrange for a meeting at our offices, as a professional courtesy, with you and Christine this afternoon. I took the liberty of arranging it for two p.m."

"Holy shit!" exclaimed Jake. "This really has to be the most bizarre case I have been involved in and we haven't even finished the examination phase."

"I trust that you can account for your whereabouts last night, Jake, because I anticipate that you will be one of the focal points of the police investigation," Michael said solemnly. "After all, from what Christine told me about what happened yesterday and the day before, the proceedings were certainly adversarial. Coupled with the death threat you had previously received; I am assuming that the anonymous tipster probably disclosed that fact to the police as well. They have to interview you because you are one of the key parties before they can exclude you from further consideration."

"After I left the office about six thirty p.m., I went for dinner at Nick's Taverna, where we had dined the night before. I stayed there for a few hours and Nick will be able to vouch for that time. I left at about ten p.m. and Crystal called me from Vancouver on my landline at home at about eleven p.m. We spoke for about one hour and then I went to sleep. And what about you, Michael? They will probably be checking on your whereabouts as well."

"I went home to the acreage with Kathy after work. We had dinner, watched a couple of episodes on Netflix and then just went to bed," Michael answered. Turning to Christine, he added that he did not think that she had a serious issue of accounting for her whereabouts.

"Both of you have better alibis than me," Christine replied. "I just went home after work. I did not see anyone. Did not speak with anyone at all and I did not even watch any television. I just read a couple of chapters of a Jo Nesbo novel and went to sleep."

"*Jo Nesbo*?" asked Jake.

"He is a Scandinavian noir fiction writer. From Norway, I think," Michael said, clarifying that matter for Jake. "But let us get back to the situation at hand."

"Have you contacted and advised Paradis?" Jake asked. "And what about Layton? He seemed more pissed off with McQuaid than with me by the end of McQuaid's examination."

"I have a call into Marcel Paradis' office," Michael replied. "But he has not responded yet. I assumed that Layton was also staying at the Delta Plaza, so I also phoned them. They confirmed that he was a guest, but that he checked out by nine p.m. last night. I also put a call into his office in Vancouver, but no response from him to this point in time."

"And then we have Marcel's colleague, Tommy Smith," Jake added. "But we do not have his contact information; we do not know which hotel he was staying at, and we do not know his whereabouts right now, either. In fact, we do not even know his real name."

"Who is this Tommy Smith guy?" asked Christine.

"We met him at the restaurant during dinner the first night of the examinations," Michael explained. "He came up to our table and asked to speak to Marcel, in private, for a couple of minutes. When Marcel came back, he confirmed that he made a mistake in revealing his first name and that his surname was not Smith. Marcel explained that he was some security guy which he had hired to ensure that Louie was safe in Denver and that he had come to Calgary to ensure his safety here as well in case Louie was going to be questioned. However, after Marcel's vulgar outburst, Layton decided to conclude his examination. This Smith guy certainly did not look like your average American Anglo-Saxon named Smith. He was probably of Italian heritage. All we know is that Smith was just a fictitious name Marcel came up with. Pretty serious-looking guy, about mid-sixties. Has some strange idiosyncrasies: he will not shake hands and seemed to be averse to any kind of physical contact with another person. He spoke with a fairly thick New York accent, and I would guess that he probably came from Brooklyn, originally."

"Oh my God!" exclaimed Christine. "Do you think this Tommy Smith is a... Mafia guy?"

"You mean a hitman," Jake said, correcting Christine's characterization. "Who knows? But I did say that this case is getting more bizarre by the day."

"And I thought that family litigation was really adversarial. Here we have fraud, a death threat, a possible Mafia connection and a murder," said Christine. "It makes family law, at its worst, seem almost prosaic."

"Let's try to summarize the possibilities before we talk to the police, Paradis or Layton," Michael stated. "First question: who do we know who had a motive to eliminate McQuaid and why at this time?"

"I would say that it had to be Paradis," Jake stated with some discomfort, since he was accusing his own client of possible complicity. "McQuaid had defrauded his nephew and insulted his family honour. McQuaid also called him a son of a bitch during the first day of examinations and though Paradis maintained his cool, I believe that his cigar gesture to McQuaid in the boardroom was intended to be a symbolical threat. Furthermore, Paradis also considered that son of a bitch comment to be a slur on his mother's honour. He does seem to have a sincere fixation on 'family honour'."

"And I think it would be safe to assume that Marcel, since he had Tommy Smith available, would not have to exact any satisfaction, personally. He also left for Denver right after the examination. His timeline seems fairly secure, even though he did have a motive," Michael added.

"Well, I have an alternate theory," Christine interjected, catching both of her colleagues' immediate attention. "What about Layton? What if Layton was McQuaid's silent partner? Layton used him as a stooge to help perpetrate the fraud on Louie Paradis. The only person who could confirm that fact was McQuaid. Only he could implicate Layton directly in the fraud, which would also make both of them jointly and severally liable for the $600,000. That link would also have Layton disbarred from practicing law.

"McQuaid did not perform that well at his examination. He was obligated to produce that alleged lease agreement. If he failed to produce it, the outcome of the trial would be in our favor. If the wire transfer to Vancouver could not be fully traced, the only person who could implicate Layton in respect of the receipt of those funds was McQuaid. When faced with personal liability for the entire $600,000, I think McQuaid would have been motivated to approach Paradis to try to make a deal. I could see McQuaid selling out Layton. After all, McQuaid did not have any prior dealings with Paradis.

"Layton would have to worry about McQuaid possibly turning on him to escape personal liability. As for Layton, McQuaid's betrayal would also mean that Mr Paradis would beat him twice in a row. I do not think that Layton would find that bearable."

"Well, we still have Louie Paradis' positive identification of Layton as being the 'dapper man' who turned over that bank draft the following morning," Jake said. "But Layton can claim that he was simply acting as McQuaid's counsel at that time. That would explain his presence and I am sure that Layton could create a plausible explanation for his involvement based on McQuaid's examination testimony."

"And if Paradis did have McQuaid eliminated, even though he claims that 'principles like family honour trump financial considerations', money is still money," Michael said. "Paradis is about $700,000 out of pocket at this point. He also had to know that killing McQuaid prematurely could very well jeopardize the recovery of those funds. He may have despised McQuaid for defrauding his nephew, but I believe that Paradis would be shrewd enough to recover his money before exacting any revenge. It just does not make sense for Paradis to have McQuaid eliminated at this point. So, I think that Christine's theory about Layton seems more plausible than Paradis simply deciding to exact revenge for his besmirched family honour. If Paradis just wanted revenge, since we now know that 'he knows people', he could have done that a long time ago and without our involvement."

The three lapsed into silence for a few moments, digesting the possibilities and their implications, until Michael finally broke their silence.

"When you consider the respective motives both men had, I would say that they were about equal. But when you consider the timing, I believe the scale tilts in favour of Layton. The sooner McQuaid was out of the picture, the more secure Layton's position became."

"I would say that both theories still have some merit based on the limited facts we know at this point," Jake added. "Let's not eliminate either possibility for the time being, but we will have to tread softly. After all, Paradis is our client and if he is culpable, while we do not want to breach any of our ethical obligations, we do not want to become accessories after the fact, either. At the same time, if Layton is the culpable party, then he is the one who probably uttered that death threat too. Perhaps he thought it would put a scare into me and that it might affect my ability to act effectively.

"If the police received an anonymous tip, Layton is probably the source as well because he would try his best to implicate me. Even if he could not implicate me in the end, he could misdirect the police investigation in the interim. I certainly do not see Paradis cooperating with the police or trying to sabotage his own action by having his own lawyer charged with the murder of the defendant who he is suing.

"If I were a betting man, I would bet my mortgage on Layton, but proving it may be another matter."

Michael turned to Jake to offer him some cogent advice.

"Jake, your timeline does pose some potential problems. You claim you left the office at about six thirty p.m., but the office closes at five p.m., so there is no one to corroborate your presence for that one and a half hours."

No worries there, Michael," Jake replied confidently. "I was answering telephone calls and e-mails which I had received during the two previous days of examination. They will speak for themselves."

"You also claim that you were at the restaurant for about three hours, leaving at about ten p.m. But the hotel is just a short five-minute walk from the restaurant. I am sure that the police may speculate that you may have gone to the washroom and then slipped out."

"It was snowing heavily last night, Michael," Jake replied. "I would have had to get my coat from the coat check. I would not be walking in that storm, even five minutes, without a winter coat."

"Good point, Jake. Make sure you mention it if that issue comes up in your police interview," Michael said. "But you could not possibly have remained in conversation with Nick for the entire three hours.

"Then there is that one hour between ten and eleven last night for which you do not have any alibi. Please do not communicate with Crystal about last night's timeline before the police contact and speak to her. You do not want to place yourself or her in a position where the police may suspect possible collusion between the two of you. I strongly recommend, as your partner and friend, that you should not even accept any of her calls until after the police have interviewed her first."

"All right, Michael," replied Jake. "I shall follow your advice, but what motive would *I* have to murder Layton? He may have been a supercilious dick, but I deal with people like that on almost a daily basis."

"Just think about this for a minute, Jake," Michael explained. "Nick can confirm your presence from seven to ten last night. Crystal called you on your landline at eleven p.m., so you had to be in your apartment by that time. We know that McQuaid was killed sometime last night while he was a guest at the Delta Plaza Hotel. When you go home tonight, time your drive from the restaurant to your condominium. Note how much time it would have taken and hypothetically, whether it would have left you with enough time to stop at the hotel to kill McQuaid and still get home in time to receive Crystal's call. Our problem is that we do not know when McQuaid was killed."

"And you should follow up on your telephone calls to Marcel and to Layton, Michael," Jake said. "So now all we can do is just wait for the police and try to relax as best we can."

Chapter 45

At precisely 1:55 p.m., Detectives Peter Krystov and Edward McKeown, Homicide Unit, Calgary Police Service, attended at the offices of Bolta & Barton. Ginger offered the two plain-clothes detectives the privilege of stowing their overcoats in the reception room closet, however, both detectives preferred to carry their winter coats into the boardroom and drape them over a couple of empty chairs.

Michael, Jake and Christine were seated as Ginger ushered them into the room and they proceeded with introductions and the standard exchange of business cards. Once those preliminary formalities were concluded, the detectives explained that they were merely interviewing people who had recent dealings with McQuaid.

As for Michael, Jake and Christine, though they were legally bound to be truthful in their responses to the questions the detectives posed, they also were intent on not volunteering any additional information which might violate their duty of confidentiality to their client, Paradis.

***

"This is just a preliminary interview at this point in our investigation into the murder of Roger McQuaid, which occurred at the Delta Plaza Hotel last night," Detective Krystov said. "But if any of you wish to have your individual lawyers present, that is your prerogative. However, we will be questioning each of you separately."

"In that case, I can advise you that I am representing Jacob Barton and Christine Breland," Michael announced to Krystov's obvious surprise. "And Mr Barton will reciprocate as my counsel."

"Well, that is a novel situation, counsel," Krystov replied.

"You stated that this is just a preliminary interview," Michael replied, reminding the homicide detective of his own statement. "I assume that neither I, nor Mr Barton, nor Ms Breland are suspects or even 'persons of interest' at this point. What I am proposing is simply convenient for both sides today. Each one of us will be represented by counsel during the interviews you conduct, and I can also assure you that we shall cooperate as much as we can. In the event it becomes apparent that this arrangement cannot continue to be feasible, we can change the representation at that time. However, I am curious. If the murder occurred last night, how did the Calgary Police Service become aware of our firm's connection with Mr McQuaid so quickly?"

"We are not at liberty to disclose that fact at this time, counsel," replied Krystov. "Nor are we at liberty to disclose the estimated time of death, in case that was going to be your next question."

"As a professional courtesy, since Jake, I and Ms Breland, are officers of the court; how much can you tell us about what happened to Roger McQuaid last night? The news media advises simply that he was shot last night in his hotel room at the Delta Plaza Hotel," Michael inquired politely.

"And as you know, Mr Bolta, since this is an ongoing investigation, there is a limit as to what information we can share with you and your clients, at this time," Krystov answered formally. "Basically, we cannot tell you much more than what has already been reported in the news media."

***

Michael noted that the detectives employed the standard police interrogation protocol. While Krystov was speaking, McKeown would simply observe and take copious notes. If Krystov paused to collect his thoughts, McKeown would immediately take over with his own questions. In that way, the interview or the interrogation would continue seamlessly for the police but afford them the occasional respite. There was no such break for the interviewee whose questioning would continue unabated, thereby making it more difficult to possibly fabricate answers.

***

"All right, in that case, we shall start with Mr Barton. Ms Breland may be excused for the time being," Krystov announced without any further debate.

***

Jake proceeded to advise the detectives of his role in the litigation, the parties to the litigation and their respective counsel and the issues. He briefly recounted the examination of McQuaid on the first day and the examination of Paradis on the second day. He also informed them of the name of the court reporter, who he advised, could provide them with transcripts of both examinations, as well as the audio recordings of those examinations.

When the detectives politely asked if Jake could provide them with courtesy copies of his own transcripts, Jake advised that though he was prepared to consent, on behalf of his client, Paradis, to the release of that information without any court order, he explained that the court reporters get paid for their time and for the transcripts which they prepare. Consequently, he felt it was only fair to the court reporter that Calgary Police Service duly pay the reporter for those copies, as opposed to Jake simply providing them with a courtesy photocopy of his own transcripts, which he did not yet have in any case.

As expected, the detectives then proceeded to have Jake account for his whereabouts subsequent to the conclusion of Layton's examination of Paradis the day before. Jake advised that the examination was conducted at their offices, and he remained at the office until about six thirty p.m., at which time he went to the Greek steakhouse. He remained at the restaurant from seven p.m. to about ten p.m. and they could contact the owner, Nick Theodorakis, to confirm same. Then he drove to his condominium because he was expecting a long-distance call from his friend, Crystal Bachman. The journey home took longer than usual because of the snowstorm, but his friend called him promptly on his landline at about eleven p.m. and they spoke for about one hour, after which he went to sleep. He provided the detectives with Crystal's contact information so that they would be able to verify that information. In response to their follow-up question, he confirmed that he had not spoken with either Nick or Crystal since their respective dealings the preceding day.

Michael did not interject or speak during the entire forty-five-minute interview. However, before ending their interrogation, Krystov asked Jake about the death threat, obviously in an attempt to surprise Jake and assess his reaction. At that point, Michael decided to exercise his prerogative as Jake's counsel and interject himself into the proceeding to afford Jake an opportunity to collect his thoughts.

"Detective Krystov, I am very interested in knowing how that particular information came into your possession. If that information also came from your anonymous tipster, that raises further issues. The knowledge of the death threat which Jake received a few weeks ago is limited to a select few people. Jake, me and then Christine since she was assisting Jake on the Paradis file. The only logical conclusion which I can draw is that the person who uttered the threat had to be the person who tipped off the police about our firm's involvement with McQuaid," replied Michael. "Has the CPS stopped to consider that possibility?"

"Furthermore, Detective Krystov," added Jake, "I reported the threat to the police and provided them with the original recording right after it happened. The report and the recorded threat speak for themselves, and they have been in CPA custody since I filed that report a couple of weeks ago. So, did you gentlemen obtain that information from your own records or from this anonymous source? If it was from your anonymous source, I would have to agree with Michael's conclusion that the person who tipped you off had to have made the threat as well."

"I am not at liberty to admit or deny anything at this point," Krystov stated neutrally, "but do you get many death threats, Mr Barton?"

"Not every often, Detective," Jake replied. "But civil litigation is adversarial and not really that civil, so it happens from time to time to some lawyers. I believe that this was my third threat in about fifteen years of practice."

"Do you have any idea as to who might be responsible for that threat?" Krystov asked by way of follow-up.

"My initial assumption was that it was probably Roger McQuaid, because he was the only new person in my adversarial life," Jake replied calmly, maintaining eye contact with Krystov until the detective looked away to his notes to ask his next question.

"Did you take the threat seriously?" Krystov asked.

"I took it seriously enough to report to the police," replied Jake. "Just as a law-abiding, tax-paying citizen should. But I agree with my counsel, if the threat information came to you from a tipster, rather than from the complaint I had filed, I would suggest that you consider that your tipster may have ulterior motives and may even have some personal involvement in the homicide which you are investigating at this time."

"Well, we shall certainly... as you lawyers put it so quaintly... take that under advisement," answered McKeown. "But you said that your initial assumption was that McQuaid had uttered that threat. Who is your alternate choice, Mr Barton?"

"I believe that it might be McQuaid's counsel, Sterling Layton, who has offices in Vancouver."

"And what is the reason for that assumption?" McKeown continued.

"He was one of the opposing counsel, in a multi-million action and a court-ordered mediation in Denver a few months ago. He was representing a company that owed my client substantial professional fees and the proceedings got quite heated, but were resolved to the satisfaction of my client, at least," Jake replied. "Perhaps he thought that an anonymous death threat might affect my ability to prosecute my client's claim. So, if you gentlemen are relying upon an anonymous source, perhaps that source is attempting to misdirect you toward other possible suspects, like me and dissuade you from considering him as a possible suspect at the same time."

"Since you are making that assumption, Mr Barton, can you think of any reason Mr Layton would be motivated to eliminate his own client at this time?" McKeown persisted.

"Well, there is some evidence to indicate that Mr Layton may have been involved in McQuaid's fraud, himself, and he would not want that information to come out. McQuaid also did not perform too well at his examination," Jake replied casually. "In fact, I would suggest that you obtain a production order for the joint account which McQuaid set up for himself and Paradis' nephew and see if you can trace and identify the recipients of the two wire transfers. Those recipients may be able to shed some light on why McQuaid was killed and who might be responsible for that murder."

"By the way, was Mr Marcel Paradis involved in that Denver mediation?" McKeown asked.

"He was!" replied Jake. 'However, he was represented by two other American counsel."

***

The detectives' interview of Michael was quite cursory and focused more on his knowledge of Paradis, than any possible personal involvement on his part. They did advise him that they wanted to speak briefly with Kathy to confirm his timeline before they left that day.
Christine Breland's examination was even shorter. Both detectives then thanked the three of them for their cooperation and advised them that they may be in touch again in the future.

After the detectives left, Michael convened a meeting with Christine and Jake so that they could review matters from their respective perspectives and brainstorm again.

***

"Well, those interviews were certainly not very informative from our perspective," Michael stated, his disappointment evident in his voice and in his posture. "Hard to defend yourself when you do not know exactly what you have to defend yourself against."

"I do not think the detectives were aware of the police report I had filed on that death threat," announced Jake.

"Why do you say that, Jake?" asked Michael.

"Krystov did not display any surprise when you suggested that their information on the death threat probably came from their tipster. That confirmed to me that it did come from the anonymous police source. But I thought I detected a slight facial twitch when I told him that I had previously reported the threat to the police. I took that to mean that they were not aware of that report and Krystov suddenly realized the implication that their anonymous source may be providing information

286

for a collateral reason and that their anonymous source may also have some personal involvement in the murder."

"So, if Layton wanted to try to point the police in your direction or in Paradis' direction, you decided to volunteer information which would point them in Layton's direction," Michael said, impressed with Jake's strategy. "Good thinking!"

"Well, I do believe in that aphorism 'what's sauce for the goose is sauce for the gander'," Jake replied smugly. "So, if Layton wants to presume to rain on our parade, I am more than willing to urinate on his."

Chapter 46

On their drive home to the acreage, Kathy was still concerned for Michael since the two police detectives spoke briefly with her before they left the office. They wanted to confirm the timeline which Michael had provided to them earlier. Her concern and her curiosity motivated her to broach the issue of the implications of the police interview that had been conducted that afternoon.

***

"Nothing to worry about, Kathy," Michael answered sincerely. "I assure you that I am not in any jeopardy. Jake's position is a bit more serious because he received that death threat and he was the one who examined McQuaid, but I do not believe that Jake is in any real jeopardy either. Christine is absolutely in the clear."

"But someone killed McQuaid the day after he was examined, Michael," Kathy replied. "In my mind, that is really serious. Who killed him and why?"

"I agree," Michael stated succinctly. "But I assure you that you and I have nothing to worry about. Jake has a more difficult position because we believe that whoever killed McQuaid may be pointing the police in his direction, but Jake was able to turn the table at the end of his interview and point the police right back."

"Who?" Kathy asked. "Who is that 'guy'?"

"Jake and I were inclined to believe that it might be Paradis, but Christine presented a fairly good argument that it may very well be McQuaid's lawyer—Sterling Layton. But we really do not know for sure. We are just speculating at this point because the police did not really tell us anything about McQuaid's murder. We do not even know when he was killed, other than the fact that he was shot in his hotel room sometime last night.

"Do you really think there is a chance that McQuaid was killed by his own lawyer?" Kathy asked, somewhat incredulous at that prospect.

"Layton strikes me as an arrogant man who thrives on an adrenal rush by taking unnecessary chances, just to prove that he can succeed and overcome those obstacles. Even the ones he has created for himself. I know it does not make sense, but you have to appreciate how arrogant he really is. We believe that he may not only be involved in McQuaid's fraud, but that it was actually his idea. The reason we suspect him is that McQuaid flushed his defence down the toilet during his examination. If McQuaid is found liable, he would probably approach Paradis and turn on Layton. In that case, Layton would become liable for the fraud and probably be disbarred as well. He may even end up facing criminal charges. So, having created this problem for himself, he may have decided to eliminate the one person who could implicate him and even testify against him. And that probably gave him an even greater adrenal rush."

"You say that you and Jake believe that he not only killed his own client, but then he tried to get the police to think that it was Jake who killed McQuaid as well?" Kathy asked.

"That's right!" answered Michael. "But Jake may have succeeded in giving the police reason to believe that not only was their anonymous tipster Layton, but that he was also their probable killer. The key may be in tracing those two wire transfers and the police can obtain those relevant records much faster than we could through a court application. We would have to serve the application on the banks and probably on Layton, since he is McQuaid's counsel of record. That would then give him the opportunity to oppose that application and delay matters considerably. The police could apply for a production order quite easily and quite quickly. And most importantly, without any notice to Layton."

"All right, Michael," Kathy answered more calmly. "Thank you for explaining the situation, though I do not think I understand fully. I shall try not to worry about you or even Jake. I may even be developing some affection for him, God forgive me!" Kathy exclaimed, crossing herself.

"Since Adam is coming out this weekend, perhaps we can go skiing together. I have taken him for lessons a couple of times, and he seems to really enjoy it."

"I would love to go skiing with you two, but I have not skied for a few years. So, I am not going down any black runs," Kathy replied modestly.

"I would not go down any run other than the elementary green runs, Kathy."

***

When Jake got to his condominium he loosened his tie, shook off his loafers, threw off his jacket and poured himself a generous serving of his favorite scotch, Balvenie Aged 25 years in the cask, and dropped a couple of ice cubes into the crystal glass to chill the scotch. Before he was able to savor his first sip, his cell phone rang, and it was Crystal.

"Hello sweetie," he replied. "God, but I sure wish you were here right now."

"Hello Jacob," Crystal replied anxiously, "is everything all right?"

"Relatively speaking, things are all right, but they could be better. They would be better if you were here beside me sipping some great scotch and running your fingers through my hair."

"I received a call from a couple of Calgary police detectives this afternoon," Crystal replied. "They identified themselves as homicide detectives, Jacob. Is there something you want to tell me or something I should know? I tried to call you at your office before closing time, but those calls were not returned."

"What did they say to you?" replied Jake, attempting to deflect her questions for the moment.

"They wanted to know if I had spoken to you two days ago and when that call took place and how long it lasted. I just told them the truth. I had phoned you on your landline, not your cell, at about eleven p.m. You were pretty pleased the way the examination had gone that day and we talked for about an hour and then we both went to sleep. I did not know why they were asking those questions and since I had not received any call from you, I assumed that being truthful was the best alternative. I hope what I said did not make things more difficult for you." Crystal sounded extremely concerned.

"Two of the many reasons why I adore you more with each passing day. Your beauty and your brains," Jake replied. "Just as you decided to trust me by being truthful, I made the same decision about you. I needed you to be truthful about our telephone conversation, but Michael suggested that I do not attempt to contact you in case the detectives assume that we were colluding together. That was the only way you could have helped me, but you had to decide to be truthful without any advice or encouragement from me. But Crystal, what would you have done if I had asked you to help me fabricate an alibi?"

Crystal remained silent for a moment before she responded slowly.

"The short answer, Jacob," she replied, "is that I would have probably turned you down because if you truly cared for me, you would not even think about putting me in jeopardy. If you would be prepared to put me in danger just to protect yourself, then that would prove that you cared more about yourself than about me or us."

"That is what I hoped you would say, Crystal," Jake answered. "I would not ask you to lie for me because, one: there was no need to lie; and two: I would not think about putting you in any jeopardy. I would probably throw myself on that proverbial sword to protect you, because I do really care for you."

"Oh, Jake!" Crystal exclaimed, "I do wish I could be there beside you right now, even though I cannot think of a witty come-back right now."

***

Jake proceeded to relate the events which had transpired over the two preceding days. Crystal did not interrupt until Jake had finished.

"Hard to believe, Jacob," Crystal finally replied. "Is this the kind of life you are offering to share with me? Death threats and murder?" she asked half-jokingly.

"No, dear." Jake spoke longingly, "this is probably the most bizarre case I have been involved with in my entire career. There are a few issues which I have to resolve, but I assure you that I will succeed in the end. I just have to be patient and follow the sage advice of my Greek friend who told me that though he was not capable of eating an entire cow at a single sitting, if he was given a sharp knife and a good fork, he would be able to consume the entire carcass within time."

"Really Jacob?" Crystal asked rhetorically. "Perhaps I had better fly out to see you this weekend because I am concerned that you may becoming either delusional or fanciful, at best."

"I would love it if you will come out, Crystal. You seem to have become a fixture in my heart and even in my soul," Jake answered melodramatically. "I do not feel either complete or fulfilled... unless I am with you... making love to you."

"Feeling is mutual, lover of mine," Crystal replied. "I shall e-mail my itinerary to you tomorrow morning. I want to see you this weekend. Perhaps we can go skiing together?"

***

The call from Paradis came in the following morning and Ginger immediately transferred it to Michael.

"Well, son," Paradis drawled. 'What's going on up there that is so urgent?"

"You have not heard, Marcel? Someone shot McQuaid sometime after the examination ended two days ago," Michael replied, paying close attention to Paradis' voice to see if it would disclose anything.

"You're joshing, right?" Paradis asked. His voice remained calm, disclosing no surprise. "What did that son of a bitch do? Shoot himself?"

"We don't know too much, but apparently someone killed him in his hotel room sometime that night. The police are not disclosing any information," Michael responded.

"How does this affect the recovery of my money?" Paradis asked nonchalantly.

"Well, it is going to delay matters, at the very least," Michael replied. "But you do not sound either surprised or concerned, Marcel."

"McQuaid was such an asshole, someone was bound to kill him sooner or later, so his killing is not a surprise. As for 'concern', I have total faith that you and Jake will recover my money. Is there anything else I should know?"

"Someone is trying to point the finger of guilt at Jake, but he has a pretty good alibi and a tight timeline for the entire evening," Michael said, then added. "But the police also asked some general questions about you as well. That would make sense since you were suing McQuaid at that time."

"I was at the airport by five pm, since it was an international flight, and I caught the first flight to Denver that night at seven p.m. Before that, I was with Jake at your office. Any idea as to who the stool pigeon may be, Michael?" Paradis asked.

"Well, McQuaid is dead, so that eliminates him. It's not me or Jake, and I am quite sure that it's not you. By elimination, that would leave our dear learned friend in Vancouver: Mr Sterling Layton, Esquire," Michael replied.

"I would not put anything past that son of a bitch," Paradis replied, still maintaining a calm demeanor, notwithstanding the unusual development in his lawsuit. "Is there anything else?"

"No, Marcel. There is nothing else to report at this time," answered Michael. "But I shall keep you advised of any developments." Michael decided that it was neither necessary, nor prudent to ask about Tommy Smith.

"You do that, son," Paradis replied. *"Adios, amigo!"*

***

The following morning, Layton belatedly replied to Michael's telephone call. It was just a terse e-mail:

"Sir.

In light of your conduct and your client's conduct during the just completed examinations in Calgary, I hereby put you on notice that I shall only communicate with you in writing—either via faxed correspondence or via e-mail.

I have no intention in speaking to you by phone or in person. Any and all future communication between us must be in writing from this point on.

I trust that I have made my position clear, and my position is non-negotiable.

Signed: Sterling Layton, Esquire"

Michael ruminated for a minute before responding via a return e-mail:

"Sir.

As a professional courtesy, since it appears that you may not be fully informed, I am obliged to advise you that your client, Mr Roger McQuaid, met an untimely demise two days ago. To that extent, please advise us of who shall be acting as the Executor of his Estate so that we may proceed and expeditiously conclude the extant litigation.

However, I concur. All future communication between you and your office, and me and my office, should be restricted to writing.

Signed: Michael Bolta"

***

Within minutes of sending that e-mailed response, Michael received a frantic telephone call from Layton.

"McQuaid is dead? What happened?" Layton asked.

***

Michael merely referred him to Detectives Krystov and McKeown. He referred Layton to their concluded e-mailed agreement and declined any further oral conversation.

However, he concluded that either Layton was not involved in McQuaid's death, or he was a very good actor, because his apparent surprise at his client's death did not appear to be feigned.

Chapter 47

There were no further developments on the McQuaid murder, but it remained a prominent matter which continued to preoccupy Michael's mind for the remainder of the week. Jake was less concerned, since his mind was focused on Crystal coming out for the weekend. Michael and Jake had decided that both groups would go skiing together that weekend. They agreed upon a half day at Lake Louise, which would permit them to have dinner at the luxurious Post Hotel on the way home.

Crystal and Kathy seemed to develop a friendship quite quickly. On the hill, Jake, Crystal and Kathy skied as a group, since Michael tried to trail behind Adam. It was a lot easier for him to go down to assist his son, rather than clumsily trying to trudge back up the slope to reset a ski if it became separated.

Adam's skis were short and quite maneuverable. By late afternoon, his confidence had grown substantially. On the last run down the hill, Kathy's threesome had already made it down and they were watching Adam and Michael — who were about one hundred meters from the end — complete their run.

"Dad let's race. I bet I can beat you down the hill," Adam announced without any warning.

With that statement, Adam pointed his skis down the hill and accelerated. Michael delayed his response because he assumed that Adam would lose control and that he would have to come to his rescue. To his surprise, Adam maintained his balance even when he lowered his body into a racing crouch with his poles tucked snugly beneath his armpits. What was most shocking was that when Michael finally attempted to catch up to his son, he was unable to do so. In a final desperate attempt to catch up to Adam, Michael proceeded to descend in a straight line down the hill. Unfortunately, he hit a rut and became airborne when he lost control. He could hear his companions collectively gasp their concern. He hit the ground, losing one ski and landing on one of his poles, which no longer remained straight.

Though the impact with the compacted snow winded Michael, he could not prevent himself from laughing at his foolish attempt to outrace Adam.

As he lay prone on the ground trying to recapture his breath, he could see the four of them trying to make it back up the hill. Another skier came by with a grin on his face. He facetiously complimented Michael on his airborne maneuver and asked if he could provide him with any assistance. Michael declined politely and assured his would-be Samaritan that he could only feel pain when he breathed.

Shortly after that exchange, Adam and his other skiing companions reached him and asked him if he was all right.

"And I beat you, Dad!" Adam exclaimed. "I beat you. I am the champ!"

"I am all right," Michael replied, trying to reassure everyone. "The only thing I appear to have injured is my pride."

"And your ski pole," Jake added, holding the bent pole skyward.

"Congratulations, Adam," Michael said. "You beat me, and you are the racing champ."

"So, what do I win, Dad?" Adam asked. "My choice of dessert for dinner?"

"That sounds fair to me, Adam," Michael answered, wincing as he got up beside the rest of the group.

***

The dinner at the Post Hotel was subdued. Everyone took turns answering Adam's innumerable questions.

"Why is it so dark in here, Dad?"

"It is part of the ambience, Adam. The subdued lighting gives everyone more privacy," answered Michael.

"Why is everyone speaking so softly?"

"They just do not want to disturb anyone else's dinner, Adam," replied Kathy.

"So, what is everyone going to eat? I am just famished! I could probably eat a horse, but not really."

"We can let the waiter know what we like and what we don't like and then ask him for his recommendations. Then we can make up our minds," answered Crystal.

***

When the waiter came to take everyone's order, Adam asked to be last so that he could have the benefit of hearing what everyone else was going to order first. Finally, it was his turn.

"And what would you like to order, young man?" The waiter asked solicitously.

Adam had been listening in to the conversations at the adjoining tables and he had picked up some pointers on restaurant etiquette.

"What would you recommend this evening?" he asked politely.

The waiter tried to disguise a smirk and proceeded to go through the menu, inquiring as to Adam's gastronomical preferences. Finally, the waiter and Adam settled on a shrimp appetizer, and a six-ounce filet, with mashed potatoes and fried mushrooms.

Once the entrées were completed, the waiter ignored the adults and asked Adam what he would prefer to have for dessert.

"And what would you recommend?" Adam asked again, trying to affect as much maturity as he could.

"Well, we are quite famous for our pecan pie. I can tell you that it is one of my favorites."

"All right, I will have some of your famous pecan pie," Adam announced proudly.

"And would you like to have it with ice cream or whipped cream?" the waiter asked.

This decision stymied Adam for a moment, so the waiter cheerfully made his final recommendation for the evening.

"Why not have the pecan pie with both the vanilla ice cream and the whipped cream?" the waiter cheerfully suggested.

Adam quickly looked up to his father for final approval, forgetting momentarily that he had won his choice of dessert. Michael merely nodded his approval, but he directed a cautionary condition for the benefit of the waiter.

"Could you bring my son some pecan pie, with a *little* ice cream and a *little* whipped cream?" Michael requested. "With emphasis on the *'little'*, since I will be picking up the tab and determining the tip."

"My dad is a big tipper, aren't you Dad?" Adam interjected quite seriously.

"I would say that I am a fair tipper, if my instructions are followed appropriately," Michael replied, looking directly at the waiter and trying to will the waiter into compliance.

"Instructions received and understood, sir!" the waiter replied with a knowing smile, but then he shared a wink with Adam. After all, *'little'* was a subjective limitation. Adam attempted to wink back, but their conspiracy was obvious to the remaining parties at the table.

***

The drive back to the city was quiet and even though Adam had drifted off to sleep, the remainder of the party kept their conversation casual. No one dared to raise the events of the preceding week.

Jake and Crystal picked up their car at Michael's acreage and proceeded back to the city. Michael carried Adam into the residence. After undressing him, he decided to forego the usual mandatory requirement of having his son brush his teeth and say his evening prayers since Adam had fallen into a deep slumber. He was exhausted, not only by the physical exertion of the day, but the excitement of being able to share a formal dinner in a dark, fancy restaurant with four adults.

"Adam is so sweet, Michael," Kathy said. "You should be really proud of him."

"He can be adorable, can't he?" Michael agreed. "I just hope that the divorce does not affect him too much. Everything is going well so far, but you never know. Marlena has enrolled in the winter session, and she intends to complete her degree. Sooner or later, she is bound to meet someone. I hope that she finds someone who can make her happy, but I am also concerned that all these changed relationships may have an adverse effect on Adam because he is so young. I have heard some real horror stories. I am trying my best to get along with Marlena. Fortunately, she is more upset with Alexa's duplicity than with me right now, but you never know.

***

By the time Jake and Crystal reached his condominium, they were quite tired, but Jake's ardor had been invigorated. It seemed that his desire to make love with Crystal was becoming insatiable. He loved exploring her body and uniting inside of her. Crystal was compliant with his suggestions and requests, and he reciprocated in turn. Finally, when they were both spent and still entwined together, Crystal broached a topic which they had never discussed before.

***

"Jacob, have you even considered starting your own family?" she asked quietly, her lips affectionately nuzzling his neck. "Adam was so adorable this afternoon."

"To be truthful, I never considered it," Jake replied. "My life was fulfilled, and that notion never crossed my mind. Kids were for other people... to propagate our species."

"And what about now? Has your life changed somewhat?" Crystal asked softly.

"Well... you seem to have changed my life," Jake replied seriously. "What about you, do you want to have kids?"

"Like you, Jacob," Crystal replied. "I thought my life was fulfilled as well. The thought of having a family by someone I was involved with, never materialized before."

"Are you saying that you are considering it now? Jake asked, somewhat anxiously. "Would you consider having a child with me, then?"

Crystal pulled herself away from Jake's embrace so that she could watch him when she spoke to him.

"For the first time in my life, I have decided that I would like a child, preferably by you but a sperm bank donor may have to do if you are not

299

inclined. I believe that you can even get a Nobel laureate as a donor," Crystal replied mischievously.

"Really?" Jake asked indignantly. "You would settle for a Nobel laureate sperm donor, instead of me? I am trying to visualize that Nobel laureate watching some porn on the internet, masturbating vigorously, trying desperately to ejaculate into a specimen jar without spilling any of that precious fluid or having it squirt onto the screen or dribble onto the keyboard."

"Well, I believe that they do come with high IQs. and intelligence is very important to me," she replied, disingenuously.

"So you think that a flatulent geriatric masturbating to some porn is a demonstration of higher intelligence?" Jake asked mockingly. "I think it is just self-absorbed ego. After all, I bet his parents were not Nobel Peace Prize winners."

"You may have a point there, Jacob. But perhaps they are just very proud of their accomplishment, and they want to share their DNA with other people?" Crystal responded teasingly, since it was obvious that the suggestion was irking Jake.

"So, physical appearance is not important to you? How about a sense of humor or a convivial personality, not to mention modesty, my best quality?" Jake inquired, feigning mild outrage. "And I seriously doubt if any Nobel laureate could get you to climax by having his sperm injected into your vagina with some syringe or whatever the hell they use."

"So, I take this indignation to be an affirmative response to my question?" Crystal asked coyly.

**

To their mutual surprise, their short verbal exchange had rekindled their passion. Jake mounted Crystal and maneuvered her legs over his shoulders to maximize his penetration. Their lovemaking was vigorous, as if each party wanted to totally subdue and overwhelm the other.

"If this is make-up sex, Jacob," Crystal said breathlessly, "I suggest that we argue more often, but you have not answered my question… verbally, that is."

"Honey, I am not only willing to accede to your proposal, but unlike that Nobel figment of your imagination, I am even prepared to make a direct personal deposit."

Chapter 48

Three weeks had elapsed since that initial interview with Detectives Krystov and McKeown. On the twenty-second day, Michael received a call from McKeown who asked for a second interview with him and Jake. Michael agreed and scheduled it for two that afternoon. After taking the call, Michael went to Jake's office to discuss the matter.

"Morning, Jake. Guess who called me just now and requested a further *'chat'* with the two of us."

"When you phrase the question that way, it could only be our dedicated members of the Calgary Police Service," Jake replied nonchalantly. "I was waiting for them to get back to us, but did they indicate what they wanted to discuss specifically?"

"No!" replied Michael. "They play their cards close to their chests, but obviously there must be some new developments."

***

Precisely at two p.m., the two detectives arrived and were ushered into the boardroom by Ginger. Jake and Michael joined them before they were able to take off their winter coats. After the usual reciprocal greetings, Michael offered the detectives some coffee before the interview commenced. Both officers accepted the offer and asked that their coffee be black—no sugar or cream. Michael decided to join them, but Jake declined.

***

Krystov commenced the proceedings by advising that he and McKeown had several telephone conferences with Layton and that they wanted to pursue some new matters which had arisen.

"For the record, gentlemen," Michael stated firmly, "I do not believe that it is either fair or appropriate for you to interview us without sharing some relevant information. Therefore, if you are not more forthcoming with some relevant background facts, this is going to be a short discussion."

The two detectives did not even bother to exchange a glance. Obviously, they had discussed what approach they were going to take this afternoon and Michael's position had been anticipated and discussed before they showed up.

"Naturally, Mr Bolta," McKeown replied, "we are prepared to share some of the information which has come into our possession, however, we may not be at liberty to share everything, because we do have to maintain the integrity of an ongoing police investigation."

"Who do you wish to interview first?" asked Michael

"We do not believe that we have to examine you further, Mr Bolta." Krystov replied. "Though you were one of Paradis' solicitors of record, you did not participate in the examinations and your timeline, as corroborated by Ms Clemmons, pretty well eliminates you as a person of interest."

"And I guess you are telling me that I remain a person of interest?" Jake asked. "I was a party to the examinations and perhaps you are of the opinion that my timeline is a bit more porous and perhaps my alibi is not quite that ironclad?"

"Keep in mind, Mr Barton, that just because we may consider you as a person of interest, that does not make you a suspect," McKeown replied, attempting to sound as innocuous as possible. "It may simply mean that we believe you may be in possession of information which may prove helpful in our investigation."

***

Even though both detectives attempted to affect an innocent, casual demeanor, like a teenager exiting the confessional booth thinking that his admissions were accepted by the priest as being at least plausible, Jake still harbored a subliminal feeling that their intentions may not be as innocuous as they were intimating.

***

"Well, gentlemen," Jake announced casually, as he sat down beside Michael, "please ask away, but that does not mean that I will be inclined to answer any and every question you may ask."

"We would like to deal with your timeline, Mr Barton." Krystov stated formally. "Exactly what were you doing at your office between five p.m. and approximately seven p.m. on the day in question?"

"As I told you before, I was in my office trying to catch up on matters… e-mails and correspondence and voice messages… which I was not able to attend to during the two days of the examination."

"And was there anyone in the office during that period who could corroborate your presence?" McKeown interjected. "Your own staff or possibly some of the cleaning staff?"

"As I told you before, I was in my office and I did not speak with any of my staff and the cleaning staff only get to our offices later on in the evening," Jake replied politely and calmly.

"Perhaps it is time we were advised as to what is the estimated time that you believe McQuaid was murdered?" Michael inquired. "If you believe that it occurred between five p.m. and seven p.m., then your questioning is appropriate. But if you believe that McQuaid was murdered at some other time, then I object to this line of questioning."

Krystov and McKeown did exchange a glance at this point before McKeown responded.

"Our investigation has disclosed that a couple of guests overheard a heated argument in McQuaid's hotel room at about six that night. However, no shots were heard. There was no evidence of any argument or disagreement or struggle after that point in time."

Krystov then proceeded to follow up. "So, Mr Barton, are you able to prove your presence in your office from five p.m. to seven p.m. on that evening?'

"I believe I can," replied Jake, still affecting a calm tone. "You may check my computer and the various e-mail replies to those e-mail messages I had sent. You may also check my cell phone records and my office phone records in respect of the incoming and outgoing telephone calls for that evening. Those documentary records should adequately corroborate my presence in my office during that time frame. Probably as good as having the Pope and the College of Cardinals as my witnesses."

It was obvious that Krystov was not impressed with Jake's religious analogy.

"Perhaps we will," Krystov replied.

"No!" Jake replied emphatically. "I insist we do that right now. That information is readily accessible now. The telephone records may take a few days to obtain from the telephone company, but you can check my e-mail history for that time period right now. Let's go."

With that statement, Jake got up and left the boardroom and walked down to his office. When he got to his office door, he opened it and waited for the other three men to catch up with him. Jake's e-mail records for that evening disclosed about a dozen e-mailed responses. Most critically, they indicated that those e-mails had been sent between five fifteen and six forty-five p.m. He also reminded the detectives that there was a serious snowstorm that evening, therefore he drove his car to the restaurant and that Nick Theodorakis, the owner, would be able to verify that he got there at about seven p.m.

"In fact, Mr Bolta," replied McKeown, "Mr Theodorakis confirms that his records verify that you had ordered your first drink at 6.55 p.m. But all we have disclosed is that there is evidence that McQuaid was involved in a serious argument with someone about six p.m. That does not exclude the possibility that the murder occurred later that evening."

"Well, my whereabouts from seven p.m. to about ten p.m. should also have been corroborated by Theodorakis, because after I paid for my bill, I left," Jake added, with increasing confidence. "Since it took me about ten minutes to drive from my office to the restaurant, it would have taken me at least fifteen minutes to drive from the restaurant to the Delta Plaza Hotel. That would mean that I would have to be missing from the restaurant for at least forty-five minutes. Fifteen minutes to get there and fifteen minutes to return. I am assuming that it would have taken me at least another fifteen minutes to park, go up to McQuaid's room, shoot him inside that room and then go back down to the car and return to the restaurant. Though I may not have been missed for five or ten minutes, I suggest that a forty-five-minute absence would have been noticed by the waiter and by the owner. By the way, I have neither owned nor shot any kind of a gun in my life. And for that matter, I have neither shot nor murdered anyone either, at least to this date."

The two detectives exchanged another quick glance and this time it was Krystov who picked up the 'interrogation', because it would not be fair to continue to characterize it as just an interview.

"Well, that still leaves that one hour between you leaving the restaurant at about ten p.m. and receiving that telephone call from your friend, Ms Crystal Bachman at about eleven p.m., Mr Barton."

"Out of curiosity and out of a desire for self-preservation, when we became aware that McQuaid was shot, the next day, I timed myself leaving the restaurant at ten p.m. and it took me almost fifty-five minutes to drive home," Jake replied. "The snowstorm had stopped that next night, but the streets were quite treacherous because of the previous night's snow fall. In any case, it probably would have taken me a few minutes more to get home before eleven p.m. if it was still snowing. Crystal called me on my landline, not my cell. That would prove that I was in my home, not someplace else and the telephone records will corroborate that fact. There is no way I would have had time to drive to the hotel, park, go up to McQuaid's room, shoot him, go back down and then drive home. And by the way, what was my motive?"

"Well, as we have stated earlier," replied Krystov. "We have had several telephone communications with Mr Layton, and he is convinced that it was you who shot Mr McQuaid. He told us about your temper, which you displayed during that mediation in Denver. He told us about the acrimonious exchanges between you and Mr McQuaid during your examination of him. Finally, he told us that you would do anything to win a lawsuit and if that meant eliminating a witness, he believed that you would do it. What do you have to say to those allegations?"

"Firstly, I did not display any temper down in Denver," Jake stated matter-of-factly. "I would characterize it as mere righteous indignation. I may have called Layton and his two associates morally challenged sons of bitches, but that is exactly what they were. Just as the police have no legal obligation to be totally truthful with a suspected criminal, lawyers are permitted to get dramatic and be righteously indignant at appropriate times.

"Insofar as my examination of McQuaid was concerned, Layton was more distressed about his answers than I was. I thought that he was quite helpful at some times when Layton permitted him to actually answer a question. I probably had more acrimonious exchanges with Layton than I had with McQuaid. But I had never had any dealings with McQuaid prior to this lawsuit and this examination, and civil litigation is adversarial because you are usually dealing with liars and thieves. It is very seldom that you come across a situation where both sides are moral, and the issue is an honest disagreement about a contractual interpretation or performance."

"Do you have any more questions for my client?" Michael interjected.

However, the two detectives were checking their notes again, trying to buy some time to collect their thoughts and possibly continue the interrogation from a new perspective.

"Well, I have a question, Detective Krystov," replied Jake. "Have you gentlemen obtained that production order which I suggested at my first interview?"

"We have not got around to that at this time, but we certainly shall."

"Well, I have been able to obtain those records," Jake admitted with considerable satisfaction. "We traced that wire transfer from Calgary to Vancouver, since our client's nephew was a joint signing party on that account. Then I got one of my Vancouver colleagues to make an application in the British Columbia Supreme Court to compel the recipient bank to disclose its records. The application was supported by the nephew's sworn affidavit which was delivered from Denver. Because of the urgency, as evidenced by the murder of McQuaid in Calgary, our colleague was able to obtain an expedited order compelling the bank to disclose that information and guess what that information revealed?"

The two detectives did not respond. They realized that they may have erred in not pursuing that order themselves, but they could not bring themselves to give Jake the satisfaction of hearing them politely request that clarification.

"The recipient of that wired $300,000 was…" Jake gave a dramatic pause. "Surprise, surprise, surprise…" Jake added, handing the detectives a copy of the bank documents which had been forwarded from

Vancouver. "It was our dear friend and colleague, Sterling Layton, Esquire."

The two detectives examined the bank documents carefully before speaking. They were somewhat surprised at this development, which appeared to have undermined their theory considerably.

"Perhaps this was just a payment of legal fees for the trial?" McKeown speculated somewhat weakly.

'As you can see, the initial recipient account was in the name of a numbered company, which in turn was owned by another numbered company. The director for the first company was fictitious, but the named director and sole shareholder of the second numbered company was Layton. I would respectfully submit that having these corporate layers superimposed on each other, usually indicates a malicious intent to disguise a fraud," Jake concluded confidently.

Michael decided to interject again.

"Gentlemen, if you permit yourselves to assume the following: if Layton was not only involved in the fraud, but the acting will and mind behind it, he had a very good reason to hide and protect his involvement. The only person who could betray him on that point was McQuaid. Secondly, he had a good motive, which was revenge. He butted heads with Paradis and Jake in Denver and ended up being humiliated. Paradis never had any prior dealings with McQuaid, but if you speculate further that Layton got McQuaid to participate in defrauding Louie Paradis for a $300,000 payoff, it was critical that Layton take whatever steps he could to prevent the disclosure of those facts. Disclosure would have resulted in him being liable for the full financial loss; he would probably have been disbarred for his fraudulent conduct and possibly even criminally prosecuted. After Jake examined him, Layton knew that McQuaid was his Achilles heel. He also knew that McQuaid's morals were malleable and that he would have no qualms about turning on him. So, if you were in Layton's shoes, what would you do?"

"Did you also discover who was the recipient of the $300,000 wire transfer to that Edmonton bank account?" asked McKeown, but he had a good premonition that Jake had obtained that information as well.

"As you should have guessed by now," answered Jake, "it was no one else but McQuaid. That was his payoff for his participation in the fraud."

"We want to cooperate with the police." Michael stated firmly. "But we would like to receive some more information about McQuaid's death, in return. If you gentlemen persist in speculating that Jake was the responsible party when all of the evidence which we have provided you points more logically towards Layton, then that cooperation is ended as of this moment."

"We receive information from various sources and through various means," replied Krystov. "And we are duty bound to follow up, so please do not take this personally, Mr Barton."

"But with all due respect, I *do* take it personally," Jake responded seriously. "When you get some fatuous information from Layton about me, you elect to pursue it vigorously, but then when we provide you with other more cogent information, you elect to ignore it. After all, you are not merely suggesting that I was speeding or jaywalking. You are suggesting my complicity in a murder! A conviction means a life sentence without any parole for twenty-five years."

The detectives were lost for words, at least temporarily and Michael decided that it might be an opportune time to ask them another serious question.

"Could you share some of the details of how McQuaid was killed?"

As was their custom, the two detectives exchanged another quick glance and McKeown elected to respond.

"There was no evidence of a forced entry, so we assume that McQuaid let his killer in voluntarily. He was shot at close range with hollow-point bullets at a distance of about ten feet. Two shots to the chest and a third shot to the head. We do not see too many professional hits in Calgary, but this one certainly reeks of a professional killing."

Now it was Jake and Michael's turn to exchange a quick glance, but fortunately it went unnoticed by the attending detectives. Krystov elected to share a final bit of information.

"Since no one heard any shots, we are speculating that the gun had a suppressor, a silencer, which makes it even more probable that this was a professional hit; therefore, individual alibis may not be all that relevant."

Chapter 49

The day after the second meeting with the police detectives, Kathy called Michael on his intercom to advise him that Marlena was on the line and that she wanted to speak to him. Michael decided to take the call.

***

"Hello Marlena." He addressed her politely. "Is everything all right? No problem with Adam?"

"No, Michael. We are both fine," she replied. "I just want to meet with you... perhaps for lunch today, to discuss a couple of things."

"Of course we can meet, but you can discuss anything with me over the phone as well," Michael replied solicitously.

"I really believe that these matters should be discussed in person, Michael. Will you meet me today?"

***

Michael decided that it would be prudent to accede to her request, even though he had plans to share lunch with Kathy that day. Now he had to explain the situation to Kathy, and he hoped that she would be understanding. After he ended his conversation with Marlena, he buzzed Kathy's station and asked her to come into his office. He met her at the door as she entered his office. She appeared to anticipate that their lunch date was going to be cancelled, but she was slightly curious about the possible reason.

"I am sorry, Kathy, but I am going to have to cancel our lunch. Marlena wants to meet me to discuss something, but she was not prepared to discuss it over the phone," he explained apologetically.

"That is not a problem, Michael. I can go out for lunch with Jake's assistant," Kathy replied directly, however, her disappointment could not be fully disguised.

"I really am sorry, Kathy. Perhaps we can go out to dinner someplace instead of just going home and warming up some leftovers tonight. I would like to make up for this last-minute cancellation."

Kathy could see the sincerity in Michael's facial expression and in the tone of his voice. She came up to him and embraced him tightly. Her tongue gently licked his lips until they parted, and her tongue was able to enter his mouth and tenderly explore it. She pressed her bosom against his chest and her hips against his hips until she sensed that he was becoming aroused, at which point she slowly drew away. Michael was surprised and confused at this sudden demonstration of passionate affection. Kathy leaned forward and gave him one final farewell peck on his lips. She smiled coyly.

"Just so you do not forget about me entirely while you are having your lunch today," Kathy announced confidently and smirking coquettishly, she turned to leave his office. She wanted him to know that though she trusted him, she was not that sure of Marlena's motives.

"I am thinking about phoning her back and telling her that something has come up… and it has," Michael replied with some embarrassment at the ease with which Kathy was able to arouse him.

"No, Michael," Kathy stated firmly. "You go and do your duty. Find out what Marlena wants and if she needs your help, do not hesitate to give it. Then you can make it up to me by taking me to that French restaurant we went to a couple of weeks ago and then you can continue to make it up to me after we get home."

"You know that I cannot and will not ever forget you, regardless of who I may have lunch with, Kathy."

Michael attempted to reach for her so that he could kiss her again, but Kathy restrained him by pushing him away with her arms against his chest.

"No! Michael," Kathy replied. "I want you to leave wanting me, so that you will not dally and so you will come running back as fast as you can. And do not worry, I do trust you."

***

312

Marlena wanted to meet Michael at her favorite bistro a few blocks away from his office. When he entered the restaurant, he was able to see that she was already seated, perusing her menu. When he reached her table, she looked up at him and smiled broadly, sincerely happy that he had come. Michael could see that she took extra pains to ensure that her hair and make-up were perfect. He also noticed that she deliberately enhanced her appearance by discreetly disclosing some decolletage, for his benefit, no doubt.

"Hello, Marlena." Michael greeted her warmly as she rose to meet him and extend her cheek for him to kiss dispassionately. "You look truly beautiful. How are things? And what did you want to discuss?"

"Oh, please sit down and order some wine," she replied. "We can discuss those matters over lunch. You are looking pretty good, yourself."

***

They proceeded to order their wine and lunch while they exchanged meaningless comments. Marlena did mention the last telephone conversation she had with Alexa. Michael decided not to respond, because it would inevitably lead back to their separation and recent divorce. Marlena also mentioned the courses that she had selected for the next semester, and she appeared to be sincerely looking forward to resuming the academic career which she had interrupted when she became pregnant with Adam. Michael did not speak too much, merely restricting himself to monosyllabic acknowledgments or silent nods of agreement. Marlena insisted that they order a second six-ounce glass of wine, instead of coffee after they had finished their lunch.

"Marlena." Michael spoke kindly, hoping to prompt her to disclose the real purpose for their luncheon meeting. "You said this morning that there were a couple of things which you wanted to discuss with me."

"Yes. I did say that, didn't I?" Marlena replied, her tone suddenly became more serious. "I have had a long time to think about what has happened to us and the mistakes that we—no, that *I* have made. Believing that Alexa was my friend and that she was being truthful with me was one of those mistakes. I want you to know that I still have feelings for you, and we do have a son and if you can forgive me, perhaps we can try again?"

Michael could see the tears welling up in her eyes and he reached for his handkerchief and handed it to her.

"Marlena," Michael replied kindly, "please do not take my comments as patronizing, but I care for you now just as I had loved you before. Just as I was faithful to you throughout our marriage. I realize now that I had contributed to our breakup by becoming too preoccupied with my work and I see now, in hindsight, that I neglected you. So when Alexa came along, she took advantage of both of us. Why she did what she did, I do not think I will ever understand, but I can never forgive her for her betrayal of me and of you. Especially you, because she masqueraded as your true friend, and she totally betrayed your trust. We were never that close, so her betrayal of me is not as painful as her betrayal of you."

"But if you still care for me, why can't we try to make it work again, Michael?" Marlena asked, carefully trying to dab away her tears to avoid smearing her make-up.

"Just as I fell in love with you when I first met you and I saw you smile, Marlena," Michael solemnly confessed, "I have to be totally honest with you right now. Those feelings have gone. I still care for you, and I want you to be happy, but I cannot honestly turn back the clock and undo the things we have done or take back the things we have said. You were my wife and I loved you. You are the mother of our son, and I adore you. But even though I cannot say that I love you now, I did love you for that while and you shall always remain an important part of my life."

"Oh Michael," Marlena exclaimed emotionally. "I really screwed up our life. No, my life. I knew that we could have had a wonderful life, gradually going old and grey together, watching Adam grow up and start his own family."

Michael put his arm around her shoulders to console her and he could feel the shudder of the emotions flowing through her body, just as the tears were now flowing freely down her face.

"I just have one last request, Michael," Marlena said emotionally. "No, I have two last requests."

"If I can do them, I shall, Marlena."

314

"I should not have had that second glass of wine, so would you take me home? I know that I can take a taxi, but I do not want a stranger asking me questions why I am crying and why I am so sad."

"Of course I can drive you home," Michael replied. "And what is your second request?"

"Can you promise me to try to remain my friend? I know that it may be an easy request to ask, but a difficult request to fulfil?"

"I promise you, Marlena, that I will not only try, but that I shall remain your friend. We have a wonderful son to raise together, and I know that you will find someone who will love you as I once had and adore you, as I adore you right now."

***

When Michael returned to the office, Kathy watched him anxiously, hoping to see something in his walk or in his demeanor which would give her some indication of what had transpired between the two of them over lunch. After all, he had returned to the office almost an hour later than she had expected. When he got closer to her, she could see that he looked melancholy and tired.

***

"Hello Kathy," Michael stated calmly. "Can you come into my office, please?"

Kathy followed him into his office and though she was concerned about his apparent sadness, she felt no trepidation for herself. They sat on the office sofa and Michael simply collapsed into a sitting position, clasping his hands together, obviously distraught, his chin hanging down on his chest. He turned to Kathy slowly and she moved forward to embrace him. She could feel his body shudder with emotion and when she looked up at his face, she could see that his tears were welling up in his eyes and she tightened her embrace.

Michael explained what happened during his lunch with Marlena. He apologized for becoming so emotional in her presence, but he explained that he felt so sad for Marlena... so sad that he could not bring himself to lie to her and tell her what he knew she wanted to hear. That he still loved her. He observed how that inability on his part affected Marlena, but he was powerless to prevent it and he felt such enormous guilt. Kathy merely held onto him and caressed his cheek and then lovingly kissed him. She could taste the bitter brine of his tears as they streamed down his face and onto his lips.

"Why don't we just go home early today, Michael?" Kathy finally announced. "I am not really hungry for dinner today. We can have dinner another evening. I just want to go home with you right now, run a warm jacuzzi and pour you a hearty serving of your favorite brandy and then just make love to you."

Chapter 50

A few days after the second meeting with the police detectives, Jake received a call from Denver. It was Marcel Paradis.

"Hello Jake. So when am I going to get my money?" Paradis asked jokingly. "I received copies of those bank and corporate records, so we know that McQuaid had sent half of my money to Layton and then sent the other half to himself," Paradis inquired calmly. "By the way, are you two guys freezing up there yet?"

"Not freezing at all, Marcel," replied Jake. "It's gotten warm here and most of the snow has melted away. Almost Bermuda shorts weather."

***

In light of the information which was disclosed by the detectives as to their theory that McQuaid's murder was probably a professional execution and in light of their unusual introduction to Tommy Smith, Jake and Michael decided that they had to exercise extreme caution until they knew more about how and why McQuaid got killed.

***

"As for your money, McQuaid's death was a mixed blessing," Jake elaborated. "On the one hand, he is not around to contradict Louie's evidence or compel us to go through a complete trial and then endure a possible appeal. On the other hand, his death has complicated matters. We will have to apply for a couple of court orders. We have to establish that McQuaid either committed a fraud, which would compel Layton to disgorge the $300,000 which he had received since it can be traced back to those defrauded funds. That would also compel McQuaid's estate to return the $300,000 which he had paid to himself. Alternatively, we can claim that McQuaid is in breach of his contractual obligations under that lease agreement he described at his examination and that this agreement should be rescinded because he is not in a position to fulfil his contractual obligations. His estate would receive the return of that fifty percent interest in that placer mining concession in the Yukon, if it actually exists, and you would receive your money back. But I am working on it. In fact, I was going to contact Layton and explain why it would be preferable for him to just return the money which he had received. Then I can focus on the estate."

"What can you offer Layton in exchange to encourage him to be more reasonable?" Paradis asked.

"I suggest we offer that we would not join him as a defendant in your lawsuit, which would make him a potential witness and permit us to apply to have him removed as McQuaid's counsel. We could also offer that we would not report his conduct to the BC Law Society, never mind the tax department for possible tax evasion," replied Jake.

"I could live with that, Jake. The best persuasion is when you can offer someone a little carrot but hold a big stick in your hands at the same time. That approach usually seems to improve the other guy's clarity of perception. Are there any further developments on McQuaid's murder?" asked Marcel, changing the topic.

"No new developments to my knowledge. But the police's new theory is that someone may have hired a professional to carry out the execution and that complicates matters. Though I, Michael and even you, all have good alibis for that evening, the police seem to be implying that any one of us, including Layton, hypothetically, could have arranged a murder for hire. So our respective whereabouts at the material time may not be that relevant but proving that theory is another story. However, it does appear that McQuaid had a number of disgruntled former business associates, any one of whom had the motive and the probable means to do that hiring too."

"What about Layton actually carrying out the killing himself?" asked Marcel.

"Possible, if you want to assume that pigs can fly, then anything is possible," replied Jake. "What makes it improbable is that the police are only aware of an argument in McQuaid's room at about six p.m. No one heard any shots, but he was shot three times. Once in his back, which the police speculate spun him around and then he was shot again in the chest and finally in the head. The police believe that the gun had to be equipped with a silencer and that is why no one heard any shots. Furthermore, he was shot with hollow-point 9-millimeter ammunition and at that distance the police say that you could put your fist in the exit wound. The first shot was probably fatal, so why the need for the second shot and then the final shot in the head?"

"They knew each other," replied Paradis. "So McQuaid would not have a problem opening up his door to him. I could see that Layton was upset with McQuaid's performance during his examination. That should explain the argument. And if your assumption that Layton used McQuaid to help him defraud me for a $300,000 payoff, he could have become concerned that McQuaid could leave him holding the bag. Layton could have become very angry and just proceeded to shoot McQuaid in a frenzy. You told me that Layton was a guy who got an erection by taking risks... even deliberately creating risks for himself, sometimes. McQuaid posed an obvious threat to him since it appeared that their defence was failing. If that happened, I believe that McQuaid would rat out Layton to try to save himself. If I were in Layton's position, I would feel extremely vulnerable, but then I do not go around trying to deliberately defraud other people. And if Layton did not do it himself, he would have had to have it arranged in advance of the examination, but how would he know if McQuaid would perform well or not until after his examination was finished? I am assuming that it would not be easy to hire a professional in Calgary to eliminate McQuaid on a couple of hours notice, so that is why I think Layton did it, himself."

***

Once again Jake felt that Paradis was attempting to bounce a new theory off him to counter the tentative theory the police were currently pursuing. It was as if Paradis were putting words in his mouth which he expected Jake would repeat to the police. Jake did note that though Paradis denied trying to deliberately defraud other people, he did not bother to make a similar disclaimer about arranging to have someone eliminated. If that was what Paradis was attempting to accomplish, then Jake decided to play that game himself.

"By the way, Marcel," Jake asked seriously, "if Layton decided to eliminate McQuaid, what about Louie?"

"What about Louie?" asked Paradis.

"Louie met Layton in Calgary, when he presented that bogus $600,000 matching contribution to that joint account. He could identify him and implicate him indirectly. If Layton would be prepared to execute McQuaid in his hotel room, he may be prepared to do the same thing to Louie. After all, it seems to me that Louie may be a loose thread. And if you pull on a loose thread, it may cause everything to unravel."

"Sometimes a loose thread just breaks off, Jake," Marcel replied. But Tommy has assured me that Louie is perfectly safe. No need to worry about him."

"Well, it would be nice if the police could identify that it was Layton arguing in the room with McQuaid that night," Jake ruminated casually. "But the police do not appear to have that kind of evidence or at least they have not decided to share it with us at this point."

**

After the call ended, Jake decided that it was time for him and Michael to review the situation and decide how they should proceed. He walked over to Michael's office, knocked once and then went in.

"Just got off a phone call with Marcel," Jake said. "He has provided me with a very interesting theory as to why it has to be Layton, personally, who killed McQuaid. I got the impression that he was trying to convince me that it could not have been a professional hit."

"We have a number of issues we have to deal with at this point," replied Michael. "First thing is that we have to proceed quickly to recover Paradis' money. It may be easier to recover the money Layton received, first. Then we can deal with the McQuaid estate, but we should obtain a preservation order to ensure that those funds remain in that account or be paid into court. I just have a feeling that the sooner we can separate ourselves from our client, the sooner our lives shall improve."

"The preservation order is already being looked after, Michael," Jake replied. "I am using our agent in Edmonton to arrange for it. Louie's supporting affidavit has been e-mailed to Denver for execution, notarization and return. Once that original affidavit is returned, our agent will proceed with the application to preserve those funds."

"The second thing I believe," Michael said, "though Layton had the best motive and the most to gain from McQuaid's death at this point, in all probability I am not that sure that he had the means to carry it out through a third party. But he was a guest at the same hotel, so he definitely did have the personal opportunity, probable access and the motivation.

"The third thing is our dear client's possible involvement and the implications which flow from that if it turns out to be a fact," Michael continued. "Paradis does not strike me as a forgiving individual and if he believes that Layton was the brains behind this fraud, I cannot see him just walking away from this affront to his family honour. If he was involved in McQuaid's death, someone with whom he had no previous dealings, why would he just leave Layton unscathed?" Michael said, completing his analysis.

"The one good thing is that we do not have any personal knowledge of any involvement by Paradis, either directly or indirectly, at this time," Jake replied. "I agree that we should try to recover his money as quickly as possible. If it is ever established that Paradis was involved in McQuaid's death, then we simply notify him that we are ceasing to act. He is smart enough to figure out why we would not be able to continue to represent him."

"I agree, Jake," Michael replied. "So let's proceed accordingly. How do you think we can persuade Layton to refund his $300,000?"

"I am thinking that we should use some appropriate leverage mixed with some moral suasion," Jake replied. "But you mentioned that Layton had a death wish about deliberately engaging in needless risks, even creating some risks himself, just to demonstrate his egotistical superiority. Is there some way we can try to utilize it against him? There may be a limit to the amount of risk he would be prepared to assume."

"We can call him and try, but he has advised me that he will only communicate with me in writing," replied Michael.

"Well, he never told *me* that was his position, so let me call him and see what he has to say."

Jake buzzed his paralegal and asked her to call Layton's office and then put the call through to him in Michael's office. Considering the fact that Jake knew that Layton was trying his best to implicate him in McQuaid's murder, he assumed that Layton would be unaware of what the detectives may have disclosed to him, but it was still going to be a gamble as to whether or not Layton would believe him. Furthermore, though it was contrary to the Code of Conduct to mislead another counsel, in these circumstances Jake felt he was entitled to bend that rule as far as he could.

***

"Good morning, Mr Layton. This is Jacob Barton, and I am with Michael Bolta in his office. I would like to put you on the speaker so that the three of us can try to resolve the litigation. I believe we have a proposal for you which you should find difficult to refuse."

"Well, I am not sure… Mr Bolta and I had agreed that all communication should be in writing," answered Layton. However, it was evident that he was curious about the proposal which Jake had referenced.

"We need to talk right now, Mr Layton, and not waste a lot of time exchanging e-mails, faxes or letters," Jake answered tersely.

"All right, what is this proposal which you think I will find difficult to refuse?" Layton inquired smugly.

"I believe that you should refund that $300,000 which you had received from McQuaid to our trust account before close of business today."

"And what makes you think that I would find that proposal difficult to refuse?" replied Layton, chortling to himself.

"We have just obtained bank records which confirm that McQuaid wired those funds to a Vancouver bank account which was in the name of a numbered company, whose sole director appears to be fictitious. The sole shareholder was another numbered company which appears to be wholly owned and controlled by you," Jake replied calmly.

"So what!?" Layton exclaimed. "It was just in prepayment of my fees for that action."

"I expected that would be your response, Mr Layton, but that reply raises additional issues for you. Firstly, if it was in payment of legal fees, there would have to be an account and I appreciate the fact that even if there never was any such account, you can probably produce one now. But I am equally sure that the personal representatives of the McQuaid estate will not be able to locate one at their end when they try to justify and reconcile a $300,000 payment to you or... in this case, your numbered company."

"I am not impressed, Mr Barton!" Layton replied confidently.

"Well, Mr Layton," Jake replied, "I am sure that if we can prove that McQuaid received that $600,000 by fraud, then the $300,000 you received, which can be traced directly to those defrauded funds, also constitute the proceeds of a fraud and the court will order their return."

"I am still not impressed, Mr Barton!" Layton said, though with less certainty.

"Then you have the issue of trying to explain to the Canada Revenue Agency why you would have a client render payment of an account to a specious numbered company which was controlled by a fictitious director, which, in turn, was owned by a numbered company which was, in fact, owned and controlled by you. Perhaps this corporate structure was just a novel tax-avoidance scheme, but I am quite sure that CRA would be interested in pursuing this line of inquiry and even possibly conducting an audit of you and your firm as a whole."

"McQuaid and I had certain business dealings over the years, and he simply wired those funds to the wrong account." Layton replied smugly, believing that he had neutralized this issue.

"But those funds were wired to that account a few months ago and it is quite evident that you must have become aware that either McQuaid overlooked paying your account or more probably, that you were engaging in a tax fraud, at the very least."

"Is that all you have, Mr Barton?" Layton scoffed. 'Well, I can advise you that I still have not found it difficult to turn down your proposal."

"Then let me advise you of the following additional matters," Jake replied, unaffected by Layton's rejection of the issues he had raised to that point. "If you do not wire that $300,000 to our trust account by close of business today, we intend to amend our claim and join you as a co-defendant and a co-conspirator with McQuaid. That would also make you a witness in this proceeding and disqualify you as counsel for the defence in this action. We would, concurrent with making you a party to this action, proceed to file a formal complaint with your Law Society for breach of various rules of your Code of Professional Conduct."

This time Layton did not respond. He was trying to assess the collective implications of what Jake had just told him.

"And if you still find it difficult to accept my modest proposal, Mr Layton, I can also advise you that if the Calgary detectives are able to identify you as the party who was in McQuaid's room during that loud argument, that could create a very serious problem for you. The evidence shows that McQuaid had let someone into his room voluntarily, so the visitor had to be known to him. They may even be able to locate a witness or witnesses who may be able to identify that person, if not actually leaving that room, then at least leaving that floor shortly after that argument. But I do know that you left the hotel quickly that evening and according to the airport records, you purchased a stand-by ticket to fly back to Vancouver. Obviously, that earlier return to Vancouver was not pre-planned by you."

Since Layton was not responding to Jake's final statements, Michael decided to interject.

"If you still find Mr Barton's proposal difficult to accept, would you prefer to endure the close scrutiny you will be receiving from us as a defendant in this action? And you may also have to deal with your Law Society, the Canada Revenue Agency and possibly the Calgary Police Service."

"Hypothetically, what would you offer in exchange for my cooperation?" asked Layton. "Assuming that I am gullible enough to accede to this outrageous blackmail."

"Threatening a civil action is different from threatening a criminal prosecution, as you should know," Michael replied pedantically. "The former does not constitute extortion. Reporting a breach of your Law

Society's rules is just a performance of our civic duty, as is reporting this suspicious fee payment to the tax department. But we have no control over what the Calgary Police Service may or may not do. Therefore, we are not trying to blackmail you, Mr Layton. We are just trying to afford you the opportunity of fulfilling your professional and personal moral duty and avoid a possible vexatious close scrutiny at the same time."

"If, and I repeat *if*." Layton finally replied, "what assurances will I receive that you two will fulfill your part of this… bargain?"

"It will have to be short and sweet, Mr Layton," Michael replied. "In consideration of the return of the $300,000 on a forthwith basis, we will accept same in full satisfaction of any and all claims which our client may have against you. Obviously, we are not in a position to reference those other collateral matters, since they involve third parties over whom we have no control. Your refund of our client's funds will be deemed by us and our client a sufficient atonement for any and all sins you may have committed in respect of this matter."

Layton finally responded reluctantly. "Please have your assistant e-mail me your trust account's transit number and account number. The funds shall be wired to your office today subject to the trust condition that I receive your written acknowledgment that those funds are paid in full satisfaction of any and all claims which Mr Paradis may have against me or my firm."

***

After the call ended, Jake and Michael shared a 'high five'.

"I wish we had some scotch or brandy in the office to celebrate, Michael," Jake said enthusiastically. "Having that morally challenged son of a bitch blink and get flatulent certainly makes my day. Almost as good as a great orgasm. I tried to be careful about suggesting what the Calgary Police may know, but the operative words were 'may know', not 'do know', so I do not think I crossed any line. If Layton chose to interpret that statement differently, that is his problem."

"Well done, Jake, but now you will have to focus on getting McQuaid's $300,000 released," Michael replied, sharing Jake's enthusiasm. "Hopefully we will be able to recover those funds quickly and close this file and get on with our lives. And if Marcel Paradis ever darkens our doorstep again, we shall not be able to accept any further work from him, regardless of any proffered retainer. Agreed?

"Agreed, my friend!" Jake replied happily. "After all, I may be a father in the near future, and I really would love to simplify my life."

"A father, Jake?" Michael asked curiously. "Am I to believe that you are finally going to give up the pursuit of frivolous fornication?"

"It ended as a potential competition between me and a Nobel laureate, but I won," Jake replied with a self-satisfied smirk. "We should go out for a drink after work and I will tell you all about it, my friend."

Chapter 51

It did not take Jake long to persuade the representatives of McQuaid's estate to refund the $300,000 which he had wired to himself from that joint account, since they were unable to locate any written lease agreement corroborating McQuaid's allegation that Louie Paradis was merely purchasing a half interest in that placer gold mining concession in the Yukon. They were also unable to locate and verify the existence of any such concession. However, they were finally persuaded by the recorded telephone conversations and those transcripts in which McQuaid had unequivocally represented that he was obligated to deposit a matching $600,000 to that joint account. They were satisfied that, at worst, McQuaid was involved in a fraud and at best, he was in breach of his contractual obligations. Jake decided that it was time to report the good news to Paradis and arrange to have the $600,000 wired to his bank account in Denver.

***

"Morning Marcel, it's Jake Barton calling from Calgary. Just wanted to advise you that further to Layton's refund of his share a couple of weeks ago, McQuaid's estate has just wired the other half of your funds to our trust account. So if you e-mail me your banking particulars, I will have our office wire the full $600,000 to you in Denver."

"Well, its always good to hear that a project has been successfully concluded and even though it cost me $100,000, it was money well spent," Paradis replied, and Jake could visualize him with his ostrich cowboy boots resting on top of his desk, chewing and turning that unlit cigar in his mouth. "Any new developments on McQuaid's murder?"

"Have not heard a thing, Marcel," Jake replied. "But it is nice to know that I am not the primary target in their proverbial crosshairs any more. I can contact the police and see if they are prepared to offer any new information and get back to you."

"You do that, Jake," Paradis said. "Any don't worry about wire transferring those funds to me. I am coming up to Calgary in a couple of days, so I can pick it up in person."

After that call, Jake telephoned Detective Krystov's cell and inquired as to the status of their inquiry. The detective was surprised to receive his call and even asked Jake if someone in the department had alerted him to some new developments in the case. Jake assured him that his call was simply coincidental.

Detective Krystov then proceeded to advise him of those new developments. It appeared that McQuaid had scratched his assailant because he had some skin tissue under a couple of broken nails on both hands. Furthermore, they were able to locate a guest of the hotel who was going down in the elevator to the front desk to check out. A disheveled man had pressed the descend button by mistake and he was muttering a profuse apology for stopping the elevator. That guest had a good look at the person who was trying to go up in the elevator. This incident had occurred at about six p.m. The guest took note of the fact that the other person was not only excited, but that he had bleeding scratches on the left side of his face and on the right side of his neck. The most prominent feature he could recall was that the agitated man was totally bald. He had related this information to the clerk at the front desk in case that man needed some medial attention.

The detective continued to explain that they were unable to locate and interview this individual in conjunction with other hotel guests who were either checking in or checking out that night or just guests on that floor. It turned out that he had flown to New York and then on to London and he had just recently returned to New York.

During their telephone conversation with him, they e-mailed him some photos of Layton and three other bald men who had similar features and the witness positively identified Layton as the individual he had seen that evening. Consequently, the two detectives had flown out to Vancouver to interview Layton in person the previous week.

They noticed that Layton still had some facial scratches which were almost healed. He denied that he was in McQuaid's room that evening or that he had argued with him. He explained his scratches as minor injuries he sustained when he had gone skiing. He had lost control and skied into a spruce tree. To that extent when they asked him to provide them with some DNA samples, to their surprise he readily obliged. He advised them that he had been in McQuaid's room previously, but he denied having anything to do with McQuaid's death. Unfortunately for Layton, the police had just received DNA confirmation that the skin under McQuaid's nails came from Layton.

Krystov explained that since they now had that DNA match, plus the positive identification from that witness, coupled with the fact that Layton had lied to them meant that they finally adopted Jake's theory about Layton killing McQuaid. The theory was not only logical, but they believed that it was provable beyond a reasonable doubt. He had motive: his fear that McQuaid might reveal his involvement in the fraud. He had opportunity: they could place him in that room that same night at the appropriate time. They could prove that the argument which other hotel guests had overhead was between him and McQuaid. And the most incriminating factor was that Layton deliberately elected to lie to them about those facts.

"What about the weapon? Have you found it? What about the shots no one heard?" asked Jake.

"No, those are just minor missing links, Mr Barton," replied Krystov. "But our investigation has been able to confirm that Layton was a member of a gun club in Vancouver and that he participated in target shooting on a regular basis, so he was familiar with guns. We believe that he obtained and disposed of the gun in Calgary, since he would not be able to board any flight to or from Calgary."

"But what about your theory that it was a professional hit?" Jake asked. "The fact that the gun had to have a silencer, since no one heard any shots, coupled with the fact that hollow-point bullets were used and that McQuaid was shot three times, with the last shot being a kill shot to the head."

"It was an expedient theory at that time because it conveniently answered a lot of critical questions. But there is more than one way to suppress the noise of a gun shot," answered Krystov. "But now we know that Layton and McQuaid had that vicious argument during which

McQuaid attacked Layton, which was evidenced by his facial and neck scratches. Layton may have had some intention to either defend himself or shoot McQuaid that night because he brought that gun with him. The gravity of their argument was overhead by other guests on that floor. It was followed by McQuaid's physical attack on Layton when he scratched his face. That resulted in Layton pulling his gun causing McQuaid to back off. In his anger, Layton proceeded to shoot him in his chest, which probably spun McQuaid around. Layton, in a frenzy, proceeded to shoot him again in the back. By this time Layton had to be extremely angry and agitated, so when McQuaid fell face down, Layton shot him again in the back of his head. The medical examiner had concluded that Layton was already dead after the first shot."

"You believe that you can prove all of this without having the actual gun?" Jake asked skeptically. "Having a gun for protection is understandable, but hollow-point ammunition is prohibited."

"If someone obtained an unregistered firearm, I don't believe they would worry about prohibited ammunition. So we believe we can and that we shall prove all salient facts beyond a reasonable doubt. In fact, Detective McKeown and I are on the way to the airport to fly out and pick up Layton and bring him back to Calgary. Vancouver detectives picked him up this morning. However, you may be interested in what Layton had to say about you and your partner when we had initially interviewed him. He accused you two of extorting $300,000 from him. Is there anything you would like to say about that allegation, Mr Barton?" Krystov asked politely.

"Detective Krystov," Jake replied, "you can interview me and Michael any time you want, and we will answer any and all of your questions. It is obvious that McQuaid was a mere accomplice in the fraud in exchange for a $300,000 payoff and his estate has just refunded those funds to our office. But I can advise you that neither of us attempted to commit extortion, which I believe is section 346 of the Criminal Code. We did threaten to sue him by joining him as a party to our civil action against McQuaid because we sincerely believed that the fraud was conceived, instigated and carried out by Layton. He was probably retaliating for the humiliation he received in that Denver mediation, but section 346(2) exempts a threat to commence a civil action as an act of extortion. Our threat to sue him civilly certainly does not constitute a breach of the Criminal Code. We did not threaten any kind of criminal prosecution, which is solely and exclusively in the hands of the police and the crown prosecutors."

"Uh-huh!" Krystov replied, skeptically. "But I have to admit that you have a bit more credibility with me than Layton has right now.

"One final question, Detective Krystov," Jake asked politely. "What about your serendipitous witness? What can you tell me about him? You say he is from New York?"

"Just an older guy. He really has these prominent eyebrows and this unkempt handlebar mustache. Soft spoken. Told us that he served a tour of duty in Vietnam and that he arranges security matters for some clients, but that he will be retiring soon."

Jake suddenly experienced a strange sensation. It was as if the temperature in the room dropped by ten degrees and he felt chills running up and down his spine. He had to discuss these developments with Michael forthwith and definitely before he reported back to Paradis. After ending his conversation with Krystov, Jake buzzed Michael's office to confirm that he was available and then he marched quickly past his paralegal's desk and Kathy's desk without a comment. Kathy noticed that he had a stern look on his face and that he was obviously upset by some matter.

"Michael, we may have a problem!" he announced, and he sat down in a chair in front of Michael's desk. "I just had an interesting discussion with Detective Krystov, who just happens to be flying out to Vancouver with his partner to pick up our learned friend."

"You mean Layton?" Michael asked with considerable surprise.

"Yes, I do mean Sterling Layton, Esquire," Jake replied with finality. "They had Vancouver police pick him up for homicide, but they may have an important hole in their theory since they do not have the weapon. They can prove that it was Layton who not only argued with McQuaid at about six p.m., but apparently, they also had a physical fight and McQuaid scratched Layton's face. That has just been confirmed by DNA found under McQuaid's nails."

Michael leaned back in his chair and tried to assimilate these new developments and their potential implications.

"My, oh fucking my!" Michael exclaimed, exhaling slowly.

"Don't worry, Michael," Jake replied, "it gets worse. That witness whose elevator had fortuitously stopped on McQuaid's floor and who has positively identified Layton and confirmed his facial scratches… guess what he looks like?"

Michael merely looked at Jake with his mouth agape. He could not bring himself to believe what Jake was about to reveal.

"Let me guess, Jake," Michael replied, "an older guy with a handlebar mustache and a Brooklyn accent…? My, oh fucking, fucking my!"

"And it gets even worse, Michael," Jake added. "I had phoned Marcel earlier and told him that we have been able to recover the entire $600,000. I wanted to confirm arrangements to wire those funds down to Denver, but he told me that he was coming to Calgary in a couple of days in any case and that he would pick up the funds personally."

"Do you think that Marcel's mysterious friend, 'Tommy' may have had a hand in McQuaid's death?" Michael asked somewhat rhetorically.

"That or I am going to convert and become a believer in coincidence. I will even forsake heading towards Sodom and Gomorrah, for I will have seen the light and start on the path to Damascus," Jake replied with obvious skepticism.

"It does seem to be highly coincidental that if the witness is actually Tommy, that he would be coming down the elevator to check out and he just happens to stop at McQuaid's floor and see Layton, disheveled and bleeding, shortly after his argument and fight with McQuaid," Michael summarized.

"Assuming that information to be true, though extremely coincidental," Jake replied, picking up the speculative narrative. If Marcel had given Tommy instructions to eliminate McQuaid, what an opportunity that chance meeting must have seemed to him. He could eliminate McQuaid and implicate Layton at the same time. All he had to do was come back up to McQuaid's floor, identify himself as hotel security investigating the argument which some other guests had reported. McQuaid would have let him into the room, probably without even checking for any identification. Tommy enters the room and kills him. He then exits the room and proceeds to check out. He probably manipulated matters at the front desk by mentioning that he had just met a distraught, bleeding guy on McQuaid's floor. Then he flies to New York and on to London, before finally returning to New York. The front desk would have passed that information on to the detectives, who were able to contact him eventually and give him an opportunity to tell his story and exonerate himself at the same time."

"And I am sure that if the police conducted any investigation into Tommy, they would find that he did have a 'security services company'. His presence in Calgary would be substantiated by our own client that he was here to ensure security for Louie Paradis. And who made that security recommendation to Paradis? - Bolta & Barton," Michael concluded. "Which raises another question: why would Bolta & Barton make such a recommendation in the first place?"

Both men lapsed into silence, thinking about the possible incriminating implications of what they had just finished reviewing.

"If we are even half correct, we are accusing our client of possible complicity in a murder for hire," Jake replied. A murder which did not simplify our case, it complicated it. But you are a student of human nature, Michael, what do you think was Paradis' motivation?"

"Remember what he said about family honour when we had that first meeting with him and his nephew. That it was important to recover the money, but they had to eke out some form of retribution because they had to maintain their family honour. And when McQuaid insulted him during his examination by calling him a son of a bitch, Paradis claimed that it was also an affront to his mother's dignity? What if he really believed what he was saying?" Michael replied.

"On the other hand, what if Tommy was simply proceeding to check out and his elevator had just stopped by chance when Layton pushed the wrong button?" Jake theorized. "McQuaid did pose a serious threat to Layton and his performance at his examination was not very effective. In fact, Layton appeared to be infuriated by McQuaid's propensity to answer first and think later. There was no way that McQuaid would permit himself to be solely responsible, financially and legally. After all, what do you think their disagreement was all about since it had degenerated into a physical fight? Either McQuaid was provoked to attack Layton, who shot him in self-defence, or McQuaid attacked

Layton when he was threatened with being shot. Layton was experienced with guns and if he intended to kill McQuaid because the litigation was not proceeding to his master plan, he would not have too much trouble in obtaining a gun. If he could obtain a gun, he could also obtain a silencer, as well as hollow-point bullets. After all, if he went to McQuaid's room with a gun, three shots in a hotel room would have resulted in immediate unwanted attention. If Layton intended to kill McQuaid to eliminate the threat he posed, he would be smart enough to give himself an opportunity to get away and get back to Vancouver. He may have been prepared to take this kind of risk, but he was not suicidal," Jake concluded dismally. "He would not want to go to prison for the balance of his life."

"Can we agree that our best option, speaking morbidly," answered Michael, "is that the police have arrested the right man? If Layton is convicted by a jury, the police and prosecution must have some additional evidence to prove his guilt. If Layton is able to raise a reasonable doubt, he will be acquitted. In either case, there is no moral or legal or ethical problem which we have to deal with; however, we can expect him to try to excoriate the two of us in the process."

"Alternatively, Paradis had instructed Tommy to eliminate McQuaid, which Tommy was able to effect with a certain amount of aplomb. After all, it could not have been easy to shoot someone, implicate someone else and be a corroborating witness to the other person's probable guilt, while absolving yourself with your own witness testimony," Jake replied. "In that case we are faced with serious legal and ethical issues."

"Why don't we wait and see what Paradis has to say when he gets to Calgary," Michael said calmly. "After all, in the end, regardless of the suspicions we may harbour at this point, we do not know with any reliable certainty what actually happened that night. Perhaps it is true when they say that ignorance is bliss… sometimes."

Chapter 52

Jake was sipping a triple shot of his favorite scotch from a cut crystal glass waiting for eight p.m. It was his second triple of the evening, and it was his way of adhering to the promise he made himself after that barroom incident at the end of his first year at law school: no more than two drinks at any one time. The time difference between Calgary and Vancouver was a one hour, and he wanted Crystal to have sufficient time to finish dinner before he called her at her apartment. At precisely eight p.m., he called her cell and she responded on the second ring.

"You sound sad, Jacob," Crystal observed. "Is everything all right?"

"I am tired, and things could be better, but I shall be all right. I was thinking of taking a couple of days off and flying out to see you. I appreciate that it is in the middle of the week. If you have to work, I can preoccupy myself during the day and we could spend the evenings together, if you are interested," Jake replied wistfully.

"Of course I am interested. How could you possibly think otherwise? I miss you too, you know," Crystal replied. "But are you drinking? Your speech seems a bit slurred."

"Cross my heart, I am only on my second drink," he replied, sheepishly, a bit guilt-ridden at his half-truth.

"*Humm*, I would be prepared to bet that your drinks are not singles, Jacob, but if it helps you relax, I am not displeased. I know how hard you have worked on that last file of yours."

"And I may not be prepared to take that bet," Jake replied.

"But you told me that you were able to recover the money your client had lost."

"As for the case, an unexpected problem has arisen, but Michael and I are going to deal with it," Jake replied. "The reason I am thinking of coming out to see you in the middle of the week is because our Denver client is going to be coming here this weekend and if I do not come out tomorrow, I will have to put it off for a couple of weeks."

"The weather out here is cool and wet, Jacob, but at least you will not have to slog through any snowdrifts. I can meet you at the airport at five p.m. if that will work for you."

"I am starting to love Vancouver. It is always so green and clean that I don't mind the lack of sunlight or your eternal rain. Sweet dreams, Crystal and I shall see you tomorrow."

***

Michael and Kathy had prepared a simple dinner for themselves and decided to eat it in the living room in front of the fireplace. Outside the snow started to fall again, but it was not very cold.

"You seem preoccupied, Michael. Is everything all right?" Kathy asked solicitously.

"A problem came up on the Paradis file, but we do not know if it is going to be a big problem or something which is more benign," Michael replied solemnly in between mouthfuls. "There is not much to say at this point, because we really do not know all of the facts."

"You may discuss it with me, Michael, if you like, even though I am only a mere woman who probably cannot fully comprehend these complex, intellectual male matters," Kathy answered facetiously, sighing sweetly. Her mischievous smirk accentuated her dimples.

"You really are adorable, Kathy," Michael replied, then added his own pejorative comment. "But then your intellectual powers are not your most endearing attribute."

Kathy feigned indignation and proceeded to steel a baby carrot off his plate in retaliation.

"I suspected that your attraction to me might be merely physical. So I suppose it will have to suffice," Kathy replied joylessly.

"You know that you are as intelligent as I am, dear madam and you probably have more common sense," Michael replied. "But your physical attributes and bedroom virtuosity really endear you to my heart."

"Madam?" Kathy replied, feigning outrage. "You called me 'madam'? Oh well, I forgive you, this time. But seriously Michael, can you share what is bothering you right now? I really do not want to be shut out and you never know, even if I cannot help you, sharing this burden with me may lighten your load. I want you to see me as a companion, not merely some carnal toy which satiates your more prurient interests."

Though Kathy was only being half-serious, after Michael summarized the potential quandary confronting him and Jake, she became aware of the enormity of their potential problem. On the one hand, if their client was involved, directly or indirectly, in McQuaid's death, they had serious ethical and legal issues to resolve. On the other hand, the alternative was relatively benign, however, it was too coincidental to be plausible, never mind probable.

***

"So it all depends on what, if anything, Mr Paradis tells you when he comes to Calgary this weekend. Then there is really nothing else you can do at this point, is that right?" Kathy asked seriously.

"That appears to be the situation," replied Michael.

"If there is nothing you can do at this point, you should try not to worry so much because that is just going to stress you needlessly. Once you are certain of what happened, I know that you will deal with it appropriately," Kathy stated firmly. "So let me put the dishes away and you go take a quick shower and I shall join you in the bedroom, shortly."

Michael followed Kathy's instructions. He was lying under the duvet, watching the light seep under the bathroom door and gently illuminate the room. He was listening to the running water, and he fantasized about the streams of warm water cascading off her body as she preened under the shower head. Finally, it was too much to bear... and definitely too long to wait. He decided to join her.

"Say lady, is there enough water for the two of us?" Michael asked innocently, as he opened the shower door and joined Kathy under the shower.

"There will always be room for you, Michael," Kathy replied, as she proceeded to embrace him and kiss him.

Michael rested his hands on her buttocks and pressed her against him. He could feel her firm breasts compress against his chest as he became aroused. Kathy reached under with her right hand and commenced to massage his erection with long, firm strokes, as Michael moaned. Then she swiftly threw her right leg over his shoulder and mounted him. Michael lifted her left leg over his right shoulder so that he would not have to bear her weight with his arm. Kathy maintained their kiss, parting his lips with her moist tongue and exploring his mouth. Michael commenced to lift and lower her fused body in an ever-accelerating rhythm until they both moaned in unison. Kathy remained mounted, her hands clasped behind his head, looking intensely into his eyes. The concern she noticed earlier had abated… at least for a while. Slowly she could feel him soften inside of her and as she slipped her thighs off his shoulders, he slipped out of her as well.

"Well, isn't this convenient," Kathy observed ingeniously. "Now we can finish showering and go to bed. I trust my virtuosity was sufficient for you tonight, Michael?"

***

Jake seemed distant and preoccupied as Crystal drove him to her condominium. Every time she said something to him, he would respond by apologizing and ask her to repeat her statement. Finally, in response to her question as to what was preoccupying him, he gave her an abbreviated version of the problem which was confronting him and Michael.

"So, if I understand correctly…" Crystal spoke seriously and deliberately. "If this client of yours was involved, directly or indirectly, what are your legal obligations?"

"We have the issue of client confidentiality, for one thing. But we are also officers of the court, and we are obliged not to become accessories after the fact and not to mislead the court, specifically, and the legal system as a whole," Jake replied.

"And if he is not involved, there is no problem?" Crystal asked, somewhat relieved.

"Unfortunately, that alternative is really unlikely."

"But you do not know, at this time, what the real facts are. Isn't that correct?" Crystal persisted.

"That is correct," Jake replied unenthusiastically.

"Do you have any legal obligation to inquire and inform yourselves?"

"No, we do not. The problem is that if the police, the prosecutor or the judge asks us, we cannot divulge confidential information which we may have, but we cannot mislead or deceive the authorities at the same time. We can be disbarred and sued for the former and disbarred and criminally prosecuted for the latter."

"But if you do not know anything positively, they cannot ask you about you may be assuming, can they? Mere speculation cannot be relevant, can it?" Crystal persisted, attempting to identify a palatable alternative.

"No, mere speculation is not relevant. But if our client decides to disclose his involvement in the murder to us this weekend, then he can effectively checkmate both of us," Jake replied.

"Why would he do that after you won his lawsuit for him and fairly quickly at that? I heard that lawsuits can go on for years."

"Sometimes clients do not know when to keep their mouths shut. And sometimes they are not satisfied unless they can brag about their exploits and who better to brag to, than someone they know cannot disclose it to anyone else? If either Michael or I knew what our client was planning in advance, then we could have retained a third-party lawyer to pass on the warning to the police. That lawyer would be bound to keep our identity confidential, but the authorities would be able to use the information to ensure that the crime would not be carried out. The prospective target would be protected. But this is different. This is after the fact."

"I just do not understand why you and Michael are in any jeopardy if your client confesses his involvement to the two of you, since it would be after the fact," Crystal replied, obviously quite confused.

"The police have charged someone else; a lawyer, in fact. The lawyer who was defending the murdered man. What happens if our client decides to confess to us and then this accused, who we would know is innocent, gets convicted? The penalty is life with no parole for at least twenty-five years. How do we maintain our duty of confidentiality to our client and yet not facilitate a miscarriage of justice since we are officers of the court?"

"I get it, Jacob! I finally get it, but you do not know one way or the other at this point, right? My gratuitous advice, which is probably worth what I am charging you, is that you do not permit your client to implicate the two of you, in the first place and then you just permit course of justice to unfold as it shall, in the second place," Crystal exulted triumphantly. "Perhaps I should have gone into law?"

***

Jake could only smile at the simplicity of Crystal's naive analysis, but it did contain a kernel of truth. When they reached her condominium, he did not even give her an opportunity to disrobe herself. He lifted her up in his arms and carried her directly to her bedroom.

"And what, pray tell, sir, is the meaning of this?" she asked coquettishly.

"I am about to render payment for your gratuitous, sage advice and I am also going to fulfill my responsibility as your preferred sperm donor. So, just hush up, kiss me and love me all night long."

***

Later, Jake brought some carbonated water flavored with some tonic to satiate their thirst. When he finally drifted off to sleep, Crystal heard him talking in his sleep. He kept stating that he had to protect Michael, at all costs. That if it came down to it, he would assume sole and total responsibility, but for what, it was not clear. He also kept repeating that he had an obligation to protect Michael. After all, Michael protected him years earlier and that protection permitted Jake to become a lawyer. He intended to fulfil his responsibility and repay Michael for the support he had rendered those many years ago. He repeated his regret for the fact that an opportunity had not presented itself earlier so that he could demonstrate the gratitude he felt he owed Michael.

***

After Crystal dropped Jake off at the airport, she was driving back to the city core when she had a sudden and intense realization. Jake's nocturnal soliloquies had to relate to this conflicted problem of client confidentiality and professional responsibility as an officer of the court. Jake had decided that if the issue materialized, he was going to protect Michael by assuming total responsibility for any consequences, even at the expense of his own professional career. She decided that she had to share her concern with Michael, so that he was aware of what Jacob was thinking of doing.

Michael took the news with mixed feelings. He was extremely grateful that Jake was prepared to sacrifice himself, but he was equally decided that he would not permit his classmate, friend and partner to make that kind of sacrifice. They would stand shoulder to shoulder and confront whatever was going to happen together, and hopefully come out successfully in the end or they would both go down together. If Jake felt so strongly about trying to protect Michael, the very least Michael could do would be to reciprocate.

Michael found Crystal's concern endearing and reassuring. It was his first experience that one of Jake's girlfriends had bothered to demonstrate such a concern about his personal welfare. Perhaps Jake had finally found a keeper.

Chapter 53

Jake and Michael were waiting in the boardroom for Paradis to arrive, since it was closer to the reception, and it was Sunday, and the rest of the staff were away. Paradis and his nephew finally arrived, and Jake ushered them into the boardroom and offered them some coffee or iced water.

"Hello fellas!" Louie exclaimed exuberantly. "I just want to thank you both for a job well done... and so damn fast at that."

Louie proceeded to shake their respective hands vigorously and then he enthusiastically hugged each of them in turn with a surprising strength which practically expelled the breath from their lungs. Paradis was obviously pleased, but thankfully, more subdued.

"And you both have my most sincere thanks... and my gratitude as well," Paradis announced, as he also shook each lawyer's hand and then gave them a quick familial embrace. "A job well done, yes, sirree!"

"Well, we have something for you in return, Marcel," Michael replied, as he handed Paradis a $600,000 bank draft made payable to Marcel Louis Paradis.

"As I have said my whole life, winning is always better than losing but winning and getting paid is even better."

The euphoria in the room being exuded by each man in the room became infectious. They not only smiled, but they also beamed at each other. Even Paradis looked as if he was prepared to launch into some Louisiana victory dance. They finally got seated at the boardroom table across from each other.

"Well, gentlemen..." Paradis announced. "... and I use that expression seriously and sincerely. Is there anything else that has to be dealt with before we close this file for good?"

Even though it was Jake who had performed the bulk of the work on the file, Paradis set his gaze on Michael. The two men's eyes met and locked. It was if both were engaged in a high-stakes poker game. One player had to decide whether to call, raise or fold. Then the other player, in the event of a raise, would be obliged to decide how he was going to respond.

"Any new developments on Layton?" Paradis asked neutrally, turning his cigar over in his mouth with his tongue.

"The Calgary Police Service has decided to charge and arrest Layton for murder," Michael replied. "He is in Calgary police custody as we speak. Detective Krystov shared a couple of bits of information with Jake as they were about to fly out and pick him up. One bit was that Layton and McQuaid were the ones who had the argument in McQuaid's room that evening. Apparently, the argument got quite heated and McQuaid even physically attacked Layton, scratching his neck and his face, which has been confirmed by DNA analysis. Detectives Krystov and McKeown were able to get Layton to give them some personal samples during their initial interview. Why he agreed to provide those samples, I do not understand. He had to realize that they would come back as a match."

"Layton always struck me as arrogant son of a bitch. You know the type. They really do believe that their excrement smells of roses and that they are superior to everyone else. Besides, you told me that he was even inclined to create additional risks for himself, just to prove that he was smart enough to extricate himself. However, even though I do not gamble, one of my dear friends told me that no matter how lucky or smart you may be, or you may think you may be, if you keep playing with fire, then one fucking day you are bound to burn your own butt," Paradis replied.

"Well, there was an additional piece of information which Krystov decided to share with Jake," Michael added in a neutral manner. "It appears that Layton, after he left McQuaid's room, mistakenly pressed the down, instead of the up, elevator button, and he was greeted by a gentleman from Brooklyn who was on his way to check out. Krystov described him as in his mid-sixties, prominent dark eyebrows and a handlebar mustache. That Brooklyn gentleman observed that Layton's face was bleeding and he appeared to be very agitated when he apologized for the inadvertent stop. The Brooklyn gentleman proceeded to check out of the hotel, but he mentioned this meeting to the hotel clerk. Layton apparently checked out in a hurry later as well. However, he did not catch his scheduled flight back to Vancouver. He proceeded directly to the airport and purchased a stand-by ticket for his flight back. He got lucky, because there was a cancellation, and he took that seat."

Paradis smiled a Cheshire Cat smile at Michael and decided to ask the obvious question.

"And you think that this 'Brooklyn gentleman' may have just happened to be my associate, Tommy... er, Smith, Michael?"

Jake came to the realization that Paradis and Michael were engaged in a word game, and he decided to sit back, watch and listen for a while to see how it would unfold. However, in his heart and mind, he was committed to protecting Michael at all costs. Even at the cost of his career and possibly his liberty.

"It would seem that the physical description of this Brooklyn witness would seem to match Tommy, wouldn't you say, Marcel?" Michael decided to respond to Paradis truthfully, but neutrally. "And though I am not interested in Tommy's real last name, let's stop referring to him as 'Tommy Smith', please. Since we both know that it is not his real name."

Paradis knew that this proverbial cat-and-mouse game he was playing with Michael had serious implications, but he could not help but toy with Michael a while longer in any case.

"The description does seem to be extremely similar," Paradis agreed. "And I can confirm that it was in fact Tommy. Jake had suggested that Layton's involvement in McQuaid's fraud not only put McQuaid in jeopardy, but that Layton may have decided to eliminate Louie as well."

"What!" Louie exclaimed indignantly. "Uncle Marcel, you never done told me that."

Paradis decided to ignore his nephew's outburst, since it was not germane to the discussion he was having with Michael.

"I retained Tommy's firm, which, by the way, is a long-established firm, with several employees, to arrange for Louie's security in Denver. Since Louie was acting as my agent, Layton also had the right to examine Louie as well. In the event Louie would have to come to Calgary, I had Tommy come up here to ensure his security in your city as well."

"So it was just a coincidence that both Layton, McQuaid and Tommy were all staying at the same hotel?" Michael asked.

"No, it was not a coincidence," Paradis replied. "Once Tommy determined that McQuaid and Layton had both booked into the Delta Plaza Hotel, he arranged to obtain a room on the same floor as Layton. You know what they say… keep your family and friends close but keep your enemies closer. It is Tommy's standard operating procedure that if he was to conduct a surveillance on an individual, he would try to be as close as possible because in the event the target saw him, it would not appear to be an out-of-the-ordinary event. The target would not become suspicious of his obvious presence."

"So was it just a coincidence that Tommy met Layton right after he had that argument with McQuaid?" Michael asked a bit incredulously.

"As coincidental and unlikely as it may seem right now, Michael," Paradis replied. "Sometimes, just as shit happens, so do 'coincidences. It was a pure and simple coincidence. Since the examinations were over and Layton did not request an examination of Louie, Tommy's services were no longer needed.

"A fortuitous coincidence though, because Tommy could identify Layton as the man who probably just left McQuaid's room after McQuaid had raked his face and neck with his nails during their fight. And what kind of a pussy fights like that? Scratching someone's face like a girl, instead of simply kicking him in the balls, followed up by an uppercut to knock some teeth out of that motherfucker's face?

"But without that evidence, the police would not have any reason or right to request any DNA sample from Layton. That sample not only confirmed his presence in McQuaid's room, but that he was a participant in that fight with McQuaid."

"You realize that Tommy is going to have to come back and identify Layton, don't you?" asked Michael.

"Of course! Both I and Tommy understand that full well."

"And you realize that both Jake and I will probably have to testify as to our involvement in the case as well?" asked Michael.

"Of course! You were my lawyers trying to recover my money from McQuaid, who happened, apparently, to be involved in that fraud with Layton."

"And if we are asked a question as to whether or not we had ever met Tommy previously, I trust you realize we shall be obliged to tell the truth," Michael asked.

"Of course!" Paradis replied, without raising his voice to underscore his lack of concern and emphasize that Michael's sundry issues were without any substance. "You had met him at the restaurant after the first day of McQuaid's examination. He came to our table and requested a short conversation with me. And perhaps I should identify Tommy fully now, but he does not like me to identify him by his legal name when he is working on a project for me. His name is Tommy Consella. founder and president of Consella Security & Investigations — Brooklyn, New York. The company has a good reputation and has been in business for almost forty years. He only hires ex-servicemen who meet his criteria, which are competence and men who are also in need of personal rehabilitation. Considering what Tommy had gone through after he left the service, though he was able to make it on his own, he knew that there were many more of his comrades-in-arms who needed a helping hand."

"Jesus Christ, Almighty!" exclaimed Jake. "Marcel, do not know how Michael and I have been sweating nails and bullets for the past couple of weeks over this crap?"

"And why would you think that I would not understand and appreciate your positions?" asked Paradis. "Perhaps you two do not understand my position in such matters: I am loyal to my faithful employees and to my independent contractors, such as yourselves. Secondly, I am also grateful. Consequently, regardless of what I may decide to do or not do, personally, I would never put any of my employees or my independent contractors in any jeopardy. No sirree! I would cut off a finger with a rusty butter knife first. And as you can see, I still have all of my digits."

"And if the police and the prosecution have sufficient evidence to convict Layton, I am not going to lose any sleep," Paradis continued. "That also goes in the event that cocksucker gets acquitted. The fact that the son of a bitch got arrested and has to defend himself, is sufficient satisfaction for me. So Louie and I are going up to the Yukon to check out some legitimate placer gold mining concessions to see if my dear nephew can make a few million of his own this coming spring… with a little help from his loving uncle."

At that point, all four men rose in unison and shook hands in farewell. Louie left jubilant, obviously counting and spending the millions which he had yet to earn. Paradis left with his Cheshire Cat smile firmly fixed on his face, but otherwise, he remained largely noncommittal. Jake and Michael, if they had a mirror to check their respective expressions, would have found themselves to be largely dumbfounded by the events which had just occurred.

"Perhaps this is not the most appropriate time for me to share this information with you, Jake," Michael stated firmly, "but I want you to know that Crystal had called me the day you came back from Vancouver. You were pretty restless and talking in your sleep. You kept talking about sacrificing yourself to save me, in gratitude for something I had done for you years earlier. She called me out of a deep concern for you, Jake. I sincerely believe that you have finally found a keeper. Treat her well and be honest with her. She will repay you tenfold."

"She did that for me?" Jake asked incredulously. "She really did that for me?"

"Yes, she did, my friend," Michael responded unequivocally.

"And Michael, did you believe everything which Marcel told us this morning? I mean, everything fits together so well… almost too well," asked Jake, skeptically.

"You have to remember everything he said. He said that he would never place someone who trusted him in jeopardy," Michael replied. "As for believing 'everything' which he did say, I would say that issue is now moot and irrelevant.

Chapter 54

After Michael had explained to Kathy what had transpired with Paradis and his nephew, Kathy understood from the obvious relief on Michael's face that the potential dilemma which had been confronting him and Jake had been resolved satisfactorily. But she had her own dilemma confronting her. She felt that she could either choose to ignore Marlena and her continuing presence in Michael's life and in Adam's life, which might fester with the passage of time, or she could possibly meet her and have a discussion about how the two of them can learn to share Michael and Adam, although in different ways, so that everyone's life could be enhanced. There was no assurance that if she tried to reach out to Marlena that she would not be rebuffed or even possibly insulted. She understood that if she tried, she may still not be able to achieve that result, however, she was positive that if she did not make the effort, failure was guaranteed. Consequently, without informing Michael, Kathy decided to reach out and telephone Marlena.

***

"Hello, Mrs Bolta. This is Kathy Clemmons calling." She introduced herself tentatively. "May I speak to you on a personal matter?"

Marlena was surprised by the call and unsure of how to respond initially.

"A personal matter?" Marlena inquired softly. "What personal matter?"

Kathy was relieved that Marlena's initial reaction was neutral. It assured her that there was a chance that she might be prepared to discuss the matter, perhaps even meet in person.

"I would like to say that this is difficult for me, as it may be for you. But events have caused our lives to cross and it would appear that we will be dealing with each other, one way or another, for the foreseeable future."

Marlena remained silent. Kathy had not clarified what the personal matter was, but she seemed concerned and sincere. She decided that she had nothing to lose if she continued to listen.

"Ms Clemmons," she replied, politely, "you said that you had a personal matter to discuss, but you have not explained what that personal matter is."

"Yes, I did say that, and I apologize. I have no intention of being obtuse," Kathy replied earnestly. "As I said, since fate has caused our paths to cross, I was hopeful that we could talk, possibly meet. It was never my intention to hurt you in any way, Mrs Bolta. I know how it feels to have your marriage destroyed, but in my case, it was destroyed by my husband. He was not only unfaithful, but he also got his girlfriend pregnant while refusing to have a child with me. I had spent years trying to support him financially and emotionally, but it was still not enough in the end."

Kathy decided to limit making assumptions as to what Marlena may be feeling or thinking. She decided that it would be more prudent if she simply opened herself up to her and saw how Marlena would react.

"Why do you want to talk or meet, Ms Clemmons?" Marlena asked, obviously conflicted as to how she should respond.

"It is my sincere hope that we can get to know each other better," Kathy replied. "After all, Michael will continue to play a part in your life and then there is Adam. You should be very proud of raising such an adorable child. He is solicitous and respectful, and yet he can be so deliciously mischievous and playful. It is truly a joy to be able to spend some time with him. You should be very proud of him, and I want you to know that I have no intention of trying to replace or supplant you in his life. He truly adores you and Michael. I just hope that you will permit me to play a minor part of his life."

"Perhaps we should meet, Kathy," Marlena finally replied. "You are right. Fate has caused our paths to cross. I have no desire to have you as an enemy. I have seen and felt how destructive hate can be, personally. You will be a part of not only Michael's life, but our son's life as well. I would prefer to have you as a friend and if that is not possible, then I would like to have at least a civil relationship with you. It would not only be better for Michael and for Adam, but I feel that it would be better for each of us as well."

They agreed to meet for lunch the next day.

***

Jake could not keep Michael's description of what Crystal had told him about his nocturnal musings out of his thoughts. She was only the second person in his entire life who had demonstrated an interest in his personal welfare and who had taken active steps to try to ensure it. Michael, all those many years ago when Jake got drunk and then committed the incredibly stupid act of throwing an empty beer glass against the barroom mirror. Now it appeared that Crystal had a similar concern for his personal welfare, and she did not owe him any favor either.

Jake had grown up as the only child to an aloof set of parents. Notwithstanding his best and most earnest efforts to please them, it was never enough. And even when they were pleasantly surprised or pleased, they never provided him with any confirmation or assurance. Eventually, he started to emulate them and respond to them in a similar fashion. Consequently, going through grade school and then middle school, Jake was shy and antisocial. He did, however, pay close attention to how his fellow classmates interacted with each other and he tried to learn. By the time he reached high school, he formed some core beliefs.

Regardless of what his fellow classmates may have felt or thought about him, what was important was what he felt or thought about himself. Secondly, you only got disappointed or betrayed by others if you permitted yourself to nurture expectations of them or if you decided to repose your trust in them. But his most important awareness was that if you believed in yourself, that would result in those other people believing in you as well. And if those other people would not believe in you, then you could make them envy you. If they envied you, whatever they felt or thought about you became irrelevant because he believed that, in the depths of their souls they wanted to be like you. In fact, they wanted to be you and it contented him immensely to know that their wish would remain unrequited.

However, that mindset made meaningful relationships difficult, if not impossible, to foster. Michael was an exception. He had come to Jake's defence when he had no obligation to do so and at a considerable personal and professional risk. Could it be that Crystal was another such exception?

He had told many women on many occasions that he loved them, but it was a meaningless expression to him. It held no more significance than telling a woman that she was beautiful, when she was not. It was only intended to give them some false assurance if they chose to believe him and they usually did.

Jake tried to analyze and understand his feelings about Crystal. He found her physically attractive, intelligent and witty. He enjoyed her company and he enjoyed her physically, but she got drunk in New York and ended up betraying his affection and his trust. He had attempted to reciprocate and exact some revenge, but it was not fulfilling. In fact, it was disappointing. He'd thought that he would be using that couple, but it ended up that they used him.

He felt so grateful when, as events unfolded, he and Crystal were able to reunite. It was not that he had decided to forgive her. No, it was because he wanted to forgive her, just as she had chosen to forgive him.

He reviewed his personal life, and it did appear to be as barren as his parents' life and that was something he wanted to avoid at all costs. Contemplating suicide seemed a more palatable alternative to their stoic existence which was not only devoid of joy and expectation, but even sadness and disappointment.

Michael had told him that you cannot have one without the other. Perhaps it made sense to take a calculated gamble, like trying to fill an inside straight after your opponent made a large raise. You were obliged to call before you had the opportunity to draw that elusive fifth card and it was an expensive risk to take. You knew that there were only four cards remaining in the deck which could perfect your hand, but you first had to make that call just to have the opportunity. And making that call, by itself, was no guarantee of success. The odds were against you, but if you decided to make that call, at least you had the chance to make a winning hand.

The critical factor was timing. If you paid attention to the flow of the cards, sometimes you knew that a longshot call at the right moment was the indisputable correct decision you had to make. Perhaps in life the same principle applied.

***

Marlena and Kathy arrived at the restaurant at the same time, rather embarrassingly. Both women were even apologetic, reciprocally, for being punctual. Those mutual feelings helped to diffuse the tension. They even chose to laugh at their awkward introduction when they simultaneously first extended and then withdrew their hands, in obvious confusion as to what the appropriate protocol was in these circumstances.

"We should just sit down before we trip or fall or break something," Marlena announced.

"And you will not mind if I address you as Marlena?" Kathy asked somewhat awkwardly, as they were being seated in a secluded corner of the restaurant for more privacy.

"Not at all," Marlena replied. "Though I admit I thought I should despise you, but you did not take Michael away from me. In fact, *I* was the one who drove Michael away because I foolishly chose not to believe him but believe that vile sister of his. If fate would have it that he was driven into your arms, so be it. I believe that you are a good person and that he will be happy with you. I do not believe that you will disappoint him or hurt him. I want him to be happy. He is a good man."

Kathy examined Marlena carefully before responding. "Thank you, Marlena. You are too kind. And I would like to share something with you. After you and Michael had that lunch, Michael came back to the office emotionally drained. He asked me to join him and after I closed the office door, he broke down emotionally because he could not bring himself to deceive you. Even though he knew he was going to disappoint you and hurt you, he knew that if he was not truthful, he would hurt you even more. Regardless of how he responded, he knew that he would be hurting you and it hurt him. He does care about you, and he wants you to be happy."

"Now you better stop that before I start to cry," Marlena responded softly, dabbing at her eyes with a small silk handkerchief.

"Ladies!" announced their waiter a bit effeminately, "my name is Armand and I have the exquisite pleasure of not only serving you and ensuring that you shall have a scrumptious luncheon, but I intend to try to become your good friend as well."

Then he bowed down and in a conspiratorial fashion, cupped his hand by the side of his mouth so the secret he was about to reveal would not be overheard by anyone else.

"And we are not going to count, in fact, we are not even going to think about the possible calories you two beautiful ladies are about to consume."

Kathy and Marlena exchanged a quick, knowing glance and smiled. It was obvious to the two of them that they could not have selected a better server.

"In that case, Armand," replied Marlena, "we are going to leave ourselves entirely in your capable and competent hands. You may select our wine, appetizer, entrée and dessert. We assure you that calories are not going to be a consideration today."

"Wonderful! Wonderful! Wonderful!" Armand exclaimed, almost ready to execute a pirouette in his joy. "But will it be permissible to ask a few questions as to your possible preferences? Modest though I am not, I am not clairvoyant, either."

After their waiter settled on their wine and asked them a few cursory questions, he advised them that each course would be selected by him and presented individually as a 'Chef Surprise', but he was confident that they would not be disappointed because if they were disappointed, *he would just die,* and they were ready to believe him.

***

"Adam is a wonderful son, Marlena," Kathy said. "I enjoy watching him interact with his father. He so yearns to be older and more mature, but he is truly adorable, even when he is trying to be mischievous."

"Yes, he is a good son," Marlena replied. "And he does try act beyond his years at times, but he can also be quite perceptive at times as well. That evening I came out to Michael's acreage when the three of you were having dinner… after you left, and Michael and I ended our conversation, I asked Michael if Adam could come home with me because I did not want to be alone that night. Naturally, Michael complied, but what was truly adorable was to observe Adam trying to console me because I did get a bit teary. He held my hand as we walked out to my car, and he told me that he did not want me to be sad."

"And I do want to assure you that I have no intention of trying to replace you. I just hope you will trust me that I can be a good friend to your son," Kathy said sincerely, getting choked with emotion.

"And I want to assure you that having met you, having shared this 'scrumptious luncheon' with you, to quote our erudite server, and having spoken with you, that I do believe you and I hope we can not only be acquaintances, but that we may become friends in time. Though I believe that most other people will find that shocking that the ex-wife does not resent her ex-husband's paramour and vice versa, but that will be their problem, hopefully, not ours."

The waiter approached them with feigned sadness and a sigh, wringing his hands.

"And you two beautiful ladies just have a wonderful afternoon and I hope that you shall grace us with your exquisite presence soon or you shall break my little heart. You truly will."

"You need have no fear of that, Armand," Marlena replied, as she and Kathy exchanged a smile and a gentle embrace before they parted.

***

Jake decided to fly out to Vancouver and surprise Crystal. He showed up at her office with flowers for her and chocolates for her staff. There were two other clients seated in the reception room and the receptionist was busy at her desk, but she looked up at Jake as he entered the room.

"Excuse me, but is Ms Bachman in this afternoon?" Jake inquired politely of the receptionist.

"Ms Bachman is in, but she is busy at this moment. Who shall I say is calling?" she asked inquisitively, looking up sweetly from her seated position.

"Just a good friend, but I would like to surprise her," Jake replied. "Could you put the flowers in a vase for me and here, the chocolates are for you and the rest of the staff."

"You wouldn't happen to be the 'flower guy' from Calgary, would you?" she inquired, trying to suppress a smirk.

"I may be," Jake announced proudly, sharing a conspiratorial wink. "Why? Does Ms Bachman receive flowers from other guys as well?"

"Not lately," she replied. "And thank you for the chocolates. I am sure that we shall enjoy them."

"Would it be possible to phone her right now?" Jake asked.

"Well, you can try. But if she is busy, she may not answer."

Jake proceeded to call Crystal's cell and she picked up on the third ring.

"Jake, what are you doing calling me in the middle of the day? I thought you were a lawyer who works seven days a week, not a banker who works four hours a day," Crystal answered, a bit surprised at receiving his call so early in the day.

"I just wanted to hear the sound of your voice and I wanted to feel the gentle beating of your heart. I just want to hold you in my arms right now and kiss you all over," Jake replied, winking at the receptionist again.

The receptionist was desperately attempting to suppress her laughter with one hand at Jake's childish attempt to woo her employer, but she was encouraging him to continue like an orchestra conductor with her other arm.

"That sounds nice, Jacob, and I assure you that my feelings are the same, but since that is not possible at this moment, what do you really want right now?" Crystal asked politely, trying to indulge him as best she could.

"Crystal, I have told you what I want, but I would prefer to characterize it as what I 'desire'. Mere 'want' is so pedestrian. I 'desire' you!" Jake replied emotionally, clutching at his heart with his free hand for the benefit of the receptionist who was enjoying his performance immensely.

At that moment, Crystal exited the lab and entered the reception room, still holding her cell phone to her ear. Her premonition was correct.

Jake was facing the receptionist and not aware that she was right behind him. Crystal gestured to the receptionist to play along by putting her forefinger to her lips to maintain their secret.

"I have a surprise for you, Crystal," Jake announced, winking at the receptionist again.

"A surprise?" Crystal replied, putting her cell phone in her back pocket. "For me?"

Jake spun around in surprise. "Not fair to sneak up on someone behind their back, Crystal. *I* was trying to surprise *you*, not the other way around."

"Let's not worry about that right now. I believe you said you have a surprise for me," Crystal replied. "All right, out with it. I see that you brought some flowers and some chocolates. Is that it or are you modestly referring to yourself, as well?"

She approached him slowly and wrapped her arms around his neck and kissed him on his lips.

"I did bring little me and a little something else," Jake replied, pulling out a small jewelry box out of his jacket pocket and slowly opening it up to disclose an elliptical radiant Tanzanite ring, encircled by an array of small diamonds. The rich purple/blue luster of the stone was enhanced by the sparkle of the diamonds. The ring was truly dazzling, and it complemented Crystal's violet eyes perfectly.

Crystal was not only surprised. She was truly shocked. She looked down at the ring and then up at a smirking Jake and then back to the ring.

"Oh, let me see. Let me see!" interjected the receptionist. "My God, Ms Bachman, I do believe that he is proposing to you. Just hold that pose because I want to take a photo of the two of you."

Crystal looked back up at Jake and his broad grin, a little confused and surprised.

"What does this mean, Jacob? Are you proposing? If so, I thought it was customary to get down on one knee," Crystal asked, jokingly.

Jake immediately dropped down on one knee and looked up at Crystal, whose mouth was opened wide in pleasant surprise.

"Crystal Bachman, will you marry me?" Jake asked, becoming serious and solemn for a moment, before relapsing to a more jocular attitude. "But if you do not say yes, you have to give the ring back."

Crystal's emotions were a mixture of surprise and satisfaction. She paused, examining Jake's facial expression and vocal tone to try to discern his sincerity, then she looked back at the ring with delighted approval.

"I guess in that case I'd better say 'Yes'!" she replied with feigned resignation. "After all, if it does not work out, I still get to keep the ring, right Jacob?"

"You get to keep the ring, but I am never going to let you go!" Jake replied with genuine sincerity.

Crystal pulled him up to his feet and embraced him. She shared a wink with her receptionist who was on the verge of tears and then she kissed Jake intensely. They were only interrupted when the receptionist and the two other clients sitting in the reception room commenced to applaud them vigorously.

***

Kathy was preparing dinner and Michael entered the kitchen to offer some assistance. Kathy decided to disclose her lunch with Marlena. Though it caught Michael by surprise that Kathy did not reveal her intentions in advance, he could tell by her radiant face that she had made the right decision.

"I am glad that the two of you had the courage and the strength to meet and talk," Michael said. "It could not have been easy for either of you, but Marlena is a good person. She has a good heart. She was just duped by Alexa, who I never want to see or speak to again. I may be able to learn to forgive her in time, but I doubt it. I know that I can never forget her betrayal. Some people are just morally contemptible. They cannot bear to see someone else be happy, so they try to destroy their happiness so that they would be as miserable like them."

"She still is your sister and your closest relative, Michael. Perhaps she can learn to change, possibly improve, otherwise she is dooming herself to a deplorable existence," Kathy replied solemnly.

"You cannot help someone who is not prepared to help themselves, Kathy," Michael replied. "I choose to preoccupy myself with you and with Adam."

CPSIA information can be obtained
at www.ICGtesting.com
Printed in the USA
BVHW030501220322
631814BV00003B/11

9 781800 163393